I0775687

A DOSE OF POWER

C.M. LOKKEN

Published by:

Spotted Boogin Press

I dedicate this book to my amazing wife.
Despite my many self-perceived failures, she has always
supported me.
I love you so much, Beck.

CHAPTER 1

The day had started like any other, I suppose. I woke up from a night of drinking, half naked, wearing only a grungy tee to cover my chest. The morning breeze was cold on my bare ass that was inexplicably raised in the air. Star was snoring on the bed beside me, wearing nothing herself.

I didn't remember her even showing up the night before, but given how much I had to drink, that wasn't all that surprising. We often met up, drank, and then fucked till we passed out. Sometimes it seemed like she thought that was her payment for spending the night, and while I certainly didn't mind the sex, I hope she knew it wasn't mandatory. We weren't dating in the typical sense, but she was probably the person I spent the most time with from week to week.

I sat up and brushed a tangled red lock from my face and it spilled down my back with the rest of my hair. I stretched and my entire spine popped, sounding a bit like a bag of popcorn. It was one of those good pops, the kind that just makes you melt in your own skin as your whole body realigns itself with the universe. Star didn't budge, but then she would sleep through a hurricane given the chance.

I stumbled to the bathroom, and it felt like my brain was spinning in my skull like a top. I brought my arm up to hide my face from the beams of sunlight trickling in from behind the curtains. The light leapt at my eyes like a rabid animal, clawing at my retinas. I would've had enough trouble walking without the hangover, thanks to the piles of clothes and other mess lying everywhere. I tripped over Star's backpack near the door and its contents spilled out into the hall: a variety of makeup containers, some deodorant, a razor, and a couple of sex toys.

Star was something else. With minimal effort, she could stun a room with her looks alone. She was a cute, short girl with a pleasantly padded stomach and tits galore. Sure, I had my own, but I was a B-cup at best. I couldn't help but feel underwhelming when I compared myself, I was never one of the pretty girls growing up. Girls like Star could bounce their way into any clique if they wanted, girls like me just stood off in the corners of rooms hoping people would just ignore us while we blasted loud music from our headphones. Star wasn't that type of person though, she had her own problems with self-worth, which is probably why we bonded so well.

I finally made it to the bathroom, tore off the tattered rag I was wearing that passed for a shirt, and hopped in the shower. I stood there, letting the cold-water wash over me for a while. I could feel the hangover beginning to lose its grip, and I took the time to just think about nothing at all. Centering myself with a clear mind was the only way to prepare for the day of monotony ahead.

I had a typical office job, and it was just as shitty and soul crushing as you expect. Punch in, pound the keyboard, talk on the phone, punch out, rinse and repeat. I had become just another cog in the corporate wheel, scrambling for that daily bread. I never got the loaf though, like most of us, my grind amounted to just crumbs in my pocket, more stress than money. It paid the bills though, and bought some good alcohol, and in the end that was all I could really ask for.

I couldn't deny that I had grown complacent, jaded to the grind, making my way through the days just to come home and play video games and get drunk, and occasionally fuck something. It wasn't glamorous, but it sufficed. It's not like I could just get up and find something else in this town. Asheville's desire to be a tourist town with no real infrastructure made sure of that.

Rent prices were climbing through the roof, while companies seemingly competed over who could offer the most mediocre compensation. Typically, if you found something above minimum wage with benefits, you held on to it like a child with a broken toy they aren't ready to give up. I once asked for a raise, and during the conversation mentioned the disparity between wages and the cost of living, and the HR rep expertly deflected and mentioned that the area was just so beautiful that it was practically a benefit itself. I had asked for a two-dollar increase, they gave me ten cents, and I actually thanked them before leaving the room.

I grabbed a bottle of mouthwash and splashed some in my mouth, I gagged a little when I was met with the taste of cheap liquor. Someone had apparently been rather desperate for a mixer. I frowned but used it anyway, there was bound to be enough mint to disguise the alcohol. I was sure I had gum in my purse somewhere.

I dried off with a towel that I hoped was clean enough and plopped down on the toilet for a moment. I kept my phone and a pair of sunglasses in the bathroom cabinet, mostly for mornings like this one. I scrolled through my routine of social media sites, mostly trying to see if anyone had posted pictures of me drunk and naked, it had happened before and was always a nuisance to get rid of. Satisfied that my remaining dignity was still intact, I put the phone away, finished my business, and strolled out of the bathroom.

I could hear Star still snoring from the bedroom, either that or a sawmill had been installed overnight. I decided I needed coffee, which meant navigating the minefield that was my house, dodging the relentless assault from the sun, and then surviving the descent of the crooked stairs. It would take grace and skill, but I had made the trip many times before, so I had an advantage. I made it with no casualties, and only minor injuries.

I shoved some empties out of the way and pulled out the coffee maker, the only functional appliance in the whole kitchen it seemed. I took great care of it, and for good reason: What's a girl to do without her morning cup of tar to get things moving in the right direction? I loved a good pot of coffee, regardless of the time of day, but that one first thing in the morning was serendipitous. The aroma as it percolated was enough to lift you from your feet and float you through the air, like one of those old cartoons when someone put a pie in the window. I poured a cup before the pot was even half full, the few escaping dribbles boiling away loudly on the hot plate. I couldn't wait for the rest; I unfortunately had things to do.

I staggered back up the stairs and leaned on the bedroom doorframe. Star's stomach rose and fell with each breath, gently jiggling her breasts. I swore under my breath, not enough time in the day. I contemplated calling in sick just to climb back in bed with her for another round, but remembered I got a warning for attendance last weekend. I probably wouldn't get fired, but I didn't want to push my luck.

I set my coffee down and dug through the room for something to wear. We didn't have much of a dress code since we never physically interacted with customers, which was nice. After some sniffing, I settled on a Metallica shirt and yesterday's jeans. I thought about it for a moment and then dug in the closet for my tattered denim vest. I put my hair up in a ponytail, mostly because I couldn't be bothered to do anything else with it. I had to practically crawl completely under the bed to find my black biker boots that I liked, shoving various other boots out of the way. There's always that one pair that just fits better than anything else. I flopped on the bed and laced up the boots, with more effort than I care to admit.

I looked over at Star, still snoozing away without a care in the world. She had mentioned that she was on a vacation this week and clearly had no plans of doing anything constructive with the time off. I pondered this for a moment, as I was certain she didn't have a regular job to take a vacation from. I appreciated the concept, but since the rest of us did have to work, she needed to get the hell out of my bed.

I poked her a few times and frowned when that had no effect. I reached up and grabbed her nipple just firmly enough and gave it a slight twist. She screamed and bolted upright clenching her chest tightly and glared at me. I fell off the bed laughing.

"That wasn't nice, Tri... you're gonna give me titty cancer." She whined still rubbing her breast.

"You'll be fine... now get out, I gotta get to work. Lock up after yourself, yeah?" I said climbing to my feet.

I tossed her bra at her head and strolled out of the room, chuckling to myself. Mornings were always much nicer with company, even if I had to resort to having my own fun. My brain enjoyed the antics, using the activity to help wake myself up. That combined with the caffeine would be enough to get the day moving along.

I made my way down the stairs, and as I reached the bottom, remembered I had left my coffee back up in the bedroom. I frowned, going back for it would be risky and honestly too much of a hassle. Star was probably already drinking it, so I decided to just get another cup. I poured the coffee over ice and mixed it with a little hazelnut syrup, the sugar free kind that was probably still unhealthy but at least it didn't have any calories.

I gathered up my keys, my ID card, and some loose cash for lunch and headed outside. My purse was more for holding miscellany than it was being an actual purse, so I left it in the car most of the time. Star always warned me that it was a good way to get it stolen, but considering how little value it held, I wasn't too concerned. I kept my wallet in my pocket anyway, and the garage door was always closed.

I hit the button to raise the garage door and growled when it got stuck halfway, as it does only when it knows I have somewhere else to be. I'm never convinced the damn thing isn't sentient. Then again, if it were, my rent would be higher. Against my better judgment I gave it a swift kick, which hurt my shin and would likely leave a bruise. The door opened the rest of the way, and I swear I heard it laugh.

Inside the garage sat a satin black 1984 Chevrolet Camaro. I'd always been a fan of American muscle. That deep-bass roar of the engine, the blocky body, the smell of octane, it all really got me going. Even as I child, I loved watching my dad work on cars, though he usually spent more time drinking, yelling, and cussing at me than he did working on the car. Despite that, I still had a fondness for anything with an engine that could shake my bones when the engine revved.

The car had seen better days, though. The satin black paint was peeling, and there was some body rust, she had a solid frame though. There was a hole in the hood where the blower stuck out, but it was in rough shape. Only two of the three barrels worked, but she ran just fine, when she felt like it. That was something I could relate to. It was probably a little past due for an oil change as well. Still, it was more than enough to get me from place to place.

I never had the money for a real new car, but I had picked this baby off craigslist for a less than two grand. With a little help from a friend, and more than a couple paychecks spent on parts, I got it running well enough to be a daily driver. She purred like a lion with a respiratory infection when she idled but give her some gas and she would set off all the alarms of weaker cars two streets over. It always made me a little giddy.

I crawled in through the window like a racecar driver, partly because it made me feel cool, partly because the door was nearly rusted shut and I didn't want to risk it falling off if I worked too hard trying to get it open. I held my breath as I fumbled with the ignition and said a little prayer as I turned the key. I heard the engine turnover and gave the gas pedal a little tap to finish the job. She started up with little fuss and roared to life, scaring the shit out of the neighbor's dogs. They scrambled and yipped in confusion over the sudden eruption of sound, but I couldn't really hear them over the rumbling of the engine.

I always hated leaving the house this early, especially to go to work, but the car made it worth it most days. I threw it into gear and let the car pull itself out of the garage. It crept casually towards the end of the driveway, and I tightened my grip on the steering wheel, feeling a smirk forming on my face. Perhaps a little reckless driving would help get my blood pumping. The neighbors were mostly deaf old people, so I wasn't worried about upsetting them, it wasn't like they'd hear it anyway.

As the front tires reached the edge of the drive, I slammed my foot down hard on the gas and cut the wheel. The engine roared fiercely, and the back tires screamed while frantically trying to maintain grip on the pavement. The rear of the car began to spin to one side as I inched forward out of the drive, smoke billowing from the wheels. The tail end just barely missed the mailbox as I slid out onto the street and straightened the wheel. The tires finally got enough grip to launch the car forward, and I grinned devilishly for just a moment.

Today was not going to go well it seemed. A few feet down the road something resembling the sound of a bullet hitting a cast iron pan echoed from the engine bay and even the hood jumped. The car shut off suddenly, the roar of the engine replaced by ticking and hissing noises while smoke billowed out from the hood. The car coasted a little from the initial force but didn't make it very far up the hill before it started rolling back towards the house. I felt my mood darkening.

Cursing loudly, I beat my hands on the dash in protest, as if it was somehow not my fault for acting like a dumbass with a car already on the verge of death. I reluctantly let the poor beast slink back to the driveway, defeated. I retried the ignition a few times and received only clicks from the starter as a response. I sighed, and cursed, then got out to push the car back into the driveway.

I popped the hood and more smoke billowed out to greet me. I didn't know much about cars, especially broken ones, but didn't let that stop me from standing confidently over the engine bay looking as if I was prepared to beat the car until it submitted to my will and started working again. I looked things over as if somehow the secrets would reveal themselves to me out of sheer force of will, but ultimately had no success. I dropped the hood and pouted, still cursing under my breath.

Star had popped out of the house wearing a flowery sundress. She puffed happily on her vape, tilting her head towards her scooter.

"Need a lift?" She said through a cloud of vapor as I approached. I waived away the smell of blueberries and grumbled at her from behind my sunglasses.

"Fine, if I'm going to be late, might as well show up smelling like a hippie. We're stopping for a bagel though, and no I'm not buying yours." I said.

I had already hopped on the back of the little flower print, sticker-ridden tragedy she used for transportation. She grinned and took her spot in the driver's seat as I slung my purse over my shoulder. I winced as I felt the tip of a pen stab at me through the fabric. It was turning out to be one of those days.

About an hour later we arrived at the office building of my job. It was a pleasant drive along the bank of a river of questionable cleanliness. The waste treatment plan was up stream and regularly leaked actual human shit into the river. For some reason that never stopped people from using it every warm season, usually tubing at one of the various businesses that likely never checked or disclosed the current E. Coli levels.

Asheville is a very interesting place, set in the heart of the mountains; it is a liberal bastion of weird surrounded by the otherwise conservative Bible-belt. Unsurprisingly, it had become overrun with hipsters pretending to be locals once the craft beer fad gained ground. At any given time, you could be run down by a wild herd of green-fueled food trucks offering everything from tofu to blood sausage, and all sporting some new local brew. It was quaint.

My job was your typical corporate bullshit call center. Everyone shows up for their scheduled nine-to-five, deals with the unreasonably rude customers on the phones so the people making the money don't have to, and then they go home to drink until they forget where they were for the last eight hours. It paid more than minimum wage, but in this economy, which wasn't saying much. My rent was paid, and I never went hungry, but living paycheck to paycheck, or more often paycheck to a few days after paycheck, was getting old.

The employees here were like a family, dysfunctional as it may be. We weren't close really, but we all commiserated about the utter bullshit we each had to deal with each day. Someone always knew which bar had the cheap beer special each night. I often wondered if the plan was just to hire us, break our spirits, and then wait for alcoholism to kill us so they could replace us with someone else that would work for a lower wage.

Like most corporate jobs, my duties were very basic, but over scrutinized, and as such caused the highest possible amount of stress over every detail. I had been promoted several times, but most of them were sideways moves if we are being honest. Instead of dealing directly with the customers, I fiddle with numbers on spreadsheets for most of the day. The company was a large one, and on more than one occasion I had to shuffle around more money than I could make in a decade just to balance out a few accounts.

I flopped down at my desk and flicked on the computer to start the day. Given how my morning was going, I half expected the CPU to instantly overheat and explode itself through the back of my desk and burn a new hole in someone's lap. The day was just starting however, things could change. I could hear various coworkers chatting away with each other or on the phone with customers, general day to day call center work.

It was amusing to me how mediocre the call center was in the American job market. We had partners overseas in the Philippines and to them working at a call center was prestigious. They all wore suits and carried briefcases and bragged about their high-paying American job around town. In some places people were even required to attend a call center college for two years before they could work in one. It was one of the most sought-after jobs over there. My wage overseas would have me living and eating like a queen, but here I was making only a few dollars more than minimum wage and had to scrape by, hoping no big expenses popped, like my damn car breaking down on the way to work or something.

A few hours passed as I mindlessly typed away at my numbers and chewed on my bagel. A little message popped up on my screen reminding me to take one of my required breaks for the day. Most days I hated the fifteen-minute breaks, sure they were paid breaks, but they always seemed to interrupt my flow of work right as I got into a good stride on a project. Today was different, I had to get out of the building and get some fresh air. A girl can only stand so much filtered and recirculated butt stank with a lingering hangover.

I grabbed a soda from the break room and went to plop down under a tree outside. The sun was still far brighter than should be legal, but the air smelled fantastic. There was a spring shower building in the mountains and the freshness was wafting down into our valley. It practically gave me an olfactory orgasm.

I always tried to appreciate the small things in life, the smell of rain and the sound of thunder. Thunderstorms had always captivated me as a child. It didn't matter how bad things were at home, sitting on the porch and watching a storm would calm me down. I loved to watch the water race down the glass door, and if the storm was close enough the sound of thunder would drown out the loud voices behind me, if only for a few seconds.

As an adult, listening to storms was still one of my favorite ways to relax. I even had an old mp3 player full of rainforest thunderstorms hooked up in the bedroom for the nights I had trouble sleeping. I managed to position the speakers just right so that it sounded like the storm was in the room with me. I even bought a candle that smelled close enough to real petrichor that if I closed my eyes, I could picture myself sitting on that porch as a child again, enjoying the moment to myself. Sadly, the rain didn't make it down to the building until well after my break was over.

I spent the rest of the day emailing copies of the spreadsheets I corrected to the various middle management in the building. Chances were if my work revealed anything important, they would just take my name off it and show it to their superiors as their own findings. They would get a raise; I would get a pat on the back and asked to find more. It was nothing new, just life as a cog in the great corporate wheel, ever turning, keeping the squeaking to a minimum so as not to get replaced.

Finally, after what seemed more like months than minutes, the end of the day rolled around, so I clocked out and headed outside. The rain had subsided, but the smell was still there, and I decided to walk down to the gas station at the corner. They had a little diner-style restaurant attached to it that served something that mostly resembled food. It wouldn't kill you, and honestly didn't taste that bad. It didn't taste that good either, but it was cheap and if you didn't examine it too closely, it would go down easily.

As I stepped through the door, the smell of bacon sizzling on the flat top hit me like a truck, and my stomach trembled to remind me just how hungry I was having only a bagel and a few sodas to get me through the day. I loved hole-in-the-wall joints like this and looked for them whenever possible. It didn't matter if the food was any good, each place was its own little experience. This one, for example, was decorated with kitschy little figures, plastic plants, and every surface had some kind of red and white checkered tile. Old license plates and signs with farm animals or equipment lined the walls, a distinctly southern bit of Americana décor. You had to wonder how racist the regulars were, but you also knew the grits would be delicious.

I took a table in the back corner, near the coffee machine, and waived at a few familiar faces, our whole staff usually visited since it was so close to the office. I ordered a BLT sandwich and some hash browns without even glancing at a menu, and the server brought me an empty cup and a mostly fresh pot of coffee while I waited. It was still warm, and only a little bit greasy.

I absent-mindedly stared at her ass as she maneuvered back into the kitchen to shout my order at the half-deaf cook, then whipped out my phone. I scrolled through social media looking for something interesting to occupy my time. There wasn't anything terribly exciting, just the usual: memes, cat pictures, conspiracy theories, memes about cats having conspiracy theories, and of course the unrestrained personal drama from that one friend we all have. The one you keep on your list just so you can watch them spew bullshit and start fights they have no chance of winning, mostly because it's better than anything scripted on TV.

With the well of entertainment on social media tapped out, I decided to scroll through my dating apps to see if anything interesting popped up there instead. Being a redhead, I was practically a walking fetish that apparently needed constant reminders of my role as a sexual object. My DMs were always full, but the messages were mostly dick pics from underwhelming men that really didn't have much to show off. There was the occasional impressive one, but usually not for the reason they expected. Honestly, who wants that much metal flopping around down there?

My food arrived, and I shared a good laugh at one with the server who had apparently gotten the same picture a week ago. I made mental note of her single-and-looking status and started in on my sandwich. The bread was toasted just enough to not be considered plain bread and was saturated with so much "butter" that it dripped when I picked it up. I told myself the lettuce was wilted from the heat and not because it was old, and that the tomato was mushy and flavorless because my tongue was focused on the bacon.

I gazed around the diner while I ate, observing my surroundings out of habit. People-watching was always a fun game. I found it useful to know exactly who and what was around me in case something went awry in my general vicinity. You never know who's going to take an extra dose of crazy before heading into a public place. Someone wakes up on the wrong side of the second amendment and suddenly decides they need an AR-15 to buy a damn sandwich.

There wasn't much to see today. It was mostly empty, save for a few elderly people having their abnormally early dinner. For some reason little restaurants attached to the side of a gas station never seem to be popular with the younger crowds. Sure, it wasn't five-star cuisine, or the newest and hottest spot on the block, but it was cooked from fresh ingredients if you believed the poorly laminated paper sign by the door, and it stuck to your ribs. It was just greasy enough to cut through a hangover that lingered around far too long, which should be enough of an appeal to those around here. This was a beer city, after all.

I found myself staring at some crows fighting over scraps in the parking lot as I finished my food. I stood and dropped some cash on the table for the bill with a nice tip. I decided to take a chance and left my number on the receipt for the server before heading out the door. She was always friendly with me but that's more indicative of her career than her sexual preferences.

I made my way over to the gas station and stepped up to the counter. The sign above the scratch-offs was illuminated and boasting the prize totals for the various drawings. It had been a while since anyone had hit the jackpot, so the total for the Supreme-O-Million had jumped up over seven hundred million dollars. My heartbeat sped up a little thinking about the number. I imagined the wonderful life I could live with money like that, picturing myself lounging by the ocean in a cabana filled with liquor and naked bodies.

The lottery was run by the state's education board, supposedly to help fund state schools. I hadn't figured out the math behind it completely, but it seemed like they pooled all the money from the ticket prices, paid for the printing, set aside a percentage for the prize pool and pocketed the rest for the school system. Though, it was more likely that the money was dumped into the stock market and profits were deposited in personal accounts first with only small donations to the school board. The fact that the prize amount had gotten so high without anyone winning should have said something for the odds, but the thrill of possibility was enough to get anyone's blood pumping. Hell, they have the hotline for gambling addiction printed directly on the tickets.

I didn't gamble often, but every now and then when the prize got high, I'd take a chance and buy a ticket. It was cheap, and the money went to a good cause, in theory anyway. I selected my numbers and ran the ticket through the machine, while it processed, I picked out a couple scratch-tickets. They never seemed to amount to much more than a free case of beer from time to time, but it gave me something to fiddle with while I waited on the drawing in a few days.

I strolled outside and plopped down on a bench, pulling my phone from my bra. I texted Star for a ride home, she said that morning she would be around when I got off, so it shouldn't take long for her to pick me up. I pulled a coin from my purse and looked over the two scratch tickets. One boasted a grand prize of two million dollars, and the other claimed you could receive five thousand dollars per week for life.

The latter was far more exciting, as it meant I could quit my job and easily transition into a life of wealth with a steady stream of income higher than I would ever possibly need in a week. Bulk prizes were nice, but I was certain I could spend 2 million in a weekend with enough thought and be right back to being broke, only in a nicer house that I wouldn't be able to afford the taxes on. With five grand a week, every week, I could start investing and building up to things more easily while focusing on a hobby or starting my own business instead killing my soul in my dead-end job. I often thought about what it would be like to work solely for my own benefit instead of making rich people richer.

I frantically scribbled the coin across the surface of the card, revealing the numbers needed to win first. I memorized them and then took to the task of scratching the boxes in the game field looking for matches. A few times I found a number just one away from a match, but no winners. I huffed and tossed it in the trash can, looking over the other card for a moment.

I scratched off the list of numbers first and then started working on my numbers and my heart skipped a beat when I found a match. I trembled, butterflies the size of school buses fluttering in my gut as I stared at the matching number. Could this be the day I finally get out of this shithole of a life? Would I reveal the box to be the grand prize and walk away from this gas station in bum-fuck-nowhere a millionaire?

I was giddy with the potential, the realist in me trying to reason with myself, reminding me of the odds and insisting it was nearly impossible. I moved the coin towards the prize area and pressed down, gently biting my lower lip in preparation. I closed my eyes and rubbed the coin over the prize area, eager to see what lies beneath but too scared to look. I lifted the ticket up and blew the dust off, and then slowly opened my eyes.

I had closed them so tightly my vision was blurry at first. My heart was racing, my breathing hastened as the focus returned.

"Aw, motherfucker...." I exclaimed loudly, startling a few passersby.

The ticket almost seemed to mock me, proudly displaying five dollars in the prize box. I had spent ten to buy the damn thing, so that didn't even break even. I growled under my breath as I went back inside to redeem the prize and traded the credit out for a five-dollar ticket. I scratched this one off at the counter, and just as I figured, it came up empty.

I chucked the losing tickets in the trash as I headed back outside. I shouldn't have gotten my hopes up, but that was the thrill of it after all. Anticipation, chance, the adrenaline high surging in as you let your imagination run wild. I checked my phone, but still no answer from Star, so I sat back down on the bench and waited. I spent the next couple hours just watching people coming and going.

There was a lady pumping gas that seemed rather underdressed, even for a warm day. If she was anyone else, I'm sure she'd be badgered by horny guys being generally rude in public but looked like she might chew the head off anyone with the balls to try. She had an aura of "fuck around and find out" to her. You could have told me one of her parents was a bear and I'd only curiously wonder which one.

Across from her, some kids were dangling out a car window bashing each other in the head with stuffed toys and squealing loudly while their mother just stared blankly into the distance while pumping her gas. She looked like a damn zombie. Her eyes were completely bereft of any life that may have once blossomed within her. It was as if her humanity had been sucked right out of her.

I was a little torn as I watched the children play, I knew I wanted kids someday, but wasn't certain I was ready for the responsibility. I felt like I didn't make enough money to support a child either, they were expensive little bastards, always needing to be fed and what not. I wasn't sure if I wanted to adopt or have my own. If so, did I want to be inseminated, or try to find a man I could tolerate for more than his penis?

These were decisions that were best left for another time, I thought to myself as a very large and very loud pickup roared into the gas station. I liked to call them "little-dick" trucks, as they were clearly compensators. I knew that much was true, my Camaro was compensating for mine. In fact, my penis was so small it was a vulva.

A short, stout, young man hopped out wearing a sleeveless flannel shirt, faded blue jeans, brown work boots and safety wraparound sunglasses and I nearly choked on the irony. The man was a walking stereotype for the south; all he was missing was a cheating wife and baying hound dog, and maybe some tassels. He spit a mouthful of tobacco into the trash, well, mostly into the trash. A large wad of the nasty stuff rolled down the side of the can. Utterly disgusting, this is exactly why I prefer dating other women.

This vagrant display of fragile masculinity was thankfully interrupted by the sound of Star's scooter sliding into a nearby parking space. She had changed into a nearly transparent white dress with tiny flowers and skulls scattered about over top of light blue panties and a matching tank top. Her hair was up in pigtails behind a set of rider's goggles, and she had a lollipop stick hanging out of her mouth. She had some elbow-length, fingerless, leather gloves and knee-high leather boots adorned with some bronze and silver cogs. Her appearance was naturally sexy but fashionably disjointed.

She was a freelance model, working mostly on her own through paid websites and social media, but she took gigs with photographers from time to time if she needed the cash. She must have given up on her supposed vacation and took a gig during the afternoon. It was likely that she just threw on the first bit of clothing she pulled out of her backpack after the shoot.

I was a little jealous of her from time to time. I was stuck in a shitty job, slaving away for someone else, while she just took pictures of herself and posted them online. I knew there was more work involved, but I often simplified it in my head out of frustration. There were hours spent on marketing and deciphering website TOS loopholes about nudity. There was learning how to set up lights to make the scene look natural but still emphasizing her body in the right way. It was art, and art takes time and effort I just never seemed to have.

It really just confused me more than anything, not because of the work, but how carefree she seemed. She didn't have a meticulous schedule to worry about, so she was constantly spending her time as she wished. Despite everything though, it didn't garner her a lavish lifestyle by any means.

She had a nice phone, and of course she had that scooter, but I had never once been to her place. I wasn't sure she even had one. It seemed she just bounced from couch to couch, occasionally doing favors for meals but never really asked for anything in return. She just seemed to always be available. She was certainly reliable, almost to a fault, and always tried never to let anyone down.

I knew her better than most people did, and I knew that lifestyle occasionally took its toll on her. We would get together, have a few drinks, and then head back to my place to fool around. After the fun, when we just lay there in the dark with our sweaty bodies pressed together staring up at the ceiling, we would talk. She would tell me about things in her past, her childhood, and her family life that were almost unbelievable when you considered how bubbly she was day to day.

Her sister was half psychotic and total asshole, and like most families her parents had their own issues that weighed heavily on her. She had been through a lot, even as a teenager, which would make the average person cringe. I could only lay there and listen and tighten my arms around her when she started to cry. I had nothing to say to seal the wounds but letting her vent to me seemed to help.

She would cry herself to sleep a lot, and it made my heart ache. I cared deeply for her, and it was because of those fragile intimate moments where she poured her soul out to me. It was probably easy for her to talk to me because we had such similar pasts. We both grew up with less than great situations, bullied in school for various reasons, and abused at home by family. I could relate to her pain, because I had felt something similar myself.

We weren't officially dating; in fact, the subject had never even come up. I wasn't seeing anyone, just the occasional fling, and Star did the same, but we slept with each other far more than anyone else. Admittedly there was something deeper going on between us. Many nights we didn't even have sex, we both just wanted someone to commiserate with and talk away the stress of the day.

She roused me back to reality with a poke on the head and a bright smile. I'm not sure how long I had been sitting there lost in thought. I stood up and gave her a peck on the forehead. It had been a long stressful day at work, and it was nice to see her.

We hopped on the scooter and headed off towards the house, and I held onto her maybe a little tighter than usual. That may have been due to her driving though; she was clearly in a good mood, coasting in and out of lanes going around slower or stopped traffic. We even dipped off road a few times despite my shouting for the contrary and to watch where she was going. She simply giggled and sped up faster, seemingly racing against some invisible opponent, and loving every minute of my despair.

We stopped at a light, and I could hear my stomach growling over the idle of the bees in a tin can that passed for the scooter's engine.

"Hey, if you're done trying to kill me, can we grab some food?" I asked over her shoulder.

"Mmm, okay. What did you have in mind? Wanna hit up something downtown? I hear there's a new noodle shop that cooks authentic Korean dishes." She suggested.

"Oh, I heard about that, didn't it open up where the pastry shop used to be?" I asked, "That could be interesting. I'm always in the mood for Asian food."

She nodded and revved the engine to keep it from dying out while we waited on the light. It changed, and we cruised off towards the infamous downtown Asheville.

The city part of Asheville was typical of a smaller scale city. It's no Charlotte, or Atlanta to be sure, but it has its charm if you're into that sort of thing. I personally preferred the quieter, more rural areas. However, if you wanted to eat something that wasn't from a franchise or chain, downtown was the place to go.

There were numerous bars, pubs, and taverns to crawl due in great part to the various breweries in the area. Asheville had been nominated Beer City, USA a few years in a row due to its booming micro-brewery scene. If you could think of something to make beer from or in, chances are someone in Asheville had already done it and was turning a profit. As you would expect, all that craft local beer brought on the hipsters in droves, but that was a recent change.

The real face of Asheville was truly and delightfully weird. In a ten-foot span of sidewalk, on just about any street, you could see hippie girls with flowers in their dreadlocks, giant multicolored mohawks, thick bushy beards, and a mile of tattoo ink, and it was glorious. Sometimes you got a weird combination of those things rolled into one person, and that was just normal in Asheville. Cars rolled around with bumper stickers bearing the legend KEEP ASHEVILLE WEIRD for a reason. We were all a little off here, and we enjoyed every moment of it.

We cruised down an alley way, Star was a fan of shortcuts on her little scooter whether they were legal or not. She would drive anywhere the thing fit and dare anyone to question the decision. Occasionally a police officer would say something about her driving habits, but she would just smile that innocent little smile of hers and then apologize with a bit of a pout, and they tended to look the other way. She had stolen one of the local police support stickers that were given to donors to the force and displayed it proudly amongst the various Peace Frog and other beach stickers on the scooter's limited real estate. It helped, the cops would always thank her for her support, and she'd smile and giggle to herself.

We skidded to a halt at the end of the alley and Star hopped off excitedly. She always loved going out to eat, didn't matter with whom. Depending on the establishment she rarely ever paid. Given too much of a chance and the girl could flirt her way out of anything.

Her favorite technique involved flirting with the young male servers, playing off their hormonal frustrations. A little eyelash batting, some pouting lips, and a cute voice saying "pwease" would get her way with most of them. Eighteen-year-old boys are also quick to buy a girl's meal if she offers to buy them booze later and gives them a phone number. Whatever works.

Star had clearly spent too much time around me and my deviousness had rubbed off on her. Most of the time she gave out numbers from old boyfriends or flings, expecting a hilarious phone conversation. One time she accidentally gave a guy his older brother's number, which didn't go over so well. I imagine the next family gathering was a little awkward.

Occasionally she'd add a note that just said 'sext me' with a little winking smiley face, and then hang out with whoever owned the number she gave. Mostly, that person was me. She was responsible for more unsolicited dick pics than any of my dating apps. It usually made for entertaining conversations as we got drunk and reviewed the attempts. One particularly desperate weekend resulted in a booty call for me, so I guess it's not always an annoyance.

We made our way into the restaurant and waited to be seated. The delicious aromas assaulted me, something about the smell of soy sauce and sesame oil just made me happy. I love Asian food, doesn't really matter what kind. I had recently discovered soup dumplings and had in one sitting spent seventy-five dollars on them just for myself. It wasn't my proudest moment, but damn if they weren't delicious.

As most places were downtown, the place was packed. People dipping in and out to pick up to-go orders, servers darting around avoiding people and raking in tips with the dirty dishes, tourists staring through the window like they feared something eating them if they went inside. It was the typical Asheville restaurant experience.

We looked over the menu for a little while, and finally settled on sharing a large plate of something I couldn't pronounce but the ingredients made it sound interesting. It appeared to be what I like to call the kitchen-sink menu item, a large plate with a heaping pile of food consisting of a little bit of everything else the place offered. I was an adventurous eater, and if you set something in front of me and called it food, chances are I'd try it. I had always wanted to travel the world one day and just eat until my heart or stomach exploded, either would be a glorious death sure to echo in the great feasting halls of Valhalla.

The food arrived quicker than expected, and we dug in like we hadn't eaten in weeks. A few of the staff stared with mouths agape as I attacked the pile of food like a starved animal that just found a brimming trashcan. I doused my portion with the hottest stuff I could find, and then shoveled the food into my face with an almost unnatural quickness. Star was a little slower but not by much, and within mere moments the mountain of food had been reduced to a molehill.

We both leaned back in our chairs, patting our stomachs. Star belched, loudly, and I'm almost certain I heard the window rattle. It was a pleasant dinner, despite the awkward stares. We sat there for a little while longer sipping on our drinks, chatting about our day, and picking at the remaining food before ultimately asking for a to-go box. We wrapped up the remaining food and I met Star outside the door after I paid.

It had gotten dark out, and the city's face was changing. As night fell you would see the street performers and buskers fade away and the houseless people settling onto benches or underpasses for the night if they couldn't make it to the shelter in time. The businesspeople in their smart suits were gone as well, replaced by the night club goers cruising around in their cars, blasting their music as if trying intentionally to compete with the surrounding noise. I liked the city a lot less at night as the people on various substances became belligerent and harder to cope with.

We hurried to the scooter and worked our way through the traffic to get home. I didn't live far, nothing is all that far from downtown in such a small city, but it still took a while to get home due to the frequent traffic jams at the city exits. There were far too many people coming in to have fun at the late-night attractions of the city for my liking. I only ventured into the bars on occasion if I was looking for a hookup, and that usually meant I was desperate.

I like to go to concerts now and then, but I can't dance, and overly drunk people get on my nerves, especially in crowds. They got even harder to tolerate when I got drunk. I honestly preferred to drink at home where, if I had a bit too much, I could retreat to my room and pass out without having to worry about other people getting in the way. If I didn't make it, it was my house, so it didn't matter how naked I was or on what stair I was drooling.

We pulled into the driveway and as the headlight panned over my car I growled. I had almost forgotten about it breaking down this morning. Thankfully I had the next few days off and could fiddle with it, and then call someone over that actually knew what they were doing. That was a problem for tomorrow though.

I loved to drive my car; it was certainly fun. Upkeep on a vehicle was just so tedious, all the fluid and tire changing and what not. Science really needed to get on top of making a car that never needed basic maintenance. Seemed like something Elon Musk would steal the idea for and then claim Tesla invented.

My foot was only just past the threshold of the front door before I took off my pants. During the warm season I liked to lounge around the house in my jammies, and it was always my priority when getting home. I kept a pair on the couch just in case I didn't feel like walking all the way to the bedroom to change, tonight was one of those nights. Star followed suit, taking of her heavy leather gloves and boots and reducing her attire to just the tank and panties. I pinched her butt playfully.

"Don't you have a home to go to?" I asked as we flopped down on the couch.

"Aren't I already there? " She smiled back and grabbed the remote for the TV.

"Seriously though, Star. Do you even have a place? Where do you sleep when you aren't crashing here with me? Are you renting somewhere?" I asked thoughtfully.

It occurred to me again that I had never stayed over at her place. I was curious as to whether she was paying for a place that she never stayed at, which would be kind of silly. She looked distant for a moment before responding.

"I keep some things at my parent's house, but I'm not really staying anywhere. I tend to just crash on couches or sleep with someone for a place to stay for the night. I know my modeling seems glamorous, but I don't make that much money doing it and rent is so high around here, it's hard to find anything I can afford." She replied.

I looked at her for a long moment, a little shocked and confused. I hadn't considered she might be houseless. It explained several things that I had wondered about, like why she always had her bag full of clothes and toiletries, or why she was always asking to use my shower. I reached out and put my arm around her.

"I'm sorry, I didn't know."

I paused and felt a certain heaviness in my chest as I prepared for what I was going to say next. My anxiety was building fast. I was never any good with this sort of thing. I wanted to say it, and my brain thought of what seemed like a million ways at once and I was having a hard time deciding which order of words I wanted to use.

She turned and looked directly into my eyes, and I could practically hear her asking for help from those deep blue pools.

"I have a spare bedroom, you know. There's no bed, but plenty of room for your stuff…" I stammered, "I mean, we already sleep together regularly. Do you want to make it a thing?"

"Are you asking me to move in with you, and to be your girlfriend?" She asked and then paused for a moment.

"All at once too, damn Tri you are making progress. Next, you'll be asking me to marry you and have your babies." She smirked.

She knew I was uncomfortable, probably heard the anxiety in my voice when I spoke, but she was trying to lighten the mood by picking at me.

"Ha-ha, mock me all you want, I was just offering you a place to stay. Everyone needs a place to call home.

See if I'm ever nice to you again, I've got half a mind to... hey, get off!"

I was cut off by a sudden attack as Star pounced on me and began tickling me relentlessly. She managed to get me on my back and pin me beneath her. I struggled to get free, and she just pinned my arms above my head. We were both laughing hard at this point and starting to pant a little from the exertion. She leaned her face close to mine and looked deep into my eyes for a moment and as I paused to enjoy the view, she closed them and pressed her lips against mine.

Her kiss tasted ever so slightly like cherry, her favorite gloss, and her lips were as soft as velvet. She pressed my head back against the cushion and began to slowly rock her hips. I just let everything happen, enjoying the bliss and spontaneity of the moment. Her hair fell around our faces like a curtain, letting only glimpses of light through from the television, trapping me in a little cage that I never wanted to leave.

My heart was already racing before she even started moving her hands down my body. She caressed my chest with the most delicate touch, carefully tracing around my nipples with her fingertips. Each of her movements had a certain rhythm to it that was just perfect. I exhaled slowly and then gently bit her lower lip as her hand continued lower. She shifted her position just enough to get her hand under my waistband and between my legs.

A few seconds later I was launched into a state of euphoria. My eyes rolled back in my head as she worked her magic, and I felt like I was somewhere else. I was suddenly lying in a great sea of silk, with ribbons of it crashing over my naked body like waves and gently pulling away like the retreating tide. My senses were overloaded with ecstasy, and I couldn't help but cry out to the sky above.

She tugged my clothing away and the sensations changed as she replaced her fingers with her tongue and the warmth of her breath washed over me. I was soaring through the sky with the sun setting in the distance. I was carried through the clouds by a pair of wings that had sprouted from my back and my muscles tensed with every movement. Each thrust of the wings moved me higher through the vast blue sky until I was able to see over all the clouds. It was beautiful, and I hung there for a moment taking it all in.

I could feel an urge building. Something within me was getting very warm. Had I followed in the folly of Icarus and flown too close to the sun? Every inch of my body tingled, and I felt as if I could burst into flames at any moment.

I tucked my wings and let myself plummet below the clouds. The rush of the free fall was exhilarating. As I broke the cloud cover, I could see the ocean below, and the burning sensation drove me towards it. I needed the cool release of the water washing over me. It would be my only solace from this heat. I cried out and I could feel my pulse hastening, my chest heaving with each breath.

I had lost all sense of my physical self, caught up in the intense sensations my body was feeling. I clenched my eyes shut as I plummeted through the sky towards the great sea below. I could feel the wind on my face as I rushed forward, my nerves felt like they were on fire now. Then in a moment, I felt the water rush over me dousing the heat.

The release was so intense I could feel my entire body convulsing. The cold water embraced me as if I had always belonged there, the currents gliding over my skin cooling every inch of my tired body. The waves lapped at me, drenching me with moisture as I relaxed.

I opened my eyes as Star rose back up to give me another kiss. She was smiling from ear to ear, and I was panting like I had just run a marathon. I was even a little dizzy.

"I'd love to move in with you, Trianna. I've never felt more at home anywhere else." she said quietly, laying her head down on my chest.

We laid in silence, gently caressing each other. Star was always great in bed, but this was different. That was something magical, there was a connection that I had never felt before. I must have been tired, I was getting all sappy, but I knew I had made the right decision. I was ready to settle down, and Star was the best possibility.

I smiled and kissed her forehead, careful not to wake her, and then let myself drift off to sleep. I had the most wonderful dreams and slept better than ever before.

CHAPTER 2

The light of the morning sun pounded on the windows, begging to get inside. A few crafty rays managed to sneak past the blinds and blast into the room. They crept along the floor searching for a way to leap into my eyes. Inch by inch they moved across the room until finally they found something reflective to bounce off and leap to the edge of the couch. The light moved more vigorously now, seeking its goal. My head rolled to side, and that was all it took. Within in seconds the photons rocketed directly onto my face, the little bastards. I groaned and covered my face with my arm, but the damage had been done.

I wiped the sleep from my eyes and lifted my head, squinting to take in my surroundings. Star was beside me on the couch, still snoozing peacefully. I envied her ability to sleep so soundly and carefree. She barely even stirred when I slipped out from under her and slammed my shin on the coffee table.

I rubbed my leg, yawned loudly, and made my way to the kitchen, pausing to stare at the coffee pot for a moment. I had left the pot on all day yesterday when I left for work, and there was still enough for a cup. It was warm, sure, but it was probably a little burnt having sat there so long. I debated whether it was worth drinking or just waiting while I made more. I decided to drink it out of desperation, poured a cup, and then started brewing a new batch.

I leaned on the counter and stared out at the glass doors that lead to the deck out back. The back yard was mostly trees and bushes and other sorted plants, not much of a yard at all really. The thickness of the foliage did however encourage visits from all kinds of animals. That was my favorite part about living in Asheville.

The city proper had almost everything you could ever want to spend money on, but if you just wanted to relax and enjoy nature, then the outskirts were the place to be. We had plenty of forested areas that promoted wildlife to flourish and flourish it did. We had birds, squirrels, chipmunks, snakes, frogs, turtles, deer, foxes, wolves, bears, coyotes, raccoons, possums, and who knows what else that all liked to forage through the wooded areas. It certainly wasn't uncommon to find one or more of them rooting through your trash.

It was beginning to look like a nice day outside. The weather was almost always tame in the mountains, for the most part anyway. All year round we experienced relatively mild weather conditions, save for a few months where we seemed to hit some interesting extremes. The last few years we had barely gotten any snow, and it seemed to be less and less each year, which was sad. I really like snow.

The summers got quite hot in the later months, but nothing compared to other places. Late July and August were usually the worst of it, but even then, not terrible. The mountains were a really nice place to sit around and do nothing and just soak in the natural world. Which, honestly, is how I would have preferred to spend my day.

I sipped at my coffee, grimacing slightly at the burnt taste, and thought about the day. I needed to look at the car and figure out what the hell went wrong this time. Laundry could probably wait another day; I still had a few things to wear. I checked through the fridge and kitchen cabinets to see if I needed groceries. I had a decent supply of canned and boxed foodstuff, so I wouldn't starve.

Aside from the car it looked like I had a day to relax after all. I had recently gotten a new zombie game I was eager to try out. It was one of those games where you mindlessly ran around and collected items while doing side quests because the main story was a little lacking. Still, it was pretty fun having a couple brews and blasting open some rotting skulls. I enjoyed the simple things, after all.

I looked around for my phone, so I could try to find someone to help with the car, it was painfully obvious that I wouldn't have much luck on my own. I found it in my pocket, and of course the battery was dead, having not been charged since the night before. I pouted and looked around for a charger to take with me out to the garage. I pulled one from the wall in the living room and glanced out the window as I stood back up.

The mail truck was outside, and the postman was hefting a stack of things into my mailbox. I cracked opened the door and a gust of air reminded me that I wasn't wearing anything from the waist down. I fumbled around looking for my panties to climb back into, and then strolled out to the mailbox. I don't have the typical concept of modesty, especially on my own overgrown property. The neighbors barely left their houses anyway, they were old and spent most of their days rotting in front of their televisions.

At the box, I retrieved the stack of things the mailman had so gently crammed inside like how you would stuff a turkey, that you hated, while you were drunk. I often got piles of junk mail, as if someone had put me on a mailing list, or seven. Probably an ex. I flipped through the envelopes tossing out the obvious junk, there were receipts for my bills that were on auto-pay that I've repeatedly set on paperless, and a couple magazines I had cancelled a while back, but they kept sending me issues anyway. They were probably just excited to have something to do with their physical copies in the internet age.

I was excited to see a couple of small packages in the very back of the box. I had a bad habit of getting drunk and then pulling my phone out to shop online. I usually forgot before the next morning that I had bought anything, so it was like having a little drunk elf depositing gifts every couple of weeks. Sometimes it was things that I actually wanted or needed, but usually it was dumb shit that drunk me thought was hilarious, like an egg separator shaped like a nose. It was gross and didn't really work all that well.

As I bent over to reach into the mailbox them, I heard some snickering from the neighbor's yard. The neighbor's grandchildren were apparently visiting and had decided to sneak a peek at the neighbor girl walking around in her panties. I rolled my eyes, dirty little boys that probably didn't even know what to do with anything they were seeing. I tossed a stern look directly at the bushes they thought they were hiding behind and heard them scurry off.

I walked back into the house and into the garage, plugging my phone in to charge for a while. I tossed the mail on the counter and tore open one of the packages. It was the new CD I had ordered, from one of my favorite metal bands, Gorehowl. Yes, I still buy CDs, eat me. The album was called The Bloodied Path to Victory, its cover depicting a poorly stereotyped and oversized Viking wading through piles of bodies moving towards a glowing citadel. I love dark and heavy music, the kind of music that makes prudes clutch their pearls and hurry off to church.

I quickly opened it and popped it in my beat-up stereo, a little death metal always brightens up the day. I cranked up the volume and bobbed my head along with the beat. The band's vocalist was a stunningly beautiful woman named Alexis, she had a voice like an angel, and I'm talking the biblical kind that starts conversations with 'BE NOT AFRAID' and have too many eyes. Her harmonies were sweet and lovely, and she backed them up with a scream that could chill to the bone.

I opened the next package and was delighted to see it was a bag of specialty coffee. The beans were cured in a whiskey barrel, which imparted some flavor to the final roast. It had an aroma of aged wood and caramel and boasted a caffeine level high enough that it could likely kill someone. I think they lean into that idea for marketing in the hopes that it will stave off any lawsuits.

I stepped back inside to put away the mail and to put on some shorts before heading back out to check out the car. I passed my cat, Echo, on the stairs who mewed at me lazily, barely lifting her head. She was a Siamese and certainly had the troublemaking personality most people expect from the breed. She was kind of an asshole sometimes, but I found that endearing and relatable.

Once in my room I quickly slipped on a mostly clean pair of shorts and then headed over to the cat bowl by the closet back in the hallway. I scooped some dry food into the bowl hoping the offering was enough to spare my life for another day. She came bounding into the room, very excited by the sound the kibbles made bouncing into the metal bowl. She purred loudly and it was clear I had pleased my master. With my life no longer in immediate feline danger I stepped into my flip flops and headed back down to the garage.

I cranked up the music a little more, head bobbing along as I moved over to the toolbox and flipped it open for easy access. Inside was everything you would expect to need to work on the most delicate and intricate problems around the house: A hammer, five mismatched crescent wrenches, six screwdrivers, a broken tape measure, some random sockets, and handfuls of various bolts and screws that I would never use for anything. Ever. Clearly a masterful and expertly curated set of equipment.

I walked over to the car and plopped down into the driver's seat. I turned the keys and tried to crank it up, hoping that somehow it had magically fixed itself overnight and I could claim that I had painstakingly fixed every part of the engine to get it working again. People would gather in the street to cheer and swoon at my adept abilities as a master mechanic. Hell, maybe I'd even get a statue.

Sadly, that was not the case. The engine stirred but only just and then puttered out at once. There were some clicking noises as the relays and lights tried to urge the rest of the car to start, but she sat quiet and still as I released the ignition. Perhaps the fanfare needed some time to amass.

I hopped out, popped the hood, and moved around front to take a closer look at things. I checked the things I knew a little about, fluid levels, spark plugs, all seemed fine. I scratched my head and tried to think of what else could be the problem. The effort was fruitless however, as I had about as much movement in my head as I did from the engine.

Resigning myself to the idea the problem must be elsewhere, I went back to the garage table and grabbed the jack. Maybe if I lifted the car up, I could see if anything seemed out of place there. I poked my head in first to see if anything was leaking or obvious. The ground was dry, and nothing was hanging down, so I crawled underneath despite every alarm in my head blaring that I was more likely to be crushed under the car than gain any useful information.

Swallowing my nerves, I was able to find the flywheel and the starter, two parts I had to have replaced previously. I checked to see if anything had broken but from what I could tell everything was in order. I poked around at various things trying to tell what purpose they served but only managed to get my fingers covered in grease. I decided I would likely need to cancel the parade.

I crawled back out from under the car and lowered the jack putting the car safely back on the ground. I huffed and blew the hair from my face, my brow furrowed partly from thought, partly from frustration. I grabbed my phone now that it had time to charge a little and started looking for some help. I posted a message up on a couple social sites in hopes that someone I knew could look at it without me having to get it towed somewhere. I went inside and poured a fresh cup of coffee while I waited for an answer.

The TV was on, signaling Star had finally decided to wake up. She was watching some documentary about a serial killer, as she often liked to do. I could hear the voice-over describing a grisly scene of a disemboweled prostitute and couldn't help but think I had heard it sampled in a metal song somewhere. We each had our own twisted interests.

My phone loudly vibrated a few times on the steel worktable, indicating I had a message, so I hurried back out to the garage to check. One of the guys I used to work with said he was in the neighborhood and would be glad to stop by and check it out for me. He was a car hobbyist and likely would be able to identify the problem with ease, so I told him to head on over.

"Star.... Put on some clothes, we're gonna have company soon. Jackson is going to come check out my car, see why it's not working." I yelled through the door.

"Ugh... yes master." She responded sarcastically. Clearly, she was not interested in leaving her show unattended.

"I should go pick up my things anyway if I'm moving in. I've got stuff in a few places. What's wrong with the car?"

"Hell, if I know. If I did, I wouldn't need Jackson's help, now would I?" I shot back over my coffee. She enjoyed pushing my buttons.

"Okay, okay, don't have to be an ass about it. You need anything while I'm out?" she asked in between huffs while she got back into her tall boots. They looked awesome but looked difficult to get on.

"Nah, I think we're good, unless you wanna pick up some booze or something." I replied.

I set my coffee down to bang my head and play air guitar to the song blasting from the garage. It was a real headbanger. No matter what kind of problem I was having, some face-melting, loud-ass, djenty death metal always made it a bit easier to cope. I went back out to the garage and killed some time fiddling with things that needed to be cleaned up.

I had a lot of random stuff that just seemed to collect in piles for no reason. I threw some things away and tried to organize others. That passed enough time for Star to leave and Jackson to arrive and check out the car. I was thankful for the aid.

Jackson was an interesting fellow; he kept his hair buzzed short, but his beard was wild and unruly. He was tall but stocky and had a bit of a beer belly forming behind his grungy plaid shirt. I met him when I worked at my last job. It was a warehouse job where I moved boxes from one stack to another all day, not all that different than what I did at my current job, just with numbers instead of heavy boxes.

He popped the hood and wiped some grime off a few things, poking around with his flashlight. He closed the hood and shook his head. I didn't like the look on his face as he walked towards me wiping his hands on a rag.

"Whoa, hey now... you don't look like someone who is about to tell me my car can be easily fixed with some duct tape and sheer force of will." I blurted trying to stave off the dread of the impending bad news.

"Well, that would work if you meant duct taping a bomb to it and forcing it off a sheer cliff." He replied not hiding the grim reality.

"You threw a rod, and in the process managed to crack part of the manifold. She's dead in the water I'm afraid. Replacing the whole engine is probably the cheapest fix at this point. Though judging by the shape of her, you might be better off getting a new— "

"DON'T!" I cut him off, fighting back tears. "Just don't say it. I know. Fuck! I can't afford this shit right now." I was steaming.

I kicked the side of the car out of frustration and the pain quickly reminded me I was wearing flip flops. I sat down and leaned against the car feeling a bit defeated. Jackson grabbed a couple beers from the fridge in the garage and sat down beside me, handing one to me. We cracked open the beers and sat in silence for a few moments while I sobbed to myself.

Growing up poor I was no stranger to problems with things breaking down, but no one had ever really taught me how to deal with big ones like this. Twenty-six years old, and I still couldn't figure out how to deal with life's curveballs when they were thrown at me. I didn't

even know how much an engine cost, but I was certain
that it would be more than I could scrounge up quickly. I
would likely have to save from the next several paychecks
to pay for it. That or skip rent for the month, I'm sure that
would go over well.

I chugged the rest of my beer and sighed deeply.

"Well, thanks for looking at it for me Jackson. Not
the news I wanted, but at least I know what's wrong now. I
guess I'll start looking around for a new engine, or a car I
can afford, though chances are slim I can get anything that
runs for what I can afford to spend. Unless of course
you've got a car lying around that you would spare for
about eighty bucks?" I asked.

"Nah, but I'll keep an ear to the ground for you."
He offered. "I know the car meant a lot to you, so I'll try to
find an engine. '84 was a popular model, I'm sure I can find
something for a reasonable price. Might even be able to fit
a 'Vette engine in it. Not sure about finding one with a
blower though. I'm gonna head out, I'll make some calls,
poke around, and let you know if I find anything." He
stood up and brushed the dirt off the back of his pants.

I nodded my thanks and just sat and stared at my
empty beer for a little while. It took more effort than I care

to admit getting up and then heading back inside to flop onto the couch. I needed something to take my mind off reality for a while because there was no sense moping about the car all day, might as well reschedule that and focus my energy on more important things. Things like drinking some more craft beer and killing zombies.

Echo mewed loudly and hopped up onto my lap as I grabbed the controller for my PlayStation. She could tell I was in a bad mood and was trying her damnedest to cheer me up and steal my attention away from my game. She was far too adorable and persistent to ignore. I picked her up and rubbed my cheek against hers for a moment, scratching at her belly before letting her lay down in my lap.

I started up the game and let myself zone out for a while, immersed entirely into the game world. There was something cathartic about shooting mindless zombies for hours on end. The troubles of day to day life seemed to just melt away each time I blasted some poor undead fiend. Sure, it was only temporary, but it let me escape from anything dragging me down and let the simple existence in the game just wash over me. Escapism at its finest.

I sometimes fantasized about how much simpler life would be if the zombie apocalypse were to occur. Nothing to worry about except basic survival and living free. Sure, you'd be on the run all the time, and things would be constantly trying to kill you, but it seemed easier to deal with than wasting away in the nightmare of capitalism where you are forced to sit still while things are constantly trying to kill you with poverty wages and rent increases. No billionaires, no bigoted laws, no more counting pennies for bills and food, just the wild world and a pile of ammo.

I liked to think all the zombie movies I'd seen and games I'd played were just training for the real event. I had to be an expert with all this practice. I'd be decked out in salvaged gear, probably running my own little enclave of survivors, surrounded by a harem of beautiful people that relied on me for safety and survival. I'd have a team of mercenaries that respected me for my skill and would throw themselves at any of my enemies just to ensure I would lead humanity itself to victory over the undead.

Realistically my survival skills were sincerely lacking, and it was much more likely I'd end up dead within a month or two. Probably wearing a bath robe while sobbing on the sidewalk outside of some busted up fast food joint, clutching a rusted kitchen knife and covered in poison ivy rashes while hallucinating from some wild mushrooms that I had convinced myself were totally safe. I'd be surrounded by a hoard of raccoons I tried to tame as companions that had chewed off at least one of my fingers and probably a toe. Truly a glorious death.

After a few hours of slaughtering my way through unending zombie hordes, I was roused and forced back to reality by the sound of someone pounding on the front door. My first thought was that I had the TV up too loud, and the neighbors had heard all the yelling and cursing and called the cops, again. I groaned and prepared myself for the arduous task of explaining things as I walked to the door. When I opened it, instead of an annoyed police officer I hoped wouldn't accidentally shoot me I was surprised by a pile of clothing and boxes bound together with bungee cords. Star pushed past me and dropped the pile on the floor beside the chair.

"Phew! That was much heavier than it looked. Thanks, pookie." She said wiping some sweat from her brow.

I stared at the massive pile, flabbergasted by how she managed to carry it, let alone get all that stuff secured on her scooter. I figured that without at least a master's degree in physics, or possibly quantum mechanics, I wouldn't be able to reach any feasible answer without suffering a brain hemorrhage. I shook off the thought before it made me sick, and then closed the door. Some mysteries are best left unsolved.

I walked back over to the couch to find that my spot had been commandeered by Echo. Nothing is more enticing to a cat than a warm butt spot on soft furniture. Cats, when unobserved, will in fact teleport to any warm space regardless of how it may inconvenience their subjects. If you listen carefully, you can almost hear the rushing of wind to fill the void left behind wherever they were before the space became available.

I reached down to gently move her over, and quickly found my hand encased in a live bear trap, tips of teeth and claws ready to plunge deep into flesh. I apologized and slowly retracted my hand, opting to sit beside her and give into the whims of the divine.

"So, what's up with the car is it working now?" Star asked, unwinding the mass of bungee from her pile of stuff.

I growled slightly, not wanting to remember as I laid down to cuddle Echo for comfort.

"It's dead, needs a new engine. No idea how I'm going to pull that off." I said, hiding my head with the cat, who casually licked my nose.

"Oh, that's no good. Well, I can give you a ride in the meantime, I don't mind. We'll figure something out." She said and rubbed my leg gently. "Now quit moping about and help me carry this stuff upstairs. I'm not sure where to put it. "

I sat up and looked over the pile and could've sworn it had grown while I wasn't looking. I grabbed an armful and escorted Star up the stairs to the spare bedroom. There was an empty dresser and a random chair that didn't match anything else in the house. There was also a walk-in closet with a few boxes of old junk I kept around for who knows what. I set the bundle of Star's things down on the chair and turned to face her, a small smile forming on my face.

"Well, it's not much, but it's a room. If the boxes are in your way I can put them in the garage, but feel free to put whatever you'd like in here. The cabinet under the sink is empty too if you have anything to put in the bathroom." I gestured to the rooms as I spoke.

"Thanks, I've got some furniture I'll have someone bring over too, but I wanted to at least get some of my clothes over first. Just what would fit on my scooter, anyway."

She said 'fit on my scooter' casually as if it wasn't a feat that would baffle modern science. She set some things down and dug in one of the bags producing a bottle of vodka.

"Got some booze too." She added.

I smiled my approval, and we headed back downstairs to unwind. I hadn't realized how long I had spent playing my game until we went outside to sit on the deck. The sun was starting to dip behind the mountains giving the sky a gorgeous color. My stomach growled, and Star nodded when I asked if she wanted something to eat.

I was in the mood to cook suddenly, my natural southern reaction to having a guest in the house. Probably a habit I picked up from my Granny. I tossed some steaks on the grill while Star worked on making some instant mashed potatoes she found in my cabinet. I was pretty sure they weren't expired, so I didn't protest. A nice dinner in would be good for a change, I ate out far too often for my own good.

We ate our flawlessly cooked dinner and just sat and talked for a while. Not about anything specific really, just talking and enjoying each other's company. I was enthralled in conversation with her, hanging on to everything she had to say. It was going to be nice having her around.

After dinner we headed back inside and decided to watch a movie. It was some foreign flick with a name I'll never remember, about a haunted forest where teenagers kept getting lost, and then being found hanging from a tree at the forest's edge. It was actually pretty good, but I ended up dozing off halfway through. Star poked at me to keep me awake, but it didn't help much. I woke up just in time to see a set of bloody hands planting an acorn at the edge of the forest to some haunting music, just before the credit roll.

I sat up and rubbed my face sleepily while Star switched the TV over to the news. I hate watching the news, it's always so depressing. They prop up a couple of talking heads with virtually no personality just to read stories off a teleprompter. Usually, it's just a bunch of fear mongering or corporate pandering focusing on some tragedy and using it to push a political agenda from one side or the other, not there's much of a difference in the US. You can tell the stories are cherry picked from the internet and heavily edited by the network before airing to spin things just the right way.

Honestly, you'd be better informed if you opened the trending tab on twitter and scrolled through people arguing it one way or the other. The real news story was always hidden somewhere in the middle of the 'right' and 'left' babbling anyway. Network news just wants enough of the graphic details to try and boost ratings rather than tell the truth of the situation. Anything to compete with the internet I suppose.

The local news was a slight improvement at least. They managed to talk about some things going on in our area that would have a more direct effect on our day, before giving another watered-down version of the national news. Sometimes it sounded like they said the same things word for word as another network which always filled my head with troubled thoughts. I think there was a big fuss a few years ago when someone recorded a bunch of sister networks reading the same script on a bunch of smaller news channels.

In between the macabre puppet shows the local news had a few interesting things to break it all up. My favorite part was a segment that talked about new restaurants opening in town or nearby. It was just finishing up that segment as we flipped over to the station. The image cut to a woman in a smart looking dress standing beside a machine with a bunch of numbered ping-pong balls jostling around inside a spinning container.

"Hey, didn't you get a ticket for this, Tri?" Star said prodding at my leg.

"Yeah, I did, actually... I think it's in my pants from yesterday. They're still over there on the floor. Toss 'em to me." I said stretching my back.

She threw them over to me and I dug through the pockets looking for the little ticket with my sets of numbers on them. The lady on the screen began calling out the numbers as the balls were collected at the top of the machine.

"The first number is… Seventeen!" she announced loudly, smiling brightly for the camera.

I emptied out all the pockets but couldn't find the ticket. There was loose change, my ID card for work, and a receipt from the diner. I was starting to wonder if I lost the damn thing riding home on Star's scooter.

"Ugh it's not here… oh maybe I left it in my purse!" I exclaimed and scrambled to the table I had left it sitting on.

"The second number is… Thirty-Four! Oh, looks like we got two for one this time, so the third number is… Forty-Nine!" The announcer called out proudly.

She seemed to really enjoy this job, and I wondered if she got kickbacks from the prize pool. I dug through my purse frantically trying to find my ticket. I was determined to find it before she called out the fifth number, so I didn't have to look up the numbers online.

"Our fourth number for the Supreme-O-Million jackpot is… Five! Only one more to go, will anyone win the grand prize on this week's drawing, or will we see the amount increase even higher?"

I dumped the purse out on the table, various items clattering across the surface and falling to the floor. I shuffled through what felt like a few pounds of loose paper. It was like a little dragon lived in here hoarding receipts and doodles I drew on sticky notes at work to pass the time. Finally, I pulled it from a rather obvious spot poking out from a side pocket and thrust it in the air as I grimaced at the mess on the table.

"Got it! I found it, what were the numbers again?" I proclaimed dashing back to the tv.

"The fifth winning number for tonight's jackpot drawing, a grand prize of Seven Hundred and Fifty Million dollars is... Twenty-Six! So, the set of numbers for tonight's jackpot are Five, Seventeen, Twenty-Six, Thirty-Four and Forty-Nine! Check your tickets closely folks, this jackpot is the highest..." Her voice trailed off as I stared at my ticket and then back at the numbers on the screen. I read the numbers again a couple of times as my stomach churned.

Five, Seventeen, Twenty-Six, Thirty-Four, Forty-Nine.

My heart was pounding, my face dripped with sweat, and I felt a whirling haze setting in on the edges of my vision like I had too much to drink and was about to promptly puke and pass out. I could even taste that pre-vomit saliva starting to creep into my mouth as my nerves began going haywire. I fell on the couch and turned to face Star. She was staring at me with a look of confusion and eagerness on her face.

"Star.... Oh my god... oh my fucking god, Star... I WON! I FUCKING WON! I'M A MILLIONAIRE!" I screamed and unconsciously bounced up and down on the couch.

"You're fucking with me!" She exclaimed.

She reached out for my hand trying to read the mix of emotions on my face. I was shaking, my body wasn't ready for that much chemical activity in my brain. I tried to stand but buckled and threw up into the small trashcan I kept by the couch. I handed her the ticket to see for herself as I wiped my lip.

She squealed loudly as she confirmed the numbers. I finally managed to stand up, wobbling with the rising adrenaline taking control of me. Star grabbed my hands and we both jumped up and down in unison screaming loudly and laughing like a pair of sugar-fueled children. We jumped, laughed, danced, and hugged as we both processed what had just happened.

Never in a million years did I think something like this was possible, things like that didn't happen to people like me. Literally that morning I was crying into an empty beer bottle because my car broke down and I couldn't afford to do anything about it. But it had happened, it happened to me, I won the fucking lottery.

I stopped jumping and ran to the kitchen and flung open the liquor cabinet. I dug around to the back and pulled out a bottle of champagne that I had bought to make mimosas with but never remembered to use. I looked in the cabinet above the sink and pulled out two champagne flutes that I had stolen from a party at a hotel and called Star into the kitchen.

"Here's to a new life, and never having to work a day in our lives ever again!" I shouted as if speaking to a large audience.

Star giggled as I tried to pop open the champagne. I was failing humorously because my hands were still shaking too much. She took the bottle from me and ripped off the foil with ease and expertly popped the cork, sending it rocketing off down the hall. Echo chased after it, playfully batting it around like a toy.

We poured some drinks and tapped the glasses together, the champagne spilling over the edges of the glasses, but I didn't care. I wasn't even going to clean it up either. I didn't care about this shithole house anymore. I could just have it steamrolled and replaced with a mansion if I wanted. Star wrapped her arm around mine and we slurped down the fizzy liquid and laughed.

"Music! We need music to celebrate the occasion, and none of your angry metal..." Star announced and ran to the living room to pull up some music.

I tipped the bottle of champagne up and took a swig as I followed her. She turned on some bass-heavy house music and we danced as if we didn't have a care in the world. Honestly, in that very moment, we didn't. I hadn't felt that way since I was a child, and it felt amazing.

I suddenly didn't care about my car, or my bills, or anything. I didn't care about my past, the terrible abuse I had suffered growing up, or even the questionable decisions that led me to a dead-end job just to survive. I was free. Free from all the stress that weighed on me and it was so refreshing.

We laughed and danced, we drank and took off our clothes. We fooled around and then drank and danced some more. We partied and enjoyed ourselves as much as we could until we eventually moved into the bedroom and passed out. I slept like a log and had the most pleasant of dreams while snuggling Star tightly.

Seven hundred and fifty million dollars had just fallen into my lap, and everything about my life was about to change. I didn't have a clue just how much would change, however.

CHAPTER 3

The next morning, I awoke in my usual haze. I carefully pulled my arm out from under Star's head, hoping not to disturb her, and sat up yawning and stretching away the aches from the night before. That seemed to happen more often the older I got. It was disconcerting. I rubbed the sleep from my eyes and made my way to the bathroom for my morning ritual.

I sat on the toilet and scrolled through the social media sites, eager to say something about my win but not wanting to give it away before I claimed the prize when someone could come steal the ticket or something. I opted not to say anything and continued to scroll, pausing to skim through some click-bait article about science and robotics, mostly to see if we had reached one of those 'oops, went too far' moments. One slip up with the AI and we could easily activate Skynet or something.

Satisfied that I wasn't going to be hunted by living liquid-steel anytime soon, I finished my business, stood up, and caught a glimpse of myself in the mirror. I looked amazing. I stared for a moment, not used to liking my appearance. I had a sort of glow around me, though that could just be the grease on my face. Still, I didn't feel an ounce of stress and it showed.

I flicked on some music from my phone and hopped in the shower to freshen myself up. After all, I had big plans for the day and wanted to look fierce. Today was going to be huge! I was going to quit my job, and there were quite a few people I had words for.

Once out of the shower, I cleared the steam from the mirror and started the arduous task of making myself look fancy. I pulled up some hair tutorials on YouTube, picking one with the fewest steps to make it easier on myself. It was a simple but bold and reminded me of something you might see on Audrey Hepburn. Impressively, I managed to not ruin it completely, and mostly pulled it off.

I ran to the spare room and borrowed some of Star's makeup, as I didn't really have much of my own other than some foundation and lipstick. I looked up a few tutorials to at least try to make it look like I knew what I was doing, even though I certainly did not. The internet told me that contour was everything, and that I could pretty much just make everything else up from there. I managed.

I really wasn't a make-up girl most of the time, it was just too much effort. Today was important though, so I told myself it was just like war paint, and by the time I was finished I was ready to take on the world. I looked amazing and I couldn't help but smile. I strolled out of the bathroom with my head held high and went to dig through my closet for an outfit to continue the look.

I found a nice dress that I had only worn once before for some business gathering. It was a lovely shade of green and fit me like a glove. It was a little low-cut, not too revealing, though I didn't have a lot to reveal anyway. It rested just above my knees with a little slit up the side to allow better leg movement, and it made my ass look fantastic. I dug out some nice chunky heels to wear with it, and even decided to find some jewelry to round things out.

I stood up straight and looked at myself in the full mirror on the bedroom door, I was beaming. I didn't dress up often, I felt so much more comfortable in just a T-shirt and jeans because they made it easier to hide the things I was insecure about. Looking at myself now though, I had to smile. I clean up pretty good when I try.

Star stirred in the bed behind me, and I turned around to face her. She bolted up and rubbed her eyes, staring open-mouthed at me.

"Holy shit... Trianna!? You look amazing! I barely recognized you, thought I was still dreaming or something." she exclaimed, rubbing her eyes again.

I chuckled and tried to make a sexy pose, then stumbled and tried not to fall over.

"It's a special day, I'm going to quit my job! Had to look my best for such a wondrous event." I giggled some more despite myself.

"I'll be back in a little while, after I'm done making a scene at the office. I'm going to rent a car, so we can go pick up my winnings, I think we have to drive to Raleigh to turn in the ticket." I said, turning back around to admire myself in the mirror again.

Star got up and wrapped her arms around me from behind, nestling her head between my shoulder blades. I caressed her hands gently, and then turned and gave her a peck on the forehead. She looked up at me and smiled and I just held her for a moment. I was glad I had decided to bring her into my life more permanently.

We had already been through so much together; she was one of very few people that knew of the terrible things that I had been through as a child. I was abused by my father, and it had lasting effects that I often just repressed. In fact, she may be the only person not directly involved that knew any of the darker details. She'd even talked me off the ledge a few times, figuratively speaking.

With as many times as I had turned to her for comfort since we met, I'm not sure why it took so long to reach this point.

Despite everything, she was willing to try to make things work with me before I had money, if I had waited even another day, I would have to question that. This felt like the universe was rewarding us for making that choice when we did. I leaned down and kissed her goodbye and then left.

I looked up the nearest car rental place, called the number, and requested a rental with pick-up, as I was certainly not getting on Star's scooter looking this nice. The man on the phone assured me that was no problem, and we discussed what type of car I wanted. I asked about muscle cars and was pleased to discover they had a new Dodge Challenger available. It wasn't a Camaro, but it would do.

After a quick credit check and a pause that only made me moderately nervous. the man informed me that the car would arrive in less than an hour, then they would have me sign some papers and the car was mine for as long as I needed it. I absently agreed and zoned out listening to the stream of information he was legally required to give me next. I was used to that sort of thing from my job and offered positive grunts of affirmation where needed.

I made some coffee and spent the next hour mostly just staring at my winning ticket and fantasizing about what to do when I got to the office. I grinned at the idea of me standing triumphantly over the burning rubble of the office, but then shook that away as it wouldn't do any good to get arrested before I even collected my winnings. Maybe I could get away with just destroying that damn printer though. No, that would be too cliché, thanks a lot Office Space. I rolled my eyes and sipped my coffee.

I had just tucked the ticket away, hidden between the back of my phone and the protective case, when the rental car pulled up outside. I filled out the paperwork and took the keys from him. He jabbered some more legal jargon at me, shook my hand, and took everything back to his follow car and they drove off while I looked over the beast sitting in my driveway.

"Fuck yes." I muttered under my breath.

The car was a sleek metallic green with black accents, and it just radiated ferocity. I slipped into the leather seat and ran my hands over the steering wheel. It felt alive with power, and as I turned the key it roared to life as if it had been waiting for me. I stepped on the gas and the whole car shuttered as the engine revved, eager to be free. Something about the sound of American muscle cars just made me tingle in all the right places.

I hopped out and grabbed my new CD from the stereo in the garage. Sliding the disc into the drive in the dash, I felt my adrenaline starting to spike. The metal blasted from the speakers and my skin crawled with excitement. The sound system was pretty good, there was even a subwoofer in the back, steadily vibrating the mirrors as I backed out of the driveway.

Learning absolutely nothing from the earlier excursion, I threw the car into gear and stomped on the gas. The car roared loudly, and the tires squealed as they tried to grip the pavement. I laughed and cheered as the beast lurched forward and sent me loudly on my way.

I raced down the back roads of my neighborhood, eventually finding my way onto the interstate where I could let the machine really shine. It took no time at all to reach the speed limit, and I looked around to see what my surroundings were. The road was relatively clear of traffic and the usual spots where the cops like to hide and wait for speeders were all empty. I took the opportunity to have a little fun and test the car's limits.

I tightened my grip on the wheel and once more stomped on the accelerator. My speedometer climbed quicker than I expected, and the engine purred as if it had been waiting for this all along. Within seconds I was doing over a hundred miles per hour and loving every second of it. I howled and focused on the stretch of road ahead.

My adrenaline was pumping as I pushed the car a little more, one twenty. I could feel my heart rate increasing, one forty, I hungered for more. I carefully weaved between lanes to pass a couple cars, the occupants of which likely startled and irritated, now cursing the madwoman racing past, and found myself rewarded with a long stretch of open road. One fifty, one fifty-five, one sixty, the needle buried in the red and I could feel the power of the engine starting to shake the car. The raw power was exhilarating, and I cheered out loud as I pushed the car to one sixty-five.

At one seventy I lost my nerve though and took my foot off the gas to let the car coast its way back down to a reasonable speed. I was panting and laughing, feeling a little high from the rush. I passed a few more cars and then hit the brakes as I neared my exit. That was fun, but I needed to chill for a bit. I didn't want to die before I got to be rich after all.

I made it to the office without further shenanigans and pulled around to the side of the building where my boss's office was located. There was a little awning that stuck out over the area outside of his windows. I backed the car right up to it, making sure the back end was as close to the building as possible, and put the car into neutral. I checked the rearview mirror and could just see through the blinds enough to ensure he was sitting at his desk, caught up in whatever it was that he was pretending to work on that day.

I grinned as I slammed the gas pedal down and the car boomed, rattling the windows, and scaring the absolute shit out of him. I laughed as he nearly fell out of his chair and his papers scattered across the office as he flailed around to keep from falling. He glared out the window as I cut off the engine and climbed out of the car, giving him a fake little 'oops, sorry' wave. I watched his expression shift as he realized he recognized me despite my dramatic change in appearance.

I scanned my ID, pushed open the doors and walked into the building like I owned the place. You could almost hear people's heads poking up from their desks to watch as I made my way to Mark's office. It was clear to everyone something was about to happen, and no one wanted to miss out on office drama. Drama and gossip were like the backbone and lifeblood of conversation in this hell hole.

Mark was the biggest douchebag I had ever met in my entire life. His short, salt and pepper hair was cut in a style that clearly indicated he thought he was much younger, and he sported a greasy little soul patch under his bottom lip. He always wore a thin gold necklace, and you just knew he never took it off. He carried himself with an aura of sleaze-ball and Old Spice so thick that you could cut it with a knife. He made it a point to hit on every woman he met. He was like a living golem of disgust and yet he carried it all with an uncanny level of confidence that tricked people into overlooking the layer of sleaze so he could try to win them over with his con-man charm.

He had been married at least three times that we knew of and had tried to fuck every girl in the building at least once. His marriages always ended due to his infidelity, and it was a wonder to me how someone like him got one woman to fuck him let alone multiple women. I shivered at the thought of that little gold chain bouncing off their foreheads as he flopped around on top of them, the mental image alone was enough to make me gag.

It was still clear that my stunt with the car had rattled him, but he was already slicking his hair back and building up his sleazeball bravado. I stared him in the eyes as I approached unable to be swayed by whatever nonsense he was about to blurt out of that sloppy blowhole of his. I could see him undressing me in his mind as I approached, but I wasn't about to let that discourage me. I didn't even bother to ask him into his office first and I just smirked as I stopped directly in front of him, knowing he hated the fact that I was taller than he was.

"Hey Mark, I wanted to talk to you about a few things. You are by far the most ignorant, pig-headed, fucking sleaze-ball I have ever had the misfortune of working with." I started, and his eyes bulged with shock and disbelief.

"Even being this close to you now makes my skin crawl, and the smell radiating from your office makes me want to puke. We've all tolerated your lack of professionalism for too damn long, well not me, not anymore. I refuse to stay silent about all the inappropriate comments and glances you've given me and the other women working here. You're a fucking pig, and I hope you realize that you are going to grow old and die alone, wallowing in your own self-pity, probably after sticking your dick in a microwaved cantaloupe." I exclaimed.

I spoke loudly enough that everyone on the floor could hear me, and I noticed that most people had stopped working and stood up to watch things play out.

"You can't fucking talk to me that way, Trianna! Have you lost your damned mind woman!? You are fi— "

I cut him off before he could finish.

"You wish, asshole. You can fire me all you like, but I only came in today to quit. But while you steam about your shitty life and cry yourself to sleep tonight over a bottle of cheap whiskey and pain killers, I'll be in Raleigh celebrating, and you know why? I just won the fucking lottery and I never have to see your misogynistic ass again." I boasted loudly.

I could hear people starting to laugh quietly to themselves. I turned around and started to walk away and I could hear Mark growling and cursing under his breath because he couldn't think of what to say back to me. I paused and decided to add insult to injury, still riding high on how powerful I felt in the moment.

"Oh, and one more thing fuck-face. Melissa in accounting showed me those pictures you sent her. The heart-shaped pubes were certainly an interesting choice, but I don't think I would be so proud if I had such a shriveled mess hanging down there." I added.

That was all it took to put the office into hysterics. A roar of cheers and laughter echoed behind me as I made my way to my desk. Despite the show, I still needed to gather a few things. I probably should have taken care of that first, but this was too good to pass up.

Mark's face flushed with rage and embarrassment, and he demanded everyone to shut up and get back to work, slamming his door behind him. He shouted and slammed things around in his office. I had wanted to put the man in his place for quite some time, and I couldn't help but enjoy the moment. It was long overdue.

I quickly went through my desk and grabbed the things I wanted from it. I had some pictures and spare cash that I needed to take, I left most of the toys and decorations. I could always buy new ones. I grabbed the few that held sentimental value but decided to leave everything else to the desk-pickers.

Every office job has them, the greedy people that lurk around people's desks when they leave, looking for what supplies they can salvage for themselves. I could already sense them circling, eager to see what I was leaving behind.

"I've got all I need, fellas. The rest is fair game, help yourselves." I called back over my shoulder as I strolled away.

Nothing but vultures, I tell you.

I made a point of stopping by and saying goodbye to the few people who I would actually miss working with, and all of them were excited to congratulate me on such a grandiose exit. Several people joked about me lending them money, many of which I questioned if they were joking. I would undoubtedly share the winnings with close friends and family for sure, but it was unlikely to be anyone here. I made my way to the exit and paused to turn and look back.

The office was slowly returning to its normal day to day life, and I felt a bit sad for a moment. As much as I hated the monotony of the job, I had formed a bond with the people I worked with, and it was very likely I would not see many of them again. I had to laugh at myself, but I actually was going to miss the place a little.

Just a little though.

Not much.

CHAPTER 4

I rode around aimlessly for a while after leaving the office. It was nice to have the simple freedom. There was an entrance to the Blue Ridge Parkway not far from where I worked, and I decided to take a short drive up to one of the lookouts. The parkway was popular, especially amongst bikers. Slow speed limit, beautiful views, and fresh air, I couldn't blame them.

I liked to go up and sit at the lookouts and just soak in the scenery. Depending on where you went, you could see pretty much the whole valley that Asheville sat in and get a real appreciation for how small the city really was compared to other places. I sat on the hood of the car looking out over the valley and watched a flock of birds flying by a bit further down. I reveled in the fact that I could go places like this any time I wanted to from now on, without being burdened by having to go to work.

I didn't stay on the parkway long, I still needed to get back to the house and pick up Star and a few of my things, so we could head to Raleigh and collect the winnings for my ticket. I pulled out my phone and made some hotel reservations, so we could spend the next few days there. This trip was going to be a drain on my savings and credit cards, but I'd be able to recoup the loss soon enough. I had never been to Raleigh before, so I wanted some time to explore the city and city what it was like.

I climbed back in the car, started it up, and headed back to the house. I sang along with the music as I drove, which always got me the most interested looks from people at red lights. Something about a woman blasting metal seems to catch the locals off guard, as if heavy music was just a boy's club. I guess they expect me to be engrossed in the latest pop music, or even worse the local country station, but I couldn't stand any of that sappy bullshit.

As I pulled into the driveway, my phone rang, Jackson was calling. He probably had a lead on an engine or something for the car. Not like I needed it now, but I answered anyway.

"Hey Jackson, what's up?" I asked cheerfully as I shut off the car.

"Hey Tri, got some good news, I managed to get my hands on a sweet V8 with a four-barrel blower on it from a project car I picked up. If you want it, I can sell it to ya pretty cheap." he said proudly, thinking he had come to the rescue.

"Hey that's cool, good job Jackson. I won't be needing it though."

"Oh? Did you find one already or did you manage to get another car?" He asked.

"Neither, you're not going to believe this Jackson. I won the lottery. The big one. Seven hundred and fifty million bucks. I'm on my way to Raleigh now to collect!" I exclaimed.

It was hard to contain the excitement in my voice as I said the number aloud.

"Holy shit... you're fucking with me. You serious, Tri? That's fucking amazing! Hey, keep us little people in mind when you are living the good life, yeah?" He said, clearly shocked.

"Oh, I will, Jackson, I will. Hey, on the subject, do you want the Camaro to work on? I'll give it to you if you come pick it up. Hell, I'll even give you some money to fix it up when I get my winnings. It'd be nice to see her in all her original glory.!

"Uh, yeah! That'd be awesome! I haven't rebuilt a Camaro in a while. You don't have to give me any money though Tri, you won it." He said being delightfully modest.

"It's cool, I'm about to have more money than I'll ever know what to do with. I'm probably going to be giving a lot out to various people, and you've always helped me out of a bind when you could. I remember things like that buddy."

"Well, it's your money. I can't say I couldn't use it. Any who, I just wanted to call and let you know about the engine, I'm about to head to work. Have fun in Raleigh, and congratulations. I still can't fucking believe it. I'll see ya around, girl."

"Later Jackson, I'll see ya when I get back." I said and swiped the screen to end the call. He was a good friend and my list of people to share the wealth with definitely included him.

I climbed out of the car and went inside to pack up a few things and print off my hotel reservations. Star was elbow deep in a bag of chips and lost in another dark documentary; this one was a series depicting the last twenty-four hours of the lives of famous people before they died. This episode appeared to be about Jim Belushi. What a waste, the world lost a true comedy legend with that one.

I headed up stairs and dug in the storage hole in my closet for my suitcase. I filled it up with some clothes, toiletries, and other necessities and then set it on the bed, so Star could toss her stuff in too. It was far bigger than I needed for this trip so there was plenty of room but knowing her she'd probably fill it up and then fill one of her own.

"Star... come pack up, we gotta get going." I said as I sat down at my computer. I needed to look up how to collect my winnings, I honestly had no clue.

"Okay Tri, I'll be up in a minute!" She called back halfheartedly, still clearly consumed by her show.

I pulled up the lottery website and skimmed over the information. Winners had to meet at the head office in Raleigh within seven days of the drawing to supply the ticket and some other personal information for tax purposes. Aside from that and the address there wasn't much information to gain from it. Mostly it just talked about the odds of winning and reminded people of the dangers of gambling, supplying a couple of hotline numbers at the bottom.

I saved the address to the GPS on my phone and went downstairs for some coffee. Star passed me on the way up and I playfully pinched her butt. I was still in a giddy and playful mood after my stunt at the office. She swatted my hand away and grinned at me over her shoulder as she headed to the room to pack up.

As I poured my cup of coffee, I could hear Star crashing around upstairs as she dug through her things for whatever she felt she needed to pack. I couldn't immediately think of a reason we would need to bring a couple of elephants with us, but she had, from the sound of things. Perhaps we'd detour through the alps and terrify the Romans at Trebbia. I chuckled to myself, enjoying my own joke like a dork.

I glanced around the house, eyeing the various piles of dust and other mess, but found myself unbothered. I kept telling myself I was going to spend a weekend really putting in the elbow grease and get the place all clean and tidy, but I never got further than picking up clothes, washing dishes, and sweeping up wads of cat hair. Now though, I had a better excuse to not clean anything: I could just pay someone else to do it for me. I could let a professional do all the dirty work, and just take care of picking up my things when I packed up to move into a new place.

I had always wanted to move to an island or a beach, somewhere that I could be near the ocean. I had some reservations about it, like the worry of everything being swept away in a hurricane or something, but the benefit of being able to walk to the ocean whenever I felt like it outweighed most objections. It had always felt like a fever dream, but now I could just buy a private island and have my own personal beach if I wanted. I sipped my coffee, closed my eyes, and slipped into a daydream.

I took a deep breath of the ocean air and sighed happily as I opened my eyes. I wiggled my toes in the pristine white sand as I looked out over crystal-clear water. The waves crashed gently on the shore, and I could hear the gulls chattering in the sky overhead. The wind rustled the palm trees behind me, and I strode towards the water, slipping out of my clothing as I walked.

I jumped naked into the water and let out a slight gasp as the coolness met my skin. It was the perfect temperature, partly cool water rolling in from the deep mixing with the shallow waters warm from the direct sunlight. The water was deceptively clear, I far enough from the shore that the sandy bottom of the bay was well below me, but it looked only inches from my feet. I could see turtles gliding along the bottom snacking on the plants, and schools of fish shimmering as the sunlight reflected off their scales.

I dove under the water and was quickly joined by a couple of dolphins eager to play. I held on to their fins and we blasted through the sea leaping in and out of the water without a care in the world. I could hear them happily chirping and clicking at me as we swam across the water's surface. The clicking noises got steadily louder and then began to sound more like… snapping? I shook my head sad to find myself no longer in the ocean but leaning against the table in the kitchen. Star was snapping her fingers in front of my face to get my attention.

"Hello, earth to Trianna! Your presence is requested planet side, come in!" she said jokingly.

I bit at her hand playfully and grinned.

"Sorry, just lost in thought, hey you look great!" I said, admiring the adorable human that had replaced my imaginary dolphin friends.

Star had changed into a flowing black skirt decorated with a colorful skull pattern and a tight white blouse with a delicately drawn skull and flower image that wrapped around the left side. Her long blue hair was up in a tight bun, and her makeup looked cut from a painting, so vibrant and perfect, all rounded out with a naturally innocent smile. I leaned over and gave her a peck on the forehead.

We gathered up our things and loaded them into the car. The day was gorgeous, so I let all the windows down and opened the moon roof as we drove. It was about a four-hour drive from Asheville to Raleigh, but it felt much shorter. We sang along with the radio, played typical travel games, and took turns mooning or flashing people, like totally mature people often do when driving.

We got to the city as the sun was setting, clearly too late to go by the lotto headquarters, so instead we checked into our hotel. Since this was a special occasion, I had decided to splurge and rent a suite at one of the really nice hotels, mostly because I had never got to stay in one before. If I travelled at all, I usually ended up in a LaQuinta because they were cheap, and they seemed to care about keeping the rooms clean. None of that tonight however, it was time to treat myself to something fancy.

We walked in through the large gilded glass doors and stopped in our tracks. It was like stepping into a whole other world. The place radiated elegance, and there wasn't a speck of dust in sight. The floor was solid marble and well-polished, and the pattern circled around a large cut out area that was filled with dirt around plants and a huge tree that stretched up incredibly high towards the windows in the ceiling. I wasn't aware the front desk was in an atrium when I made the reservation.

We giggled to ourselves with excitement as we took in the view. I walked up to the counter and rang the bell sitting on the large granite countertop. A young woman wearing a very crisp uniform appeared, smiling brightly, and checked us in. She handed us our key, which to my surprise wasn't just a cheap plastic slide-card but an actual brass key.

She had instructed us to take the elevator to the top floor and follow the signs to our room. There were only a few suites on this floor, so it was easy to find ours. I pondered for a moment if there was someone famous staying in the other rooms that we might bump into during our stay. I slipped the key into the keyhole and there was a satisfyingly heavy clicking noise as the lock opened.

I pushed the door open, and we stepped into the room. The carpet was incredibly plush under our feet, thick to the point it felt like walking on clouds. The suite was very elaborate, and the hallway entrance opened into a large room, elegantly decorated with art and plants. In the middle of the room was a large fish tank with exotic looking fish swimming around peacefully. Behind the fish tank, surrounded by some very nice hardwood flooring, was a rather large hot tub and a table with ice buckets and some bottles of wine.

I was ecstatic, I had always wanted a room with a hot tub. I looked around the room, just trying to take it all in. I opened a side door and found that it contained a very large tiled bathroom with a huge clawfoot soaking tub next to an open area standing shower. I thought it was odd there were no walls for the shower, it just stood alone with its showerhead recessed into the ceiling above as if the whole room was the shower. The marble sinks had basins carved like seashells spiraling to the drain, and matching seashells carved soap that had bits of crushed flowers mixed into them.

I stepped back out to the main room to check another door. This one was the bedroom, and it was stunning. Set against the far wall was an elaborately carved wooden bedframe that held a massive bed. It looked to be somehow even bigger than a king-sized bed. There were white satin pillowcases and sheets folded over the top of a comfortable looking burgundy quilt. I dropped my suitcase beside the dresser, which was carved to match the bedframe, and flopped down on the bed. I was delightfully surprised to find that it was a waterbed. The water rolled beneath me, rocking me along with it while I giggled.

"Starrrrrr! Get in here! Check out this bed!" I called out to her in the main room.

"This room is insane Tri!" She said walking into the room. Her eyes widened as she looked at the bed. "Is that... what I think it is?"

"Yep!" I exclaimed, jiggling the surface with my hips to make the bed roll again. Star clapped excitedly and joined me, and we just rocked our bodies with the movement of the water for a little while, laughing like children.

It had been so long since the last time I had a chance to relax and live in the moment that I almost had forgotten what it felt like. I was always so stressed about everything that it was hard to just enjoy little moments like this. We laughed and chased each other around the room with pillows, getting all sweaty and nearly breaking a few things in the room. After a little while we had built up an appetite and decided to order room service and test out the hot tub.

We ordered a big fruit and cheese plate, some chocolate strawberries, and a bit of ice cream to cool down with later. We stripped down and climbed into the hot tub to relax and eat. Star opened some of the wine and we sat in the tub, enjoying our snack, and having a nice chat for a few hours.

We exchanged stories of other times we had stayed in hotels and how they compared to this one, or rather how they didn't. This, of course, led to discussions of hookups we had in hotel rooms, both exciting and disappointing ones.

"So, this guy was going down on me, and then all of a sudden his breath felt cooler, and everything started to really tingle in a way I wasn't used to." I explained.

"Turns out, he'd never given head before, and his brother had told him it would taste bad. So, he brought fucking Tic-Tacs and snuck a few into his mouth while he was eating me out!"

Star cackled, almost dropping her wine glass into the tub. We were having so much fun, I wanted the night to last forever. I couldn't remember the last time I felt this relaxed and carefree. The two of us just sitting in a tub, drinking, sharing stories, fooling around, and just enjoying each other's company felt like something out of a dream.

Night was steadily creeping in, so I suggested we get ready to turn in for the evening. We toweled off, finished the last of the wine, and curled up in bed together. Star pulled up a true crime documentary to listen to until she drifted off to sleep. I cuddled up against her and sleepily tried to plan the next day. In the morning we would have a nice breakfast, then head to the lottery building, and I didn't make it any farther than that before I drifted off.

CHAPTER 5

We awoke the next morning to housekeeping knocking on the door. I had slept later than intended without the sun's hateful rays to wake me up. The maid kindly informed us that we still had about an hour left to catch breakfast downstairs and assured us that the chef would still be cooking until then. It wasn't until we got down to the café that I understood why she had mentioned that.

To me, hotel breakfast was a continental breakfast where they laid out various things that were mostly edible on a buffet style hot-and-cold bar. Everything mostly resembled foods you recognized, even if the quality was dubious. You grabbed what you wanted, or at least what you thought wouldn't kill you before the end of the meal and went on with your day. At the Hotel Grande, however, things were very different.

We found ourselves standing in front of the counter with a pile of fresh raw ingredients splayed out before us, and a couple of smiling chefs in their fancy white chef suits and hats ready to cook something for us, to order. I was blown away by the concept, at least for breakfast. I had only ever seen something like this at the hibachi section of our local Asian buffet.

I ordered a blueberry waffle and an omelet with a bunch of mushrooms and spicy peppers. I was pleased to see they had some ghost peppers and didn't cap their spice options at jalapeno like most places. I also got a freshly blended fruit smoothie to wash it down with. Star ordered a cheese omelet with some very crispy bacon and an English muffin.

We were handed a numbered plaque and instructed to find a seat and the food would be out shortly, so we grabbed a table near a window overlooking the courtyard. Outside with us, there were rows of gorgeous flowers and plants, lovely topiaries of various shapes, and well-trimmed Japanese Maple trees, all tracing the edges of the pathways to a massive fountain at the head of a small lake on the property. Closer to the building there was a large swimming pool and a couple of hot tubs, they were not quite as nice as the one in our room. There were a few people relaxing in and around the pool, but the courtyard was calm and quiet.

After a short wait, a server arrived at the table with our food, and it was the most impressive spread of breakfast I had ever seen. The omelets were unbelievably fluffy, and everything was cooked perfectly. We thanked him, and I slipped him a tip before diving into the food. It was so good I wanted to shove my face in it like a pig in a trough but decided against it. We were in a respectable establishment after all.

Star crunched happily on her bacon that was so over cooked it made me cringe. I don't know how she stands eating it like that. It seemed like such a waste of delicious pig fat, but she insisted it made it better. It was the only way she would eat pork, as they were supposedly too cute to eat under any other circumstance.

We finished our food and headed back to the room to get ready for the day. We had just thrown on some shirts and shorts to come eat breakfast, not caring much about appearances. However, we wanted to look a little less like two people that had just rolled out of bed where we were going next. We didn't need to be fancy but looking like we put some effort in would be nice.

We showered, quickly tossed on some simple makeup, in case of pictures, and got dressed. I opted for a tee and jeans with my comfy calf-length combat boots. Star went with her usual tank-top, shorts, and flip-flops combo. Just to soothe some of my anxiety, I peeled back the case on my phone, checking that the ticket was still safely hidden there and I hadn't managed to lose it.

I pulled up the address for the lottery office on my phone's GPS as we made our way down to the parking lot. City traffic in Raleigh was a different beast than it was in

Asheville, and I wasn't entirely prepared for it. We had barely gone a block down the road before we were stuck in a traffic jam. I anxiously tapped my hands on the steering wheel to the beat of the music.

It shouldn't have taken more than twenty minutes to get from the hotel to our destination, but it did. Two hours later we made it to the building, and I could feel the goosebumps forming all over me. I reached over, grabbed Star's hand, and clenched it tightly as I turned my head to smile at her. Our lives were changing immensely, and I wasn't sure I was ready for it. Having her with me made it a little easier to cope.

We went inside and were greeted by a perky secretary who happily showed us where we needed to go. She asked us to wait in a small lobby while she rang the boss to get everything ready. Moments later, a man in an expertly tailored suit appeared, his face plastered with an ear to ear smile, and his voice boomed through the room while he congratulated us. Another man appeared, more timid and reserved than the first, carrying some documentation that he asked me to fill out while he authenticated my ticket.

I removed the ticket from its hiding place and hesitated slightly as I handed it to him. I was almost afraid he would just steal it and never come back, but that seemed silly. By the look of him, if he tried, I could outrun and overpower him anyway. He moved over to a computer at a nearby desk and typed away something to verify the ticket.

I looked over the forms he had given me, as I suspected it was a pile of papers needing my personal information for taxation purposes. There were also a couple charts explaining how much money I would receive depending on how I wanted the payout. I could get a little more if I took the annuity and let them send me small payments over the course of a few years, or I could settle for a slightly smaller, but still incredibly large, amount in one bulk payment. It was a challenging decision.

I pondered the differences, running some math in my head. I figured it was only about an eight million difference, a lot of money sure, but compared to the total amount it felt miniscule. I would lose about fifty million to tax and processing fees for the lotto system as well. After some thought, I decided on the lump sum. It was more money than I could ever spend either way, and I wanted to start piling it into savings and investment options and giving some of it to friends, family, and charity right away.

The man returned from his computer, scrolling through a tablet, and took the clipboard from me. He went back to the computer, entered my information, and compared his notes with whatever was on his tablet. After a few moments he nodded to the loud man who had been standing next to him in pure silence just smiling the whole time. I could tell working with this man would be its own special level of hell.

"Well miss Trianna von Drake, I have splendid news. Everything checks out with your ticket, and it appears that no one else purchased a winning ticket so the grand prize is all yours! Congratulations! Now if you will come with us, we have a bit of a ceremony we like to perform with our jackpot winners." The smiling man in the suit boomed.

The sudden outburst made me jump a little. He chuckled and gestured towards a set of wooden double doors at the far side of the room. He went first, pushing through the doors and we followed him through. The timid man put away his tablet and followed us as well.

Inside the room there was a big banner with the lottery logo on it and streamers hanging from the ceiling. There was a little stage full of lights and cameras, and a full staff of people applauding as we entered. It was like a surprise party had been planned for us. We moved onto the stage as the man in the suit grabbed a microphone and composed himself. A camera moved into position in front of us, and the operator gave us a thumbs up as a little red light flickered on.

"Ladies and Gentlemen, my name is Buck Winston, president of the North Carolina Education Lottery, and today it is my pleasure to announce that we have a winner of our Supreme-O-Million grand prize! The jackpot had grown to an unprecedented seven hundred and fifty million dollars over the course of the last few months. Not a single person managed to claim a winning ticket leading us to this exceptional jackpot. Today that has changed, and we finally have a grand prize winner! Come here young lady, what's your name?" He gestured towards me.

"Uh... Trianna." I said nervously, I didn't much like being in front of the cameras.

"Well Trianna, I would like to be the first to officially congratulate you on winning the largest grand prize our organization has ever awarded! It is with great honor that I hand you this check for seven hun...ed and f... fty... mill.... dollars!" His voice faded in and out as I felt my head spin.

The moment the giant cardboard check touched my trembling hands, I felt like I had been pushed off a cliff. The whole room went dark then, and the floor rushed up to meet me. The excitement was too much for me to deal with and I blacked out on the spot.

I awoke sometime later propped up in a chair, Star holding my hand as a paramedic flashed my eyes with his flashlight.

"You scared the shit out of me, pookie!" Star said squeezing my hand.

The paramedic checked my vitals, and gave me a clean bill of health, recommending that I drink a soda or something to get my blood sugar up a bit. Star nearly toppled me over rushing in to clutch me tightly in a bear hug.

"I'm fine, Star. Relax. I just got overwhelmed by the gravity of the situation."

"It's not uncommon," said the medic. "They keep a couple of us on standby for times like this. People get understandably over-excited and then faint. You're okay though, no concussion or anything." He assured us as he packed up his kit.

I had been moved back into the office with the timid man and his computer. He was busy checking paperwork and typing the information into his terminal. I stood up, taking a moment to steady myself, and made my way over to him.

"So, when do I actually get the money? " I asked eagerly.

"Well, we are going to give you a couple thousand today in cash, to get you by in case you quit your job like most people do, and then deposit the rest into your bank account. Depending on their procedures you should see the full amount within a few days, though most banks will place a hold on large deposits to verify they are legitimate, if you take this paperwork to your local branch, it should help speed up the process." He answered, monotonously.

He handed me a folder with some official looking paperwork in it, and then made his way over to a safe in the wall. Reaching in, he pulled out a stack of money and a counting machine. He came back to the table and set the machine down and started dropping bills into it. After a few moments he put the stack of cash inside and envelope and handed it to me.

"There you go! Ten thousand in cash, don't blow it all in one place!" he forced the joke out as I took the envelope from him.

"I might, just for spite." I said casually.

Buck had returned to the room carrying a bottle of champagne and a couple of glasses.

"Ladies! How about a toast before you leave?" He offered, and I nodded.

It would be rude to decline a gift from the man that had just given me a fortune. Part of me worried that if I did anything to upset him, he would take the money away and kick us out on the sidewalk empty handed. We toasted good luck and drank the champagne which was much better than the bottle I had at home. Buck swallowed his glass in one big gulp and offered us another, which we declined politely explaining that I had plans to drive around for a while once we left.

After a few minutes of awkward and forced conversation, they indicated we could leave. We thanked everyone and waved as the secretary walked us back to the front door. I was eager to leave and see the city, especially with the wad of cash I'd just been given. We headed out to the parking lot and hopped in the car. I sat there for a few minutes, holding Star's hand and tried my best not to burst into a mix of tears and laughter, not fully able to process the gravity of the situation.

We cruised around the city for a while, taking in the sights and exploring since neither of us had ever been there before. Aside from the size it wasn't too much different from Asheville, though the people walking the streets downtown were less odd by comparison. Depending on which direction you looked that was. Asheville liked to cling to its weirdness, in many cases boasting it, but it wasn't exactly unique in that sentiment.

We pulled into the local mall and hopped out, excited to go shopping. I didn't go shopping often but I was making an exception for the occasion. It was mostly Star's idea; I would have been happy watching a couple movies and eating food all day. Not having to worry about prices would make it more tolerable though.

We spent hours running between different stores and trying on crazy outfits. Sometimes I just sat down and let Star model things for me, enjoying the fun she was having. We tried on dresses and shoes and pants and skirts, and more. We even made a stop at the lingerie store and picked up a few lacey things. If this had been a movie, the entire afternoon would be cut into a montage to some uplifting rock music where we each made faces at the other's choices until we eventually got a thumbs up and sparkles appeared in the mirror around us. In reality, I spent about two thousand dollars on clothes and stood by the car making faces at the receipts until I was interrupted by my stomach demanding food. We did find a decent amount of clothes that I would actually wear, which was a pleasant surprise, but it was definitely time to refocus and get something to eat. I sat down in the car and looked for restaurants on my phone while Star stuffed our bags in the trunk.

We rode back to the hotel to deposit our haul and change into something nicer. I had found a few nice restaurants to try out, but they looked like the type to reject us if we didn't dress up enough. Fancy restaurants liked to be snooty about their appearances in the front, as if they didn't have a bunch of burly, sweaty, foul-mouthed people running the back of the house. I never understood the idea of wearing nice clothes just to eat in, but then I also had mustard stains on half of my shirts.

Luckily, we had picked out a couple of fancy evening dresses while shopping that would get us in just about anywhere. Mine was a sleek, black, open backed dress that fell at my knees in the front and down to my calves in the back. Star's was a dark red ankle length gown with sexy little cut-outs down the sides that prevented her from wearing anything underneath. Not that she was planning to anyway. We touched up our makeup and then headed back down to the car.

I managed to make reservations with my phone, apparently it wasn't a busy night for them and there were still a few tables open. I had picked a highly recommended fine-dining restaurant that boasted a chef and owner that were featured on the cooking channel. It was a little hard to find, the place was a little off the radar. It was one of those places you hear about, the ones that you only know how to find if you are supposed to be there. I was eager to see the menu and to be able to sample all kinds of dishes crafted by master chefs, instead of the greasy fast food or chain restaurants I normally shoveled into my gullet.

We pulled up in front of the very non-descript building and the valet hopped out of his shack to greet us and park the car. He gave us a ticket and drove off as we entered the building. I looked around in awe as we entered. The whole place had an incredibly romantic feel to it, and the smell was amazing.

The maître d' stood behind his podium with his head held stereotypically high, looking perfectly disinterested in the world around him. It was a nice touch. We approached him, and he raised his eyebrow to inspect us. After a moment waiting for us to leave, he forced a smile and asked if we had a reservation, I replied with an exaggerated 'yup' just to make his skin crawl.

After sighing audibly and checking his book, he summoned a server to seat us at our table. I made it a point to sniff loudly and point my nose upwards as I walked past him. Star giggled once she realized what I was doing. The server, in stark contrast, was very cheery and insisted on bringing us several different wines to taste while we read over the menu.

I knew we were in for an interesting night when I noticed there were no prices listed anywhere except the wine bottle menu.

"So, what? How do we know what we are going to pay?" Star asked staring confusedly at her menu.

"It's a classy place Star: 'if you have to ask you can't afford it'. Supposedly the prices are figured by what the chef does with the order, but I imagine that's just a rumor. They probably buy fresh ingredients for each day's menu and base it on that." I said still browsing.

The menu was relatively small, but each item was packed with ingredients, most of which I had never heard of. Growing up poor in a small town, my options at restaurants were limited, so you can understand my confusion when I saw things like Roast Chicken with Harissa and Schmaltz or Lavender Poached Pears with Poire Williams Pudding. I didn't know what half of the options, but I was nearly drooling over the thought of trying them.

The waitress brought us some water and we each asked her questions about the menu. We chose a simple appetizer, bread and flavored olive oil with some kind of seasoned meatballs. I decided we should gamble and let the server pick our entrees, and she was more than happy to oblige.

We quietly gazed around the dining room while we waited for the appetizers to arrive. I felt rather out of place, the room was packed with very well-dressed people that just looked important. I didn't see anyone that I recognized as incredibly famous, but I'm not exactly well versed in today's who's-who.

There were a couple faces that looked familiar, that I might have known from television, but couldn't be certain. In the far corner I recognized a food journalist from the cooking channels, one of those guys that goes around eating at all different kinds of restaurants and then tells you how to make their best dishes at home. I wasn't that good at cooking, so I usually just made a sandwich while watching the show. Sometimes I would add a parsley garnish to give a little pizzaz to my 'hand-chopped egg with relish and mustard aioli' sandwich.

After a short wait, our appetizer arrived. The bread was warm and crusty, the olive oil had fresh herbs, crushed pepper, and sea salt. On a separate dish were four delicate meatballs coated in marinara and parmesan cheese. It tasted amazing, and the only way to explain the flavor with any accuracy would be the expletive that escaped quietly from my mouth after the first bite: "Holy fuck!"

Once we finished our appetizer, the server returned with our main course, and they had gone all out to impress us. The chef even came out and delivered it himself, I recognized his face, but couldn't place his name. He didn't have his own show that I knew of, but always seemed to be a judge on many of the competition shows. I felt like it would be too awkward to ask for his name in his own restaurant, so I didn't.

My plate was an extravagant set of Asian-fusion inspired tacos with wagyu beef and ginger, accompanied by a roll of brightly colored sushi, and a black garlic soup. I couldn't help but squeal with excitement. Star's meal was a mixed pasta dish with lamb and shrimp in a pesto sauce. It wasn't anything I would have expected, but each bite exploded with flavor. We sampled each other's plates and danced in our chairs with glee. Neither of us had ever eaten food this good in our lives.

We flagged down the waitress and asked for some desserts before we had even finished our meals. Star got a tiramisu, to keep with the Italian theme of her meal, while I opted for some sort of frozen thing with fruit in a tall glass. I wasn't sure what it was, and the name was impossible for me to pronounce, but it looked delicious. It was somewhere between sorbet and smoothie with some bananas and strawberries folded into it.

With some effort we both finished all our food and sat back in our chairs with audible sighs of satisfaction. I rubbed my stomach hoping to ease the cramp from over-eating as I glanced over at the check. I felt nervous about checking the amount, knowing it would be far more than I was used to spending for a single meal. I knew I could afford it, but that didn't help to ease the anxiety. I flipped open the little black booklet and slowly moved my eyes towards the total. My eyes popped wide open as the numbers registered.

The receipt wasn't even itemized, just a single line for the entrees and dessert, the bottle of wine, and a suggested gratuity. The wine was nearly half of the price which I expected but three hundred bucks for two people still seemed steep. I sighed heavily, paid with cash with extra for the tip, and left before they tried to bring change.

We strolled out of the restaurant past the snooty maître d' again I held my nose high and sniffed, unable to help myself. The valet greeted us, checked my ticket and had our car brought back around.

"Thank you so much for coming!" he said.

"You too!" I smiled and handed him a tip as the realization of my awkward response set in. I quickly climbed into the car and closed the door to hide my embarrassment.

"It's been a hell of a day, don't ya think?" I asked, looking over to Star who had reclined her seat to ease the stress on her full stomach.

"Today has been amazing, pookie. I can still hardly believe any of it is real." She replied.

She slipped her hand into mine and gently caressed it with her thumb. She gave me a loving look but seemed a little nervous. I could tell she had something on her mind.

"I've been meaning to ask though, Tri..." she hesitated slightly.

"Why did you decide to include me in all this? You could've just as easily told me to hit the road and come out here alone and started a new life. All this money, the freedom you'll have, you could meet all kinds of men or women in the world, why me?" She sounded almost sad as she asked.

I stared at her for a moment, unsure of what to say. She had caught me completely off-guard with that question.

"I... Star the money has nothing to do with anything. I wanted you in my life before any of this, so of course I'm going to include you." I explained.

"Look, all those nights we spent together talking about our pasts really meant a lot to me. I got to know you better than I know anyone else, and you know things about me I've never told anyone. I thought about it for a long time because it hurt me to know when you were off in someone else's bed, when you could be with me." My eyes were starting to water a little, and my voice cracked with emotion as I spoke.

"I'm in love with you, Star. Simple as that. I brought you with me because I wanted you to be with me. Nothing is going to change that, okay? I love you." I said, wiping a tear from my cheek.

She started softly crying and wrapped her arms around me.

"I love you too, Trianna. I just haven't had the nerve to tell you." She sputtered through her crying.

I held her tightly, a little in shock that I had finally come clean about my feelings for her. It was nice to hear the words out loud instead of just rattling them around in my head, waiting for the right moment. It felt like butterflies left my stomach and carried a huge weight off my shoulders. I hugged her tightly for a moment, and then we pulled just far enough apart to kiss deeply forgetting the world around us in a raw moment of bliss.

A horn outside reminded me that we were still sitting in the valet lane. I glanced out the window to see the mostly teenage valets crowded around the booth to watch. I blushed, and then quickly snapped my eyes forward pushing the car into drive and burning out a little as I pulled away. I could hear a few rowdy cheers from the boys as I squealed away.

"Perverts! Can't even have a touching moment without some adolescent little prick sticking his nose where it doesn't belong." I said as the car bolted down the road.

Star laughed as she wiped the tears from her face. She rested her hand on my thigh, caressing it slowly with her thumb. We made our way back to the hotel and scrambled up to our room. We had barely made it into the room before we started tearing each other's clothes off.

Star giggled as I chased her into the bedroom and threw her down on the bed. I quickly peeled off my underwear and pounced. Pumping adrenaline and raging hormones made me high as I breathed in her scent. Our lips touched, triggering an explosion of ecstasy. I don't remember when the music turned on, but we rolled around with our bodies pulsing to the beat.

It was the most passionate night we had ever spent together, our hands and tongues exploring one another as if they were on an expedition. Leaving no inch of each other untouched we moaned, laughed, and thoroughly enjoyed ourselves. We took our time and experimented with new tricks and positions we had seen in porn, but most were too awkward or painful, so we improvised. After our second orgasm, we still weren't sated.

Star reached into her bag and pulled out a surprise. She tightened the straps around her waist as she guided me to the edge of the bed and got behind me. I closed my eyes and squirmed slightly as she pushed the silicon toy deep inside me. It felt so good. She clearly knew what she was doing, and I began to shudder.

We changed positions several times, finding which way we fit together best. We moved around the room, trying different surfaces along the way. I begged loudly for her to go harder, and then we nearly knocked the TV off the dresser. We moved back to the bed after spilling the ice bucket, and I climbed on top of her. It wasn't long before we shared another orgasm.

Eventually we settled down and lay sweaty and breathless in the wrecked hotel room. Star nearly fell asleep drinking her water and I had to grab the bottle before she got the bed any more wet. She giggled and snuggled up against me, I kissed her head. I watched the stars through the window for a short while before drifting off to sleep, still tingling.

CHAPTER 6

The next three months seemed to fly by in a blur, as my entire world changed. I was living my life as a rich woman in love.

I bought a house on the coast of South Carolina with its own private beach. I gave my good friends money or bought them things they really needed. I even let Jackson have the old Camaro and enough money to properly fix it up. I paid off my lease so the landlord would leave me alone while I prepared to move out of my apartment. I donated some money to charity, mostly things related to sick children or animals. I'm kind of a softy for things like that.

We threw a big going away party with our friends and family in the area, and it was bittersweet. It was likely that we wouldn't see most of them again. They would get caught up in their day to day lives and not be able to find time to visit for one reason or another. I understood, which is why I had given them all what gifts I could.

I had been in their shoes most of my life. I wouldn't get mad at them, because I knew they felt trapped and just wanted to keep their heads above water. I would still miss them though, and it pained me to say goodbye. I couldn't stay here any longer though.

After we moved, life really started to change for us as we evolved and adapted to our new location and lifestyle. We didn't have to work, but we both found hobbies to occupy our time. Star spent a lot of her time working on elaborate steampunk outfits. She would still do photo shoots occasionally, but mostly made stuff to sell online. It was incredibly lucrative, and she was excited to share her ideas with the online community she had made.

I started up a budget friendly tech repair company, hiring a few local tech grads at competitive wages and basically let them run the shop how they saw fit. I offered low rates on repairs, and we made most of our profit selling parts and custom machines on the side. I hired an accountant to run the numbers, so that I didn't have to, and in the end, I didn't have much to do with the day-to-day, but I could say I owned a successful business, which had been a dream of mine for a long time. I even had plans to open in multiple cities over the next three years.

My relationship with Star was growing steadily. We relished the ability to drop everything and venture out on impromptu date nights. We caught all the new movies we wanted, ate classy food, bought expensive things we didn't really need just because it was fun. Many times, I would sober up the next morning and return things that we either already had or were just too impractical. I'm still not sure how we wound up with four different rainbow polar bear statues.

One day while relaxing on the beach with Star, I got it in my head that I wanted to marry her. Gay marriage was legal in most places now, so it wouldn't take much to get the knot tied. Still, I was perplexed because I had never really considered marriage. Being with Star had changed my opinion of many things, rainbow polar bear statues included.

Later that week I took her out to eat at our favorite restaurant. It was a little Italian place, run by first generation immigrants, tucked away in an alley where you had to really be looking for it to even find it. We had literally tripped and stumbled into the place one night while out drinking and were just blown away by the food.

I'm still not sure if she ever noticed, but I had been a nervous wreck the whole day. I had the ring in my purse, hidden way down at the bottom, and we had spent most of the day out and about. I arranged to have a private table set up and waiting with candles and wine and the appetizers. Star looked over the table and then at me questioningly.

I had a whole speech I wanted to give, but in the moment, I was so nervous I fumbled through the whole thing, barely got a word out. I nearly fell over trying to get on my knee to propose, and tears began streaming down Star's face. I pulled out the ring and finally managed to stutter the question. She tackled me as she shouted 'YES!' and we fell to the floor locked in a kiss. I was worried I might need the waiter's help to get her off me, so we could eat, but Star's never been one to pass up good Italian food.

I'll remember that night for the rest of my life.

This new life was great, and things were going better for me than I had ever imagined. I was the happiest I've ever been. I didn't know it then, but things were about to change in a way neither of us expected. My sudden wealth solved many of my problems, but it was attracting attention I had never expected.

CHAPTER 7

I hadn't realized it at the time, but I had overlooked a gravely important detail when picking out the new house. I wanted the bedroom to have bay windows and a balcony, so I could look out over the ocean from the comfort of my bed. I loved the view but did not realize this meant the sunrise was free to claw at my face every morning. The oversight just might be my undoing one day.

Sure, I could have bought thick blackout curtains for protection, but there was something particularly stunning about watching the sunrise over the ocean from the comfort of your own bed. I awoke, like most mornings, under direct assault from the first rays of morning sun cresting over the horizon eager to end me. However, this time the light was shining around the silhouette of Star standing out on the balcony.

Our new house was hidden in its own little cove, surrounded by trees on one side, and it was set against a cliff on the other. We had the beach all to ourselves and a long drive to the house from the main road that discouraged people from sneaking onto it. We often lounged on the balcony or even on the beach wearing nothing. It kept our tan even and the ocean air on a warm summer night feels amazing on bare skin. Star was in fact nude on the balcony, probably having just climbed out of bed. She smiled as I wrapped my arms around her from behind and rested my head on her shoulder.

"You're up early…" I said, running my hands across her skin lovingly.

"Yeah, I wanted to watch the sunrise, this is the first time I've managed to do that since we moved. It's beautiful. I still can't believe this is our life now. It feels like just yesterday we were struggling to make a living back home, and now… Now I'm standing naked on my bedroom balcony looking at the sunrise over my own private beach." She laughed slightly to herself, turning to face me.

"Thank you so much Trianna, for sharing this amazing life with me."

I just held her tightly for a while, and we watched the rest of the sunrise together. We eventually broke away and went downstairs to eat breakfast. Star had learned to cook, and was quite good at it, and chose to cook most of our meals. I helped occasionally, but it was nothing compared to what she pulled together.

"I'm going to go check the mail, back in a bit!" I said pulling on some shorts I had left lying on the table in the den.

The mailbox was at the end of the drive, so the mail person didn't have to drive all the way to the house. It didn't bother me really, gave me an excuse to get a little exercise first thing in the morning. I strolled down to the garage and grabbed my bike. I had bought and restored a couple antique Schwinn bikes for us to ride around town.

The roads were very flat here, which made it much easier to ride, compared to the hills back in Asheville. I couldn't handle riding up and down steep inclines, so I never rode a bike much after I grew up. But here it was a really nice way to get around if you weren't in a hurry. The ocean air made it seem more like relaxation than exercise.

I pedaled my way up the driveway, winding back and forth around plants and trees. In a straight line through the woods, we weren't very far from the main road, but the way the driveway snaked up to the house was almost half a mile. I liked that it was secluded. It meant I didn't have to deal with nosy neighbors.

There was the occasional animal that would wander across the property. They didn't seem to be bothered much by my presence. I had to watch out for snakes or alligators, they liked to stray from the lagoon at the far end of the property from time to time. They rarely bothered anyone though.

I coasted to a stop beside the mailbox and flipped open the box. Most of the mail was addressed to Star, she ran her business online but somehow still got a large amount of physical mail forwarded here for it. Thank you letters or gifts and pictures from her clients mostly. I set the mail in the basket on the front of the bike as I flipped through it.

A particular envelope caught my eye. It had an air of importance about it, nice quality paper with bordered edges. It had a hand-written address, and I was a little shocked to see it had been sealed with wax. It seemed like something out of an old movie.

The emblem looked to be two wireframe boxes that were tilted just the right way that you couldn't determine top or bottom. There was no return address either, which puzzled me. The bubble mailer has some heft to it for its size, maybe it was a new phone or tablet.

I set it in the basket with the rest of the mail and turned around to head back to the house. I had no clue what was in the package, and the ride back was wracked with nervous anticipation. I wasn't sure if I was more nervous or excited. I pedaled faster, eager to reach the house and find out what was inside.

I rolled up to the house, snatching the mail from the basket, and ran up the stairs in the garage to get back inside. I made my way over to my desk in the den, setting the stack of other mail down, clutching the mystery package. Star, hearing the commotion I made coming back in, strolled into the room carrying our plates of breakfast. I could smell the tantalizing scent of waffles and warm syrup, but they would have to wait.

"Hey babe, check this out. We got something weird in the mail." I said as I picked up my letter opener. "It feels like a tablet or something."

She set the plates down on the table and moved over to join me as I slit open the envelope and peered in. I had been right, it was a tablet, there were no charger cables or anything else included which was odd.

"Did you order a tablet?" Star asked curiously.

"Nah, my phone does pretty much everything I would need one for. It doesn't even have any cables with it, I wonder if the battery is charged."

I pulled it out of the envelope and on the screen was a sticky note that read: 'Power on, press play.' in very neat handwriting. I removed the note from the screen and hit the power button. It took a moment to boot up and then loaded automatically pulled up a video. Star leaned in to watch as I hit play.

The video was strange, it started with the sound of a film reel and the old style black and white count down, beeping as each number changed. The film was also in black and white, and showed us a very sleek futuristic looking building at the end of a cobblestone driveway. There was a voice speaking, and he sounded like the old newsreel announcers from before World War II era movies.

"A marvel of modern times stands before you now. Behold the illustrious headquarters of the Paradigm Corporation! Within these walls, Paradigm has created wonders like no one has ever seen before in the history of mankind."

The image changed to a woman on a stage. She appeared to be creating flames in the palms of her hand and forming them into balls. She threw them into the air above her where they then burned themselves out. She bowed, hands leaving tracers in the air from the flames she still held.

As she left, a man entered, wheeling out a Tesla coil. He started the machine up and began swatting at the energy coming off the orb at the top. He then grabbed one of the bolts and pulled himself up into the air. My jaw dropped as he positioned himself above the orb upside-down seeming to hold himself in place with his hands holding on to the bolts of energy as if doing a handstand.

"We have invented a way to challenge the elements themselves in a manner sure to inspire awe and boggle the mind! Given your status in society, we here at Paradigm cordially invite you to our headquarters for a tour of the facility where you can meet the scientists behind these amazing feats of human ability."

The image changed again to a laboratory full of tables covered in beakers and vials, and various electronic lab equipment. Men and women shuffled around in long white lab coats clutching and writing on clipboards while observing various chemicals in beakers. A small crowd of well-dressed and obviously wealthy people stood behind a railing watching the scientists at work. Then the screen cut back to the building from outside again.

A man in a very smart suit walked onto the screen and smiled raising his arms as if to show his pride in the building behind him.

"Paradigm, making the world a better place by making a better you!" The announcer finished as the screen faded out.

The screen then displayed an image of the Paradigm logo, which I noted was the same emblem from the wax seal. I raised an eyebrow and looked at Star, puzzled.

"Well, that was weird... what do you suppose this is about?" She said looking in the envelope for something that might explain.

"I'm not sure, seems like we are being invited to check out whatever this Paradigm place is. Why did it look like a propaganda film from the 40s?" I asked.

I poked at the screen to try and find anything else, but there was no response. I set the tablet down on the desk, leaning back in the chair to think. Just then the tablet vibrated and displayed an incoming call. I furrowed my brow at it and slid the green icon to answer the call.

A camera feed popped up displaying the man in the smart suit from the end of the video, and I almost pulled a double take.

"Ah, the Lady Von Drake, a pleasure to meet you." The man said as I picked up the tablet again.

I stared for a moment still caught off guard by the situation.

"I see you have received our invitation, good. I will send a car around shortly to bring you to our private hangar." He said.

He seemed to be gesturing to people in the room with him, but the camera was fixed mostly on his face, and I couldn't see much else.

"Whoa, whoa, whoa. What are you talking about? I don't know who you are, I'm not going anywhere without some explanation." I said.

The balls on this guy, thinking I would just hop in a car because he sent me a tablet in the mail. He smirked.

"Your hesitations are understandable. Forgive me, allow me to start over more appropriately. My name is Sebastian Artosis, but you can call me 'Bach'. I represent the Paradigm Corporation." He explained.

I didn't hide my surprise or subsequent dismay at his classical music pun of a name as he continued.

"We cater a unique, specialty service to young wealthy individuals like yourselves. We offer a product that we guarantee you have never seen before, however due to our strict non-disclosure policy I cannot tell you any more about it without having you sign an NDA form here at the facility. I can tell you that what you saw in our video is but a taste of what we can accomplish. I think you would be very interested in what we have to offer."

He exuded confidence, like that of a used car salesman, but it was rounded and polished with that experience you see from career politicians. I stared at him curiously as he spoke, unsure of his intentions. He did manage to pique my interest.

"How do I know this isn't some scam, or some plot to get me to your place so you can rape or kill me or something?" I said, judgmentally.

"Do you believe in magic, Ms. Von Drake?" he said, dodging my question.

I didn't answer, waiting for him to acknowledge my concerns.

"I can assure you my intentions are purely business, and I mean you no ill will. I must run; the car should arrive shortly. I hope to see you at the facility for your free tour. Before I go, I would like you to ponder just one thing..."

He raised a single, leather-gloved finger in front of the camera and smiled. The air around his finger seemed to shimmer for a moment. At first, I thought it was something wrong with the camera feed. Then, suddenly, a small light formed just above the tip of his finger, which quickly grew into a small flame like a lit match.

I watched in awe as it began to curve into a ball of fire balancing in the air just above his finger. Once fully formed, it looked like a tiny raging sun. The video call ended then, leaving me just sitting in my chair holding onto the tablet with my mouth agape.

I was baffled at what I had just witnessed. Surely it was some trick, but I wasn't sure if you could edit a video call like that. I looked up at Star who appeared just as confused.

"Did that dude just create fire out of thin air?" she asked, dumbfounded.

"I'm not sure... he was wearing gloves, maybe it was some fancy lighter trick." I said.

"Well, what do you think, should we go check it out? He doesn't give off too creepy of a vibe... but he does kind of seem like he could work for the government or something." Star said, pulling out her phone and poking furiously at it looking for something. I moved over to the table and popped a piece of bacon in my mouth, chewing on it as I thought about the situation.

"I am curious, I have to admit. Seems super fishy, but I think I want to at least see what it's about. I'm bringing my gun with us though, just in case."

I started working on the waffles Star had made for us, thinking hard about what I had just seen. I wasn't sure what he meant when he asked if I believed in magic, but to follow it with that display. Was he trying to tell me that magic was real? That he could use it? That he could teach us? It was all too strange. How did he know to call the tablet at that exact moment? I needed answers.

I hopped up from the table and went back up to the bedroom to get dressed in more appropriate clothing. Despite my new-found wealth, I hadn't changed my style very much. I just bought nicer brands of clothing. I slipped out of the shorts and tank and dug around in the closet for my black cropped denim vest and a sleeveless band shirt featuring the saw blade Whitechapel logo. I slid into some tight black denim jeans and a pair of biker boots as well. It worked for me and made me feel like a bit of a badass.

Star had come up to change as well, slipping into some short shorts and her long steampunk boots. She was fastening up a custom corset she had made that had a frilly knee length skirt attached. It really drew the eye to her chest, which is why I walked into the wall on my way past.

I grabbed a key off the nightstand, using it to open the locked drawer that I kept my handgun in. I had a nice black leather leg harness for it that strapped onto my upper thigh. I wanted to make sure they knew I wasn't someone to be messed with, so I was going to wear the gun in plain sight. I checked the gun to make sure it was loaded properly, and that the safety was on, subconsciously whispering the steps my instructor had taught me at the range.

I looked at myself over in the mirror, even without the gun I looked like a badass. I looked like I meant business. I didn't trust these strange people, but my curiosity was certainly piqued. They'd have to show me more than tricks to win me over, however.

I made my way downstairs and out onto the front porch. I looked out towards the far end of our long driveway. You couldn't see the whole thing from the house, and the trees blocked the view of everything from the road for privacy. Sure enough, just as 'Bach' said, I saw the car approaching.

I was baffled on how the man knew to time everything the way he did. Calling the tablet just as we opened it, sending the car just as we got ready, how did he know? Just a few of the very pointed questions I wanted to ask him in person. If he was somehow monitoring my house, there would be hell to pay.

Star joined me as the car finally pulled up to the front of the house. It was a long black limousine, and I laughed at the stereotype. You'd think someone would eventually break the mold and send a more modest vehicle. Maybe just a nice coupe or something.

The doors opened as soon as the car came to a stop, and two men wearing stark white suits climbed out. They appeared to be twins, same height, same face, and same long red hair over pale skin, it was unnerving. They had a look about them that just screamed private muscle, but they weren't very large in build. The sides of their heads were shaved, and there were mystical looking symbols tattooed in intricate patterns from their temple all the way down into their collars.

"We are from the Paradigm Corporation. We have been sent to escort you to the facility for a tour. Please, have a seat when you are ready to go." said one of the strange men.

He gestured to the car as the other person opened the rear doors of the limo. His voice was very flat, and almost robotic. I looked at Star and raised an eyebrow. She shrugged in response, and we made our way down to the car and climbed in the back seat.

Inside, the car was just as lavish as you would expect it to be. Leather seats, red velvet carpeting, a small bar set into one of the bench seats, it had the works. As we took our seats and the doors closed, I realized we were not alone in the back of the car. There was a woman sitting at the other end of the car.

She was dressed the same as the men outside, save for the obvious gender differences. She also had the strange tattoos. I was beginning to worry this was some kind of cult. She sat very still looking straight ahead, as if patiently awaiting an order.

I waved to her politely and said 'hello' to try and break the ice, but I got nothing more than a quick nod. She clearly was not the slightest bit interested in conversation. Star gave me a curious look, clearly intrigued herself. I made a face back, indicating I was stumped as well.

I heard the doors close at the front of the car and the engine started up. We were quickly on our way to wherever we were going. I hoped it wasn't far, as it didn't seem like it was going to be a lively trip. I shrugged and poured a whiskey sour from the bar. Might as well take advantage of the available resources.

Some time passed, Star was busy with something on her phone, and I had just put mine away. I tried to look out the windows, only to find they were tinted so dark I couldn't really see anything. It appeared they didn't want us to know how we were getting to the facility. Paradigm seemed to have a thing for secrets. Star leaned over to me held her phone out.

"I'm not sure this is a good idea, Tri. I can't find anything about these guys on the internet. Not even conspiracies. It's like they don't exist at all." She whispered.

This, however, caught the attention of the woman riding in the back with us.

"Rest assured, Paradigm is legitimate. Due to our desire to protect the privacy of our clientele, we keep ourselves hidden from the public. You will be expected to sign a non-disclosure agreement regarding your trip to the facility." She explained.

Her voice was the same flat, almost lifeless tone as the men. She did not elaborate and maintained her position in her seat. She resumed staring straight ahead from behind her dark sunglasses. I looked at her for a few moments, expecting her to say more but she didn't. I looked at Star and we both shrugged.

The car came to a halt then and I could hear the engine shut off as the front doors opened. I slid towards the door as the men opened it, but they stood in the opening preventing us from getting out. I felt nervous for a moment, and the hair on my neck stood on end briefly.

"Before you go further, I must ask that you sign this." The woman spoke.

She handed us two clipboards, each with a large stack of papers on them.

"You can read them if you like. They are non-disclosure agreements, stating that you will not discuss anything regarding the events that occurred in this car. You will agree to never speak to anyone outside of the Paradigm Corporation about anything that was seen or heard, including but not limited to the route taken to arrive at this private airport. This is a legal contract, and breaking it is punishable by law. By signing the top page, you agree to these terms and may proceed to the facility via helicopter." She explained.

I looked at the thick stack of pages bound to the clipboard, and then back to the woman. There was something about her voice and the way she spoke that bugged me. It reminded me of Data from Star Trek, like she was an android or something.

I decided I didn't want to bother trying to read the pile of legal jargon that she had handed me, picked up the pen, and scribbled my signature on the line. I handed mine back to her as Star did the same and the men moved from the door allowing us out of the car.

"Thank you. You can proceed to the helicopter now." She said.

I looked around as I stepped out into the sun. We had been driven to a small airfield that I didn't recognize. There were no signs or logos anywhere to identify it. There was one single runway that looked like it was designed for use by very small planes, and there were a couple helipads on either side of it.

A helicopter was landing on one as Star got out of the car to join me. The men closed the door and then got back in the car and drove off while two more men climbed out of the helicopter. They, too, had tattoos on the shaved sides of their heads, but the designs appeared to be just slightly different. Their faces were just as calm and emotionless as the previous people as they gestured for us to climb into the helicopter.

We climbed into the back and were met with another woman dressed in white. She too barely acknowledged us. I didn't bother to say hello, realizing it likely would not get me anywhere. No point in wasting the breath.

The trip was very similar to the car ride. We sat in silence most of the way, the woman stared at nothing, and we couldn't see where we were going. Star was still digging around on the internet trying to find anything she could about Paradigm. Still, we came up with nothing.

After a short time, we began descending back towards the ground. The woman handed us another stack of papers and I groaned slightly as I quickly scribbled my name on the line while she gave nearly the same speech as the first woman. Star signed hers as well and the men set the helicopter down on the pad as the rotor slowly wound its way down. They helped us out of the doorway, and we looked around.

We were now standing in front of the building I had seen in the video on the tablet. There was no parking lot that I could see, and certainly no vehicles. We had landed on a pad in middle of a small field, and the rest of the compound seemed to be surrounded by trees. There was a large mountain behind the structure with the building extending into it.

The men ushered us up the path from the pad towards the front of the building. I couldn't see an exit anywhere. There no roads or anything approached the building. I could smell the ocean on the air, so perhaps we were on an island.

We began up the stairs and the doors to the facility opened. A man and woman, still dressed in white and adorned with tattoos, emerged. Behind them was a man in a smart black suit and sunglasses. I was distracted by something moving in the trees but couldn't see anything clearly. As the group approached, I realized the black suited man was the one from the tablet video.

"Ah, the Ladies Von Drake, so glad you could join us today!" he said, extending his arms in a welcoming manner.

I looked him over as he approached. He was a little taller than me and had an average build. The perfectly tailored suit fit him like a glove, and he wore that cheesy smile you see on politicians and salesmen.

"Before we begin, I must have you sign a non-disclosure agreement. You are about to witness something many people will never see. And to protect our assets and our clientele we must ensure you will not share this with anyone outside of Paradigm." He said, as the woman presented us with two more clipboards.

"We've signed a lot of these today... I'm starting to get very suspicious, Bach, was it? If I flip through this one, I'm not going to find something giving you permission to sell us as slaves, am I?" I said as I scribbled my name. He waited until my signature was finished to speak.

"Certainly not, if we needed to sell off anyone as slaves, we would start with the drones... but that's not what we are here to discuss today." he said dismissively.

"You two lovely ladies have been selected to take a tour of our facility, and if all goes well, perhaps we can add you to our very exclusive list of clients. You brought the tablet with you, yes?"

Star pulled it from her purse and handed it to Bach. He set it down on the pavement and took a step back just before it began spitting out sparks and melting. We looked at him, thoroughly confused, and he just smiled.

"Thermite! Wonderful stuff. Now, let us head inside, I'm certain you are eager to get started. If you will follow me inside, we will have some quick refreshments and then begin the tour." He spun on his heels and made his way inside, the twins gesturing for us to follow him.

He led us down a short hallway to a lavishly decorated little room containing a small table and two pod-like chairs. The drones pulled out the seats for us and we sat down. Bach appeared with a towel over one arm like a waiter and placed two cups before us. He picked up the pitcher from the table and poured us each a cup of the most delicious smelling coffee I had ever encountered.

He clapped his hands and one of the men appeared with a covered tray in his hands. Bach lifted the lid and retrieved two small plates and set them down beside our cups of coffee. On each of the plates was a small pastry dipped in strawberry yogurt with the Paradigm logo drawn on the top with chocolate. They looked freshly made.

I took a bite of the pastry, and my eyes involuntarily rolled back in my head. It was delicious, and paired with the coffee I was in heaven. I had tasted some extravagant desserts in the last few months, but this was the best thing I had ever eaten. I watched Star bite into hers and experience the same delight.

A bit of the crimson liquid from the middle of the pastry ran from the corner of her mouth, and I wiped it with my finger and licked it off. It was pleasantly sweet, but I couldn't help but notice a slight metallic aftertaste, like copper. I shrugged, perhaps an effect of the salty air over the course of the flight in. I quickly devoured the rest of mine, savoring each bite.

Bach cleared our table back onto the covered tray and sent the man off with it, who disappeared down another hallway.

"Now that the refreshments are out of the way, ladies, prepare yourselves. You are about to bear witness to advancements in recreation, unheard of by the common man." he said eagerly.

"We here at Paradigm have developed something, that will blow your minds. What you are about to see will cause you to question all you know as real and leave you hanging on the edge of your seats."

He grabbed the back of our chairs and spun us quickly towards the wall as he spoke, and suddenly the floor began to move.

We found ourselves on a rotating platform moving into a dark room. As we moved into the room, I could see we were facing a large pane of glass that separated us from a room full of scientists and equipment and I recognized it from the video.

"Welcome to Paradigm labs, ladies. Here our scientists are constantly working on new ways to improve our product. What is our product, you may ask? The answer may confound you." Bach mused.

"We here at Paradigm have revolutionized what it means to be human. We have developed a drug that grants human beings a set of certain special abilities. Our formula is top secret! Not even our NDA's will allow you to know just what started it all. Suffice to say we made a ground-breaking discovery within the human genome that allowed us to awaken hidden powers inside of all humans." He continued.

"We've unlocked the ability to use those powers in extravagant ways. Ways that you will soon see." He cleared his throat before continuing.

"Our team has found that, by modifying certain aspects of our DNA, with a very specific series of compounds, we can make individuals see the world in a whole new way. From that new perspective, we can enhance their natural abilities, granting them the power control the world as they perceive it." He explained.

"Some say its super-science, some call it playing god, some call it a trick, but I call it... Magic!" Bach said with a flourish.

He spoke with a practiced tongue, delivering his speech like a sales pitch.

"Imagine, being able to see the world for what it really is, being able to see the energies that flow around and through the planet and every living thing on it, like a great net of ether. Now, imagine being able to reach into that ether and draw power from it. Being able to manifest that power in yourself and command it to your will. Let us leave the scientists to their work and bear glorious witness to a few brave souls that dared to look into the heart of the universe itself, bending the forces therein to their bidding." he said as the room began to move again.

The next room that appeared before us was dark and contained an empty stage. I leaned forward a little in my chair trying to decide if there was anything lurking in the shadows. Suddenly, there was a blast of light from the darkness as a ball of fire rushed towards us. I ducked and screamed despite myself, and I could feel the heat as it drew near, but seconds later it slammed up against a barrier of some sort just before us.

The flames danced across the invisible barrier as they dissipated. There was a bit of a blue shimmer in the air that seemed to ripple from the impact. I sighed with relief and sat back up in my chair. Star clapped excitedly, clearly enjoying the show.

A woman's figure now stood on the stage, glowing slightly with an aura of fire. The flames died out darkening the stage. Moments later, a spotlight snapped on, revealing the figure. A young woman stood before us, ready to perform.

She had a large spiked red mohawk and wore tattered biker leathers. She grinned wildly at us as the spotlight on her dimmed, raising her hands to her sides. Her hands began to glow as she quickly became engulfed in a raging fire. I could feel the heat radiating from her.

She made a quick gesture with her hand and the fire formed into two tight spheres above her palms. They left small trails in the air behind them as she slowly moved her arms in intricate patterns around her. The orbs stayed just inches above her hands as she moved. She raised both arms above her head and pushed the balls of fire together forming one larger ball as they combined.

Then with a wink she pulled the fire down before her, creating a great arc that rushed towards the invisible barrier before us. Again, I felt the heat, but the flames slammed into the barrier, fading away before it could touch us. When the flames cleared the girl was gone from the stage.

I was dumbfounded by what I was seeing. Was that girl actually able to summon and control fire at will, or was this just some elaborate hoax? I couldn't decide. I didn't have much time to think about it before something else began happening on the stage.

A large metal ball descended from above the stage. As more of it came into view, I could tell that it was attached to an elaborately constructed tower, all of which appeared to make up a tesla coil. My suspicions were confirmed when lightning began arcing from the sphere. It crackled loudly on the air as it struck metal rods that had risen slightly out of the stage.

There was a pause in the flashes for a few moments and a tremendous buzzing noise began to emanate from the sphere. Suddenly there was a cacophony as beams of lightning began slamming into all the rods at once, repeatedly. One final strike hit the rods, and held itself, blasting energy into the rods to the point that they began to glow red hot and deform themselves. I didn't notice at first, but the sphere was opening.

Inside the sphere sat a cross-legged man wearing nothing but a piece of white cloth wrapped around his waist, covering his genitals. His body was covered with tattoos of amazing detail. Strange patterns of tribal lines and circles, symbols that looked strange and powerful. They were all glowing bright blue, the same color as the lightning pumping from the sphere.

The lightning stopped, and the glowing man emerged from the sphere, never uncrossing his legs. He floated forward as the sphere rose back toward the ceiling and the opening closed. The man's arms rested on his knees, and his eyes were closed as if he were locked in deep meditation. His body was clean and smooth, no hair to be seen aside from his bushy eyebrows.

He opened his eyes then, and I gasped. The tattoos on his body pulsed, and as his eyelids opened, they revealed swirling blue storms within his eye sockets. He opened his mouth, bellowing a deep monk-like moan. I could see tiny bolts of energy arcing from his teeth to his tongue.

He leaned his head back and a huge beam of lightning raced from his mouth to the metal orb above as he continued his deep pitched moan. I could feel my hair standing on end as energy began to arc and swirl around his body. Then, suddenly, his head snapped back forward. All the lightning stopped at once, and I could see the metal ball was red hot and starting to drip downwards. He floated down to sit on the ground just underneath a large portion of the molten metal that was inching towards him.

Just then another person stepped out on to the stage, and with a wave of her hand began to shape the molten steel. She gestured with her hand, and I could hear wind blowing and the metal began to twist and cool. She pulled her hand back towards her and the steel stretched out as it curled and cooled more. Finally, she lifted a bucket of water with her other hand, thrusting it towards the steel which hissed and steamed as the two collided.

When the steam cleared, I could see that the steel had been shaped into a vine complete with leaves and thorns, and at the very end was a rose blossom. The girl gripped the stem and snapped the thin brittle steel, handing the metal flower to the man who rose to his feet to accept it. I noticed a few sparks arc from his fingers as he grasped it and the girl's hair stood on end for a moment until she let go. They each smiled and bowed to us.

Bach began to clap slowly and loudly as Star and I sat awestruck.

"Fantastic! Simply astounding work, no?" he asked, rhetorically.

The room began to move once more, and he continued his speech.

"The individuals you just witnessed are demonstrating the powers they attained thanks to the work we have done here at Paradigm. They are all employees of the corporation that volunteered to test out new forms of our wonderful product, and as you can see, they have achieved amazing results."

He adjusted his wrist cuffs as he stood, as the rotating platform brought us back to the lobby in which we had started. Bach checked his watch and nodded to himself.

"Well ladies, that concludes the tour of the facility. I know it seemed short, but we don't like to be too flashy here. Now, if you will follow me, we have arrangements to discuss."

He gestured for us to follow him as he made his way towards a door at the side of the room. He led us into a large hall, complete with a receptionist desk, it looked like a fancy hotel lobby. The woman at the desk adjusted her hair and smiled brightly at us as we approached a table. Bach motioned for us to take a seat on the large padded chairs on the opposite side of the table.

He sat down as well and one of the strange women in the white suits appeared, carrying a binder full of papers. She handed the binder to Bach before turning and leaving the way she came.

"So! Exciting stuff, eh? Let's get down to business. I don't want to beat around the bush, so I'll be straightforward with you. The research we perform here requires quite a lot of financial backing. We have our investors of course, but to keep our anonymity, we need to make sure we aren't making waves in the world. We don't want just anyone strolling up on the compound begging for the miracle pills that we manufacture here. We want to remain a secret, but business is business."

He flipped open the book as he spoke and turned it, so we could see the pages. It looked as if he was trying to sell us on a spa package. There were pictures of people doing yoga, getting massages, etcetera.

"Here's what I'm offering ladies. Spend two weeks here at Paradigm, just two weeks, and we will have you doing things you've never even dreamed of." He pitched.

"We will not only let you get a taste of what we've been developing here, but we'll teach you how to use it. We'll give you training sessions to help master it, make you into something amazing. We provide room and board, you ever stay at the Hilton?"

He paused a moment, more for dramatic effect than expecting an answer.

"One-star shack compared to our facility! I mean you'd think they rented dumpsters after a night in one of our deluxe suites. Truly the best."

He flipped through some pages showing off more pictures, this time of the people we saw on the stage, showing off their fantastic abilities.

"Now, this kind of service doesn't come cheap, but I'm sure you guessed that by now. Ten million dollars... hear me out, ten million gets you two weeks of living like a king, being pampered around the clock. Two weeks of training with our magical master and we throw in five pills, for each of you, of the star of our little show here, the amazing substance we've come to call Opulentia."

He reached in his pocket and pulled out a small box, opened the lid and set it down on the table before us. I leaned back in the chair.

"This... is a lot of money we are talking here." I said thinking over the prospect.

"This is true, but, when you consider what you are getting out of it... You saw those people on the stage, commanding the elements to their will! That could be you! They have been taking Opulentia for only a few months and have already achieved so much." He said, sliding the box a little closer.

I sighed and investigated the box. It was well crafted, but decidedly plain. No fancy designs or marking in the mahogany. There were two little pills resting inside on top of a crimson red silk pillow.

The pills were translucent gel caps, containing a dark red liquid with a little bit of a black swirl. They almost seemed to pulse with life as we leaned closer to gaze upon them. It was almost like something was calling out to us, begging us to consume them. They were mesmerizing in a haunting way, as if there was something ancient and powerful about them.

"What if it doesn't work?" Star interrupted, "What if we take the pills and nothing happens? Are we just shit out of luck while you laugh and take off with our money?"

Bach shook his head.

"We have had no cases to date where the Opulentia did not perform. There have been no cases of allergic reactions, no strange side effects; all our testing has proven the pill to be one hundred percent effective and safe. Now, to further prove my point, I'd like each of you to raise your right index finger, point it straight up, like so…"

He raised his finger in front of him and waited for us to do the same. Star raised her finger, and I hesitated for a moment, but raised mine as well. I was a little confused, but curious.

"Now, I want you to focus on the tip of your finger. Clear your mind of anything else but the sound of my voice. Focus… think of your finger as a torch, a small unlit torch. Picture yourself in a dark room, void of all light, pure pitch-black darkness."

His voice was quiet and calm as he spoke. This was clearly a practiced speech.

"You need to be able to see to leave this room, and the only way to see is to light your torch. Focus on your fingertip, your torch, your salvation from this world of darkness. Envision your torch being lit, springing to life to let you escape from the blackness around you."

He paused, waiting for something to begin. I was staring intently at my fingertip, trying to picture what he was describing. I felt a strange warm sensation in the back of my head and my vision blurred slightly. I could hear his humming resonating inside my skull, and it seemed to echo like thunder in a valley.

I could feel sweat forming on my forehead as I concentrated. Then, suddenly and without warning there was a flash of light. Star and I gasped almost simultaneously. At the tips of our fingers a pinpoint of light appeared.

"Don't lose focus! You need more light to see in this pitch-black room! Envision your torch light blazing like the sun!" Bach called out.

We concentrated, and the tiny ball of light began to grow. I could see Star's finger out of the corner of my vision and perched atop the tip of it was an orb of yellow light, roughly the size of a ping pong ball. I gritted my teeth a little and focused harder on my own light. It flickered momentarily, and then it seemed to disappear.

I was beginning to sweat again as I stared at my fingertip. I could feel the warm sensation in my skull again, the strange humming returned. This time something felt different. I pictured my finger as a torch, and as I visualized it igniting, I felt warmth on the end of my finger.

Instead of a ball of light, my finger erupted with a blue flame. It swirled from the base of my knuckle all the way to the tip of my finger. It rushed upwards, forming a ball of blue fire about the size of a baseball. I could hear Star's surprise as she leaned back, the ball of light disappearing from her finger.

I held my hand a little further away from me and stared in amazement at the blue flames dancing at my fingertip. It was stunningly beautiful. Bach began to applaud.

"Well done ladies, well done. You especially Ms. Von Drake! I have never seen anything quite like that. Especially on a first attempt!" Bach said, his voice sounded genuinely impressed.

"But... I don't understand. We haven't taken any of the Opulentia" Star said as I shook myself out of the daze.

I was still trying to wrap my head around what had just happened.

"Yeah, she brings up a good point. What's going on here?" I said accusingly.

I waved my hand and the flame disappeared as abruptly as it manifested.

"Well, actually..." Bach said behind a sly grin. "I must admit, I have been deceptive. The pastries I provided earlier were injected with a small dose of the Opulentia fluid. It takes a little while to take effect, so I wanted to give you enough time for it to kick in before our conversation. I apologize for my deceit."

I glared at him as he spoke, trying to reconcile the information he gave.

"You drugged us without our knowledge, and then expect us to give you money?" I shouted, "For all we know you could have given us some kind of tranquilizer and locked us in a crazy dungeon! You are a fucking creep!"

I stood up and slammed my hands on the table. Star grabbed my arm softly, to try and calm me down. Bach leaned back in his chair.

"Please, I would never dream of such a thing. Yes, it was roguish of me to give you the drug without your knowledge but look at what it has done for you! You can't dispute results like that." he said smugly, shrugging.

Star held up her hand and stared at it for a moment, and the ball of light returned. She giggled innocently and waved it around a little. I watched her, and I had to admit I was thoroughly impressed. I had just, through sheer force of will, created fire out of thin air. All because of a strange little drug.

I looked down at the box with the pills again. To think those mysterious little capsules could open such a crazy new world.

"What do you think Star, should we trust him? He did just drug us without our consent." I asked.

I looked over at Star while she played with the ball of light in her palms.

"I've had worse things slipped in my food... besides this is so cool! I want to learn how to do more with it!" She said.

She laughed as she tossed the ball of light into the air and poked at it with her finger. The ball burst like a balloon, spewing tiny sparkles everywhere.

"Alright, say we agree. What's to stop you from just running off with our money? " I asked, trying desperately to ignore the first part of Star's answer.

"I told you Ms. Von Drake, this is a business. Paradigm needs customers to thrive. We will provide you with the Opulentia while you are here, and teach you how to use it, all while you have a pleasant vacation in our resort." He explained.

"At the end of the first week, if you have any doubts about my sincerity, you can walk away without paying a dime. We will cut our losses and seek out another wealthy individual to offer our services. You remain quiet about what you've seen here, like you agreed in the contracts, and you'll never hear from us again."

He smiled at me, his teeth almost glinting in the light. He reached into his pocket and pulled out an electronic keycard, sliding it across the table towards me.

"Here, take the elevator to the top floor. Look at the room we have prepared for you. See what luxury we guarantee for your stay and take some time to think the offer over. When you've decided, meet me back here in the lobby. I'll wait patiently for you to decide." He said.

He gestured to the elevator doors beside the reception desk. I picked up the card and thought about it for a moment. The offer was incredibly tempting, but was I ready to spend that much money on some crazy drug? I looked at Star who seemed very much ready to explore.

She bounced excitedly as I sighed and stood up.

"Okay, we'll look around, and I guess I'll think about it. You'd better not try any more tricks though. I don't take kindly to being deceived." I said lightly patting the gun on my hip.

Bach just smiled.

"A thousand apologies, and a thousand more. I shall not deceive you again. Enjoy the view." He replied.

Star grabbed my hand and dragged me towards the elevator, clearly eager to see the suite. The receptionist smiled and waved as we passed her desk to enter the elevator. We entered, and Star was quick to press the button for the top floor. I looked at all the numbers on the panel; it seemed the top was the twenty-sixth floor. I didn't remember seeing the building go up that high from the outside, but sure enough the elevator climbed for quite some time, playing its quiet but cheesy elevator music.

Star clenched my hand tightly as the elevator rose. She was so excited she could barely contain herself. I had to admire her free-spirited attitude. I was still mad about Bach slipping us a dose of the Opulentia without telling us, but she seemed to be completely unfazed by the whole ordeal.

The machine finally came to a halt, giving me that slight uneasiness in my stomach that elevators do when they stop too quickly, and the inertia rolls through you. The doors slid open, and we walked down the hallway towards a very large and ornate wooden door. The hallway was decorated with massive paintings that appeared to be very old. They depicted scenes of people dancing in the courtyard of a great medieval castle, reveling and carrying on at some wild party.

As we neared the door, the scenes got a bit more risqué. They digress to depicting the party goers enjoying more than just the company of those around them. One man appeared to be really enjoying the King's daughter. I appreciate fine art.

We stopped in front of the door which stood a good twelve feet or more in height. It was delicately carved with the shapes of all kinds of animals. They all seemed to be migrating towards the center of the door where the image looked a bit strange.

There was a large lake in the center, and some of the animals were crawling into the water. In the middle of the lake, it was like the water was falling into a deep pit, and in the very center of this void a small orb appeared to be hovering in midair. I stared at it for a moment, trying to figure out what it was, and Star poked at me impatiently.

"Come on, come on! Open the door already, pookie! I wanna see what's inside" she said.

She was eagerly pointing at the card reader on the door handle. I rolled my eyes and smiled. This girl.

"Okay, okay... keep your panties on, at least until we're in the room." I said, playfully pinching her butt.

I swiped the card on the reader and turned the handle. Despite the size of the door, it swung open easily. My jaw dropped as I considered the suite. It was all one large room, and it was massive.

The ceiling and walls were glass, and I realized we were looking out from the other side of the mountain behind the main building. One of the walls was clearly the rock from the mountain itself. There was a little waterfall tricking down into a basin forming a small lake by the wall's edge. In it were koi fish, swimming around the roots of some beautiful plants emerging from the water's surface.

Outside there was a massive waterfall careening down the side of the mountain to a river far below us in the forest. The mist floated in the breeze past the great window that made up the wall of our room. The furniture looked like it was straight out of a Victorian era castle, lots of deep crimson fabric over dark, hand carved wood. It was all so beautiful I couldn't help but gawk at it all from the doorway.

Star bounded into the room and pressed up against the glass to look out over the valley. Some eagles flew past us screeching before descending towards the trees. I was awestricken by the view, mother nature's raw beauty seemed to stretch out for miles before us. I had no idea a place like this even existed. I looked around to the other side of the room where the bed was. I was bigger than any bed I had ever seen, easily twice the size of a king bed. I had to wonder where they found sheets to fit the damn thing.

I walked over to it and caressed the large wooden posts, they had designs carved into them as well. They were just as beautifully crafted as the rest of the furniture. I flopped down on the bed and felt like I had tripped and fallen into a cloud. It was so soft and comfortable, way better than the bed we had back at our house.

Star joined me after a few minutes of poking around the room, and we just laid there in silence enjoying each other's company. It was nice to relax, it allowed me some time to think. I played with her hair a little, idly twirling it around my finger. I thought about what I had seen and done downstairs.

I could hardly believe that I had made fire appear out of thin air. This Opulentia was amazing stuff, too good to be true, yet it seemed to be. I couldn't wrap my head around what they must have been studying to uncover such a thing. I figured it might be best if I didn't know for sure.

Star had dozed off while I was lost in thought, reliving the day in my head. I smiled, watching her sleep. She was always so peaceful and at ease with the situations in which she found herself. I admired that about her.

After a long while, I made up my mind. I wanted to see what more I could do with this Opulentia. I wanted to see how far I could push the limits of my humanity. I also wanted to learn more about this mysterious Paradigm Corporation and why they felt the need to hide this breakthrough from the rest of the world.

I looked out the great window at the darkening sky. We had spent a long time here and the sun was setting. I could already see a few of the brighter stars poking into the clear sky above. My eyes began to droop, and I let myself slip away to sleep.

Bach could wait until morning for our answer. I smiled as I pictured him waiting in the lobby all night for us to come down. It would serve him right. Creep.

CHAPTER 8

The next morning, we awoke to the sound of someone knocking on the giant wooden door. I slowly opened my eyes expecting to be assaulted by the sun's murder beams, but to my surprise the light was not very offensive. I peered to the windows and realized they had automatically tinted themselves to reduce the light coming through them.

"Holy shit... I need some of those."

I rubbed the sleep from my eyes as I moved towards the door. The knocking continued.

"Calm your tits, I'm coming...." I muttered, making my way across the room.

The decorative rugs between the door and the bed felt so soft on my bare feet. I opened the door slightly and poked my head through. A young woman in a maid's uniform stood outside the door smiling brightly.

"Good morning! Mr. Bach has requested you join him for breakfast in the dining hall on the second floor. I have brought clean robes for you to change into, and fresh coffee to enjoy on your ride down. Do you need anything else?" she said politely motioning to her cart.

"Oh, no that will be all. Thank you!" I said and pulled the door open to let the cart in.

The maid bowed her head and headed back down the hallway and slipped into one of the elevators. I could smell the coffee from the jug on the cart and I was already beginning to salivate. The robes on the cart looked giant and fluffy, I was pleased to see they were as I picked one of them up. The fabric was so soft I thought it would melt in my hands. I quickly stripped down to just my panties and slipped into the robe. It felt amazing against my skin.

Star poked her head up from the bed as the smell of the coffee reached her. I tossed the other robe at her.

"Our presence has been requested at breakfast, milady. These robes feel like they were woven from the hair of angels!" I said as I poured a cup of coffee.

Star wriggled out of her clothing and slid into her robe, snuggling it to her chest and then joined me at the cart for coffee. I poured her a cup and we headed towards the elevator. We sipped at the coffee as we descended. It was just the right temperature for a morning cup of coffee. Warm enough to feel it going it down, but not hot enough to boil your tongue out of your head.

We arrived on the second floor and strolled towards the open door to the dining room. The smell of the food hit us a few steps into the hallway, and it smelled like heaven on earth. As we stepped over the threshold into the dining room, I could see why. In the middle of the room there was a large banquet table, packed full off all kinds of food.

There were bouquets of fruit and cheese flanking either end while the middle was filled with stacks of various pastries, pancakes, waffles, and more. There were piles of eggs, some scrambled, others boiled and peeled. There was a whole tub of bacon arranged by level of wellness, chewy on the left, burnt on the right. There were sausages and gravies, jellies and jams, it was incredible! I didn't know where to start.

I grabbed a plate and started piling on various foods. Some of the exotic cheeses and fruits I didn't even recognize. Whatever they were, I was hell-bent on eating them. They looked so good, how could I not?

Star piled up an equally impressive plate of food. She stuffed a large strip of bacon into her mouth as we looked around the room for Bach. He was sitting at a table on the other side of the buffet, and we moved over to join him. He was browsing the news on a tablet as we approached and didn't seem to notice us at all.

We sat down and began working on our mounds of food. Everything was delicious and cooked to perfection. I had eaten at some of the nicest restaurants in the world, and this was still possibly the best breakfast I had ever had the pleasure of devouring. I knew I probably had bits of egg and fruit on my face, I had no regrets either.

Star made plenty of pleasant cooing noises as she tried the various foods her plate had collected as well. She even had a second plate consisting only of bacon. Bach finally looked up from his tablet to greet us.

"Quite the healthy appetite you ladies have, I must say I'm impressed." He spoke.

I had finished my first plate and was eyeballing more of the cheese and fruit.

"I trust you slept well? That room is one of my favorites. The waterfall is just delightful." He continued, "Have you given any further thought to my offer?"

He put away his tablet and sipping at some tea.

"We have. I thought about it a lot, actually. I have to say I'm a little nervous, everything that's happened so far is hard to believe even after seeing it for myself, but I am curious. Ten million dollars is still a lot of money, if we aren't impressed after the first week we can walk away?" I asked, snatching a piece of Star's bacon.

"No questions asked." Bach assured, "I have the utmost confidence you will be pleased with the experience. I can send someone to keep an eye on your house while you are away if you'd like."

He picked up his tablet again. Star chimed in before I could respond.

"Make sure they feed Echo, I don't need our fur-baby starving before we get back." She spouted between bites.

"Not a problem. Here, type up a list of any personal effects that you have need of, and I'll have them retrieved. Or new ones purchased, on the house. Don't worry about clothing, there is a rather large wardrobe on floor seven for you to peruse. We rotate the selection by the season, so I'm sure you can find something to your liking."

He handed us the tablet and went back to his tea. We chatted with each other over what we might want on an impromptu vacation while we snacked on our food. After some debate we managed to type of a list of basics and handed the tablet back to Bach. He sent the list to one of his people and then put the tablet away again.

"Alright ladies, I'm sure you are eager to get started, so once you finish your meals head back to your room and get changed. There will be training outfits waiting for you. When you are ready head to the fifth floor in the western wing. The facility is divided between two towers, with the majority being in the mountain on the west side. There is a map in your room."

He finished his tea, standing up to leave.

"If you need anything at all, the intercom system beside the elevator and the door in your suite can be used to reach the receptionist at all times. Ladies, welcome to Paradigm." he said, bowing his head slightly to us before heading out of the dining room.

We ate more food and sipped on fresh coffee and tea before heading back up to our room. When we opened the door, there was a cart waiting for us just inside with the training outfits hanging on it as well as a selection of training bras in various sizes. The outfits themselves appeared to be simple karate uniforms but made of a rather fine silk-like material. The fabric felt nice against my skin.

We got changed and made goofy Kung-Fu poses and noises at each other. Star came at me, yelling 'hi-yah' and swinging her hand in a chopping motion. I caught it and spun her around pressing her back to my chest and clenching her nipple tightly with my other hand. She squealed, and I let her go, and we chuckled at each other before heading back to the elevator.

We rode the elevator down to the fifth floor, and I braced myself in preparation for the queasy feeling. It didn't help. The door opened, and we stepped out into a large room with wooden floors. I paused to take in the décor.

There were a few decorative pillars here and there, but for the most part the whole room was open and had a very Kung-Fu movie dojo feel to it. There were stands along parts of the wall adorned with samurai armor and various ancient weapons and paintings hung on the walls. All behind protective glass, I noticed. The floors were very polished, and various decorations were stunning to behold.

"I think we should do this with the basement" Star said breaking the silence.

"This is why I love you." I said, giving her a smile.

I pinched at her butt playfully and moved into the room to see if there was anyone waiting for us. As I moved further into the room, I noticed someone sitting on a pillow on a raised platform in the middle of the room. He appeared to be wearing some sort of decorative kimono emblazoned with a great dragon on the back. I felt my inner karate kid getting excited.

We made our way over to him, and without even turning to face us he spoke and told us to sit. There were two large pillows sitting on the floor in front of him. His head was bald save for a long grey braided ponytail that reached down to the pillow he sat on, and he had a long flowing matching grey beard hanging from his chin. He looked like that Chinese legend, Pai Mei.

His eyes were closed, and he seemed thoroughly relaxed and lost in his meditation. I couldn't help but feel like I'd walked into a movie, and I loved every second of it. It made me think of the training sequence from Kill Bill. I hoped we didn't have to punch a board until we broke our fists though.

We sat down on the pillows, crossing our legs and trying to match his position. I figured he wanted us to meditate with him, and I was so caught up in the atmosphere it seemed like the appropriate thing to do. He whispered something I couldn't understand, it sounded like some other language entirely, and I broke my concentration to look at him. My jaw dropped as I watched the man slowly rise into the air.

His mouth was moving as if uttering ancient words of power, but no sound emerged. His body, never changing position from his meditative pose, lifted itself easily a foot off the pillow. Even his beard began to wave in the air, almost as if it were underwater. It was astounding to gaze upon. Here I sat, in this beautiful dojo, watching a man levitate, I was ready to explode with excitement.

Just then there was a bright flash, and I had to shield my eyes. The light faded quickly, and the man was standing before us, his hands touching palm to palm before himself. We clapped excitedly, and he took a bow.

"Welcome to my dojo. I am Master Khan, I will be your instructor. I will guide you through your journey to master the secrets of the Opulentia. Please, state your names." He said returning to his full posture.

"My name is Trianna Von Drake, Master Khan." I said, bowing my head.

"Star Morrison. Pleased to meet you." Star replied cheerfully.

Master Khan nodded to each of us in acknowledgement and then hopped back up onto his pillow with practiced ease, resuming his previous position.

"A pleasure to meet you both. You have much to learn, and I'm sure you are eager to begin. I must advise you that we have a long journey over these next two weeks, and even then, it is likely you will not command the Opulentia's power to the degree that you witnessed in the tour. You may be able to produce some flashy tricks, but it will take much practice to unleash your potential."

He reached down to the front of his platform and opened a small drawer, pulling out a small decorative box.

"These capsules contain a small dose of what we call Opulentia, which has the ability to unlock sleeping powers within us. Everyone reacts differently, and you may find that each of you can command different abilities that the other cannot." He explained.

"In our research we have found most of the powers are tied to various elemental forces. I have mastered the ability to manipulate air currents, and as such have found the ability to levitate my body, as you have just seen."

He opened the box revealing two capsules of the Opulentia and offered them to us as he spoke.

"You have already received a small dose, less than a quarter of what is contained in the capsules you are about to take. This first dose will take time to activate in your system. However, by the end of our first week's training the effects will be almost instantaneous and last much longer. Please swallow these now, and we will begin." He said retrieving two bottles of water from the drawer as well for us to drink.

Star and I took the capsules from the box and stared at them momentarily. Even after all I had seen, I found it hard to comprehend that this pill would give me magic powers. Star popped hers into her mouth with little hesitation and swallowed. I shrugged and followed suit. No point turning back now.

"Good. While we wait for the Opulentia to work its way through your system we will start with some exercises to prepare your body. Personally, I find that a little bit of yoga helps things begin to flow." He said.

He climbed down from his perch and moved towards a more open area. We followed him and spent most of the next hour twisting our bodies into various positions at his guidance. I had never done yoga before, so I found many of the positions rather difficult. Star on the other hand took to it with ease.

Her body seemed almost completely fluid as she poured herself into each position. Her focus was impressive, she never broke concentration on what she was doing. I couldn't help but watch her bend and flex her body into the exotic positions as I struggled to match them. She was just so beautiful in everything she did.

As time passed, I could feel something warm growing within me, spreading through my body. My head began to swim a little, and I had to plop down to steady myself. I closed my eyes tightly for a moment letting them readjust when I opened them again. I felt a little high.

Star sat down beside me and rubbed at her face; she was feeling something strange as well. I could only assume that it was the Opulentia taking effect. Master Khan slid out of the position he was in and stood before us.

"Ah, it would seem you are feeling the effects of the Opulentia. Do not worry, the dizziness is only on the first dose, it will pass momentarily."

He thrust a palm towards us, and a small breeze blew the hair from our faces and felt so refreshing.

"That is certainly a delightful trick." I said leaning my head back to let the breeze roll down my neck.

"Indeed, I find that air and the wind can do many astounding things. It can carry a feather, gentle and carefree. Then just as easily blow over a house or car, wreaking havoc as it sees fit. Understanding and finding a balance between grace and destruction allows me to commune with this great force of nature and, with the help of Opulentia, seek its aid for my desires. I respect the power it grants me, and in return I can perform many such feats."

He gestured with his hands as he spoke, and the wind grew stronger, lifting us slightly from the ground.

"Others do not see things in the same light. They seek to command their elements, bending the forces to their will, expecting to achieve greatness through force. I do not believe this is wise." He explained,

"I ask the air permission to perform what I wish, and out of respect it is granted to me. Others bark harsh commands, demanding their element act out their desires, and while they may perform under such harsh nature, I feel that there may be consequences to be had that are yet unseen." He said, a distant look in his eyes.

"How you control your power is entirely up to you of course. Whatever your end goal may be, it can be achieved through either method."

I nodded as he spoke. I felt the air currents lower us back to the ground as I thought about his words. He seemed to believe that it was not the pills that gave him the magic powers, but that they simply allowed him to connect with the natural world on a different level. I appreciated that point of view, it made the concept less alien to me. Perhaps he was right, who could really say?

Maybe magic has always existed in the world, but mankind was just unable to communicate with it. At least without the aid of this strange drug. It was something to think about. I snapped out of my train of thought when Star leapt to her feet beside me.

She smiled and then closed her eyes, concentrating as she raised her hands before her. She brought her palms together, pressing them tightly together and then took a deep breath. There was suddenly a presence in the air around us, and I could feel my body hair starting to stand on end. She began to slowly pull her hands apart and my eyes widened as I watched.

Arcs of lightning were forming between her hands. Energy crackled on the air and rolled across her hands and arms. Her hair stood up waving wildly with the electrical currents surging in and around her body. She looked as if she were holding one of those static balls.

She giggled slightly as she opened her eyes to see what she was doing. Energy surged behind her eyes, and small arcs even formed from her tear ducts to her cheek bones, giving her a very dangerous look. My jaw dropped as I watched her, stunned by what I was seeing. Everything seemed so much more real now that it was someone I knew and loved performing such incredible feats.

She lowered her arms to her sides and pointed her palms towards the ground. Electricity arced and rolled across her whole body and moved downward towards the floor. She focused the energy downwards, around her feet. A moment later, I realized what she was attempting.

She wobbled slightly trying to maintain her balance. The static force began gently lifting her from the ground. She hung there in the air for a moment, struggling to keep herself upright. Unable to maintain it, she let herself drop back to the floor and all the electricity disappeared.

Master Khan clapped slowly and nodded his approval.

"Nicely done, Star. It would seem you have attuned with the electrical energies of the world, very impressive. There are many avenues you can take with such power, as living things operate through a series of electrical synapses." Khan said.

"What about you Trianna? What element has chosen to listen to your call?" he asked, turning his curious gaze on me.

I held up my hand and stared at it for a moment. I didn't really have any clue how to summon my powers. We had done it before by picturing a torch in a dark room, but I hadn't really made any connection with the actions I was taking to summon the light.

I lowered my hand to my side and stood up, closing my eyes. I thought about what Khan has said about asking the elements for aid and decided that would be my best approach. I focused for a few moments, trying to figure out how to proceed. I visualized myself and tried to call out with my thoughts. I could still feel that strange warmth within me, so I decided to focus on that and tried to call it to the surface.

I clenched my fists at my side as I concentrated, and I could feel the warmth building. Suddenly, something clicked in my brain, like a piece of a puzzle sliding into place, and I opened my eyes. Somehow, I just knew what to do in that moment, like I had always known but had just forgotten. I took a deep breath and focused my mind.

Blue flames began to circle around me, starting near my feet and spiraling upwards around me, encasing me behind a shield of flames. Star and Khan both took a step back as the flames spun around me. I could feel the heat, but it felt calm and comforting, as if it wanted to protect me. I could feel the intensity of the flames growing as they swirled around me. I raised my arms and the vortex warped around me. Then, as the flames rose with my arms, I heard a faint click.

Seconds later the sprinklers in the dojo erupted, dousing the room with water and I lost my concentration. The flames disappeared, and Star shrieked as the cold water surprised her. I couldn't help but laugh as the water poured over us. Master Khan waived his hand, and a pocket of air appeared around us to keep the water away.

"An impressive display! I dare say we may need to perform tomorrow's training outside!"

Khan laughed as he motioned us towards the door. The door swung open, and we could hear the fire alarm sounding outside in the hallway. A few of the strange drones had arrived with fire extinguishers ready to address the situation.

"It's alright boys, just a training exercise. You can cut the system off." Khan said as we exited into the hallway.

The two nodded and one pulled out a tablet, poking at it intently. A moment later the alarm stopped, and the sprinklers shut off.

"Don't worry about a thing, ladies. We'll have the dojo cleaned up in no time. There have certainly been worse messes made in there." Khan explained.

"I believe that is enough for today however, you both have performed admirably for your first run. We will meet up tomorrow on the lawn to continue the training, today I want you both to relax and enjoy yourselves. I will send for you once I am ready to begin."

Master Khan patted our shoulders and turned down the hallway to leave. I watched him as he walked away, he was an interesting person. I looked forward to spending more time with him in the coming days. As he reached the end of the hallway, I noticed Bach step out to meet with him.

They exchanged words briefly and quietly, Khan motioned towards us, and Bach nodded. I watched curiously, trying to determine what they were discussing. Khan seemed to be describing what had occurred, animatedly moving his hands as he spoke. Bach simply nodded and poked at his phone as he listened.

Finally, he handed Khan an envelope and Khan tucked it into his robes and walked away. Bach raised the phone to his ear and strolled off as well. Something about that conversation seemed incredibly fishy. There was something about Bach that always left me feeling unnerved.

Star grabbed my arm and pulled me towards her, leaning up to kiss me excitedly.

"Pookie! That was incredible! I levitated, you turned into a fire-nado! Amazing!" She said, bouncing.

"Yeah, it was... I'm still kind of in shock. This is a lot to take in. You wanna grab a drink or something?" I asked, watching her bounce.

"Yeah, that sounds good, we should probably get out of these wet clothes first though, don't want to ruin the fun by catching a cold!" She replied.

I nodded, and she took off towards the elevator. I couldn't help but smile at her bubbly mood. We made our way back up to the room and changed into dry clothes. We decided to do a little exploring, so we examined the map left on our table.

The building had all sorts of things to occupy our time with. We decided to stop by the sixteenth floor and check out the Imax theater. We had a selection of movies to pick from and opted for a gory slasher flick. We grabbed a few beers at the concession booth, staffed by another set of the drones. The movie was decent, nothing extravagant, but the special effects looked amazing on such a massive screen.

After the movie we visited the seventh floor, which housed a giant wardrobe. We walked through row upon row of various clothing styles. We spent a few hours just trying on different outfits, just for the fun of it. It reminded me of playing dress-up as a kid. Though back then we didn't fill out the clothes as well, and the shoes were way too big. We picked out a few things we really liked and had the drones deliver them to the room.

I wasn't sure what the deal with these strange people was. Bach had called them drones, but then changed the subject. They seemed to be everywhere, apart from the varying hair colors and genders, it was almost impossible to tell them apart. I made a mental note to question Bach about them the next time I saw him.

We made our way to the dining hall again and got dinner and a few more drinks. Star figured out she could magnetize her cutlery and I roasted some vegetables right on my plate. We goofed off a bit and mostly just enjoyed ourselves for the rest of the evening. We walked around the garden beside the compound and watched the stars for a little while after dark.

The sky was so clear here without anything around to pollute the sky with lights. As we walked, I kept getting the feeling that someone was watching us. I brought it up with Star, but she pointed out the security cameras on the corners of the building and called me out for being paranoid. I was still a bit uncertain of everything going on here, but for the moment settled on the explanation she gave.

Eventually we made our way back to our room for some more private fun and drifted off to sleep in each other's arms. We were so far from our beach house but as I lay there holding Star while she snoozed peacefully, I couldn't help but feel right at home. Something about her just had that effect on me.

The rest of the week was much of the same routine. We would wake up in the morning, eat breakfast and wait for Master Khan to send for us. We would meet with him outside for our training, taking another dose of the Opulentia and warming up with a little yoga or a quick jog. I enjoyed the training sessions quite a bit.

He would tell us stories about what he thought the origins of the Opulentia were. He told tales of magic power dating back centuries. He believed there were certain words of power that could amplify the user's abilities beyond comprehension. He claimed he had not yet discovered any but spent most of his free time researching them.

He also taught us different approaches to using our new abilities. We learned to use them both offensively and defensively. We learned to form balls of energy or fire and fling them at targets, but also how to shield ourselves with them. The range of what we could accomplish seemed limitless.

Star practiced levitating and after several days really got the hang of it. She managed to keep herself floating a solid foot off the ground a few times. She could go higher if she got close to a wall or tree that she could cling to with her electric tendrils but would slowly descend if she moved away from it. I found it hard to do much with my fire powers other than destroy things.

Khan told me that the blue flames were something he'd never seen before, usually anyone that manipulated fire had standard looking red-orange flames. He mentioned the flames I summoned seemed to be stronger and hotter as well. He suggested that I had a rather unique reaction to the drug, but nothing to be alarmed by.

I could throw some mean fireballs, but I found I could also shoot beams of fire that had a great deal of force behind them. I discovered that I could lift myself off the ground with them but had to be careful about it. Even if I tried it on the sidewalk, the flames spilling out from the point of contact would set the grass beside the path on fire. Khan had started bringing an extinguisher to our sessions.

By the end of the week, I figured out how to use the fire to boost myself off the ground without setting too much of anything on fire. I then learned I could use smaller bursts to guide my direction as I moved through the air. It wasn't flight by any means, but it was impressive. I felt a bit like the human torch, but with fewer one-liners.

Star was using her levitation skills to float just above the ground and move incredibly fast like a magnetic powered train. Occasionally she would leap high into the air and hang there for a few moments, tendrils of electricity reaching for anything to hold to keep her afloat. I like watching her in the air, like an electrical butterfly. I was as mesmerized by her as always.

The days were long but eventful and we were having a blast training with Master Khan. He wasn't just teaching us ways to control the magic, he also taught us yoga and basic martial arts. Somedays we met back in the dojo and spent hours practicing stances and movements that Khan explained would open our inner chakras and allow us to commune with our abilities much easier. Star preferred to use the positions to flirt with me, pointing parts of her body at me as we stretched to tease me.

Once we had fully stretched our muscles and aligned our chakras or whatever, I never bought into that crystal healing crap, we would move on to sparring with

Khan. He was an expert at martial arts and made quick work of us being the novices we were. He guided our strikes with small bursts of air to try to get our muscles to memorize the optimal path for a palm strike or kick to connect.

I had been in a fair share of brawls when I was younger, I knew how to throw a punch, but Khan showed me that brute force could easily be redirected and turned against the user. He asked me to try and punch him in the face as hard as I could. I complied, and before I realized it, he had me by the wrist flipping me over his shoulder on the mats.

"Power" he said, "need not to come by force, but rather precision."

We would be catered meals on training days, lavish amounts of food brought to us by the drones designed specifically to replenish our energy to continue training. In the evenings we would sit by the water fall and meditate, or rather Khan meditated, I took a light nap. From there Star and I would venture back through the hotel for dinner and usually a movie, so we could make out in the cool dark theater.

Saturday came along, and when we were getting ready to go meet Master Khan something felt strange. I couldn't quite place the feeling but from the moment I awoke I just felt like something about the day was off. We got dressed and made our way to the lobby, where we ran into Bach.

"Ah, good morning ladies! Hope you slept well, how has your first week been?" He asked through his best salesman smile.

"It's been a blast!" Star answered cheerfully, "I never would have thought that I could do anything like what we've been doing this week. Truly amazing stuff you've come up with!"

"Great to hear it. Well, we are nearing the end of the first week, it is time to make your decision. Would you like to continue the training for the agreed amount, or do you wish to walk away?" he asked, turning to face me.

I stared into his eyes for a moment while I thought about it. So far, we had been treated like queens, just as he had promised. We were given magical powers and trained to use them, just as he had promised. It was still such a tough decision, ten million was a large sum of money, even with the lottery winnings.

Sure, we would still have plenty left over. My investments and business would refill it after a few years, but it was still such a large sum to just drop on something at once. Even if it was literally the ability to use magic.

I looked over at Star for reassurance. She was biting at her lower lip with anticipation, clearly eager to hear what my response would be. I could tell her answer would be yes, but she didn't want to pressure me into anything. I looked at my palm and summoned a small flame that danced around for a moment before I extinguished it. I nodded and looked back to Bach.

"We'll do it. I want another set of Opulentia though, for each of us." I said.

I gave him a strong look to let him know I was serious about haggling. He met my gaze with a practiced smile.

"Normally I would say no, but I think for a pair of lovely ladies like yourself, I can make an exception." He replied.

He reached into his coat and produced a tablet and business card. Something about his willingness to comply felt strange. I figured he would at least try to barter with me for more money. I worried he was up to something.

"Here you go, if you would just contact your bank to have the funds wired to the account listed on the card, we will extend your stay and I will grab another set of Opulentia for you and have it delivered to your room." He said handing me the tablet.

I sat down and pulled up my account and initiated the transfer to the account number he provided me. The website stated it would take a few hours to process through and I relayed that to information to him.

"Wonderful, I'll let you get on with your day's training then, I'll monitor the transfer and let you know once it has completed." He said.

He bowed to us politely as he took the tablet back, tucking it away in his jacket. I furrowed my brow, trying to figure out what he might be up to. The whole exchange felt weird. We left him to his business and made our way outside to meet Master Khan for our training.

As we made our way to the field that we practiced in, I felt that strange feeling again. It felt like something sinking inside me, like when you hit that first drop on a rollercoaster and it feels like your stomach is about to jump ship. I couldn't quite shake it, even as I looked around for something that might be causing it. Was it just a weird side effect of the Opulentia? Maybe it was like when smoking too much weed makes you paranoid.

Master Khan was floating in the field, waiting for us to arrive. He looked as calm and centered as always as he meditated in midair. He opened his eyes and pushed a small box towards us as we reached him. We opened it and found our days dose of the Opulentia. I looked at them for a moment, it seemed like there was something different about these, but I couldn't quite place it.

We popped them into our mouths as usual, but as soon as it hit my tongue, I knew something was wrong. The capsule immediately burst, filling my mouth with a foul metallic taste. It reminded me of blood, but there were other flavors mixed with it. I could feel something foaming in the liquid as well and before I realized it my vision was blurring dramatically. I was beginning to stagger, my legs felt weak and rubbery. I couldn't make out my surroundings, the edges of my vision were starting to fade to black. I felt both hot and cold at the same time, and a cool sweat forming on my brow.

I tried to call out but was muffled by the foaming liquid and struggled to keep from choking on it. I reached out for help with my hands, but something fell on me and knocked me to the ground. I grabbed onto it, finding that it was Star's body. She too must have been experiencing the reaction, and probably blacked out.

Her body convulsed, but there was nothing I could do to help her. My vision was all but gone by then, and my swimming head fell backwards onto the grass. I clenched tightly to Star's shirt as I slipped out of consciousness, but still I felt so alone and afraid.

CHAPTER 9

My head was swimming, and I felt like I was having the worst hangover ever. My body ached, and I could only just barely force my eyes open. There were bright lights positioned above me that seared at my eyes when they did finally open. I tried to move my head, but it was

strapped down, I found the same was true for my arms
and legs.

I tried to scream but I couldn't get the sound out. I
felt something stab into my arm, but the pain was distant.
I could hear sounds of beeping and machine fans spinning.
There were a few muffled voices as shadows moved across
the large bright lights.

It was like a science fiction movie, where they
perform an autopsy. I was crying quietly at this point; I
could feel the warm tears rolling down my cheeks. I had no
idea what was going on, I barely knew who I was. I was so
scared, terrified by what was happening.

I could feel cold metal objects poking at the top of
my head and various other parts of my body. I couldn't
even remember how I got here. I tried thinking back but
my mind was so scattered with fear I couldn't piece
anything together. I tried to scream again and something
plastic clamped over my mouth and nose. I faded out
again after a few seconds.

I opened my eyes sometime later. I was lying on a
bed in a dimly lit room. My captors had stripped me of my
clothing, and I was wearing one of those flimsy hospital

gowns. My hands were chained to the bed with thick rusty shackles, and there was an IV in my arm.

I felt weak and alone, with good reason. The bed felt dirty, as if many other people had been chained to it, and it had never been cleaned. I could hear what sounded like heavy breathing from the corner of the room behind me, but I couldn't get turned around well enough to see who was there. I tried to call out, but my throat burned like someone has poured gasoline down it. I cried softly to myself.

I could hear a faint slapping sound along with the breathing, both sounds quickening. I couldn't tell what it was, but it sounded moist, and my eyes widened when the realization hit me. There was a grunt followed by a splat on the floor, and then a zipper. I was shaking with anger and fear as a man stepped out from behind me, adjusting his grungy looking guard uniform shirt back into his pants as he walked towards the door.

I was disgusted, as if it wasn't bad enough to be kidnapped and chained to some grungy bed, now there's some pervert jerking off over my helpless body. I tried to hide my face behind my arm as I cried and tried to slip my hand through the shackles. It was no use; they were too tight. I screamed softly despite the pain in my throat and thrashed around on the bed in frustration.

I was too weak to accomplish much, but it eased some of my anger. I lay still after a few moments, catching my breath and trying to ease the swirling sensation in my head. What the hell was going on? I struggled to remember what had happened to me.

Hours passed, though they felt like days as I slipped in and out of consciousness. I thought about Star and prayed that she was not met with the same fate. Or worse. I could see her loving face in my mind, and it was the only thing I could cling to for comfort in this hell I found myself in.

I thought about the smell of her hair and the feel of her skin and smiled despite myself. I would find a way out of here and find my Star. Whoever was responsible for this would pay dearly when I got out, if I got out that is. I heard a noise and opened my eyes to see the door opening again.

A nurse walked in, her face was covered, but she looked incredibly familiar. Her skin was pale, and her hair was stark red poking out from under the little nurse's cap she wore. There was a tattoo running down the side of her head and neck, and I realized why I recognized her. She was one of Bach's drones, or whatever they were, the strange staff of Paradigm that had escorted me to this place.

My face twisted into rage as she drew near to the bed. I thrashed and tried to break free of my bonds to get to her, but before I could get any momentum up, she rushed at me. She pinned me to the bed with her knees pressed into my stomach. She gave me a stern look from behind her facemask and gestured with her finger over her mouth for me to hush.

She replaced my IV and then turned my head to look at the side of it. The skin on my neck and head burned slightly. She nodded and then got up to leave. I spit at her, the only action I felt I could take to show my anger and disgust.

Tears were streaming from my eyes again as I tried to scream at her. She paused at the door and looked back at me, and something in her eyes seemed almost sad. I stared at her, still fuming, and she looked into my eyes. There was a deep sadness behind her eyes that seemed to look deep inside me.

She knew something about what was happening to me, and she did not seem to approve. She raised a hand and gently touched the tattoo on the side of her head and then looked away from me as she left the room. I shook with terror and fury as I lay back in the bed. I felt so defeated, so alone.

I'm not sure how long I was in that room, alone and scared. There were no windows, and my concept of time was horribly distorted. Periodically the nurse would return and change my IV and check the sides of my head. Occasionally she would clean them with a rag that smelled of alcohol, and I would see small amounts of blood on the rag as she pulled it away. I had gone mostly numb to the pain, feeling so helpless about my situation that I had started to question my own will to go on.

Guards would sometimes poke their head into the room to see if I was still alive, and I winced each time, dreading that it would be the one from before. More time passed, and I spent my time either sleeping or trying to work my wrists out of the shackles. They were beginning to rub themselves raw, but I ignored the pain, my drive to escape overpowering it. I was trying to plot an escape, but it was difficult without knowing what exactly was beyond the door to this horrid cell.

I relaxed after a few hours of failed attempts to get free of the shackles and drifted off into a dreamless sleep. The rest was short lived though. I hadn't even heard the door open this time. Before I could realize what was going on, he was on top of me.

I tried to scream but he clamped my mouth shut with one strong, smelly hand. He ripped off the nightgown with his other hand and moved himself between my legs. I kicked at him, but it was of little use. I was too weak from being trapped down here; I could barely lift my knees.

He began to rub at his groin, preparing himself for what he had in mind. Terror washed over me as I tried fruitlessly to free myself of my bondage. If I didn't think of something fast, this creep was going to rape me. How had I gotten myself into such a mess?

I had debated for so long on whether to accept the offer or not. On grounds that something exactly like this might happen. Panic set in, as I thought about Star and if this was happening to her as well. No more.

Suddenly, I felt a deep calm within myself. I couldn't feel his pudgy body between my legs anymore.

The pain washed away from my face, and I felt a comforting warmth building at the back of my skull. The sensation spread around the sides of my head and down my neck and something stirred within my muscles.

I clenched my fists and there was a flash of light as the shackles burst open, freeing me. I clamped my hands on either side of the guard's head, much to his surprise. I muttered strange words, in some language that I did not comprehend. My body seemed to be acting on its own and my hands began to glow with a faint blue light.

I could smell something burning as small flames began to swirl around my arms. The guard cried out in agonizing pain, as his head filled with flames. I could see the fire burning behind his eyes, and light glowed from within his nostrils and screaming mouth. I pressed harder on his head and tilted his agonized face towards the ceiling.

Seconds later, a fountain of blue fire spewed from every opening in his skull as his screams of pain ended abruptly. Most of his hair singed off. The flesh around his eyes and mouth blackened and peeled away from his skull. The smell reminded me of frying bacon.

I let go and the body collapsed to the floor beside the bed, the smell of charred flesh rushing into my nostrils. I vomited as I broke myself from the shock of witnessing what I had just done. I stared at my hands and arms expecting them to be charred as well, but they were unharmed. My skin was paler than usual. I was unsure if it was from being trapped in the room without real food, or some side effect from whatever strange things were happening to me.

I stood up, trembling slightly and stepped over the mess I had made of the man that had tried to violate me. I didn't feel sorry for him, but I couldn't believe that I had killed him in such an insane manner. I pinched myself, thinking maybe this was all just a horrible dream that I could wake up from, but to no avail. I decided it was best to move on and try to escape. I could sort this business with the fire out later.

I moved towards the door and poked my head out to see if there was anyone waiting. The hall was dimly lit and just as dirty as the room I was in previously. I stepped out into the hallway and tried to look for some sign of where I was or where I should go. There was absolutely no indication of where I was being held, so I began walking down the hallway.

There were no other doors that I could see, and the hallway seemed to snake around to nowhere in particular. I followed it for a while, checking behind me constantly to ensure nothing was sneaking up on me. So far, I had been completely alone, when suddenly I heard footsteps. Heavy boots on the cold cement floor beneath my feet from around the next corner. I hunkered down against the wall and peered carefully around the corner.

There was a guard sitting in a chair leaning back against the wall beside a large metal door, another sitting at a table a few feet away playing cards, and a third pacing back and forth fiddling with his phone.

"There's never any fucking signal down here. It's bullshit. Why do they even need four of us on guard for some tiny little bitch anyway? Not like she's going to do anything strapped to that bed."

"Boss says we guard, we guard. If you're that bored, why don't you go help Cage keep her entertained?"

"Hah, I might, though I don't know if I want that fat fuck's sloppy seconds. Plus, she's been down here so long she's probably pissed herself. I bet it smells terrible."

"Yeah, but with a body like that, I bet it would still be worth it. She's got tits like a porn star, and I heard she's a dyke so it's probably nice and tight too. I'm probably gonna head in there on my next patrol and show her a good time. She deserves it after having Cage's flabby ass flopping around on her. I bet he came before he even got it in her, the fucking chud."

"Haha! Right? Ugly fucker probably hasn't ever gotten laid; he probably squirted all over the floor again just looking at her."

I growled under my breath, anger swelling up inside me as they spoke. They were just animals, nothing but disgusting pigs. The whole lot of them just living piles of trash. The strange calm sensation washed over me again, and I rose to my feet and stepped around the corner.

"What the fuck!? Well, well, how did you get out? Got tired of Cage's tiny cock already? Decide to come and party with a real man, eh? Why don't you slide that pretty little ass over here then? Let daddy show you how it's done."

He grabbed at his crotch as he spoke and gestured for me to come over to him.

I smirked briefly as the warm sensation crawled across my skull again, and the strange words flowed silently from my lips. The three men approached me, hungry looks in their eyes, but I felt no fear. I glared at them, and they seemed to pause for just a moment, as if even they realized something was off. They lunged at me, and I closed my eyes and stood very still.

I heard my voice, and felt my lips move, but I wasn't in control. Something inside me was taking over. There was a flash of light and when I opened my eyes the three men lay on the ground around me. Smoke slowly rose from their skulls and charred bodies.

I collapsed to my knees as the calm feeling rushed away from me. I was shaking, and I felt dizzy. Whatever this strange power was, it took a lot out of me when it happened. I stared at my hands, they tremored like the rest of me, as I thought about what I had become.

Something changed in me while I was trapped in this place. I'd become something else, some kind of monster. I had now killed four men and didn't hesitate even for a moment. They deserved it, they were real monsters. I took a deep breath and told myself I had done what was necessary.

I told myself that I could deal with this later, I needed to find Star. She might also be trapped in a room, strapped to a dirty bed. Maybe getting raped by these disgusting guardsmen. I couldn't let that happen to her, I had to save her.

I rose to my feet, still trembling slightly, and moved towards the door. I opened it slowly, peeking in to see what lay on the other side. There was a set of lockers at the base of a staircase leading up to another floor. Had they taken me underground?

I shivered more from cold than anything. I had forgotten that I was walking around naked. The fire could only keep me warm when it surrounded me. I decided to check the lockers for some clothing.

I searched and found a duffle bag in one of the lockers that had my training clothes in it. I slipped into the uniform and shoes and stood up. I felt a bit more secure with my clothes on, less vulnerable at least. There was a mirror on the inside of one of the locker doors and I caught a glimpse of my reflection.

I turned my head and realized they had shaved the sides of it, and now I had strange tattoo designs running down either side of my head and onto my neck. The pattern appeared to stretch down my back as well. I decided I would have to examine them later. I needed to get a move on to find Star.

I raced up the stairs, as best I could. I still felt a little weak, I wasn't sure if it was from the powers, or being chained to the bed for who knows how long. I peered upwards, and the stairs seemed to stretch on forever. I hoped that I didn't have to climb them all, but I would if that was what it took to find her.

"Hold on baby, I'm going to get us out of here." I muttered as I picked up my pace.

A few flights up and I came to a platform with another door. There was a sign that read 'Restricted Access' and that seemed like a good place to check first. I moved over to the door and looked through the window. No guards, just an empty hallway leading to another set of doors.

I turned the handle, and to my surprise it wasn't locked. I made my way across the hallway as quickly as possible, sticking to the wall in case someone came through the doorway. There was no window on this door, so I paused for a few moments to prepare myself. I had no way of knowing what I might encounter on the other side of the door, but I had to try to find Star. Once I got her to safety, I planned to burn the whole damned place to the ground.

I took a deep breath and slowly pushed open the door just enough to slip through. I found myself inside some sort of observation room. There were some monitors on the desks displaying various information and charts that all seemed to be updating in real time. They looked medical in nature, monitoring heart rate and the like.

There was a window wrapped around the wall behind the monitors that looked out into a large room. In that room sat a large vat of what looked like Opulentia. It was hooked up to a weird machine with a plethora of tubes and cables. I could hear the machines beeping as they displayed information on screens across the laboratory.

There were a few scientists walking around the large room fiddling with computers and writing things on their tablets. I pressed my face up against the glass to get a better look as one of the large machines started moving. It was some sort of crane, and my heart started racing as I realized what was happening. There was a body hanging by straps on the end of the crane, Star's body.

She was naked, and there were various wires and tubes sticking out of her. The sides of her head had been shaved and tattooed. She looked like one of the strange women from before, the drones. Is that what they wanted from us?

I screamed her name despite myself and slammed my hand against the glass. It was very thick however, and the sound did not reach her. I watched in horror as they lowered her into the vat of red fluid. Her body began to convulse, and the scientists began tapping madly at their computers, the sick bastards had the audacity to smile while they watched her.

I could feel my rage boiling inside me, and I rushed over to the door. It was locked and wouldn't budge. I punched it crying out with anger, and I could feel the temperature in the room rising. A warm sensation ran down the sides of my head, small at first but it built into a searing heat.

I raised my arms towards the window, and I could hear that now familiar sound in my mind. It spoke words of an ancient language I couldn't begin to understand. It felt as if something was compelling me to act. Something very old and powerful.

The strange blue flames began to circle around my feet, forming into an orb that spiraled upwards around me. It picked up speed as it reached my shoulders and whipped around my arms lunging at the windows. The glass boiled away as the orb passed through melting a massive hole. The orb itself blasted into the row of computers and scientists; their screams were brief.

I leapt through the hole and rushed to the tank; I could see Star still writhing within the Opulentia. I held up a palm to the glass and a wave of heat radiated from it, causing the cement base of the tanks to crack. The fluid came rushing out like a tidal wave. I felt it rush over my legs, chills running up my spine. I was paralyzed as I fell to the floor with the thick red liquid rushing over me.

My eyes rolled back in my head as my vision faded. I felt my muscles rapidly tightening and releasing. I was having a seizure of sorts and silently hoped that I wouldn't drown in this hellish place. I could hear alarms pounding, but they sounded distant, the sound began to fade into music.

I suddenly felt very serene, a great calm washing over me. It did not feel like I was convulsing on the floor of the lab. I was instead being whisked away to somewhere magical. A pleasant smell hit my olfactory senses, spicy but almost sweet.

I opened my eyes and found my sitting in a field in a circle of trees. The air smelled like fresh cinnamon, it reminded me of those scented brooms you find around the holidays. I took a deep breath, the calming scent washed over me relaxing my mind and body. This place was wonderful.

I heard a rustling in the trees, as if something was moving through them. I looked up as a figure emerged across from me into the clearing. It was tall and dressed in black robes. The hood of the robe hanging over its face obscured my vision of the face inside.

As it moved calmly towards me, I felt unafraid, at peace. The figure stopped a few yards from me, staring at me from the blackness within the large hood. I gazed into the darkness; it was like staring into the abyss of space. That cold black hole seemed infinite, barely contained by the cloth hood.

After a moment, there was a faint blue light, dim at first but growing. I could feel heat on the air as the light quickly grew brighter. A wave of heat burst from the figure as the robe rippled like a flag in the wind. The blue light burst upwards, burning away the hood as blue flame rocketed into the sky above me.

It swirled with the force of a tornado, the trees bending backwards with the force. I could smell the leaves starting to burn. I rose to my feet, something compelling me to embrace the power building above me. I could hear those strange ancient words again as the fiery vortex in the sky twirled downwards and engulfed me.

I lifted off the ground, held aloft by the dancing flames. I felt something stirring within me, like the fire was awakening a power deep within me. It was a comforting power, radiating from my very core. I embraced it, welcoming it to the surface.

The fire encroached upon me, slowly embracing me with its warmth. I gently returned to the ground as the flames absorbed into my skin. There was no pain, no searing flesh, only the deep serenity as I took the power into me. I felt whole, complete, as if I was missing this power my entire life.

I clenched my fists, reveling in this new feeling. I looked up to the figure, wanting to thank them for this power. When I gazed upon them this time, they felt cold, even evil. Something wasn't right anymore. I heard maniacal laughter echoing through my head.

I awoke on the cold laboratory floor beside the now empty tank of Opulentia. I felt that warmth and calm from my dream still lingering within me. I knew that power was a part of me now. I could still faintly hear that laughter as well.

My vision was blurry, the bright lights from the ceiling blasting out my vision. I struggled to keep my eyes open as a shadowed figure loomed over me. They kneeled beside me, gently caressing my cheek.

"Star...? Is that... you?" I stammered, trying to regain composure.

"Oh, not quite, love. She's with me now, and soon you will be too." A voice whispered.

I could hear his sly grin in his words as he spoke. Even without being able to focus my vision on his face I knew it was Bach. His impression would forever burn in my mind. Rage quickly bubbled up inside me.

I balled up a fist to strike him, but before I could move hands wrapped around my throat. The hands lifted me from the ground, as I struggled to breathe. I tried to kick my legs to break the hold, but something held me in place. I worked my eyelids to try and clear my vision.

When I opened my eyes, I realized it wasn't even Bach holding my throat. Bach stood beside me, smiling his devilish salesman grin. The hand that held me belonged to Master Khan. He too smiled at me, and I could feel a slight breeze on the air. He was manipulating the wind to lift me rather than brute strength.

I looked around for Star, but there was no trace of her anywhere. I struggled against the force Khan was using to lift me and managed to gasp out a few words.

"Where.... where the fuck.... is she?!" I sputtered.

"Safe." Bach replied as he turned to walk away.

"She has been taken to the medical facility to recover. She has exceeded our expectations, and further research is required. We intended to make you both drones, but it seems that will not suffice. You both show great potential, but only time will tell."

"You fucking creep! I'll kill you for this!" I shouted. Bach simply laughed and continued to walk away.

"You too, will join us. Though you may need some rigorous personality training. So hostile."

He pushed open the door, turning to blast me with a smile once more.

"She's in good hands Trianna, my hands."

He laughed and took his leave. I stared at Khan, my anger boiling wildly inside me. He simply grinned as he waited for Bach to leave the room.

"He hasn't been completely honest with you, but that's a salesman for you." He said as he released his grip, holding me aloft with just wind rushing from nowhere.

"Your friend showed drastic reactions to the Opulentia in its raw form, much more impressive than any we have seen previously. She is more powerful than anyone else we have put through the treatment."

"What the fuck are you babbling about old man? If you hurt her, I'll turn you inside out and boil you alive!" I screamed.

Khan gestured with his hand, sending a blast of wind at my mouth to silence me.

"With the power she has shown, she may transcend into something magnificent. She may even replace our source, and if so, she would be more valuable to us than you could imagine."

He laughed, lifting me further into the air. Wind poured over my body preventing me from accomplishing much more than lightly flailing my limbs. I couldn't concentrate long enough to try and call my fire to help me. I tried desperately to free myself, but before I managed to find a window Khan decided we were done talking.

In one swift motion, he flung me backwards across the room. His winds carried me hard and fast, sending me tumbling through the air. I couldn't maintain any semblance of balance, thrashing wildly as I flew. I slammed into the wall, and everything went dark.

CHAPTER 10

When I awoke, I could feel tape over my mouth, and something bound my wrists. I was being dragged down a long featureless hallway, possibly the one from before, but I was too delirious to tell. My head ached fiercely, likely a concussion from striking the wall. My mind flashed back to Khan's face as spoke, revealing bits of an evil plan like a bond villain.

I glanced up to see who was carrying me, as if I couldn't just guess. Two male drones on either side of me, following the nurse from before. Something seemed strange about her, she was nervous. It couldn't have been because of me, if I looked anything how I felt.

We rounded the next corner, and I could see her growing more tense. I watched curiously as she came to a dead halt in the middle of the hallway. The males stopped just as quickly, almost as if she had commanded them. She hesitated for a moment, taking a deep breath in preparation for something.

She turned, momentarily gazing into my eyes. I could once again see the sadness in them, as I had before. She held my gaze for a moment, as if she wanted desperately to tell me something that she couldn't. I realized there was life behind her sullen eyes, something I hadn't seen with the other drones.

The sadness in her eyes suddenly gave way to resolve. She nodded subtly to me, clearly deciding whatever was weighing on her mind. She reached into the pouch on her waist, pulling out two syringes filled with some translucent fluid. She quickly flicked the caps off the needles, I winced prematurely expecting the injections.

To my surprise, she rapidly lifted her arms then slammed them into the necks of the men carrying me. Having so little time to react, I fell straight to the ground when they released their grip. They softly groaned, staggered, and then collapsed to the ground beside me. I certainly hadn't been expecting that.

The sudden impact of my head on the floor had sent me reeling once more. In the haze, I felt the tape ripped from my mouth, and then something cutting the tape from my bruised wrists. I managed to sit up, leaning against the wall.

I held my head in my hands, still in shock of what was happening.

"I'm sorry, I didn't mean for them to drop you like that." she explained, placing her hand on my shoulder.

"We need to get somewhere safe, and then I can explain. More may be coming."

She tried to pull me to my feet, tugging at my arm vigorously. I tried my best to stand, but I was so weak from everything that I collapsed onto her. Using her for support

I managed to get my legs under me well enough to walk. She did her best to usher me along quickly.

My consciousness faded in and out as we traversed the snaking labyrinth. My head was swimming worse than the morning after a week of binge drinking. I had more than a few of those for a point of reference. She led me to a room at the end of the hall, nearly shoving me inside in her haste.

She waved her hand, which caused a large cabinet to shift to the side, revealing a hidden chamber in the wall. She guided me inside, and I collapsed onto a bed in the corner while she replaced the cabinet sealing us in this hidden room.

"You can rest here; I will treat your wounds. It should be safe, no one has found me here before..."

Her words trailed off as I blacked out once more.

I found myself sitting in the clearing in the woods once more. The robed figured standing before me in the trees, staring a hole through me almost. There was a calm in the trees, no animal sounds, no insects, nothing. Just a still quiet washing over everything.

I kneeled before the figure as it approached, its dark robes dragging the ground behind it. I could feel its presence, something imposing as if not of this world. It intimidated me as much as it fascinated me. I couldn't force myself to look directly at it.

The figure extended a hand towards me as it drew nearer. The presence of the figure hanging heavy on the air. The flesh was dark and ragged, almost leathery. Each of its fingers drew out long and thin, ending in a sharp, claw-like, black nail.

It rotated its palm before my face, aiming it up towards the sky. I felt the heat before I saw the flame. Within seconds a dancing blue flame appeared. It grew, rapidly engulfing the robed figure, but they did not react in any way to the building inferno.

I could smell the fabric and flesh burning, pungent and terrible. It was so strong I could even taste it. The fire raged hotter, blinding me from viewing the figure within. The flames danced and swayed violently and then leapt towards me.

I screamed as I bolted up in the bed, but my shriek was quickly stifled by a quick hand. The nurse shushed me and gently laid me back down on the bed. She smiled at me, gently dabbing my forehead with a cold wet rag.

"You have been asleep quite some time, however, you must remain quiet. I do not wish for us to be discovered here." She spoke.

She slowly removed her hand, waiting to see if I would cooperate. I nodded and relaxed on the bed. I was unsure of this woman, but she was far nicer to be around than whatever that burning figure was in my dreams. I looked around as she fiddled with something on a tray beside me.

The room was lit by piles of candles, and various papers adorned the walls. Several appeared to be drawings of people or animals, while the rest were scrawls of writing, or newspaper clippings. There was a pile of clothing in the corner, as well as boxes full of food in cans or bags. She had apparently been hiding here for some time.

"Here, drink this tea, it should help restore your strength." She said, offering me a small metal cup of hot liquid.

I sniffed the aroma emanating from the cup and was brought back to my childhood. It smelled just like the

tea my mother used to make when we would 'camp'
under pillows and sheets in the living room and watch
movies. I fondly reminisced on those simpler times as I
sipped the delicious tea. Thanks to an abusive father, my
childhood was not always a happy one. However, my
memories of my mother were good ones.

"This is amazing, it tastes just like my mother used
to make." I said aloud.

"I'm glad you like it." She said, smiling.

I took a deep sip, letting the warmth of the liquid
flow down my throat. It felt fantastic, but it wasn't enough
to distract me from what was happening around me.

"What's going here, exactly? I thought you were
one of Bach's drones or whatever, why did you help me?"

She winced when I mentioned the word 'drone'
aloud.

"I was supposed to be part of his twisted program,
yes. However, the treatment did not stick with me. After
they tattooed me, and tried to brainwash me with their
propaganda, I didn't remember much." She explained.

"After some time, I began remembering some
things about myself. Sadly, not much though, most of my
former life is a mystery to me. I found this room to hide in

when I wasn't needed and began trying to piece together the truth." She pointed to the drawings on the walls.

"I started drawing things I could see in my memory. People, pets, possible family members. It took months before I could place names to the faces. It took much longer to remember my own."

"What is it?" I interrupted. "Your name I mean."

She looked at me fondly. "Unless my memory has failed me, I believe my name is Calliope. You can call me 'Callie' though."

I extended my hand to her, "Trianna." She shook my hand with a smile.

"Yes, I read your chart." She chuckled, "I've been working in secret, trying to aid the new recruits when they come in, hoping someone else remembered themselves too, and might help me escape. You are the first one in years to keep your wits after the treatment."

She brushed a hand down the tattoos on the side of her head. I lifted my hand to the sides of my head, tracing the scar tissue with my fingertips. I had been tattooed, marked, just like the drones.

"What are these tattoos? Why do they do this?" I asked, confused.

"They are old mystical designs; Khan draws them from some dusty old book that looks like its bound in flesh. It has a bunch of weird markings all over it. I caught a glimpse of it once, but it is in a language I don't recognize, I'm not even sure its human."

"Not human? Like... Aliens?" I asked, dumbfounded.

"Possibly. Maybe something demonic, or maybe it's just one of those languages where the letters are pictures. Like in... Egypt!"

She seemed surprised by the name, as if she just remembered it. Though from what she had been telling me, maybe she did. She jotted the word down on a notepad nearby and looked back at me.

"The ink isn't normal ink, though. Whatever the symbols may be, it's hard to say if they do anything because the ink is made from concentrated Opulentia."

I looked at her stunned, trying to understand what exactly that meant. She could likely read the confusion on my face.

"Basically, you will never have to take the pills again, you will be able to use the magic for the rest of your life, whether you want to or not." She explained.

Again, she ran a hand down the tattoos on the side of her head, lost in thought. I pondered the idea for a moment, I hadn't thought of any of this being permanent, aside from the tattoo itself. I wondered if they could be removed, but she probably wouldn't know for sure. My brow furrowed with annoyance, but after a few minutes I broke the silence.

"You said, I was 'the first one in years'... how long have you been here?"

"I'm not sure, but it's been a while. I can remember at least four years, but I'm not sure how much longer I've been here. Some girls have been brought in that look like children. I don't remember how old I am, so it makes it hard to gauge the time."

Callie looked around the room, her gaze lingering fondly on certain items. Clearly, she was thinking about her past. She seemed to hurt deeply but wanted to hide it.

"You should try to sleep. The effects of the procedure take some time to get over. I need to get back into the facility before too many people realize I'm gone."

She poured me another cup of tea and then slipped out through the hidden door. I could hear the cabinet move to secure the entrance as she left. It wasn't long after that I fell asleep. My body ached immensely, and I don't think I've ever felt more tired in my life.

I kept fading in and out as I lay there, unsure of how long I slept each time. Most of the time I would wake up alone to find some food and a fresh cup of tea waiting. Other times Callie was there watching over me while drawing or reading something at her desk. She would smile sweetly at me if she noticed me looking in her direction.

She always seemed so motherly, though she couldn't have been more than a few years older than I was. I wondered if maybe she had children before she was taken. I had to distract myself from the thoughts of what happened to them afterwards. I didn't want to linger on their possibly dark fate.

Eventually I felt strong enough to get up out of the bed and move around some. I looked over the various newspaper clippings strewn about the walls. Small town stories mostly seemed to be interested in the day to day lives of a town in rural Tennessee. She may have been from there, or at least thought she was.

I felt bad that she was unable to clearly remember herself. I was apparently lucky to keep my memory intact. I could only imagine what it must be like for her.

CHAPTER 11

I didn't have long to dwell on the thought before I heard the door opening urgently, and Callie came bursting in.

"Come quickly! They've discovered I've hidden you; we must go! It's not safe!"

She grabbed a duffel bag from under the bed, shoving some food and clothing into it. I jumped up, chugging the last of my tea.

"Where can we go? Aren't we trapped on an island?" I asked.

"There are some caves beyond the forest outside the facility, I'm not sure if they know about them. I've never seen anyone from the facility beyond the woods when I go walking. It's our best bet for now, we can likely lose them in the trees if they chase us. Hurry!"

She ushered me out of the room back into the hallway, closing the hidden room off behind us. She looked at the door sadly before turning to me. I could only guess, but I'm certain she wanted to bring more of her mementos with her, if she could.

"Let's go," she said, "there's not much time."

I nodded and motioned for her to lead the way. She took off running, and I couldn't help but notice how quickly she could move. I leaned into a full sprint behind her, trying my damnedest to keep up. We rounded a few corners and were suddenly met by a few male drones running from the opposite direction.

Callie cursed under her breath, and dropped to her knees, sliding across the slick floor towards them. Her hands shot out to her sides, and then I could feel a presence in the air. A few chunks of concrete from the walls broke free and swarmed around her as she slid forwards. Just before reaching the two drones, she thrust her hands forward, and the concrete flew ahead of them, slamming into the heads of the drones.

They dropped to the floor heavily to either side of her as she casually stood back up and continued her stride. I had slowed momentarily, unsure of what to do, but it was all over before I could react. I chased after her once more, pushing hard to maintain the pace. I heard the concrete slabs come rolling up from behind us as she rounded another corner.

As I came around the corner, I was just in time to see another spectacle of Callie's prowess. A group of three more drones were rushing at us. The woman in front had a fireball in hand, ready to attack. Not ready enough however, for what Callie was prepared to do.

The woman threw her fireball at Callie, but she dodged it easily as she leapt forward. Bouncing off the wall, she brought her foot around hard into the woman's face, sending her careening to the floor. She didn't get back up. Callie returned to her feet, ready to continue her onslaught.

The men did not have time to react before Callie lashed out at them. Her concrete chunks quickly found their way to the drone's heads with a flick of her wrists. The sound of the impact was gruesome, almost giving me pause. I could already see the pools of blood forming as I reached their bodies.

Without missing a beat, Callie continued to lead our escape. I pumped my legs hard, straining to keep up with her as she ran.

"It's not much further, there is a service door we can use to get outside to the grounds. If we can make it to the forest, we should be okay!" She yelled back at me over her shoulder.

"I hope you're right. This is getting more insane by the minute!" I said.

We pushed on, with no more interruptions from the drones. This was nice but also a little concerning. A few more turns and we slammed against the service door.

"Shit, it's locked..." she said, "Okay, back up. I can handle this."

She motioned with her hand for me to back up all the way across the hallway, and then stared at the door for a moment. She held up her hand and made a gesture with her fingers before slamming her hand forward. The concrete around the door buckled and forced its way downward, crushing the steel door and ripping it from its frame. The door slammed loudly to the ground, and she smiled as she turned to face me.

"Alright, it worked! Let's go!" she said, once more taking off in a full sprint.

We only made it about halfway across the courtyard before the rest of the compound was onto us. At least fifty of Bach's drones came rushing out after us from both sides of the building. Some were on motorcycles, clearly eager to get to us quickly.

"This isn't going to be pretty, Trianna. I don't know if you feel up to helping me out here, but if you can muster it, we may just escape."

"I don't know if I can manage anything spectacular, but I'll try..." I replied.

We slowed to a halt and turned to face the drones enclosing on us. I was already out of breath; I wasn't sure how much help I could offer. Even if I hadn't been exhausted, I still had only limited experience with my powers. Our lives depended on it, however, so I would have to come up with something.

Callie stepped forward with a determined look on her face. She pulled her arm forward from her side, finger pointed at the ground as it moved. She was focused and well in control of her abilities. There was a rumbling in the earth, and it began to crack in front of us.

The motorcycles were caught completely off guard as pillars of dirt erupted before them. The lead bike was flung backwards over the heads of those following. He crashed into a couple in the back, their bikes tangling together. The others slammed into the pile of risen rock and dirt, having no time to slow down or change course.

Callie grinned, she seemed very in tune with her abilities. I had to wonder how long she had been practicing with her powers to manage such control. The mob continued to run towards us, but Callie stood her ground.

She swung her arms this way and that, tracing intricate patterns on the air.

Columns of dirt rose from the ground, bending into powerful arches that slammed into bodies. Drones cried out sharply as they were rendered unconscious, or possibly even dead. Rocks flew up from beneath the grass, cracking skulls and laying their targets out cold. It was absolute carnage.

The drones had started to realize that their numbers alone would not stop us, and several began to fall back. I hadn't noticed, but all the women had lined up in the back and seemed to be chanting. They all held their hands in matching positions in front of themselves. Callie noticed too and cursed under her breath.

The women all thrust their hands forward in unison, and a massive ball of fire and lightning swirled to life in the air and began hurtling towards us with intense speed.

"Down!" Callie cried.

She thrust her hands up, bringing a large wall of dirt with them to shield us. The ball of magic slammed into the dirt and exploded on impact. Dirt and rocks were sent flying everywhere. The blast sent us backwards as well, but Callie took much more of the hit.

I scrambled to my feet and tried to concentrate. I called out in my mind to the fire that I had used before when training, and much to my surprise it answered loudly. Within seconds, a torrent of blue flame swirled around my body. I couldn't feel the heat, but I could smell the grass and soil burning beneath me.

The remaining drones had split up into groups of three, the two males with a leading female. They all began to move in unison, waving their arms in the air before them, like something out of a movie. Balls of fire and lightning began to appear on the air, much smaller than before, but just as focused. They launched a volley, trying to trap us within the rain of their attack.

I felt calm and focused, almost as if I had done this my whole life. I felt a presence within me, that seemed to be taking control. I had felt it before when I killed the guards in the basement. I didn't like it, but I trusted it.

My legs carried me forward, pumping hard as they could. I advanced on the drones as their spells crashed harmlessly to the ground behind me. More spells formed, but I flung my hand forward, sending bursts of fire towards them and knocking their magic from the air. A few got close, but the wall of fire swirling around me swatted them away like flies. I no longer felt any control over myself.

I leapt forward, spinning my body and the fire surged away from me, lashing at the drones. Flames danced across their bodies, burning them painfully and interrupting their casting as they cried out. It was like I was trapped in my own skull, watching a horrible movie. Whatever this beast inside me was, it was enjoying itself.

Callie had regained her footing and was flinging rocks and dirt to help. I continued to blast the drones with tubes of swirling blue fire. Within moments, all the drones lay dead or unconscious on the ground. I felt sick, the smell of death was in the air, and the flames did nothing to hide it.

I slumped, feeling the angry presence in my mind leaving me behind as it retreated into my subconscious. I was panting hard, and it felt like I may never catch my breath again. Callie got to me just in time to catch me before I collapsed. I felt completely drained and rested my head on her shoulder for a moment, but the reprieve was short lived.

A clap echoed from above us, as if to mock us. I stirred and looked around. Callie nodded her head upwards, frowning and annoyed. I followed her gaze to the rooftop, and I could just barely make out a man in a suit standing on the edge of the building.

"That was rather impressive! I knew from the moment your fire blazed blue that there was something special about you." He called out to us.

"Still a bit weak though. You look like a strong wind could blow you over. Not quite as impressive as your little flower, Star, was it?" He smirked.

I struggled to stand, having to use Callie for support. My anger was raging, but even that was not enough to keep me on my feet.

"You see, she's reacted to the treatment in ways we've never seen before. We thought it was just an overdose at first, and that we would only get to have you. But then she began showing massive signs of improvement. We kept giving her more of the drug, and she loved it! Power readings are off the chart, and after we dunked her in the tank... Well, I think you'll just have to see that for yourself!" He bellowed as he motioned behind himself.

A large tank came into view, and there was a body suspended inside. My vision was a little blurred, but I could recognize Star anywhere. I knew the curves of her body like the back of my hand. I growled, trying to figure out just what he was doing.

Bach reached over and unlatched the lid of the tank as his drones cranked something to lift Star out of the tank. Something was off about her; I could sense it even from the ground. She cried out in rage as air filled her lungs outside the tank. Bach stepped back despite himself. I could feel a strange thickness on the air, and it began to smell like rain.

Callie tried to pull me away, urging me to leave while they were distracted. I couldn't move, I was fixated on Star. She crackled with energy and began to float above the tank. Her arms extended to her side and large bolts of energy arced and rolled across her body.

Dark clouds grew in the sky above the building as Star rose higher into the air. Her eyes opened, and they glowed with electricity. They reminded me of the man at the beginning of the tour, but more ferocious. Callie pulled harder, dragging me towards the forest, I tried to fight it as I watched Star ascend, but I was too weak.

Callie hauled me to the tree line, but I continued to stare at what they had done to the woman I loved. Her body hovered in the air above the compound, crackling with immense energy as a full-fledged storm formed around her. Thunder crashed loudly as lightning struck her body, but she just absorbed the energy like a sponge. She was beyond even a force of nature, the energy just rippling through her, adding to her strength.

The last thing I saw as we entered the forest would haunt me forever. Star threw her head back, and bolts of energy burst out from her, whipping at the sky. Thunder roared, and rain began to fall as she hovered, still crackling with power. She wasn't bothered by the storm because she was the storm.

We ducked through the trees, moving as quickly as we could despite our exhaustion. Callie used her magic to cover our tracks in the dirt behind us as we moved. It was minor, but even that was taking a toll on her. The battle had taken much out of us, and it was all I could do to limp alongside her.

The woods thickened as we progressed, and eventually I had to move on my own, climbing through piles of downed trees and around bushes. The forest seemed raw, as if never touched by man. For all I knew it never had been really, out here on this mysterious island. I wasn't sure how we were going to escape, but for the moment I could only focus on getting through the trees.

Callie had mentioned a cave system on the other side of the forest. She seemed to know her way, but as tired as we both were, it was hard to say if she was still confident. I didn't question her, just wanting to find a place to rest. It likely wouldn't be long before Bach had more drones out looking for us, so I wanted to make as much progress as we could.

I also couldn't shake the feeling of being watched. There were several times that I thought I saw a figure on the edge of my vision as we moved through the woods. Anytime I stopped to get a better look though, nothing was there. I decided I was either seeing things from the stress, or we were being tracked by bears. The latter was strangely more comforting.

We climbed over a large busted up log, and suddenly Callie shrieked. I didn't have time to react, and before I knew it, I joined her tumbling down a massive leaf-covered hill. The descent was not pleasant, bouncing off trees and rocks as we fell. Thankfully none hit my head, but when we came to stop at the bottom I was still quite banged up.

I just laid on my back, stretched across the ground for a few minutes, stunned and sore. Callie had stopped not far from me and crawled over.

"Are you hurt?" she asked

"Of course, but nothing terrible I don't think." I replied.

She grinned, resting her head on my chest to catch her breath.

"I don't remember that hill being there. I'm not sure we are in the right place, but there is a cave over there."

She pointed towards a small hole peeking out from behind some heavy vines. I wasn't thrilled to hear her words, but at least we had found something that might provide some shelter. The storm from the compound had moved over the forest and rain was quickly approaching. I hoped that it was only the rain approaching.

We staggered to our feet and leaned against each other to shuffle into the cave. There was a mustiness to the air, but it was much nicer than the smell in the courtyard. I tried to block that memory from my head. I didn't want to think about what I had been forced to do back there.

Callie waved a hand and a small dirt wall closed most of the entrance to the cave. She left only a few small gaps for air to pass through. With any luck that would throw anyone off our tracks. If they had even managed to track us this far.

I held up my hand, and focused on the tip of my finger, forming a small orb of fire that illuminated the dark cave, so we could see. It looked exactly how you would expect a cave in the woods to look. Damp, dirty, and crawling with insects and salamanders. It was quaint.

I slumped against a wall and sat down to rest. Callie sat down beside me and rummaged through her bag pulling out a couple bottles of water, and some protein bars.

"Here." she offered, "It's not much, but after all that we need something to get some strength back."

I nodded and quickly devoured the bar, chasing it quickly with most of the water in a few gulps. It was more refreshing than it had any right to be given its size. It felt like a banquet to my tired body and empty stomach. I was once again thankful for her motherly instincts.

We sat in silence for a while, letting our bodies recover as we leaned against each other for support. Callie broke the silence first.

"Trianna, what happened back there... don't let it bother you too much. We did what we had to. It was survival."

I just stared ahead of me at the opposite wall. She was right, but that didn't stop it from eating at me.

"In a way, you saved them. If the treatment works, they lose themselves to it. I remember feeling like I was trapped in my head, while someone else controlled my body." She explained.

"It didn't last long, as I began to wake up and regain control, but I think that for others, they are trapped forever. Lost to Bach's whims. Now perhaps, they don't have to suffer anymore."

She wrapped her arm around me to comfort me, and I realized I was crying. I leaned into her chest, weeping heavily as my mind raced through the events of the day. The burning bodies, the smell of death. The strange angry beast inside of me that I just let take over.

Most of all, I thought of Star. I thought of what they had done to her. I could still see her naked body floating in the air, covered with lightning. It shook me to my core.

Callie did her best to comfort me as she held me. She made calming shush noises and laid her head on mine to hold me close. I cried hard but quietly, my energy still mostly gone. My body hurt, my head hurt, but most of all, my heart hurt.

"We never should have come here, and we never should have taken those stupid pills. This was insane, I had never seen real magic before in my life, and then suddenly some strange man is offering it to me on a literal silver platter." I stammered through the tears,

"And now? And now... Star is gone. The woman I love most is just gone, and it's all my fault. I dragged her into all this, and she's gone!"

Callie shushed me and wiped away a few tears with her hand.

"No, that's not true. Bach did this, that creep did this to all of us! You can't blame yourself when the man responsible is still out there, still has your Star!" She said, trying to reason with me through my hysteria.

"He did this, true, but I brought her with me. If I had just left her alone, let her live her life, she would be fine. She would still be riding around town on that ugly little moped, crashing on couches, doing photoshoots, living life away from all... from all of this"

Callie slapped me across the face.

"You listen to me. You brought her into your life because you loved her. Yes, things turned sour here, but you had no way of knowing they would. He coerced you both into this, he is a con man. He tricked us all! We will find a way to get back and save Star. We will get off this island, and send someone to clean up this mess, the army, the government, someone will help us... they have to."

I held my face where she slapped me, reason returning to me. She was right, I made mistakes, but Bach was to blame here. I would get Star back, no matter the cost. I would find a way to get her home and safe, and we could wash our hands of this, and go back to living a normal life.

I nodded to her and hugged her tightly. It felt nice to hold someone again, it felt like ages since I had. We curled up together on the floor to stave off the cold that was creeping in. The light outside was fading, and I had let my ball of fire die out, covering us in comforting darkness.

It didn't take long for us to drift off to sleep. My body was practically crying out for rest after all I had put it through. I'm sure Callie felt the same.

I found myself in the clearing in the forest again. Something felt different this time though. The figure approached me, and I knelt before it. This time I stared at its terrible face as it drew near.

Its leathery black skin glistened with blood as it extended its hand towards me. I pressed my forehead into its palm, feeling the blood leave a handprint across my face. The blood was warm and fresh. I felt it slowly soaking into my skin.

Blue flames swirled around me, and I rose to my feet. The flames engulfed the figure, burning away its robes. While the flesh burned, I watched it nod its approval. There was no sign of pain in the featureless face as the fire raged harder. I felt the essence of the creature enter my body through the blood on my face.

I stood in the clearing, arms extended at my sides, laughing. I danced as the fire continued to swirl, burning the whole clearing. My power weighed heavily on the world, demanding respect. I felt like I was becoming a god, surrounded by my terrible flames.

Suddenly, the sky darkened. Thunder crashed, and torrential rain began to pour down, quenching my blaze. The rain burned my skin like acid when it touched me. I collapsed to the ground unable to stand against the coming storm. I writhed on the ground trying to get away from the rain.

I looked to the sky; my face contorted with pain. There, hovering high above me, was Star. She was naked and pulsing with energy. The storm raged around her as she descended towards me.

Bolts of lightning crashed from her hands, striking the ground around me. I could no longer move, frozen in place with fear. As she got closer, I could see strings attached to nails that pierced through her joints. The strings traced back up to two gloved hands in the sky, working them like a puppeteer.

I cried out to her, but the thunder drowned out my voice each time. She stood over me, fist raised above her head, glowing with energy. She looked to the hands in the sky for a moment, and then back at me. Tears rolled down her face, pouring from her electrified eyes.

Her hand came racing down at my face. Everything began to move in slow motion. I could smell the electricity on the air as it drew near. Lightning arced off her arm and hand to the ground around me as her fist inched closer to my face. I stared into her eyes, and I could see the sadness behind the energy.

Everything went dark as her fist connected with my face. Lightning surged through my body, frying every nerve I had. The pain was immense, like nothing I had ever felt before, then suddenly it was over.

I felt nothing. I was nothing. My view shifted, and I could see my lifeless body on the ground. Star's fist was pressed into the ground where my head should be. I looked down at my hands. Blood dripped from them, creeping down the strings they held.

CHAPTER 12

"Wake up Trianna," Callie rocked my shoulder with her hand as she spoke, "Do you hear that?"

My head was swimming as images of my dreams echoed through my mind's eye. I took a sharp breath but held it as I heard what she was referring to. There was activity outside of the cave, but it was hard to make out quite what it was. Someone or something had found our hiding place.

"What do we do?" I asked, trying to hide my obvious fear.

"I'm not sure. The cave might have another exit somewhere, but we may be trapped." Callie said, scooting up beside me in anticipation.

There was a rumbling as the stones and dirt sealing the cave began to shift. I glanced at Callie to see if she was responsible, but the shock on her face told me otherwise. Light was pouring in as the hole began to widen, I answered with light of my own as my arms engulfed themselves in blue flames. I stood ready for a fight with whatever tried to come in after us. Callie rose to stand cautiously nearby.

At last, the opening of the cave gave way, and I braced ready to unleash a burning hell on any drones foolish enough to enter. However, once my eyes adjusted to the brightness, there were no drones to be found. Only a young girl dressed in rags with flowers in her hair. She couldn't have been older than ten or eleven. She beamed a smile at us and motioned for us to follow outside. I looked at Callie who just shrugged and hesitantly moved towards the opening.

I couldn't help but feel as though it was all a trap, but I lowered my arms and followed Callie outside, the flames still swirling up and down my arms in case anything got too forward. As we stepped out into the clearing, the little girl giggled and waved her hand, beckoning us deeper into the trees. Her hair was long, blonde, and delicately tied in braids with beautiful flowers and vines. Her clothing looked old and patched together with various earth toned fabrics.

I was curious about who this girl might be. Was she living out here in the woods? She seemed far too young to be able to survive on her own. There were likely others in the area, I could only hope they were as friendly as she seemed to be.

We followed, unsure of the situation but curious enough about our little guide. I dismissed the flames from my arms, so that I could help Callie move through the thick brush. She was staggering a bit but seemed to be regaining her composure. I needed to thank her for everything she had done for me, but now was not the time.

We had pressing matters with a possible forest fairy. I figured, if magic was real, who knew what the hell else was out there. Callie had mentioned the idea that the source of the Opulentia might even be a demon. Maybe that's how this young-looking girl survived out here in the woods.

We followed the girl through the trees and bushes for what felt like an eternity. The trip was completely silent, the girl never offering any direction other than stopping to wave us after her before darting through the overgrowth. I still had the feeling that someone was watching us, and occasionally thought I saw shadows moving behind the trees. I could never make out anything distinct though.

After what felt like months, but was likely only an hour or so, we finally came to a halt. The girl paused at a vertical wall of moss-covered dirt and rock that stretched up into the top of the tree line. It appeared to be a substantial dead end. The girl turned to us, still beaming, and gestured for us to wait.

She turned back to the wall and raised her hands. She appeared to be concentrating quite hard and then with a quick wipe of her hands the wall grumbled and began to split apart. Through the opening a small village revealed itself. The houses were built back into large tree trunks, or mounds of dirt all surrounding a large circular area in the middle with the remains of a large firepit.

I heard the movement before I saw anything, and as the trees rustled, I realized we had been surrounded. The leaves gave way to several men and women jumping down from the branches. They were all dressed in tanned leathers and wielding crude spears and bows. None of them seemed threatening, however, they all smiled at us as they gathered at the opening in the wall.

The little girl giggled and ran up to one of the men jumping into his arms for a loving embrace. As he held her tightly, he turned enough for me to realize he had glyphs tattooed down the sides of his head, just like the ones we had. He was a drone, but somehow, he seemed different. He stepped forward to speak and I felt tense.

"Welcome friends. We saw your escape from the facility. We knew you needed help. My name is Cotton, it's a pleasure to meet you!" he said, slightly bowing his head.

"Please, step into our camp. Cherry will take you to meet our leader who can explain things better."

He dropped the girl to her feet who nodded and motioned for us to follow again. The others began to climb back into the trees to retrieve the prizes of their hunt. The first few carried down large sacks full of various vegetation and berries. The other two emerged carrying a deer suspended on a stick slung over their shoulders.

We stood still in awe for a moment before Cherry came and tugged my hand excitedly. Callie let out a slight giggle, giving me an encouraging look. She was clearly unconcerned by this development, which did put me more at ease. I wasn't quite ready to trust them completely, but they seemed harmless enough.

Cherry tugged me by the arm into the clearing, but then stopped abruptly and let go. She turned around, waving her hands through the air towards the wall. The rocks and soil once more slid into place, sealing the village off from the wild woods as if the gap had never been there. I didn't think at the time to question how this small child was using magic, it was already becoming so very normal to me.

Cherry resumed her trek, beckoning us along towards a large hut near the center of the village. The structure was mostly covered with mud and palm leaves and recessed into the hill, making its size difficult to judge as we approached. I looked around and saw few others moving through the village. The place was rather quaint and quiet.

I couldn't help but wonder how long they had been living out here, or what they had to do with the compound. Everyone I could see, aside from Cherry, had the drone markings. The tattoos all seemed strange though, as if something about them had been changed. I couldn't put my finger on it though.

We entered the large hut, and as I suspected the building stretched further back than was visible from the outside. It smelled of roasted meats, fruits, with a delicate backdrop of soil. As we rounded a bamboo divider, I saw several people around a large table laying out a feast. It was an impressive display.

Seated at the head of the table was a figure dressed in a dark cloak with the hood up hiding their face. My stomach, which was just moments ago growling to notify me of its intense desire to consume, suddenly turned. Just the sight of this person made me uncomfortable. It struck me that they looked incredibly like the figure from my recent nightmares.

The figure stood and opened their arms in a welcoming manner.

"Come, sit. We feast to celebrate your freedom!" they said reaching up to remove the hood from their face.

I looked to Callie for assurance. She had been mostly quiet since we left the cave but didn't seem to be afraid. It was likely that she was as curious about the whole ordeal as I was. She for the moment seemed enthralled by the food, and I couldn't blame her. Getting here had taken much from both of us.

We sat near the head of the table with Cherry's guidance. I could feel my stomach growling, once again ready for a feast. The smell from the table was magical. I was still a little unsure of our host, however.

With the hood down, I could see that they were older than us, and covered in tattoos, most unlike what I saw on the others. Because of the robe, it was hard to see how far they extended down, but the sides of their head held all kinds of runes and symbols, and perhaps even some Kanji. Tribal lines and dots were splayed across the face in geometric patterns. Clearly the tattoos were placed with intent, perhaps even ritualistic.

"My tattoos are prototype designs for the symbols they etched on you." They spoke in an aged voice, "I will explain later. You are famished, let us eat. There will be time for discussion later."

"Thank you for all this." Callie said eyeing the pile of food before her.

I nodded in agreement, still unsure of everyone. Everyone except for Cherry, who was currently stuffing berries into her mouth at a pace that would choke a goat. She seemed so pure and out of place with everything I had seen over the last several weeks. It was refreshing.

Cotton and his team of hunters joined us moments later, cleaner and without their weaponry. We all began to serve ourselves food onto large leaves that served as plates. Coconut shells were used as cups, and a young man served us all a very delicious, and very potent, mead. The food was simple, roast pork with vegetables and fruits, but it had been so long since I had eaten anything substantial, I couldn't complain if I tried.

Callie reached for another helping of food as I decided to break the silence.

"Thank you all again so much for all of this, but…"

I paused, taking another swig of mead. I had many questions to ask but was unsure where to start.

"Who are you? I can't help but notice most of you have these damned tattoos, are you all from the facility? How long have you been out here? Where are we exactly?"

I found myself rambling out question after question, unable to restrain myself as I often am when drunk. The leader set their cup down, smiling as they swallowed a gulp of mead.

"Easy child. One thing at a time. Yes, most of us are from the compound. I was the first experiment there. I can explain, but I must warn you, the story is not a light one."

"I have been taking in a lot of bad experiences lately, might as well keep it going." I replied.

"My name is Devon. I was... involved with Sebastian when he made the discovery initially. We met at university, and he always told me about wanting to travel and see the secrets of the world that they wouldn't teach him. He was searching for something, even then, but never told me what."

I can't say that I was terribly shocked by the idea that I had found a person in the woods that used to fuck

Bach, but few things seem out of the ordinary once you can shoot fireballs from your hands.

"He had studied archaeology, and dead old languages at Uni. He expressed an interest in the occult at an early age and had never grown out of it. When the professors kept insisting that magic wasn't real, and that his quest for such dark arts wasn't healthy, Sebastian left the academy. I followed him, even though he was several years younger than me, I fell hard for him then. He accepted me for who I was, and the sex was great of course." Devon chuckled, and I noticed a few people at the table blush as they ate.

"We traveled then, to so many places I had never dreamed of going. The Caribbean, Malaysia, Haiti, Kilimanjaro, Africa, Siberia, all over the globe in search of something. Not long after we left India, Sebastian met Khan, though back then he went by his real name: Drew. Things began to change then; Sebastian's drive was stronger. Khan had come to us with knowledge of dark arcane forces, and some research to prove it. Sebastian spent less time in my bed, and more time at his desk, constantly pouring over scrolls of languages I couldn't comprehend. His work consumed him."

"Khan taught me yoga in our spare time, it kept my mind clear and my body limber. I didn't realize it at the time, but that was because they wanted to use me as their guinea pig for some ritual." Devon paused to sip their drink. Their eyes reflected a distant pain as they spoke.

"They had found something on a recent hike, something Sebastian said would change everything. He wasn't wrong, but I had no clue what he meant then. He and Khan hired a team of people to carry something back to his lab from the mountains. They were gone for several days, I wasn't allowed to come along on these types of trips, for my safety." Their eyes rolled.

"When they returned, several of the men had died, and the others refused to speak of what they had seen. Sebastian beamed with pride and renewed vigor over the discovery. He took me that night like he had never done before, passionately powerful. I could hardly walk the next day."

"What did they find?" Callie asked, seeming desperate to get away from that subject.

"He found... what they called Subject One. I am still not sure just what the thing is, but to me it always seemed demonic."

Callie's eyes lit up; she had mentioned to me before that she felt like something demonic was responsible for what had been done to us.

"Sebastian and Khan locked themselves in the lab for several weeks, all kinds of strange noises came from behind the doors as I waited, but no one ever came out. I often thought of leaving then. I was feeling very unsettled with everything and being alone for so long only made it worse. Sebastian wouldn't even let me phone my parents anymore. I miss them so. After several weeks had passed, Sebastian came back to me with a strange gleam in his eyes. I could tell he wanted something from me, but he wouldn't say what. I found out not long after." Devon's eyes watered slightly as they recounted.

"He woke me in the night, rustling around the bedroom. He was muttering, and when I sat up to ask what was wrong, he lunged at me. He pinned me down and shoved a rag in my face. It smelled strange, and I quickly lost consciousness. I awoke sometime later, strapped nude to a table, with Khan tediously stabbing me with a set of needles. He drew on me for hours, never pausing as if he was possessed by his foul work." Devon said, furrowing their brow.

"When he was finished, Sebastian joined him. They compared my skin to images in some scrolls and nodded. Khan left and then returned with a glass container full of some strange red liquid. It swirled strangely inside the glass. He took a handful of it and smeared it across the open wounds, and it burned."

"They asked me to try and focus a light on my fingertip, and when I refused to comply Khan would strike me. I felt so helpless I eventually gave in and did what they asked of me. Nothing happened when I tried, and they decided the wrong symbols were used. They strapped me down and tried again with another set of scrolls and books. This went on for days, maybe weeks. The tattoo sessions were so long and painful it was torture to stay awake, so I slept when I could."

Devon stood and removed the robe, revealing their naked body to us as they spoke. Their chest heaved with each breath, and I traced the hundreds of patterned lines down their supple breasts tipped with bone-pierced nipples. Still the lines continued downward. Their penis was the only part of their body left unadorned with ink.

Some of the shapes and symbols I recognized, macabre characters and words tangled with images of skulls and runes. There were probably over a hundred different languages scrawled in small sections of tired flesh. The pain Devon must have endured through all of that boggled my mind. I had a few tattoos here and there that Star had helped me design, but they were nothing compared to this, not even the drone markings.

Devon draped the robe back over their body and sat back down.

"Each time they tried a new scroll of symbols, the result was the same. I occasionally felt a warmth on my fingers when I tried to summon forth a light, but still nothing. I was convinced that Sebastian had gone insane, and I was going to be tortured to death by Khan for some occult ritual. But then, it happened."

"Sebastian stormed in during a tattoo session and presented Khan with a book he had found. A foul looking thing, it appeared to be bound in skin. This was apparently hidden beneath Subject One in the cave they discovered. Khan poured over the book and smiled an evil grin. He washed me carefully and then shaved me. My body apparently needed to be cleansed. He burned some foul-smelling incense and shook burning sage around me. Then he went to work putting these symbols all over my head." I could see the tattoo lines retreating into their hairline as they spoke.

"He wasn't using the same needle and ink anymore either. He swapped to some older looking set made from bone or something and was using the red liquid in place of the ink. It burned fiercely, and I cried out until my voice went hoarse. Sebastian watched from his desk, I barely recognized him. My mind felt fuzzy, details were fading from my vision, and then I heard a voice in the back of my head telling me to escape. As Khan finished the last of the symbols, my whole body started to convulse. The lights flickered in the lab as power radiated from my body."

"Sebastian stood over me, screaming at me to control it, to focus it. He wanted me to control whatever was happening within me. His assistants fled the lab as I warped the table beneath me. Glass shattered, equipment exploded, debris flew as something primal burst from within me. The straps holding me to the table melted away as I rose. I'm not sure how long I was suspended in the air, but I could feel something within me. It was as angry as I was, it felt hurt or betrayed, or perhaps I was just projecting. Regardless, I pulsed with insane power, destroying the lab in the process. Sebastian and Khan had retreated to a viewing chamber, but they smiled as they watched."

I shifted in my seat. Nothing they were telling me struck me as odd. Bach had tricked us into his game and tortured us just the same.

"And then, as quickly as it came, it went. I collapsed to the floor in a pool of blood. Very little of it was mine. My body had rejected the substance, and my rage had forced it out of me. They called me a failure, a waste of time. They drug me into the woods and left me to die."

A feeling of pain and betrayal washed over Devon's face and was echoed amongst the others at the table.

"Over time, they continued their experiments, they rebuilt the lab into the compound that stands there now. They brought in countless victims over the years. When one failed, they threw the body out like they had done to me. Most died, a few I saved. We built this camp here, and we try to help save anyone that manages to get out of the compound. You are the first to have escaped on your own it seems, and with quite the commotion!"

I sat back in my chair, still chewing a bite of meat. Callie sat staring at her plate, a look of shock on her face.

"I'm so sorry." She uttered, "I'm not sure what to say. This is all so much..."

I rested a hand on her shoulder, and she quickly turned and buried her face in my neck to weep. It was a lot to take in, and clearly it had overwhelmed her. I held her for comfort, as much for myself as for her.

Devon gave us a bittersweet but supportive smile, like a mother watching over a child learning a painful lesson.

"I didn't mean to upset you. It is a hard tale to recount. What Sebastian has done is inexcusable."

"You can say that again." I interrupted, "He took my Star from me, twisted her into something insane. She was innocent, and I got her dragged into all this nonsense. I'll kill him for this."

My hands balled into fists and a hot air began to swirl in the hut. Callie ceased her weeping and looked up at me.

"You want to go back, don't you?" she muttered.

"For her, I'd leap straight into hell!" I replied.

I regained my composure as I realized everyone was shifting nervously about the rising temperature in the hut. The cool air returned. Devon cocked their head and looked at me.

"You have a strength to you that I have never seen from one of Sebastian's recruits. They must have been improving the process over the years, or perhaps..." Devon paused, lost in thought for a moment.

"During one of my sessions, I heard him chatting with Khan about possible reactions to the substance. He theorized that something in the human DNA might resonate with it, and in some they could possibly create a power like that of the source, Subject One." I grimaced at the word source.

"Khan said that whatever they had done to Star had turned her into something more powerful than they had expected. He said she might be able to replace their source." I relayed.

I felt myself fighting back tears as I spoke. Much to my chagrin, I often cried when I was angry, though it never stopped me from putting foot to ass when necessary.

"If that's true, then you will need to act fast if you wish to save her." Devon replied.

"They would take some time to test her abilities before giving up Subject One as the source, but Sebastian focuses like a bloodhound when he's after something."

"They were parading her around earlier like a new toy. She looked... terrifying. She reminded me of a phoenix but made of electricity instead of fire. So much rage, it wasn't like her."

"The substance they use in the ritual, it is the blood of Subject One." Devon said flatly.

Callie and I both recoiled at the statement.

"They... put some thing's blood into us?! That's what gives us this power?!" Callie blurted.

That explains the taste, I thought. Devon stood and stepped away from their seat.

"Yes, however that is the reason that I may be able to help you. Blood is natural, and while the source may be something I'm unsure of, I do know of one that can manipulate natural things." Devon stated.

Devon moved behind Cherry and stopped resting hands on her shoulders, Cherry beamed with pride. Callie and I looked to Devon with curiosity. We had seen the girl use magic to seal the camp, despite being so young and having no visible tattoos. My stomach turned at the idea that Bach had experimented on such a young child.

"You see, those of us that Sebastian tainted with his rituals were attuned with a specific element. Cherry here, is not one of Sebastian's experiments. She cannot speak, but she has proven to be proficient with control over all elements." Devon said, gently patting Cherry's shoulders.

"Okay... but if she wasn't experimented on, how does she have powers?" I asked, befuddled.

Devon chuckled, "Cherry was not experimented on, but is a natural born child of parents that were. Cotton fathered her with another one of ours, Daisy, that unfortunately died giving birth to Cherry. We were shocked, as it seemed most of us had gone infertile in the process, but Cotton and Daisy conceived."

I looked over at Cotton who looked slightly smug over this information. I rolled my eyes and looked back to Devon and Cherry.

"Alright, but I'm still lost. How does this help me get Star back?" I asked.

"Getting her back will be the difficult part, if you can get her back to us here however, Cherry may be able to revert what Sebastian has done to your love." Devon stated.

Again, Callie and I looked puzzled. Devon just chortled and smiled.

"You two, and Cherry, are the only ones in this room currently capable of using magic. Cherry can draw the blood of Subject One out of a person's body. It is painful, but once removed the person gradually loses the effects of the blood. She surprised us with this ability, pulling blood from another from our village, and trying to use it to bring a dead pet back to life. She failed with that plan, but her friend, Daffodil, lost their abilities a few days later."

I tried not to laugh at the theme of plant names. I then remembered that Callie mentioned memory loss, so it was likely none of them remembered their actual names.

"So, what you're saying..." I inquired, "is that Cherry can reverse this madness in others?"

"It would seem that way." Devon nodded, "It took some effort, but Cherry seemed to understand the process better than any of us and figured it out quickly. She's quite the little wonder."

Cotton beamed at the compliment of his child like the proudest of fathers.

"I still grieve for her mother, but Cherry has helped us all so much." He said,

"Unfortunately, we did not regain much of our memories when the magic faded. Still, it is nice to feel a semblance of normality again after what was done to us."

Callie frowned at this information. Clearly, she had some hope of remembering more of her life before the procedure, and this had ruined that hope. She sat silently chewing on some cheese from her plate.

"Okay. If I can get Star back here, you think Cherry can pull the blood out of her, and there is a chance that she will return to normal." I thought aloud, "How the hell am I going to get her back here though?"

Devon nodded to Cotton, who held his fist to his chest in a salute of sorts.

"We will help you." He said.

The others around the table matched his gesture. I glanced around at all of them, bewildered at their eagerness. Devon stood and broke the silence.

"We have been discussing retribution for some time. Cotton and the others have been honing their skills for several years here in the woods. We have all lusted for a chance to get even with Sebastian for what he has done to us, and so many others like us. I believe that the time is now, aided by your fury and drive, to strike back." Devon said triumphantly clenching a fist over their heart.

I furrowed my brow in thought. The compound was a warzone when Callie and I had made our escape, but perhaps with assistance from these hunters we would stand a chance, though I wasn't convinced.

"I will help you, too." Callie said, resting her palm on my thigh.

"I knew there was something special about you when I rescued you. I may not remember all my life before Bach changed me, but if I can help you get back your lover, your life, then I must try." She said with conviction.

I looked at her, fighting back emotions of my own. She was so kind, and I couldn't stop myself from clenching her to me in an embrace.

"I can never thank you enough, any of you." I stuttered through a sob.

Devon stood at the head of the table, a firm resolve in her eyes as she spoke.

"Retribution will be thanks enough for me." The group cheered in agreement, and Callie gently kissed my cheek in affirmation.

After dinner, we decided to spend a few days preparing for our attack. Devon provided us with a place to stay in a spare hut that had been recently built. The hut was nicer than I expected, perhaps one of the people here had been a carpenter before Bach corrupted them. The bed was stuffed with straw and leaves and was surprisingly plush.

Blankets of fur made the bed rather cozy, but Callie and I found ourselves cuddled together for emotional support. My mind was full of everything that had taken place recently. I thought of Star, and how happy we had been before all of this began. I could see her smile as we chatted over wine, usually about how the expensive wine didn't really taste any better than the cheap stuff we got before. She would laugh and suggest that the carboard box gave it a better flavor.

I could practically feel her skin against mine as we rolled together in our giant bed. Her breath on my neck as we embraced. The pulse of her heart as we held each other tight. Her voice when she complained that I was holding her too tightly and she couldn't breathe. Something was wrong about her voice, it wasn't right. It wasn't hers.

"Please, Trianna! I mean it I can't breathe!" Callie blurted.

She struggled in my arms, trying frantically to push me away. I released my grip and sat up wiping sweat from my forehead.

"I'm... I'm sorry. I must have been dreaming." I said, head still fuzzy.

"You called out her name a few times. She means a lot to you, doesn't she?"

"She means everything to me. I hate myself for getting her into this shit." I said flopping back down on the bed.

"Bach tricked us all." Callie retorted, "You can't beat yourself up over it. We will find her, and Cherry will fix us, and you can be together again."

"I am worried about that too." I said. "What if she doesn't remember me? What if her memory is all fucked up?" I rolled to face Callie.

"I think she will." She said, "I think both of you reacting so uniquely to the treatment means that she kept her memory too."

"What if she hates me for it?" I asked, turning away.

"If she loves you the way you love her..." She wrapped an arm around my midsection and held me close to her. "Then, I don't think she could ever hate you."

I couldn't help but enjoy the feeling of Callie's body against mine. I had gone through so many terrible things lately, feeling something that nice was almost overwhelming. Her skin was so soft and warm, and she smelled like fruit thanks to our wonderful dinner. I wanted to give in, and kiss her, but I couldn't betray Star like that.

Callie must have sensed my discomfort and loosened her grip. She may have been hoping that I would seek comfort in her touch. She may also have just been looking for some sense of comfort and normality for herself. We had both been through so much.

"Trianna. I hope that one day I can find love like what you have for her. When we are free of this hell, I truly hope to find something like that." Callie said softly, her voice trailing off as she fell asleep.

"I hope you do too." I whispered. I lay awake for a little while longer, relishing the comfort of being held and thinking of Star. Nothing would stop me from having her again. Not a damn thing.

CHAPTER 13

Morning came and somehow, despite being in a hut in the middle of the woods, surrounded by trees, a beam of sunlight still managed to catch me dead in the face. I sat up for a stretch. The bed had been incredibly comfortable for something hobbled together out of leaves, furs, and sticks. When I managed to pry my eye open, I noticed Callie doing some yoga on the other side of the room, wearing only her shirt and panties.

I yawned and rubbed at my eyes to distract myself from the view, but it didn't help. I bit my lip, swearing under my breath. She stretched with purpose, bending her body in ways that would probably snap my spine if I attempted to imitate. I couldn't help but notice the ways her body curved as she moved.

Callie was beautiful, there was no doubt about that. Her frame was curvy, bullshit fashion magazines would probably call her fat. She held it well, thick in all the right places. She reminded me of old baroque paintings, all pale skin and curves.

"Good morning!" She said, bending into downward dog and pushing her ass into the air in front of me.

"Good morning indeed." I replied, trying desperately to avert my gaze.

"Cotton stopped by a bit ago, he had some clothing and bathing water for us." She gestured as she changed positions again.

I walked over to the table by the door and inspected the pile of clothing. They were all hand stitched leathers lined with fur like what the others had been wearing. I was impressed with the quality of the garments. They seemed durable, whoever made them had spent time on the seams to be sure of that.

I took the bowl of warm water over to the bed to get away from the loosely grass-covered door. I removed my dirty and tattered training Gi that I had found in the compound when I escaped. A slight breeze reminded me that I was wearing nothing beneath it. I tossed the smelly clothing over by the door.

In the bowl of water was a sponge, so I began to wipe the blood and dirt from my body. The warm water felt nice as I scrubbed away the filth. The tattoos on my head and neck were still tender, but I gently wiped at them to try and keep them clean. After a few moments, I felt I was as clean as I was going to be without a proper shower and returned the sponge to the bowl.

I picked up the hide tunic and slid into it. The fit was surprisingly close, whoever these had been made for originally must have had a similar build to mine. Same for the pants, with a little squeezing here and there. They were rather comfy to not be tailored, something I had begun growing used to. Over the hides, I slid into the leather armor.

It was thicker, and a little loose fitting, but had straps to tighten it into place. It was decorated with bits of twine, colored beads, and shells. The shoulders had pads, and there were even some bracers to cover my forearms. The leather boots didn't quite fit right but that was my luck with shoes anyway. I used the belt from the training Gi as a makeshift headband to pull my red hair up out of my face.

"You look rather fierce!" Callie stated. She had started to put on her armor over her shirt and scrub pants that she had thankfully put back on.

"Can you help me get this stuff on? I have no idea what I'm doing." she asked, holding up the straps to the leathers.

"Sure thing, it's not that different from a corset." I said, working the straps into place behind her back.

"Oh, I don't think I've ever worn one of those." She sputtered as I tightened everything. "A little hard to breath... is that normal?"

"You get used to it. Here, these go on your arms like this." I said, showing her how to fasten the bracers.

I had spent some time attempting to learn archery after watching the Hunger Games movies and had a pair of black leather bracers of my own at home. I had a leather corset too, but that inspiration came from an entirely different movie.

"Are you sure you want to go back there with me?" I asked, adjusting a strap on her leg guard.

"Yes." She replied quickly, "I want vengeance for how they broke my memories, and I want to stop them from doing this to anyone else."

"I've been wondering about that." I said, making a few adjustments to my armor.

"Why does he need all these drones? Is he trying to build an actual army? To what end?" I asked.

"I'm not sure, but he has a lot of them. I heard him mentioning that his other compounds were staffed by the drones as well. Seems odd to have a bunch of people that can wield magic just sweeping floors and running a couple labs." She replied, tying her hair back.

I remembered seeing the sign labelled 'Facility 7' when looking for Star. It didn't occur to me then that might mean he had multiple labs located elsewhere.

"How many facilities does he have?" I asked.

"Well, his main research lab is this one here at Facility seven, so I'd say he has at least that many, but I don't know for certain. He travels a lot to find recruits and funding. For all I know there could be hundreds." She replied, her eyes a little distant with thought.

"I hope not." I replied, placing my hand on her shoulder to bring her back. "If we can stop him here, maybe the others will just shut down. 'Cut off the head and the snake withers' or something."

"He's definitely a snake in need of decapitation." Callie replied bluntly, and I couldn't help but chuckle.

"I wonder if there is a way to save the people he's transformed." She added, "We may have to kill some to get to him, he has several that are intensely loyal to him. When this is over though, I hope we can do something for them."

"We can try. Maybe Cherry pulling the shit out of them can help them feel normal again." I replied, "We'll have to figure that out when that time comes though. For now, we need to focus on stopping Bach and Khan, and saving Star."

Callie nodded and looked into my eyes, brushing my face with her hand. It felt like she wanted more from me, but we were interrupted by a knock from the door of the hut. I headed outside to check, and Callie followed. Outside Cotton stood waiting for us.

"I figured Daisy's armor might fit you, Trianna. I haven't seen it on anyone since before Cherry was born." His voice was a little somber.

"I'm sorry for your loss Cotton." I replied glancing down at the clothing.

"I thank you, but today is not a day for grief. Today is a day for vengeance!" He clenched his fist excitedly. "Come, we must begin preparations. Devon has already begun formulating a plan of attack." He motioned towards the village.

As we left the hut and approached the village proper, I noticed everyone seemed to be focused on a variety of tasks. Some were preparing food, while others prepared weapons, reinforcing staves and spears with thick vines or fletching new arrows. Clearly, they had been busy this morning.

We followed Cotton to the main hut where we were again met with a table full of food. Fruits and breads and eggs piled in the middle waiting to be consumed.

"Napoleon once said 'An army marches on its stomach'" Devon said, gesturing to the food as we approached. "We must get our strength up if we are to assault a compound, and that begins with a hearty meal."

I got the impression that Devon loved to play host before everything with Bach happened. They seemed so inclined to present food and hospitality. With everything going on, it was a bit comforting. It reminded me of growing up in the south.

I had an aunt that never married or had kids of her own, but she threw the best gatherings throughout the year. She loved to play hostess and was always on top of everything: food, drinks, comfort, stimulating conversation. It was like an art form to her, and she was a master. I got much the same impression from Devon.

We sat down and piled up our servings. Everything tasted so delicious, it was hard to believe it was cooked in a shack in the middle of the woods. We ate and chatted much about nothing, which was a good mental preparation for the rest of the day. Cotton and his hunters, with little Cherry in tow, joined us a short time later. They too feasted heartily on the banquet before them.

The day was simple, Devon laid out a basic plan for us to just spend the day training in the courtyard until dinner where we would reconvene over a good meal and discuss how to go about attacking the compound. If it were up to me, I would have just rushed in after breakfast, but I've always been a bit headstrong and reckless. Star deserved the best attempt possible, and that meant taking things slower and with some focus.

I glanced around at the others at the table, making mental notes of everyone as we conversed. There was of course Cotton, tall and dark-haired, buff but not ripped. To his left was Holly, a blonde bombshell in a more literal sense, she was easily the most muscular person in the group. Her hair was cropped short showing off a few more tattoo designs than the ritual symbols we all had. She looked like she would rip a bear in half if it looked at her wrong, so I didn't stare.

To Cotton's right was Twig. He was lanky and seemed mostly skin and bone, so the name fit. He was shaved bald on top but had a scruffy red beard on his chin. His eyes were always sharp and focused, I had seen him carrying a bow before. With eyes like that he was likely a good shot.

Continuing to the right sat a short stout woman with a pleasantly round face. Her name was Lemon, and she was anything but sour. Her smile was sweet, and the freckles across her light brown skin were just delightful. Her eyes were big and brown, and she seemed to always be laughing or telling a joke. Her curly brown hair was braided and beaded in some places but mostly hung to her shoulders. She spun a small stick around her fingers while she talked.

Then there was Azalea. She stood about the same height as Cotton, and much the same build. Her pale skin was littered with freckles of various sizes, and her green eyes pleasantly accompanied her fiery red hair. She sliced and ate her fruit with a very sharp looking stone knife. She had several more on a leather strip across her chest. It was easy to deduce her specialty.

Next to Azalea, and currently engaged in a chugging match with Lemon, was a rather brawny bearded man named Birch. He looked to be Samoan, and his bulky arms were covered in islander styled tattoos. He reminded me a bit of Jason Momoa in Aquaman. Lemon beat him to slamming down her empty cup on the table by just a few seconds, and he roared with a playful fury wiping liquid from his beard.

They made for a lively group, and certainly seemed skilled at hunting. I hoped that was enough to take on Bach's army of magic flinging drones. These people had all given up their magic for a sense of normality, and I wondered if that would put them at a disadvantage. Though, the drones did fail at keeping Callie and myself from escaping, so it was hard to say. We might just pull this off.

After we all finished eating, Cotton led us all outside where some of the other villagers had set up some rudimentary training dummies for us to practice on. It was clear Cotton wanted his team to show off a bit for us, so we all gathered around the first dummy. The team's weapons had been laid out nearby and everyone was making their respective choices. There were some other weapons present as well, and Cotton indicated those were for us if we wanted to try using them.

Cotton picked up his spear and stepped up to the first dummy. He dropped into a crouch drawing the spear close to his body and pointing the tip towards the head of his target. With a few rapid movements he stabbed through the chest of the dummy several times, spun the spear around lopping off an arm and then finished with a flourish, ramming the tip of the spear through the head as all the straw fell out of the body. Cherry clapped excitedly for her father's performance.

Cotton motioned to Holly, who I was surprised to see was stringing a bow. The bow looked rather thick, and her muscles held taught as she seemingly struggled to bend it down to catch the string. Given her size, the draw strength of the bow had to be immense. Without moving to line up the shot, she knocked an arrow and let it fly with some impressive speed. The arrow struck the head of the dummy before I could turn my head back around to see it. The force ripped the sack of leaves and hay off the body, pinning it to the hut several yards behind the dummy.

Twig was already moving beside her, bow in hand as well. She sniffed her approval of her shot, and Twig gave her a friendly butt bump as he quickly knocked an arrow as well. He fired and knocked a second arrow, firing it just as quickly. The second arrow pierced the dummy's chest around where the heart would be, the first split the shaft of Holly's arrow. Lemon guffawed; Callie clapped along with Cherry. That was some intense accuracy, but I kind of expected it from him.

Lemon pushed her way through the group and stood before the next dummy. She held a staff over her shoulders rather casually. When she stopped smiling though, her eyes focused and she began to spin the staff around her with impressive speed. She advanced on the dummy, striking it in various places with loud cracks as each hit connected. There was force and precision behind each blow, and the dummy bled straw and feathers from the abuse. With one final thrust to the chest she stopped, returning the staff to her shoulders and sticking her tongue out at Cherry who giggled in response.

Birch stepped up to the next dummy and stared it down for a moment. He held a net in one hand, and a short spear in the other.

"This is a lot more fun when they move..." He said pointing his spear at the stationary target. Cotton rolled his eyes, and Birch shrugged. He tossed the net over the dummy, stepped up, stabbed it through the head and then with one swift kick, broke the stand in half and pinned the dummy to the ground. He dusted his hand off and turned to Azalea who had been mostly uninterested throughout the showings.

"You gonna brood, or warm up?" He asked.

She replied with a 'tsk' and pulled a few daggers from her belt. She waved her arm in one swift motion and impaled the standing dummies with a knife to the chest. She rushed at one last target, throwing another knife as she ran, and as it struck the dummy in the head, she leapt up into a flying kick that drove the stone blade deep into the target. She smirked at Birch as she retrieved the daggers.

"Well, as you can see, we all have honed some skills surviving out here." Cotton said, breaking the tension.

"Without our magic from the treatment, we have had to adapt. Wild boars are dangerous, so we practice a lot." He gestured to a ragged scar on his leg that I gathered came from the tusk of a boar.

"You two still have your magic, so you likely won't need to use any of our primitive weaponry, but we can help teach you if you'd like." Birch added.

Callie picked up a small axe from the table and looked at it curiously. She ran a finger across the stone head of the axe as she pondered.

"It's small, but that makes it good for throwing." Azalea pointed out.

"We all carry one as a survival tool as well." Cotton added.

Callie nodded and stepped up to one of the dummies and held the axe in front of her. She drew her arm back and then flung it forward. Her form was lacking in finesse, and the axe simply tumbled to the ground a few feet away from her.

Azalea retrieved it and brought it back to her. Callie frowned as she took it from her.

"I've never thrown an axe before, but I suspected I could do better than that." Callie said.

"It's all in the wrist, like this." Azalea showed her a better place to grip the axe and made motions with her wrist to show how to release it when thrown. She adjusted

Callie's stance to help her line up the throw and urged her to try again.

Callie stared down at the target once more. She moved her arm back and forth a few times, tracing the arc Azalea had shown her, and then her eyes widened with sudden realization.

"This axe is made of stone, yes?" She asked.

Azalea nodded, "I make them myself from hard stones near the river."

Callie grinned and turned back to her target. She drew her arm back and then chucked the axe with much more force than before. It spun as it flew and passed right by the dummy.

"That was much better..." Azalea started.

"I'm not done" Callie replied and gestured with her hand. The axe came flying back towards the dummy and embedded itself in the wooden stand. Callie cheered, and the group clapped.

"Well, that's one way to do it, I suppose." Twig chimed in.

"What about you, Trianna?" Cotton asked gesturing towards the table.

I gazed over the weapons and considered trying a bow. I remembered the bow I had bought with my leather armbands after watching the Hunger Games and how poorly that had ended. I rubbed my wrist remembering nearly fracturing it and decided against it.

"I think I'm good." I said.

I raised a hand towards the last target dummy. My hair fluttered as a wave of hot air swirled around me. Blue flames appeared swirling down my arm shortly after I raised it, aiming at the dummy. The flames pooled at my hand into a massive ball that shot forward and incinerated the dummy, reducing it to a charred mass in seconds.

The group took a step back, with a look of shock on their faces.

"Blue fire.... Now that's something." Lemon muttered, breaking the silence.

I turned to face them and noticed Devon had stepped out of the main hall to watch. They smiled at me and nodded before returning inside. Cherry tilted her head and raised her palm before her and summoned a small ball of fire. The flames were red and orange, much like a campfire and she turned a face at it. She waved it away and tried again to no avail.

"I think she's jealous that your fire is blue." Cotton added.

"Yeah, Bach and Khan both mentioned that was unique. Any ideas what it means?" I asked.

"The treatment affects everyone differently, there must be something unique about how your body reacted to it." Callie said.

"It certainly seems more powerful as well." Azalea added. "I used flames myself, and never managed anything that destructive."

"Sometimes when I summon the fire, I feel like I'm not alone in my head. As if there's something... deeper within me giving it more power." I said leaning against the table and staring off into the distance.

"Well as long as you can maintain control of it, seems it's useful for now. After we save your friend, Cherry can pull it out of you if you want." Cotton rested a hand on my shoulder to get my attention.

"I'll think about it. Honestly, it's still pretty fun, even if it might be demon juice." I said with a grin.

"Well, we've stood around showing off long enough, let's get some work in today so we are ready to

strike back at the assholes that left us out here to die."
Cotton turned back to the group as he spoke.

"Let's get a run in for starters, and then we'll do some sparring." And with that, he and the group took off.

"Well, they are certainly ready for action." Callie said watching them go, "Want to join them?"

I shrugged, "I suppose some cardio would be good."

We followed the group, making laps around the village for a while. Their stamina was impressive, never pausing or slowing as they did lap after lap. After fifteen minutes or so they began pulling far ahead of us, and after thirty they were passing us. After an hour I felt like I was going to burst and collapsed in a pile against our hut.

Callie, who had slowed to a light jog a while back, gave in and joined me as well. She handed me a waterskin that she had gotten from Cotton earlier. We sat for a while, panting and drinking water as we watched the others continue to hold a strong pace around the camp.

They had much more practice at this, and it showed. Their grouping had split up though, with Cotton and Holly leading, and Birch and Lemon falling behind. I noticed Twig had stayed mostly in the middle of the pack, but also seemed far less exhausted than the others. After another half hour or so, they all joined us on the ground chugging water from their own waterskins.

After we had all caught our breath, Birch handed out some jerky for us to snack on and regain some energy. The group quickly munched it down and got up to go spar. I was impressed with their focus but found myself too worn out to engage in any further activities just yet. Callie seemed to share this sentiment, laying back on the ground to stare at the sky.

"We certainly found some serious people to help out." She said stretching.

I nodded. "Yeah, I hope it's enough. I can't let Star be Bach and Khan's play thing for much longer. It's killing me thinking about what they might be doing to her." I sighed flopping down beside her.

"We'll save her. I know we will." Callie assured me.

I just lay there in silence watching the clouds pass by. I appreciated her optimism, but that was rarely a trait I shared. I wasn't sure that we'd make it back inside if we had a hundred of these skilled hunters. It was hard to guess how we would manage without knowing just how many drones Bach had to throw at us.

I could hear the grunts and growls of the group as they tussled with each other in the center of the village. My focus was fading though, I was more worn out from the run than I realized. As I watched the clouds drift overhead, I felt myself starting to doze off. I could hear Lemon mocking Birch about something and laughing as she dodged his attacks.

There was an air of companionship in this village to be sure. Callie scooted closer and rested her head on my chest. I enjoyed her presence, but as we grew closer, it made my heart hurt. I had always had a big heart, sharing love with my close friends when I could.

However, I could tell that I was growing stronger feelings for Callie, and it pained me. I felt guilty at just the idea of feeling this way for someone other than Star. We're engaged! It felt like I was betraying her, having only lost her for a short time.

I told myself it was only because I needed something to cling on to help get through the trauma. It's a natural reaction to seek comfort, to seek safety. Growing up abused, I often found myself latching onto others for support. I reminded myself that while those often turned into relationships, they all failed. My love for Star was different, it wasn't just a coping mechanism. It was real.

Sometime later I was awoken by a foot poking at my ribs. I winced at the brightness of the sun as I tried to open my eyes. Cherry stood over me, beaming her trademark grin and motioned towards the hut. I gathered she was telling me that it was time for dinner. I must have been asleep for a while.

I roused Callie as I sat up and she wiped a bit of drool from her chin. I could see the others filing into the hut as I stood up and then felt my stomach rumbling. Food was sounding better by the second. I took Cherry's hand and we walked together to Devon's hut.

Inside there was, of course, plenty of food. Smoked fish, roast boar, fruits and vegetables, bottles of water, cider, and mead. It was impressive to see how much food this small group could manage to provide while living out here in the woods. I gathered up a small helping of everything and took my seat.

Devon sat down at the head of the table and smiled to greet us. I could tell the others were eager to discuss the plan of attack, but Devon insisted on waiting until we finished our meal. Over dinner we shared small talk, Callie and I received quite a bit of ribbing about falling asleep after the run, missing out on the sparring matches. Birch had a split eyebrow that apparently Lemon gave him during their bout.

"Should've moved quicker, ya oaf!" She goaded.

"Yeah, I'll remember that next time. Maybe I'll leave the tip on my spear." He grumbled as she chucked some berries at him leaving a purple juice stain across his cheek.

CHAPTER 14

After dinner, Devon stood to gather everyone's attention. They were ready to begin covering the plan of attack. We didn't get very far before we were interrupted by a loud explosion in the distance. Several minutes later, a young man entered the dining hall, his face painted with exertion. He took a moment to catch his breath and then spoke.

"There's something going on at the compound. There was an explosion, and then they brought a big tank of red liquid out on the lawn. It has someone inside of it. There are some drones guarding it." He explained through heavy breaths.

"An interesting development." Devon responded.

"It sounds like a trap." Azalea added, spinning one of her daggers in her fingers.

"They had Star in a tank like that before, it could be her!" I blurted. Panic was setting in at the idea they were trying to soak more of the Opulentia into her.

I stood up from the table and headed for the door, Callie quickly caught my wrist to stop me.

"You can't just go charging out there alone! What about our plans?" she asked.

"I'm going now, if anyone cares to join me, we can ambush them as the sun goes down. I need to see if they have Star in that tank!" I said, wrenching my wrist free of her grasp.

"If it is Star, then this is certainly a trap." Lemon added. "Rushing in would be reckless, but a little reconnaissance couldn't hurt."

Devon nodded, "You all go check it out. If it is Star, we may be able to save her if we can get the drop on them. If its someone else, perhaps we can save them, add to our ranks."

Everyone nodded in agreement and stood to join me at the doorway. I looked them over and nodded as well. They were right, I needed the help if I was going to get Star back from this. They all gathered their weapons and waited for us by the edge of the wall.

"Patience, Trianna. We'll save her." Callie said as we walked over to join them.

"Every second she's with them claws at my heart. I have to get her back." I said cracking my knuckles. "Whatever it takes!"

Cherry came running out of one of the shacks nearby, carrying a dark waterskin over her head. She handed it to her father who opened it and gave her a puzzled look.

"Is this what I think it is, Cherry?" he asked, kneeling beside her.

Cherry nodded with a concerned look on her face as he attached it to his pack.

"I'll use it only as a last resort. Hopefully I won't need it." He told her, patting her head which seemed to calm her some.

She turned to the wall and waved her hands, opening a small gap for us to exit through. I glanced at her, then Cotton, curious about what she had given him, but he didn't seem inclined to answer. The team filed out through the opening, and we made our way into the woods.

We moved quickly, leaping through brush and over fallen logs. Holly and Twig took up the lead, Twig watching for movement and Holly moving aside leaning tree trunks for a clearer path. Azalea and Birch brought up our rear watching for anyone trying to close in behind us. I imagined this was how they stalked game when they were hunting.

Callie stayed close to me, and I could see tense determination on her face. I was thankful for her support through all of this. I would probably be dead in the compound had she not saved me. Even though I felt like I owed her so much for that, here she was still by my side, ready to dive into battle with me to save the woman I loved.

I could tell Callie had grown feelings for me too, and it pained me to have to reject them. She was beautiful inside and out, and at another time in my life I gladly would've opened my heart to her, and probably my legs. I would never forgive myself if I cheated on Star though, especially while she was being used for some sick experiment that I roped her into. Still, Callie stuck by me, as supportive as ever.

It took some time to reach the edge of the woods, but we made it with some daylight to spare. We grouped in some bushes and crawled up to a small ridge to get a look at the compound. Twig moved over to a tree, so he could stand and peer out for a better look. He and Cotton exchanged a few hand gestures that I could only assume meant something to them. It just looked like some complicated shadow puppetry to me.

"There's six drones by the tank, and about ten more patrolling the field. There may be others hiding in the hedges, but it's hard to tell from here." He relayed to us.

"Twig is a great shot, but the moment we take down one, our position is compromised. So, we need to be ready to move."

"What if we take down all six at once?" Azalea asked glancing at Callie. Cotton looked puzzled, but Callie nodded.

"The arrow heads are made of stone." Callie chimed in, "If we can get six into the air, I can direct them all to hit at once. Azalea and I discussed the idea earlier."

Twig bobbed his head to signify he thought it would work. He readied a few arrows on his bowstring, and Holly drew hers to do the same.

"Alright, we may still have to deal with the others patrolling, but this should buy us enough time to get down to the tank and see who is inside." Cotton said.

"Callie, you get into position with Holly and Twig. Birch, you and Azalea keep watch up here, make sure we don't get flanked. Lemon, you and Trianna come with me, once those arrows hit, we rush the tank and figure out the next move."

We all nodded in agreement. Holly moved to a tree on the opposite side of the group, three arrows knocked and ready. Callie kneeled just out of sight on the edge of the ridge and nodded. Twig and Holly each stepped out from behind the tree, and let their arrows fly high into the air before ducking back behind the trees. Callie quickly traced the arrow paths in the sky, and then raised her hands as her eyes moved to the drones standing around the tank.

She brought her hands down, weaving the arrows through the air, and just like that, all six connected with their targets, and the bodies dropped to the ground. Cotton, Lemon, and I were already halfway down the hill as their bodies collapsed. I glanced back to see Twig and Holly taking up positions to guard us if anyone came our way, and Callie ducked back out of sight.

I met Cotton by the tank, and we wiped the condensation on the glass for a better view. I couldn't make out who was inside, the liquid was far too thick. There was a strange humming noise coming from inside.

"I can't see through this at all, we'll have to pull them out." Cotton said, and I nodded.

Lemon held her staff at the ready and scanned the area for anyone advancing on us as we lifted the lid off the tank. No sooner did we have it off when the liquid sprayed out of the tank and the glass shattered. I covered my face to protect it from the glass, and the liquid for that matter, and when I lowered my arms, I saw a figure floating in the air, liquid rolling down a barrier around it. The barrier dropped, and the figure stood before us. Khan laughed menacingly, it was a trap after all.

An arrow whizzed past me only seconds later, but Khan deflected it with a slight gust of wind. Another came shortly after, with much more force, and was thrust into the ground between us with a wave of Khan's hand. Cotton and Lemon reacted more quickly, each slamming their weapons forward, but Khan blew us all away from him with a massive gust of wind.

"You fools! I wondered why your bodies never turned up, you all have been scavenging in the woods all these years. Your primitive weapons will not aid you here, I am more powerful than you can imagine!" He bellowed as he summoned strong winds to push us further back.

He started to ramble something else, but it was cut short by a pillar of earth erupting beneath his feet, sending him backwards.

"Light him up, Trianna!" Callie bellowed.

Flames erupted around me as I raised my arms. I pulled my hands together to focus everything between them, forming a condensed ball of fire, and then thrust them forward sending a beam of fire rocketing towards Khan as he tried to regain his footing. He sidestepped the blast at the last second, the fire burning away his robes, leaving him standing in just his pants.

His body, like Devon's, was covered in occult tattoos. Patterns of dark symbols swirled across his torso, lined with the same symbols from my tattoos. He had perfected his techniques on himself it seemed. A few of them looked fresh, as if he had recently added them. He glared at me, an evil grin on his face.

Cotton and Lemon had regained ground and once again moved in with their weapons to attack. Khan made a quick gesture with his fingers, and Cotton was encased in a small whirlwind, his spear flying off into the distance. Lemon, however, managed to get in close enough to strike. Khan moved with great speed, his flowing hair and garments revealing he was using his powers to accelerate his movements.

Each time Lemon thrust or spun her staff at him, Khan was already moving out of the way or deflecting. With each strike he moved closer to her, lashing out with his feet or his palms to answer her attacks. He was skilled in martial arts and had learned to enhance his abilities with the powers from the Opulentia. Lemon was pacing him well, hardly reacting to any of the strikes he landed, and occasionally landing one of her own.

I heard commotion from the ridge and looked back to see Callie and the others fighting off some drones that had circled around us while we tangled with Khan. The team seemed to be handling themselves, but they were outnumbered. Holly slammed a drone into a tree, rendering them either dead or unconscious from sheer force, just as I turned back to deal with Khan.

Khan managed to trip Lemon up, and as she stumbled backwards, he gestured with his hands and pulled all the air from her lungs. She gasped and gulped trying to breathe, but the wind was relentless as Khan drew her breath from her. I summoned flames around my arms and legs, giving me a bit of a forcefield to protect myself, and charged him.

My first punch landed, singing his face and beard and causing him to stagger back a few feet. I've had a hard life, I know how to throw a punch. Lemon fell to the ground, struggling to catch her breath, I would have to keep him off her for a bit before she could rejoin me. I spun around, following the force of my punch with an arcing kick, but Khan pushed me back with a burst of wind.

He had taught us some martial arts during our training, but I knew he strongly out matched me in that category. I regained footing, and once again charged fireballs from my fists, blasting beams of fire towards him. He countered with a wall of air but seemed to be struggling to hold it against the onslaught of my blue flames. I could see a dash of concern cross his face.

Using this to my advantage, I stepped forward, concentrating on the stream of flames pouring from my hands. I could hear that voice deep in the back of my mind beginning to murmur once more, and the beams grew larger and more ferocious. Fire arced up from my legs and back, flickering onto my arms and empowering the flames which seemed to completely engulf Khan. I continued to step towards him, roaring with rage and more and more fire bellowed out of me.

Suddenly, I lost my concentration and fell to the ground as something struck my knees from behind. A drone had crept up on us from behind me and knocked my feet out from under me with a sweep of their leg. I drew one arm up towards them and unleashed a torrent of flame that quickly consumed the drone. They didn't even have time to scream, as a moment later their charred remains collapsed to the ground.

Khan was on top of me quickly after that, slamming a knee into my ribcage before I could regain my footing. I tumbled across the ground, and he struck me again across the face with a kick that sent me reeling. I managed to get my arms up in time to block a third strike, but the force behind it nearly shattered one of my forearms. He stomped my stomach with his heel and knocked the wind out of me as I collapsed fully onto the ground.

I glanced around, Lemon and Cotton both were held, suspended in Khan's whirlwinds. The group had come down from the tree line, but they too were trapped by miniature tornadoes whipping at their flesh with debris. I couldn't fathom how he managed to do so much at once while still beating me to a pulp with his bare hands. He loomed over me, and a wicked grin washed over his face.

"You see? Your power may be strong, but it is raw. Mine is practiced, honed to perfection by years of training. I cannot be beaten by the likes of you and your band of misfits and rejects. I will rip the air from their lungs until

they drown in their own saliva trying to breathe. I will----"
His villainous rant was cut short.

I had barely heard the movement over his voice, just seconds before the blade emerged from his throat. Blood poured down his chest as the blade retreated, Khan dropped to his knees and then collapsed face down between my ankles. Behind him stood Devon, a calm ferocity in their eyes. They wiped the blood from the knife and sheathed it back inside their robe.

"That was a long time coming, old friend." Devon uttered, glaring at Khan's corpse.

With Khan dead, the whirlwinds ended, Cotton and the others rushed over to join us as Devon helped me to my feet.

"Everything was clearly a trap, so I decided to follow after you all in case something like this happened." Devon said brushing some dirt from my face.

"Thank you. I was sure he was going to kill us all there for a minute. I wasn't sure what to do about it though." I said clenching my ribs.

It was likely that at least one of them was broken, but I would have to deal with that later. Birch handed out some spare waterskins and we took a moment to drink and catch our breath as we stared at the compound. Surprisingly, no more drones had come pouring out to attack us. Bach must have assumed Khan's plan would work. It almost had, but we came out alive and thirsty for revenge.

Devon turned back to return to the village after we decided to continue into the compound to look for Star. Devon said they would begin preparations to heal whatever had been done to Star when we returned. Callie was tending to minor injuries on everyone from the scuffle. She tore off one of her pant legs and used it to bind my ribs for support under my armor. She tore pieces of the other pant leg to make small bandages for everyone's cuts and scrapes while Cotton devised a plan for the inside.

"Lemon, Twig, and Holly, you three clear out the floor we enter on and guard our exit. Anyone tries to come in or out, you lay them out."

"Birch, Azalea, you come with us to find Trianna's friend. We'll need Birch to carry her out, and Azalea's daggers give us something extra for Callie to use her magic on if we get in a bind. Azalea we may also need your stealth to scout things out as we move." Everyone nodded to Cotton in agreement.

"Trianna, do you have any idea where they might be keeping her?" Birch asked.

"When I found her the first time, she was in the lab soaking in a tank of Opulentia. If they are trying to run tests on her, she might be there again." I replied.

"It's as good a place to start as any." Cotton added and moved towards the door of the compound. "Do you remember how to get there?"

"I can get us there." Callie interjected. "I have most of the compound memorized from doing my rounds."

"Alright, you'll take point then once we get this area cleared inside. Let's move!" Cotton said, pulling open the door.

He waved his arm as he spoke, ushering the team in. I had expected an alarm system to go off once we entered the lobby, but everything remained silent. Only a single drone had been guarding the entrance, and Holly slammed him into the wall knocking him cold before he could do anything about it.

We circled the area making sure everything was clear, and Cotton signaled for the trio to get into position.

Lemon and Birch traded looks, as if telling one another not to get killed, but said nothing. Twig drew his bow and took up a position where he could watch the two connecting hallways as well as the entrance, while Holly and lemon moved into ambush locations near each hallway.

Callie pointed us in the direction of the east wing, and we headed off. We stayed close together, and moved quickly, rushing through the hallways in silence. Every corner we rounded, I expected to be cut off by Bach's drones, but the place seemed lifeless. It was disconcerting to say the least. Bach was clearly up to something.

We cleared more hallways and descended a few flights of stairs without ever encountering a single drone. No alarms, no visible cameras, not even any scurrying roaches. A long the way I noticed some signs of damage where Callie and I had passed through trying to escape. It felt odd retracing those steps to re-enter this terrible place.

Our surroundings had changed from the plush hotel like appearance of the main floor into drab white halls with florescent lighting that made the place resemble more of a hospital than a resort. We were likely getting close to the lab now, but still no sign of anyone trying to stop us. I was getting a terrible feeling in my gut about everything, and not just because of the pain in my ribs. That sort of sinking feeling you get when something terrible is about to happen, like when an elevator drops just a little too quickly and churns your insides.

We finally reached a set of large metal doors with a sign that read 'Laboratory' and Callie confirmed we had arrived. Birch stepped over to the door and began to pull it open. He looked inside for a moment, and then quickly shut the door again.

"We got a problem!" He shouted and pushed us all away from the door as it exploded open behind him.

Smoke billowed from the opening as the large metal door clamored to the ground. As I suspected, they were once again waiting for us. A few drones rushed out into the hallway then quickly dropped as Azalea flung her daggers into their foreheads with incredible precision.

"Behind!" She shouted.

Several more came flying into the hallway where we came from. Cotton and his team scrambled to take up positions against the encroaching forces. Callie and I peered into the lab to find it devoid of any more drones.

"We're going in, Cotton hold them off!" I shouted, rounding the corner into the lab.

I heard the group clashing with the drones shortly after, and Birch's booming laughter as he must have taken out a few. He seemed to love a good rumble. Inside the lab, Callie led me to a door in the back that led to more stairs.

"There are a few sub labs. It's more likely she's down there." She said, pointing.

I nodded and headed down the stairwell. As I rounded the first flight a ball of fire rushed up to meet me. I managed to bat it away with a flaming hand at the last second and looked down to see a set of drones coming up towards us.

"That all you got?!" I shouted, summoning balls of blue flames around my fists.

I leapt over the railing to the next landing and struck one of the drones with a flaming fist. The blow seared flesh and connected hard sending them cold to the floor. I blasted the second one with a beam of fire sending them tumbling down the stairwell burning. I was getting more confident in my ability to use these powers, I should have been scared by how it felt but at the moment, I relished it.

We burst into the sub lab, and sure enough found Star lying on a medical table. Several people in surgeon outfits stood around her in shock at our sudden arrival. Star was unconscious and hooked up to a few machines that I wasn't sure what purpose they served. The doctors didn't look like drones as far as I could tell. I guessed Bach kept some non-magical staff for certain things.

I walked over to the table, and one of the doctors reacted, grabbing a scalpel while lunging at me. I sidestepped and brought my fist up against his chin, laying him out on the floor as the others backed against the wall. Callie raised her stone axes at them to indicate they shouldn't try anything else. I looked over Star's naked body, there were some new tattoos down her sides, but it didn't seem they had begun cutting her up yet.

I ripped out the IVs and wheeled the table towards the doorway. I paused when I heard footsteps coming down the stairs above.

"Cotton? Birch? Azalea? That you?" I called

"Yeah, we cleared things upstairs. Did you find Star?" Birch answered rounding the flight of stairs only mildly winded.

"I got her right here, she's unconscious, we'll have to carry her out." I replied moving the table out into the hallway.

Callie kept her gaze focused on the doctors as she backed out to join us, and then pulled some of the cinderblocks from the wall to jam the doorway shut.

"I've got her, we should get going." Birch said, lifting Star onto his shoulders. "We heard some commotion higher up in the compound. The others might be dealing with some drones."

I nodded and quickly kissed Star on the cheek.

"We're getting you out of here baby, just hold on." I whispered in her ear.

We made our way back up the stairs and met Cotton and Azalea as we headed back to the main floor. My heart was melting to see Star again, but I had to stay focused, we weren't out of this yet.

As we entered the hallway towards the lobby, I saw Holly slamming a drone against the floor with another clutching at her back. I couldn't figure out why these drones would look at Holly and decide to try and fight her with their bare hands instead of using their magic, but they were learning that lesson the hard way. Cotton and Azalea rushed ahead to assist the others while Callie and I stayed back with Birch and Star.

The lobby was a warzone, bodies and furniture strewn everywhere. In the middle of it all Lemon stood, waylaying drones left and right with blows from her staff. These women were total badasses in combat, and it showed. Both continuously proved they were a force to be reckoned with.

Twig was propped up in the corner, clutching a wound on his side, but gave us a thumbs up as our gazes met. Cotton joined Lemon in clearing out the main floor of the lobby, while Holly and Azalea made a path for us around the edge of the room. Callie helped Twig to his feet, propping him up on her shoulder. With some effort we all pushed through, quickly dealing with the remaining drones, and made it back outside.

Cotton led the charge for the trees with Holly at his side, both ready to destroy anything in our path. Birch rushed behind them still carrying Star safely on his shoulders, and the rest of us piled in behind him. Night had fallen while we were inside, and the darkness provided us with some much-needed cover.

Or at least it did, until balls of fire came raining from the sky. I glanced up at the roof of the building to see Bach and a few drones launching a volley of fireballs at us from above. Callie and I both responded with attacks of our own. I sent up a beam of blue flame to incinerate a few drones, and Callie let her axes fly taking out two more. Bach leapt from the building sliding down a slanted rooftop and then using his fire to slow his descent of the next two stories.

We decided to keep going. If we could make it into the trees, we could lose him and set up and ambush. Cotton and the others had almost reached the tree line, Holly had a drone by the leg, dragging them through the dirt as she ran. She slammed him into a tree trunk and ushered Birch and Star past herself into the trees. Cotton was helping Twig and motioning for us to hurry.

Callie waved her arm pulling up a wall of dirt and rocks in front of Bach to slow him down and we made our break for the trees. As we made it to the tree line, I glanced back once more to see if he was catching up. He stood still between me and the compound, hand to his ear like he was listening to something. We locked eyes, and I felt the anger in his glare, but I could tell something was wrong.

Callie tugged at my arm, to try and hurry me along back to camp, but I stayed just long enough to watch Bach curse and return to the compound. He tossed a ball of fire over his shoulder towards us, and I batted it away to prevent it from setting fire to the trees. What could possibly be so important that he would just give up on us like that?

My brow furrowed in thought, and I turned to join the others heading back through the woods to the village.

"Something isn't right." I said to Callie as we ran. "Why didn't he come after us?"

"We can worry about that for later. For now, we need to get back to the camp and help Star. You got her back!" Callie replied, smiling happily at her words.

"Yeah, my guts are telling me this isn't over though." I said, still trying to think of what stopped Bach from chasing after us.

It would have been so easy to trap and kill him in the trees, so maybe that was part of it. Whoever was on that radio had stopped him dead in his tracks. With Khan dead, I was concerned over who else might have been talking to him. There was more going on in that compound than I was ready to admit, and I just knew I had to do something to stop it.

Callie was right though, for now I had to focus on Star. We had gotten her out of the compound, but after how she had looked before, I wasn't sure if she was still my Star. I was still worried that she wouldn't remember me, wouldn't remember us. That thought scared me just as much as it did to think that she would remember everything that happened, and that she might hate me for it.

CHAPTER 15

When we returned to the camp, Devon had the table in the main hall cleared off and coated with damp leaves for us to place Star on. Birch lowered her onto the table and Cherry entered with a few of the other villagers.

I watched as they began wrapping Star in what appeared to be seaweed and rubbing a mud-like paste onto the areas of her skin with no tattoos. I hadn't quite expected this much ritual to the process, but it had worked for the others, so I wasn't going to question it.

Cotton and the others had gone back to their huts to treat their wounds and recuperate, leaving Callie and I to watch over the process. Cotton mentioned he would set up a watch in the woods shortly once he got something to drink. I nodded, not looking away from Star. My mind was wracked with anxiety over what would happen when she woke up. They had sedated her for whatever procedure we interrupted, but I didn't know how long that would last.

The girls continued to wrap Star in the seaweed while Cherry walked around the table, locating all the tattoos she would be working on. She was young but was taking the whole process very seriously. After a few more minutes they finished wrapping the leaves around Star's body and stepped back so that Cherry could begin her work. Devon was busy cooking up something at the far end of the hall for when Cherry was finished.

Cherry rubbed her hands together in a bowl of water to cleanse them and then positioned herself near Star's head to begin the extraction. She held her palms up to the first tattoo and a look of focus washed over her face. She moved her fingers ever so slightly, and after a moment I noticed the red liquid starting to draw to the surface and drip onto the leaves coating the table. I watched in helpless anticipation as more and more of the liquid came oozing out of the symbols as Cherry slowly worked her way down the design stretching down Star's head and neck.

So much of the Opulentia was pooling on the table as Cherry moved to the other side of Star's head. I felt gross thinking about what that really was and just how much Star had inside of her. It seemed like far more was coming out than would have possibly been in the design of these tattoos. It was even running onto the floor by that point.

The hairs on my arm stood on end and at first, I thought it was only goosebumps from my nerves being frazzled over the procedure. It was only when I noticed Callie and Cherry's hair starting to stand up that I knew something was amiss. Just then, Star's eyes blasted open revealing a torrent of energy arcing through them. One of the girls that had helped wrap her body screamed, and Star's head snapped toward her, her face twisted with rage.

She opened her mouth and screamed with fury, bolts of lightning surged from within her and struck the poor girl before she could react. She convulsed and collapsed to the floor; I wasn't sure if she was still breathing. Callie dove to protect Cherry, and the other girls fled. I grabbed Star by the shoulders trying to get her attention.

"Star! Star! Baby it's me! You've got to relax! We're trying to help!" I shouted, trying to be heard over her guttural cries of rage.

She screamed blood-curdling cries and thrashed about on the table, fighting loose from my grip. Bolts of energy arced around the room but given most of it was made of wood and dirt, it caused little damage. I could feel my nerves tightening and my muscles clenching as small arcs of energy contacted my skin. It was getting hard to stand as the torrent of energy raged from Star's body.

She was breaking free of the wrappings now, the leaves curling and cooking from the electricity surging through their moisture. It smelled a bit like cooking fish. Her body rose from the table, suspended by a field of static as bolts of energy coursed around her body. I stepped forward, trying to reach her to bring her back down, but she screamed again, energy flying from her in all directions.

She lunged at me, energy lashing out at me and tickling my nerve endings as she tried to strike me with her fists. I was faster than she was, quickly moving from side to side, dodging her blows, but with each passing movement, lightning jumped to my body, sending my muscles into spasms and making the next dodge that much more difficult. Out of sheer reflex I summoned flames to surround me, which surprisingly caused her to fall back some. I tried to take advantage of this pause and move towards her, but she answered with more screaming and floated back into the air.

Tendrils of energy emerged from her back and clutched the ceiling like spider's legs holding her above my head. She clenched her fists and a ball of swirling energy started to form between them.

"Star... don't make me do this!" I yelled, "I don't want to hurt you!"

I could barely hear my own voice over the crackling of energies she was generating. Frowning, I summoned a ball of flame in my hands to try and deflect her attack. I noticed something strange, however, the edges of the flames seemed to be drawing towards Star's field of current. I hadn't paid enough attention in science class to realize what that might mean and continued to draw flames together. I raised my hand to launch my attack, and suddenly my vision flashed white and my whole body convulsed as it dropped to the floor.

If I hadn't slept through class frequently, I may have learned that fire contains ion gases, and that those gases can conduct electricity. When I raised my ball of fire, all of Star's electric current grabbed ahold of those ions and completed a circuit to the ground, effectively using me like a lightning rod. It would have been nice to know such things ahead of time, but I was never one for doing my homework.

When I opened my eyes, Star was standing over me on the ground. She reached out and grabbed me by the throat, the static force lifting me off the ground as energy surged through me. My eyelids and lips spasmed and my body convulsed. Colors arced through my vision and breathing was difficult. She was going to fry me inside and out if I couldn't get through to her.

With some hesitation I summoned some flames around me which distracted her but did not loosen her grip much. It gave her enough pause for me to try to speak some sense to her.

"Star listen to me. It's me! Trianna! I love you so much, please don't do this." I stuttered.

I fought against the pain and muscle spasms, trying to force my words out loud enough for her to hear me. Star turned to face me, tilting her head and I could see some consideration behind the energy swirling in her eyes. She started to release her grip listening to my voice. The muscle spasms began to ease up, and I could think more clearly.

"Remember... remember the first time we met. You nearly hit me with that stupid scooter of yours as I was coming out of a coffee shop." I stammered.

"You stopped to apologize and insisted that you buy me a cup of coffee to make up for it, despite the fact I already had several cups. I was so jittery through the rest of the afternoon hanging out with you around town."

"We went to the Grove Arcade, and you showed me all those pretty rock necklaces your friend was selling…"

Her brow furrowed in thought, and she tilted her head the other direction as she considered my words.

I continued to spout out important dates and events as they came to mind, our first kiss, the first time we had sex, the conversations about our families, the painful conversations about my childhood and the trauma it caused me. I could feel the energy surge slowing down and my muscles were starting to relax.

I brought up our nights drinking and playing video games together, the day she found our kitty Echo and brought her to my place because she had nowhere else to take her. I barraged her with all the beautiful memories I had of us, and each one brought me closer to the ground.

Callie huddled against the wall shielding Cherry from the bolts of energy still arcing through the room from time to time. Lemon and Birch had come to help, but Devon waved them back. They could tell I was gaining control of the situation.

"Star you have to remember me, remember us. Remember the night I asked you to move in with me? How nervous I was? How great the sex was? Do you remember?"

I was standing on the ground again, and Star's hand was slowly letting loose of my neck. I could see tears forming in her eyes, even they had sparks of energy in them.

"Remember when I asked you to marry me? How I completely fumbled and forgot everything I wanted to say? I nearly dropped the fucking ring I was so nervous that you'd say no, but damnit you didn't! You cried and said yes and knocked me down in the middle of the restaurant, pouncing on top of me in front of everyone. Do you remember?"

She let go of my neck and wiped away a tear. I used this break of concentration to my advantage and rushed at her. I swung my arms around her tightly, pushing her lips against mine in the most passionate kiss I think I've ever given anyone. She panicked at first, and I felt the charge of electricity surging through us for a moment, but then as quickly as it all began, it ended.

She stopped glowing with energy, her eyes returned to normal, though red and streaming tears as she returned my embrace. We stood there for several minutes locked together, both weeping out our frustrations and sharing our joy to be reunited through our kiss. She squeezed me tightly as she cried, and when our lips finally separated, I heard her whisper

"Oh, pookie..."

I couldn't hold in the chuckle; I was so relieved to hear her voice say that pet name again. I felt like the weight of the world was lifted from my shoulders and I picked her up and spun her around, both of us still gently sobbing.

Callie came over and placed her hand on my shoulder to bring me back to reality. I pulled her into our embrace without thinking. I wouldn't have managed this without her help, she deserved to share in the moment. We let go and Star sat down on the edge of the table.

"Oh, pookie. It was terrible, one minute we were getting ready for training with Khan, and then everything went black. I woke up with people poking and prodding me everywhere, and then I just remember being hurt and angry... everything is fuzzy after that."

I nodded at her and kissed her forehead.

"I know babe, I know. The same thing happened to me. We have been trying to save you and we finally did it." I said reassuringly.

"Why... why am I naked and covered with a sticky paste?" She asked looking down at her body.

"Well, that's a bit of a long story." I said.

I pulled up a chair to sit with her while I attempted to explain everything that had happened since we blacked out. I made sure to tell her everything I could remember, as well as what Devon and the others had told us.

"So, they were just using us as guinea pigs for this sick twisted experiment the whole time? Trying to make us into those drone things that brought us here. Fucking twisted..." Star said after I finished recounting.

I nodded. It was a lot to take in, but I had spared no detail. Star deserved to know everything she had missed. She took the information better than I expected, especially about the source of the Opulentia. She always was into the morbid details of stories, not letting any of it really bother her.

I explained to her what Cherry had been doing when she came to, hoping she would let them finish. She was surprisingly hesitant, but eventually agreed. The girls came back and wrapped her in more seaweed again. Thankfully the one Star attacked was not dead or seriously injured.

I decided to step outside and get some fresh air while everyone mostly returned to what they were doing before things went sideways. Callie joined me outside, sitting down beside me as I leaned back against the wall of the hut.

"That was brave of you back there." She said, "All I could do was huddle in the corner, but you risked everything to get through to her."

"I love her more than anything. She helped me get over terrible things in my past and helped me find a way to live my life again. Without her I have nothing left to lose." I said, staring up at the stars.

"I'm happy for you. Love is such a beautiful thing. I'm glad you have someone to share it with."

I could hear a sadness in her voice as she spoke. I glanced over at her and saw that her eyes were watering.

"All those wonderful memories you have, all those magical moments you shared with her to bring her back. I wish I could remember moments like that with someone. I wish I could remember anything before I was taken." she said, pressing her face into her arms to cry.

I pulled her close to me and held her while she let it out. Sometimes you need to cry to work through things. She certainly had plenty to cry about. I couldn't imagine how hard it must be to not remember much of her life or those she loved.

I felt guilty for her hearing me say those things to Star. It was necessary, but I felt bad for Callie. I held her a little tighter.

"Maybe one day your full memory will return." I said wiping some tears from her cheek.

"Don't do that." She said. "Don't give me false hope. I am sad to have lost that, but I can't dwell on it." She sniffled.

She raised a hand to wipe tears from her face, even managing to smile at me.

"I am making new memories now, beautiful memories with you." She laughed a little, giving me a light kiss on the cheek. "I am happy to have become your friend!"

"I'm happy too, you've done so much for me. I don't think I can ever repay you for it." I said, leaning my head against hers affectionately.

"Just be my friend and help me make memories. That will be enough." she said, looking into my eyes.

"I can manage that, I think." I smiled back at her.

Devon came out of the hut with a look of concern.

"There's a bit of a complication. You should come back inside." Devon said quickly.

I rushed back in to see Cherry still drawing Opulentia from Star, it was coating nearly the whole table, and pooling on the floor. Star was starting to look a little gaunt in the face. Cherry stopped and panted, shaking her head.

"I think something has changed in Star's genetic makeup. I think her blood has become infused with the Opulentia. This may be why they mentioned replacing their source with her." Devon said.

"So, she's going to be like this forever?" I asked.

"It would seem so, unless Sebastian has some way of reversing the process in his lab, but I doubt such a thought ever crossed his mind." Devon replied.

Cherry walked around the table examining the tattoos and shook her head in disappointment. She glanced at Star's face also noticing how drained she looked. Cherry sighed and began working some of the fluid back into Star's body. I frowned, feeling defeated once more.

"It's okay. I don't mind it pookie." Star chimed in, smiling at me from the table.

"It's not okay, I never should have dragged you into this mess." I said sternly.

"You didn't! I made the choice, same as you. Hell, I probably coerced you into doing it because it sounded so cool." She replied.

"It's not your fault" I said, "I can make my own decisions."

"Then it's both our faults as poor decision-making adults." She retorted.

I couldn't help but smile. She knew how to work my mood. The color returned to her face as Cherry finished up. Star sat up peeling off the seaweed and drinking the strange smelling tea Devon had made for her. She turned a face at the taste, but finished it, nonetheless.

"I'm starving, is there anything to eat around here?" She asked setting the cup down. We all chuckled.

"I have some things laying around that should fill your stomach for now. I suggest we all get some rest, and we can meet back here in the morning for breakfast. It is getting rather late, and all this heroism is tiring." Devon said.

Devon rummaged through things on the table in the back, giving Star some bread and dried meat.

"Yes, sleep would be great." Callie added. I nodded in agreement and helped Star off the table.

"I'll see if we can round up some more clothes for your friend before breakfast." Devon said bidding us goodnight as we left her hut. We walked back to our little shack on the other side of the camp. Star was busying wiping the mud off her nude body but did not seem to care that she was naked. Lemon covered Birch's eyes and ushered him back inside her hut as we passed. I could hear him grumbling, and then Lemon chastising him physically. They made for quite the cute couple, I thought.

Back in our hut, someone had left us a fresh bowl of warm water and a sponge, and I helped Star get the rest of the mud off. Callie hesitated at the door, clearly unsure of what to do.

"You can come inside." Star said, "I'm not shy."

"Are you certain? I don't want to impose, and there's only one bed." Callie replied slowly stepping inside.

Star looked at the bed and pondered it for a minute.

"Looks big enough for all three of us, if we cuddle. What do you think Tri?" Star said playfully.

I shrugged and shook my head. "You like to roll around a lot, I'm not sure the bed even has enough room for just you."

"I can sleep on the floor, really I don't mind" Callie said blushing.

"No, we are just joking. Come on, get out of that stiff looking armor and get in this bed!" Star demanded.

Now that she was clean, Star was already curling up on one side of the bed. She gestured for us to join her, once she got comfortable. Callie disrobed as commanded, taking off the leather armor with much less effort than it took to get her into it. Without the armor she now only wore her T-shirt and panties, having used most of her pants for bandages earlier in the day.

I freed myself from the leather armor as well. I winced as pain answered many of my movements while undoing the straps. My ribs still ached, my body was bruised, and I could still feel traces of electricity moving through my muscular system. Callie had to help me undo some of the armor, and I decided it was too much effort to slip out of the hides for now.

We all collapsed into the bed, curling up with one another. We were all grateful for each other's company, simple bodily contact can soothe great levels of stress. We were all certainly stressed but began to relax easily enough as we cuddled on the bed. Only moments later sleep claimed all three of us.

CHAPTER 16

Under normal circumstances, waking to find myself
in bed with two beautiful women would be cause for
celebration. However, my dreams from the night before

had not left me quite in the mood for revelry. I had dreamt about being chased by Bach, over, and over again. Each time, he stopped in the field refusing to pursue me into the trees. A wicked smile across his face seemed to indicate he knew something I didn't.

He hadn't smiled last night when these events had occurred, but he didn't seem upset either. Something elsewhere was going on that he deemed more important than us. Even after we just stormed his compound, wiped out a decent number of his drone army, and reclaimed my fiancé that he wanted so badly for his experiments. That was rather unsettling, and I wasn't sure how to feel about it.

Bach's smug grin was not the most unsettling part of my dream though. Shortly before I awoke, my dreams went dark. It was deadly silent, and then a menacing laughter began, growing louder until it boomed like a cannon echoing through the Grand Canyon. Then, all I could see were the eyes of the dark figure from my previous nightmares. It filled my vision, like some macabre Hollywood close-up.

The figure was more intense than the previous dreams. His eyes looked like pooling lava, with only a single dense black spot in the middle. The eyes seemed like they knew me, which bothered me the most. Even after I awoke, I felt like I could hear faint echoes of his laughter in my head.

Callie, in only her panties and t-shirt, lay to my left, clenching me tightly in her sleep. Star to my right, still nude, had curled into a ball like she often does, with her ass planted firmly in my sore ribs. I had laid down in the hide clothing but removed them some point in the night due to the heat of the three of us all cuddled tightly together. I can't sleep when I get too hot, and I wondered how Callie managed to be so overdressed.

I started to move, but both women simultaneously grumbled. Callie gripped me tighter, and Star flopped around to clench me from the other direction. This put far too much pressure on my injured ribs, and I yelped out in pain despite myself. This warranted only a slightly different toned grumble from them. I sighed heavily.

Looking around the room I tried to formulate a way to rouse the sleeping beauties and free myself from their grip. My eyes settled on the bowl of water sitting on the table at the end of the bed. I felt a smirk stretch across my face, the muscles still lightly twitching. My height came in handy from time to time, my long legs allowed me a decent reach. I stretched out one leg to make sure I could reach the bowl. I only had to shimmy down the slightest amount to get my toes on the edge of the bowl.

Raising my foot into the air, I glanced at the girls. My plan was certainly mean, but playful by intent. I slammed my foot down, flipping the bowl and sending the water soaring into the air towards us. I took a moment to appreciate the way the light glimmered through the globules of water as they stretched and tumbled through the air. I was laughing before the water even hit us.

Callie and Star shrieked simultaneously. Having sat out for several hours, the water had gone quite cold, and it even shocked me despite knowing it was coming. Callie jumped out of the bed, falling onto her butt beside us. Star spasmed and then slapped me playfully.

"What the fuck Tri?!" She laughed. "You scared the shit out of me."

I couldn't' respond, too caught up with my own laughter. Callie frowned, wiping the water from her face. She had caught more of the water than we did, and her shirt was completely soaked. Being a white shirt, this of course, gave us a view of her breasts through the wet fabric. I caught Star staring and jabbed her in the ribs with my finger.

She turned to me with a devious look in her eyes and leaned over to whisper in my ear. I blushed slightly at her words, nodding as I turned to look at Callie. She pouted, still wringing water from her hair.

"What are you two whispering about?" She asked.

Star smirked, and we turned our bodies to face Callie, resting our backs against the wall. Star ran her hand over her breasts, and then over mine. Her fingers danced down my belly towards my groin. I took a sharp breath, spreading my legs as I felt her fingers enter me. Callie's face flushed immediately.

"Uh... I, uhm. Should I leave?" Callie stuttered trying to look away.

I shook my head, biting my lip, I reached down and pulled her onto the bed with us. Star ran her free hand through Callie's hair and gently nudged her face towards mine where I met it for a kiss. I closed my eyes and shivered as I felt Callie's hand join Star's between my legs.

Star and I both had a healthy sexual appetite. This wasn't the first time we had brought another woman into bed with us, but given the tension between Callie and I, it was no surprise Star had asked if I wanted this. I would never have made a move on Callie without Star's consent, the fact that she wanted her as well only made it better.

I wrapped my arms around them both, Callie moved her head to my chest and Star moved in for a kiss as well. We tangled our bodies together for what felt like ages. My body quivered with ecstasy each time we tried a different configuration. It's truly amazing how many ways three bodies can fit together with a little willpower.

If anyone in the camp had still been asleep, they certainly weren't anymore. Having Star returned to me once more had reinvigorated me. Having both her and Callie together in the same bed got me the horniest I have ever felt. My hunger for these beautiful women could not be satiated with just one orgasm. We went at it for a while, until we all were too tired to move.

"That... was... incredible." Callie muttered between shortened breaths, "A memory I won't soon forget."

There was a light rapping at the door of the hut.

"If you three are quite finished scaring away the wildlife, breakfast is ready. I found some spare robes for you all." Devon said, reaching a hand through the hanging grass to set the clothing down on the table by the door.

"BREAKFAST!" Star shouted, bolting from the bed.

I couldn't help but laugh at her excitement. This was my Star, nearly always in a great mood and easily excited by nearly anything. My heart swelled to see that she had not been significantly changed by any of this nonsense. Despite everything, she was still the amazing and pure woman I fell in love with.

We took some time to stretch out and then dressed in the robes Devon had provided for us. Star bounded from the hut first, eager for food, while Callie and I followed briskly behind. I didn't want to be too far behind her, for fear of not having anything left for myself. We all had worked up quite an appetite this morning.

When we arrived into the main hall, Cotton and the rest of the team were already seated. We received several knowing grins as we took our seats and even a wink from Lemon. Perhaps we should have shown some restraint, but damnit, I needed that this morning. Callie blushed, but Star piled food on her plate completely unabashed.

Breakfast was nice, a good spread of fruits, eggs, and smoked meats. As it often does, my mind wandered while we ate. I couldn't stop thinking about my dreams and Bach. Devon must have noticed my deep thought reflecting on my face.

"I would say congratulations are in order but given that you have already celebrated, and still seem bothered, I suspect you have more on your mind." Devon chimed in, waving a hand to get my attention.

I nodded, "Last night, while we were escaping, Bach was following us, angry that we fucked up his plans. He stopped very suddenly just as we made it to the trees, and just walked back to the compound." I explained.

"Maybe he knew we would corner him in the forest. It would've been simple to get the jump on him." Cotton offered.

"He'd be easy prey on our hunting grounds." Holly added.

"No, he was listening to something, I think he had an earpiece. It was like something came up that was more important." I replied.

"More important than us wrecking his place and stealing back your friend?" Birch questioned.

"Right?" I asked, "It doesn't sit well with me. I think there's still something more going on here."

"Well, I might know something about that." Star chimed in, gulping down some cider.

I turned to give her a puzzled look, she had mentioned before that she didn't remember much of anything after we were sedated.

"Ever since Cherry started pulling that junk out of my head, I have been piecing together memories of stuff while they were experimenting on me." She continued.

"Interesting, well, what do you think is going on?" Callie asked.

"It's still kind of fuzzy, but I remember something about a conversation between Bach and Khan while they were checking the machines I was hooked up to. Khan was saying something about using me to replace the source, because my blood had shown 'dramatic reactions to the treatment' or something. Bach seemed busy with something on his phone and mentioned something about 'launching a global effort' with the Opulentia pills." Star paused to chew some more food before continuing.

"Global effort?" Azalea asked.

"Yeah, later I heard Bach talking about the black-market value of the pills if they found the right buyers. Bach was spouting off ideas like selling the drug to the

Russians or the Triads. He sounded like something straight out of an underground-crime movie. Khan pushed back, saying that it would be too hard to roll out the treatment if others were distributing the pills. He wanted to just keep recruiting people and processing them at the lab. Bach told him he was thinking too small and stormed off." Star explained.

"He's insane!" I blurted, "Distributing this stuff across the world? Russians? Triads?! I can't even imagine what would happen if people everywhere just started shooting magic out of their hands because of a designer drug. It would be utter chaos." My brow furrowed in thought.

"That may be his intention." Devon added. "Sebastian has always had lofty ambitions; I wouldn't put it past him to concoct some twisted world-domination scheme."

I looked at Devon, my facial expression begging for more information.

"Sebastian has a lot of misguided views about world governments. It was something he discussed in length at Uni, and something that got him ostracized from many of the political groups he tried to join. He always championed the idea that countries should disavow their current government systems in favor of a new singular world order." Devon explained.

"He always liked to say he valued 'A unified planet, ready to address all problems as one, rather than opulent world powers locked in a pissing match with nuclear cocks.'"

"Yeah, I remember him saying something like that too." Star chimed in.

"So... what? He's going to try and undermine the world's governments, all at once, by doping up people on the streets with magic pills? How would that work, he would need..." I paused as the realization set in.

"An Army." Callie filled in.

"The fucking drones! He's trying to ramp up his recruitment numbers so that he can build a fucking army of warriors with magic power to launch a global campaign!" I punched the table in frustration.

"I wouldn't put it past him to try." Devon replied, "Lofty ambitions."

I was trying to wrap my head around how Bach planned to pull something like this off. Especially if he was concerned about replacing his source and we had stolen his replacement. From what Star said, Khan had been trying to prevent Bach from executing this plan. With him now dead, it would seem Bach was free to move along.

"We have to stop him." Callie said, breaking the tense silence in the room.

"We can't let him do this to any more people. People deserve to have their lives and their memories intact, we can't let him keep taking that away from everyone."

Tears were starting to slink down her cheeks as she spoke. She was right, what he was doing was awful. I hated that I had contributed money to the process. I hated him for many things, I hated him for everything.

"Easy Trianna," Lemon chimed, "We just got the place put back together, don't need you burning it down."

I hadn't noticed the heat rising in the room around me, or the flames starting to swirl on my arms. I cleared my head and calmed myself to dismiss them.

"Sorry." I replied through a grin. "All this has me a little hot-headed I guess." There were audible groans in response.

"We can't just go storming back in there. We came in hard last night and still nearly got our asses beat." Twig said, gesturing to the bandaged wound on his side.

"We have to do something to stop him, but you're right, we need a better plan. Something a little more distracting." I replied.

As I sat back in my chair, munching some fruit, something more answered as if queued by my statement. The ground trembled with great force, rattling things off the shelves and tables in the hut. Panic washed over the group, and I gathered that earthquakes were not common here.

I could hear a flock of birds screeching in fear as they flew overhead. As second tremor shook even harder than the first. I didn't know much about earthquakes or aftershocks but didn't think that was how it worked. I ran to the door to see what was happening outside and I could see smoke rising in the distance from the direction of the compound.

"Let's suit up!" I said, turning back to Cotton to indicate I wanted his help again. He nodded.

"Okay Ironman…" Star said sarcastically, effectively raining on my parade. I thought I had sounded rather bad ass.

We rushed back to our shack, so Callie and I could change back into our armor. Cotton and the others did the same. Star rummaged through Callie's bag and found a dress that she managed to fit into. It was a little big on her, given Callie's extra curves, but she tied off some of the fabric to make it work.

I wasn't thrilled that she was coming with us, but I knew she could hold her own. Having someone else with powers would prove helpful. The others were great hunters, but it felt like they were still outmatched by the drones and their magic. If we were going to pull this off, we needed all the firepower we could manage.

We regrouped at the edge of the village where Cherry was waiting to open a gap for us to leave. A few of the other villagers joined her to give us moral support.

"I don't know what I'm expecting to find, but I have a feeling it's not good." I explained.

"Sebastian must be stopped for this to end." Devon chimed, "Whatever is happening may at least give us a distraction we can use to get close to him."

The group nodded in agreement, and Cherry opened the gap in the wall. We moved with silent determination, each of us ready to end this once and for all. There was a heaviness on the air, I wondered if the others felt it as well. Something foreboding hung over us as we left the camp.

I turned back to look at Cherry as we left. She waved goodbye as she closed the wall, a clear sadness on her face. It was as though she knew more than we did about what was to come. Looking back now, I wish she had a voice to warn us of her fears.

CHAPTER 17

When we arrived at the edge of the woods facing

the compound, we were met with utter chaos. It was like

walking into a dream, especially having just seen the place

unharmed the night before. We all paused for a moment to take in the devastation. Something had gone terribly awry.

The west side of the building was engulfed in flames. The rockface that had supported the waterfall we saw in our room had been pulled down in a spike through part of the south side of the building. The compound had been converted to a full-on disaster area. The black smoke billowing from the raging inferno was suddenly disturbed by the appearance of a few cargo helicopters.

I followed their path with my eyes to the helipad on the other side of the compound that we had arrived on when this all started. I could just make out several drones wheeling large crates out of the building, presumably to be loaded onto the aircraft when they landed. From what I could gather, Bach was planning to escape with his work from whatever had destroyed his compound. He was working quickly.

We rushed the building, using the smoke and hedges for cover. We could use the element of surprise generated by this commotion to get inside undetected. As we neared we couldn't hear much over the sounds of the sirens blaring their alarm. I figured everyone knew something was wrong already, but at least the alarm system worked.

Inside the lobby, the chaos continued. The damage from our assault the night before was nothing compared to the sheer state of ruin we found the place in currently. Lights flickered on and off, bodies lay strewn across the floor, portions of the walls were ripped out. It was as if a whole war had taken place here overnight.

With Callie once again taking the lead, we snaked our way through the hallways with the goal of reaching the loading exit to the helipad. These hallways remained mostly untouched, but I could hear the strain the building was under from the damage not far off. It seemed like the whole place could collapse at any moment. I just hoped we made it out before it did.

It didn't take long for us to reach the warehouse, and we could hear sounds of people moving things from inside. I peered through the door and saw drones diligently working at packing boxes full of papers and smaller boxes. At another station, hundreds of Opulentia pills were being packed into the small boxes. At the far end, near another set of doors, stood Bach, smugly observing their progress.

He seemed rather calm for someone preparing to flee a rapidly disintegrating compound. I expected him to be frantic, or fighting off something, but everyone seemed focused on their task like nothing had happened at all. The others took turns peeking through the glass to get a feel for the layout of the room.

"Okay, we have eyes on Bach. He's got at least thirty drones working on loading things in there, maybe more out on the helipad." I said, "How do we want to do this?"

"Where do those other doors go?" Cotton asked Callie.

"They lead down to the labs I think, we would have to go downstairs and circle all the way around to cut him off." She answered.

"That's not a terrible option." Azalea added, "We could split up and trap them in the warehouse, cutting off their exits save for the helipad. Catch them in a standard pincer formation."

Cotton nodded, "I like it, how long would it take to get people over to the other side?"

"Five, maybe six minutes?" Callie replied. "So long as nothing gets in the way."

"Okay. Azalea, Holly, Lemon, Birch. You all head downstairs and loop around to the other side. Once you are in position we burst in and start dropping targets. Be fast, but quiet." Cotton said.

"If you take the stairs over there down a flight, it's a straight shot across the hallway to the stairs and freight elevator on the other side. You'll be in full view of anyone in the lab though, so try to stay low under the windows." Callie explained.

Everyone nodded, and the group took off for the stairwell leaving Twig, Cotton, and Devon with Callie, Star, and myself. I took another glance through the glass at the drones working in the warehouse. I could see the flashing lights and hear the sirens, but still none of them showed any indication of worry. It unsettled me, we were missing something. I just hoped that it wasn't waiting for the others downstairs.

Several minutes passed as I watched Bach and the drones. Occasionally, he would bark an order at some drones not moving quickly enough for him, but mostly he just stood and watched. He was standing beside a small office cubical, likely for the warehouse manager. I could see a clock on the wall through the window and noted that it had been ten minutes since the others left. They should have been in position by now. Cotton was showing his concern too, pacing in the hallway behind us.

"Something's gone wrong, I can feel it." He said as he joined us at the doors.

I turned back to the warehouse because new movement caught my eye. A man in a jumpsuit came out of the office and handed Bach a tablet, leaning over to speak into his ear. Bach nodded and then looked down at the tablet, a smile forming on his face. He looked up from the table, locking his eyes with mine through the glass in the door and waving.

An icy chill worked its way down my spine, and I turned around to check the ceiling. Sure enough, there was a small domed security camera mounted on the wall behind us. I hadn't thought to check in our haste to find him.

"We've been made." I said, pointing to the camera. "I imagine the others were too."

I looked back through the door and Bach gestured for us to enter.

"Fuck." I muttered, pushing open the door to lead the group inside.

"So eager to free your little girlfriend, and now here you are marching her right back to me!" Bach bellowed across the warehouse as the alarms shut off.

"Not exactly." I replied, "This time we came to end whatever nonsense you have planned with all these pills."

I launched a fireball at a crate of pills exploding it out of the hands of the drone packing it. The drone simply picked up a new box and returned to work, ignoring their freshly charred eyebrows.

"Oh, is that the plan? Well, should I surrender now or wait for the cavalry to arrive?" he said mockingly.

"We might be waiting a while, I'd say my special forces are dealing with them as we speak." He added, "You see, we had some trouble trying to move Subject One earlier and I had to call in the big guns. These drones here are great for basic work, but when things get hairy, well I have something better for that."

Moments later a group of drones dressed in black suits and masquerade masks came through the other set of warehouse doors. They dropped the bodies at Bach's feet. I couldn't tell if they were still alive.

"Bastards!" Cotton screamed.

He charged ahead before we could stop him. Twig knocked a few arrows and let them fly, Callie directed them towards the new drones, but one of them quickly swatted them away, smirking from behind his mask. Cotton didn't make it halfway across the warehouse before two of them stepped forward and incinerated him on the spot, or so I thought.

I heard the steam before I saw the smoke rising. When the flames stopped, Cotton stood in place, shielded behind a wall of water rising from a waterskin in his left hand. I adjusted my stance, to get ready to charge, and felt something against my foot. Looking down I saw the large waterskin Cherry had given to Cotton before we left the night before. Swirling red liquid pooled on the floor at the opening. She had given him some Opulentia to get his powers back.

Bach's drones cleared the area, carrying the last of the boxes out to the helipad, while the suits began to take up a position against us. There were six of them, each moving simultaneously with a practiced precision. They had more synchronization than a marching band. This wasn't just some private security team, this was a militia.

Bach leaned casually against the wall of the warehouse, his face stretched wide with a smile. Figures the bastard would just want to stand by and watch, rather than get his hands dirty. I couldn't wait to get my hands on him and coil my fingers around his neck until it popped. He would pay for everything.

Cotton kept his shield of water up as he glanced around at the suit-clad guards as they repositioned in an arc around him. I gestured for Devon to stay back, and then Callie, Star, and I stepped forward to give Cotton some backup. I could hear Twig knocking another arrow, waiting for an opening. The tension in the air was so thick you could cut it with a knife.

Callie tried to pull the concrete up under the feet of the guards, but within seconds they countered her and pushed it back down. This took some concentration however and Cotton used this to his advantage. He stepped towards them, slamming his wall of water down on one of them. The water struck with amazing force, sending the man careening to the ground.

Not letting the opportunity slip by, one of the others launched a ball of fire at Cotton, but I was there with one of my own to deflect it, my blue flames moving with more force than they expected. Cotton advanced on the other guard countering Callie's magic and placed a hand in front of his face. He clenched his fist and drew his arm back slowly. The guard screamed as all the moisture in his skin began drawing out and collecting in a ball between them.

The pavement crackled and twisted as Callie was now free to control it, and she brought pillars up between the legs of the guards. The two fire wielders managed to doge back, but the other two took the full force to the underside of their chins, cracking teeth and jaws. The sopping wet guard Cotton had slammed to the ground was getting back to his feet. He began trying to counter Callie once more, when I felt the hairs on my arms rising.

The air crackled with static as Star began summoning her power. Bolts of energy arced off her body to the legs of the metal tables as she passed, she was like a walking Tesla Coil. She raised a finger to the guard and with a flash of energy his body convulsed and collapsed to the floor. The water he was covered in provided extra conductivity and I wasn't sure he would get back up.

The room erupted in chaos from there. Each of us flinging balls of various elements at one another, having our attacks deflected or redirected completely. Tables and shelving units exploded sending debris scattering. Shards of metal joined clouds of dust as the other two guards whipped up gusts of wind to their aid. One dropped his attack quickly however, when an arrow pierced his heart.

I locked eyes with one of the fire guards preparing a ball of fire, aimed at Star from behind, and stepped between them readying my own. I sent a beam of fire at him, and he matched me, the flames scorching debris in the air as they passed. I could feel myself giving in to the power inside, and my flames grew stronger. I charged forward, extinguishing his blast with each step. Once I was within range, I called flames around my foot and spun a kick sharply across his face, searing flesh and melting his mask to his skin.

As I spun around to regain my footing, I again felt all my hair standing on end. Star was now glowing with energy, racing along the floor from target to target with intense speed. I watched as Cotton doused each guard with water only seconds before Star reached them. Bolts of lightning slammed from her hands into the guards frying their nervous systems and leaving them in twitching heaps on the floor.

My hair began to calm down as Star drew in her energy.

"Holy shit..." I said, staring wide-eyed.

Star just grinned back at me in response, pulling her blue hair back from her face. I looked up ready to move on Bach, but he had already slipped away through the far set of doors while we were distracted.

Twig sauntered over to the bodies of our friends that lay near the doorway. He was limping, blood streaming from his wounds, old and new. He hadn't fared well against the guards. I winced at the twisted shard of metal sticking from his back.

Twig checked his friends for their pulse and began sobbing uncontrollably as not even one responded to him. Cotton was seething with rage. Twig sat down holding Holly's head in his lap, brushing dirt from her face. His hand reached for Azalea's, gripping it tightly and then he just collapsed, either from grief or blood loss.

"Grieve later, he's getting away!" Devon cried, racing past us with their own lust for vengeance, with Cotton not far behind.

We chased after them, scanning for any more guards waiting to pop out at us. Bursting through the doors, we scrambled down the stairwell towards the lab. The hallway was twisted and deformed, likely from the battle with the guards that killed our friends. It must have happened quickly for us not to hear this much destruction.

My thoughts were interrupted by a shriek and other commotion. As we charged ahead, we found Devon leaning against the corner of the hallway, holding a wound on their leg. I heard someone scream and rounded the corner to find Cotton pinning a guard to the wall, pulling water from his waterskin and forcing it down the guard's throat into his lungs.

Before I could say anything, there was a loud crack, and something buzzed by my ear. Cotton's head exploded, sending blood and bits of skull across the wall as he collapsed. I screamed in horror and whipped around to see Bach holding my gun. He smirked, and then pointed the gun at Devon, squeezing off two more rounds.

"I should have killed you the moment you started rejecting the treatment." he said, aiming the gun back at me. "Khan said you would be too valuable to waste."

I started to move towards him but froze when a team of heavily armored guards stepped around from the other hallway. They were decked out in full riot gear and were carrying assault rifles. Evidently Bach had figured that magic guards wouldn't always be enough. Sometimes your armed militia needed to be just that.

"Escort the lady Von Drake and her friends to the lab. I still need the blue haired one after we get Subject One loaded onto the aircraft." He barked to the soldiers.

A few stood in place, guns fixed on the three of us, as we each found our arms in the grasp of two others. They dragged us through the doors of the lab, each of us hesitating to resist with the other armed guards fixed on us. I could feel my heart pounding, still in shock from watching Bach execute our friends. Fear of his new underlings only added to my duress.

A few weeks ago, I had never even seen guns like this outside of an action movie. Now here I was with several of them aimed directly at me and two people I cared for deeply. I was having a hard time comprehending just how my life had gotten this fucked up by winning the lottery. It was all too much to take in.

The soldiers led us to the back of the lab where several large tanks lined the wall. Each one appeared to be made of some high-density steel. A couple of the soldiers opened the tanks, and we were ushered into them and sealed inside. There were some vents near the top piping in fresh air so that we couldn't suffocate, at least not while the vents functioned.

Bach strutted before our tanks, shit-eating grin stitched across his face. He tapped the tanks from the outside with his knuckle. The sound was faint and muffled, indicating just how thick the walls were.

"Your oxygen supplies are all run through the same line, so should one of you decide to get a little... heated, then each of your tanks will become your own personal incinerators." Bach said smugly.

A few of the soldiers remained across from our tanks, guns still drawn and ready. The others set up watch around the room, signaling each other with hand gestures to relay their orders. I could faintly hear Callie sobbing in her tank through the ventilation pipe. I couldn't blame her, things were not going well.

I shouldn't have been surprised, I thought. Rushing this compound with just a small group of hunters with primitive weapons, and a couple people that just learned to use magic shouldn't have worked the first time. Trying it twice was proving to be a suicide mission. It was stupid to have thought this would have gone in our favor. Winning the lottery tends to change your perspective on pushing your luck, I guess.

I watched through the small glass window as some drones arrived in the freight elevator, escorting a forklift carrying a rather large cargo box. They all seemed nervous, and even Bach turned to examine the box with some respect in his eyes. Something changed in the room, everyone seemed to be focused on this piece of cargo as if they were wary to be near it. Even the hardened soldiers shuffled in place as it passed.

Just then, the lights in the room flickered and everyone stopped moving. The soldiers all raised their rifles to aim at the forklift, and the drones nervously moved to check that the load was secure.

"Don't wake that fucker up again!" Bach shouted, sternly glaring at the drone driving the forklift.

The box seemed to shutter at the sound of his voice, again washing a tense panic across the room. Bach moved to one of the terminals and muttered something I couldn't hear into a microphone. He kept his eyes focused on the crate, watching for any reaction. The crate sat still and deathly silent.

The drones, now certain that the straps were tight, and the cargo could not fall from the lift motioned for the driver to continue. No sooner had the forklift started back up than the earth shook beneath our feet. A spire of stone erupted under the rear tire of the forklift, toppling the machine to its side. The soldiers all turned to focus their aim as the crate collapsed to the floor.

The boards cracked open, revealing a large tank of a thick fluid. Inside the tank, suspended by a mess of hoses and tubes was a dark figure. I couldn't make it out through the viscous fluid, but I wouldn't have to wait for long. The thick glass began to crack, a lightning pattern dancing across the surface. Moments later the glass shattered, spilling the contents all over the laboratory floor.

The figure inside looked to be seven or eight feet tall, dark wrinkled skin stretched across a gaunt frame. I noticed the metal base of the tank was labelled 'Subject One.' I froze with terror as I studied the figure. It wasn't wearing a robe and it looked emaciated from having its blood drained for twenty years or so, but there was no question that it was the same foul creature from my dreams.

Subject One slowly drew itself up on its knees, wiping the dripping fluids from its eyes with one hand and ripping tubes from its flesh with the other. Its blood dripped swirling crimson and black, and there was no denying this was the Opulentia substance. We had been ingesting and tattooed with the blood of this insane creature. I fought back the urge to vomit, Star gasped, and Callie wept harder.

Steadily the creature rose to its feet, stretching the entropy from its muscles. It reached out a hand, examining it curiously for a moment, and then gazed around the room at the drones and soldiers surrounding it. Tilting its head to the side, I could see its neck crack and pop into alignment. The creature pointed its hand at one of the drones, and then clenched it into a fist.

Green flames engulfed the fist, and then with a display of incredible speed the creature was on top of the drone, melting away the flesh from his face. The palm of its hand covered the drone's mouth, muffling his screams as he died.

"What are you waiting for?! Tranquilize it!" Bach yelled.

A few of the soldiers listened and swapped their rifles for tranquilizer pistols. One poor bastard opened fire with the rifle, firing a short burst of three shots at the creature. The shot went wide, with only a single bullet grazing the shoulder of the beast but drawing its full ire in his direction. Subject One was on him in seconds wrenching the gun from his hands and beating him to death with it.

The other soldiers starting firing tranquilizer rounds, but they failed to pierce the leathery skin of the creature. It waved its hand, pulling up a wall of broken concrete to shield itself while it bit into the neck of the lifeless soldier. I could hear the slurping, even over the cacophony of people scrambling to deal with the situation.

Drones began summoning various magics to assault the creature, but their power paled in comparison. Fireballs were swatted away, stones deflected, winds pushed back at their source with increased fury. Soldiers darted around the room, trying to land shots, but they either missed or ricocheted off shields the monster raised around itself. Nothing they flung at it seemed to have any effect against the might of Subject One.

It steadily worked its way through the drones, occasionally pausing to rip into a throat and drink more blood. One drone managed to get up behind the beast while it was feeding, blasting it point blank with a gust full of shards of glass and other debris. The creature cried out in a terrible voice as the glass cut at its flesh, it stopped itself in midair with a surge of electric tendrils from its back.

It crawled through the air towards the drone, the tendrils of energy carrying it across the floor like a spider. Its body moved in strange ways that made me uncomfortable just watching. It seemed as though the beast was starting to regain strength from drinking the blood of the drones and soldiers. The tightness of its skin was easing away, looking less dry and gaunt by the minute.

When the beast finally reached the drone, it clutched her around the neck with one clawed hand, the other drawing the blood from her body as Cotton had done with water earlier. It leaked out from every hole in her head. Crimson streamed from her ears, nose, and eyes, pooling into an orb by the creature's hand. Dropping her body, the beast drank the blood from the air.

Unable to take my eyes away from the macabre display, I had failed to immediately notice more of Bach's black-suited guards had shown up to protect him. Several more soldiers arrived, unleashing a torrent of what appeared to be bean bag rounds from shotguns. These pelted the beast, each hitting with enough force to stagger it from its grisly meal.

Bach stood flanked by two of his magic guards, and the three of them surrounded themselves in flames. They extended their arms ahead of themselves, pooling the fires into a single ball. While the creature was distracted with the volley of stun bullets, the ball of flame churned fiercely. Bach drew his arms back and then quickly thrust them forward again, sending a massive barrel of fire racing at the creature.

Flame met flesh, and flesh seared, but not for long. The creature, groaning with pain, quickly pulled up another wall to shield himself. The flames shot upwards towards the ceiling, but two more guards stepped forward, directing the fire back down with a torrent of wind. The flames coiled around the shield of rock, once again barraging the creature.

It did not simply stand there and take the abuse, however. Reaching for one of the mangled lab tables, the creature moved quickly away from the torrent of wind and fire. It hurled the tangled aluminum desk at one of the guards, pinning him to the wall dead from the force. With that movement getting the attention of the riot soldiers, the creature moved briskly in the other direction, getting a better line of sight on its foes.

"Fuck it!" Bach shouted, "Kill it, we still have the girl. I still have other things to get ready for transport."

He turned to leave with his guards putting up a barrier of flames to shield them from debris. They followed him out through the doorway leading deeper into the facility. The soldiers dropped their riot suppression guns, swapping back to the assault rifles, ready to rain hell on the creature. However, they were not fast enough.

Evidently, the creature had regained much of his power from his grim meals as it stood menacingly across the room. It gestured with its clawed hands, and within seconds the room was a hurricane of chaos. Lights burst raining mercury powder and glass into the torrential winds. Water lines burst, and gallons of water swirled into the storm. Massive chunks of concrete and stone ripped from the walls and floor, along with ragged edges of metal from destroyed lab equipment.

I couldn't hear anything over the roar of the storm and the stream of quickly fading gunfire. I could feel my tank rattling as the force of the winds threatened to rip it off the wall to join the barrage on the soldiers. Something slammed into the ventilation lines above the tanks, severing my supply of oxygen. Moments later the tempest ended, and only the creature remained standing.

I ducked down in the tank, hoping the others did the same, and that we weren't seen for fear of being eaten. I could hear the heavy steps of the creature as it moved towards the door Bach had retreated through. It paused as it neared the tanks on the wall, and I held my breath. My heart was pounding like a steam engine waiting for the creature to either move on or rip open my tank and subsequently my neck.

After what felt like ages, the creature slammed through the door in pursuit of Bach and his guards. The room fell silent, save for the sounds of a few flickering florescent bulbs, and the water dribbling on the floor from the burst lines. I fell back against the wall of my tank, my breath heaving in my chest. I could still hear Star and Callie silently weeping in their tanks, and I was thankful they were still alive.

After a few moments of catching my breath, I reached up to the vents to make sure no oxygen was passing through. The air in the tank stood still, so I called up flames around my hands and pressed them to the edge of the seal on the door. I would have to act quickly to keep from burning through all my oxygen and suffocating. I hoped my special flames burned hot enough to make short work of things.

Concentrating, I pushed the fire into the seal, melting away the rubber used to make the chamber airtight. The smell was terrible, but I managed to get the door a little loose, and I could see the latch holding the door shut. I moved my hands closer to the latch and focused the fire into a small pinpoint on the steel latch bolt. This took much longer to have any effect, but soon I could see the metal starting to glow red. A few minutes later the bolt began to melt out of the latch, and I was able to force the door of my tank open.

Outside, the stench of death hit me hard, and I again had to fight the urge to vomit. I took a moment to regain my composure and then opened the latch to Star's tank. She bolted up and wrapped her arms around me, shaking with terror. I held her tightly for a moment, kissing her forehead and sobbing lightly, just thankful she was alive.

I let her go and we unlatched Callie's tank as well. We all held each other for comfort in the mostly dark destroyed laboratory.

"What the fuck was that thing?" Star muttered.

Neither of us had much of an answer for her. Whatever it was, this was the thing Bach pulled out of the side of a mountain with Khan and Devon so many years ago. This vile creature, hidden away in some deep cavern by who knows what. I shuddered at the thought that there might be more of these things slumbering away in caves around the world and sincerely hoped to be wrong.

In the distance we heard more gunfire. The creature must have caught up with more of Bach's militia.

"We have to figure out how to get out of here." I said, "If that thing finds us, we're doomed."

"We might be able to sneak out back to the village." Callie suggested.

"I don't know, the compound is going to be on high alert with that fucking monster rampaging around. There are probably armed guards at all the exits just waiting for something to shoot." I replied.

"So, what then? We climb back in the tanks, and wait until everyone leaves?" Star asked.

"Not exactly... hiding might still be a good option though. Maybe we can get up to the suites, hide out on the top floors away from all the action and let Bach deal with the beast." I said, glancing around to make sure no one was creeping into the room with us.

"The building looked pretty torn up, do you think it'll be safe up there?" Callie asked.

"I'm not sure, but if that thing is down here, I would rather have the high ground." I replied.

They nodded, and we huddled together at the sound of more gunfire. The floor rumbled, indicating the creature was using parts of the structure for weapons again. The doors to the stairwell burst open and more armed guards came filing through, guns at the ready. We managed to scoot behind an overturned table before the unit saw us, holding our breath hoping to remain hidden.

They paused in the middle of the room, their flashlights sweeping across the tanks. The lights then began slowly tracing across the rooms. They must have been sent to retrieve us while the creature was occupied. Bach was sure he was getting out of this alive, despite being chased down by his own experiments. If we could make it to the roof unseen, we might be able to ground his helicopters and prevent that.

The soldiers began moving around the room, searching for us. I managed to peek under the table and get a look at them. Just like the others, these were in full riot armor carrying rifles. I cursed to myself in frustration, thinking about how much of my money may have gone into funding this militia currently hunting us.

We shuffled quietly behind debris, staying low to the ground to try and avoid the lights. Getting out of this room wasn't going to be easy, I wasn't even sure how many soldiers there were. Still, we had to try, letting Bach escape simply wasn't an option.

CHAPTER 18

We managed to get closer to the door, only to find two soldiers guarding it. Four lights were beginning to close in on us, as the others swept the room. A stealthy exit was not an option any longer it seemed. I sighed, wracking my brain to come up with a plan, looking to the others for ideas.

Star pointed to herself and then back to the approaching lights, then she gestured at me and the guards by the door. I was still trying to figure out exactly what she wanted when she leaned in for a quick kiss and then slipped under the table we were hiding behind.

"Hello boys...." Star announced, standing up in the middle of the room.

"Looking for me?"

I shook my head and frantically turned back to the guards by the door. All the lights, and guns, in the room focused on Star. Within moments the room began to glow with a flickering light. Star was calling forth her power which managed to divert the guard's attention long enough for me to move closer to the door. The two soldiers guarding the door had moved forward, trying to close off Star from the exit, they were not moving confidently, however.

Star's power crackled on the air and arced to the bits of metal and puddles of water scattered around the room. Raising her arms, she sent bolts of lightning to the guns carried by the soldiers. The guards dropped them instantly as the shock surged through their hands. A few rounds discharged and ricocheted around the room, causing the door guards to duck out of instinct.

I charged one, striking him hard over the head with a chunk of concrete, sending him down hard. Before I could even recover my balance, the rock was pulled from my hands and slammed into the head of the other guard. Callie gave me a thumbs up from behind the table. Star had focused her energy into her legs and was currently dashing rapidly through the room, slamming bolts of her power into the startled soldiers and reducing them into piles on the floor.

"That was reckless." I scolded Star.

"Yeah, but it worked." She smirked.

I shook my head and rolled my eyes. Star blew me a kiss and joined Callie waiting by the door. These powers were going to our heads, I only hoped our hubris wouldn't get us killed. We hadn't suddenly become bulletproof.

I picked up one of the rifles from the downed guards and looked it over. I had spent some time at the gun range with my handgun, but I had never used anything more powerful. The gun was heavier than it should have been, a device made solely for killing. I decided that I didn't like the way it felt in my hands and put it back down. These guns caused more problems than they solved, I was better off without it.

As I moved back towards the door, the ground trembled again. The rear door, that Bach and the others had fled through, burst open as a body came flying through it, skidding across the floor leaving behind a trail of blood. I watched in horror through the swinging doors as the I could make out the outline of Subject One steadily approaching.

"Go!" I shrieked, pushing the others towards the exit.

I glanced back just in time to see the creature lift the soldier from the ground and tear open his neck with its maw. I guess Bach had given it the slip somehow, and it was coming back looking for more food. We bolted through the labyrinth of hallways, with Callie leading us, heading back towards the lobby.

The creature roared behind us, the guttural sounds achieving a deep ferocity that would make any of my favorite death-metal bands jealous. It didn't inspire the same feeling those bands would though, this shook me to my core, sounding so terribly not-of-this-earth. We ran faster, pushing ourselves to new limits to ensure distance between us and the beast. I had no interest in jumping into a mosh pit with this big ugly fucker.

We raced around corners and down tattered hallways, heading towards the lobby. We came across a few drones along the way, but Callie put them down with little effort, using the available debris to her advantage as we ran. I could hear the creature behind us, still a good distance behind, but its presence loomed after us. It felt like it could reach out and grab us at any second, out of sheer force of will.

"Almost there!" Callie shouted back at me. "We can take the elevators!"

I wasn't sure that was the safest option, but as we neared them, that portion of the building seemed unharmed. It would be easier on us than taking the stairs, and we might be able to lose the monster if we ducked out of the hallways. I looked back and still couldn't see the beast, but I knew it was gaining on us.

Luckily the elevator car was waiting on this floor, and the doors opened immediately when we hit the call button. We shuffled inside, and I once again glanced back to see if anyone had seen us. Subject One was rounding the corner into the lobby and seemed locked on us as he approached. As the doors began to close, I chucked a ball of flames out to the carpet in the lobby, hoping the fire would slow it down. The fire spread to a nearby couch, quickly turning the room into an inferno.

I collapsed back against the far wall to catch my breath as the doors shut. The elevator began to rise, hitting my stomach with that uncomfortable sinking feeling. Moments later, my heart sank as well, I heard the shaft in the lobby being ripped open, the whole car shuddered as something slammed into the shaft below us.

"Fuck." I muttered.

"These elevators move quickly," Callie said, "It won't take us much longer."

Her eyes were focused on the lights counting the floors up to our destination. I could hear the beast climbing the shaft after us, growls echoing angrily through the chamber. We were moving faster it seemed, but I could hear claws frantically scraping against metal to gain a hold. It wouldn't take long to catch up.

After a few surreal moments of calm music from the speakers, the door dinged announcing our arrival at the top floor. I jumped despite myself.

"For fuck's sake." I muttered under my breath as I stepped out into the plush hallway.

I remembered the tentative glee I felt traversing this hallway when we first arrived. The thick carpet made the floor soft, flowers in vases under each window brought such a pleasant smell to the air. I felt foolish to ever be excited by this place, but I hadn't known then the extent of the horrors I would face. I could see the same look of concern on Star's face as she quietly took in our surroundings.

"Let's drop the car on the bastard!" I said, turning back towards the elevator.

I slammed the button for the first floor and let the car start moving. I struggled to pry open the protective doors, but with Callie's help managed to get them open. I held my hand out and focused a flame on the steel cable. Star stepped beside me and joined in, electrifying the cable as well. I heard the beast shriek as the charge jumped and arced down the cabling towards it in the shaft.

As the cable began to glow red, Callie sent her last axe towards it with her powers. The stone head slammed at the red-hot steel and with a few strikes managed to sever enough that the weight of the car snapped it the rest of the way. We fell backwards, narrowly avoiding the flailing cables as the car dropped, the steel cable leaving gashes in the door as it whipped past.

I scrambled back to the edge, and peered down, hoping to see the car slam into the creature and send everything crashing to the bottom floor. I couldn't see the beast, but a few balls of green fire came rushing up the chamber as the car plummeted. They continued harmlessly past me, but the elevator car found its target with a loud crash. The creature screamed loudly as the weight of the car pushed it down through the elevator shaft.

It was a long way down, but a few moments later the shrieking stopped, cut off by a loud crash of collapsing steel.

"That should slow it down, hell hopefully it killed it." I said climbing back to my feet.

My moment of celebration was cut short by a storm of green fire and white lightning streaming up the shaft behind me. We scattered down the hallway towards the suites as a burst of the firestorm lapped out of the hole in the wall. We hadn't killed it, but we did piss it off.

"Come on, let's get into a room or something. If it starts climbing back up, we can be well hidden before it makes it back to the top." Star said, clutching my hand.

"How are we going to get into any of the rooms? We don't have a room key." I asked.

"I know the override codes for the electronic locks." Called replied. "I was on housekeeping detail for a while, before I was moved down to the labs."

"Well, that's convenient." I said.

We headed down the hall towards the room that Star and I had stayed in during our first week here. It was the last in the hallway, near the service access to the roof, Callie mentioned as we walked. Once at the door, she popped open a hidden panel and entered a code to unlock the doors. It beeped, and the door confirmed with a click as Callie gave us a proud grin.

Inside the room, we found our luggage strewn across the room with everything else. Bach must have had his drones search our things after he abducted us. I'm not sure what he might have been looking for, but it did explain why he had my gun. The gun he had used to execute Cotton and Devon.

I frowned at the thought. My friendship was resulting in an unfair amount of shit for others, and that was really getting to me. I guess when you win the lottery, something must balance out the scales. I guess all the charity donations I made weren't enough.

We rummaged through the clothing on the floors and in the closet, and each managed to find something more comfortable to wear. Callie managed to squeeze into some of my clothing, my extra height giving her curves a little more room than Star's clothing would have. With some quick tearing and tying it managed to cover enough of her to keep the leather armor from chaffing her skin any more than it already had.

Star was naked before the rest of us but was having trouble deciding what to wear. She settled on one of her skin-tight leotards she had made for a photography shoot. It had no legs, the fabric below the waist only covering her crotch and some of her ass. It came up over her neck on the top, with a window to show some cleavage, and no sleeves. She claimed it made her feel like someone from a comic book and leaving her arms and legs bare would allow her to use her powers more efficiently.

"You're my favorite dork." I said affectionately, getting a chuckle from Callie.

I climbed into a pair of old jeans, a rugged pair of Doc Martins, and a Lamb of God band shirt. My penultimate outfit for comfort and concerts. Sometimes classic looks are the best. I found my boot knife amongst the carnage in the room and strapped it on as well. You never know when a sharp knife might save your life.

I decided to keep the shoulder harness, and forearm guards from the armor. They bore the most customization from Cherry's mother, and I wanted to honor that for her and Cotton. I stepped over to join Callie at the window.

The waterfall that had so wonderfully filled out this view before was destroyed. Parts of the rockface had been pulled down into spikes by Subject One, and the water simply crashed through whatever holes it could find. With time, the water would erode parts of the stone, making a new magnificent feature, but for now it was just rage and chaos.

As if queued by that simple thought, I heard sounds of destruction coming from the hallway, and our lights in the room went out. The creature had made it to the top of the shaft and was tearing up the place to find us. We each dove for hiding places, Callie behind the couch, Star in the closet, and myself by the bed.

The walls began to groan and crack by the door as panels burst through the wallpaper. Subject One peeled away the door from the frame with great strength. Whatever power he had lost to entropy was clearly returning to him. With the room dark, all I could see peeking from the bed was the massive silhouette of the beast against the light streaming in from the windows in the hallway.

I could feel a tremendous power emanating from it, as he entered the room. It was no wonder the blood of this creature would give someone magic powers, the beast itself seemed to be comprised of magic made flesh. A living golem of leathery hide and seething rage encasing a power like the world had never seen.

The room began to glow an eerie green as flames rose from the palm of the creature's hand. I tucked down low, hoping I hadn't been spotted. The light slowly crept along the walls, and I swear I could feel the creature staring a hole through my skull even from behind cover.

Something inside me seemed to want to move towards him, as if drawn by his power. I didn't dare move an inch.

The creature sniffed at the air, and I could practically feel the bat like nostrils twitching to waft in our scent. The room was full of our clothing, so hopefully that was enough to prevent him from focusing on us. My heart pounding in my chest might have given me away were it not for the sound of the helicopters rising near the windows.

Fuck, I thought, Bach made it back outside!

The creature turned and moved over towards the window, clearly focused on this new nuisance. I took the opportunity to scramble for the door, Callie had done the same. I then realized Star had not left the closet. As Callie moved out into the hallway, the helicopter rose directly outside of the room's large window. I crept over to the closet and reached in for Star's hand to escort her out of the room.

Just as we made it back to the door, the helicopter turned to present its side to the window. The creature watched; head tilted to the side in confusion over what he was seeing.

"Oh shit.... run!" I muttered to Star and Callie, as I entered the hallway.

The helicopter was turning so that it could aim a very large minigun at the window to the room. It was already spinning up as the chopper found its position. The creature called flames to his hand with an angry growl, but that sound was cut short by the whirl of the gun, the shattering of glass, and the torrent of bullets.

The girls and I hit the floor, sliding for cover on the opposite side of the hall, as bullets shredded through the walls of suite. Fragments of wood and glass rained through the hall as the gunner panned the minigun across the room hoping to catch as many shots on the beast as he could. All I could do was hold my head down and ball up against the wall with the others, trying to stay as close to the floor as possible.

After what was likely a solid minute of constant fire from the minigun, the hail of bullets finally stopped. I glanced up, and I could see into the room through the gaping holes in the wall. I hoped to see the creature laying in bloody piles across the floor. Instead, I saw the creature, crouching unharmed behind a wall of stone and steel debris it had summoned up to shield itself.

The beast leapt from its hiding place and launched itself out of the window before the pilot or gunner could react. I watched as the creature tore into the gunner's chest with its bare hand, and then used his body as a club to assault the pilot. The helicopter spun out of control, blades slicing into the side of the building sending more debris at us down the hall. Once enough of the blades had broken off, and nothing was holding it aloft, the chopper careened to the lower floors of the building, rocking the foundation and sending a tremor through the whole tower.

I scrambled to one of the holes in the wall to find out if the crash had stopped the monster, but I wasn't holding my breath. I wasn't wrong either, out of the wreckage the beast crawled, seemingly unscathed. Not for long though, as a group of soldiers closed in from all sides, a torrent of bullets raging from their rifles.

From atop the building, the carnage that ensued below looked almost like art. Muzzles of guns flashing, soldiers moving in a steady pattern, and elemental rage dancing across them all. Pillars of earth rose under feet, spraying blood across the grass in delicate arcs. Bursts of wind moved bodies in unison, slamming them against flaming helicopter debris. Green flames racing from the creature to the soldiers, dancing with an illuminated ghost image underneath itself.

Grotesque and macabre, it was fascinating to watch. Or it might have been, had it not been so teeming with horror. Whatever Subject One may be, it was certainly primal and vicious. When I called flames to my hands, I had to focus on the act, perhaps even drop my guard to concentrate. The flames this creature called seemed to just be there when needed, with no effort at all.

I watched more blood decorate the ground as the beast sank its teeth and claws into another body, draining it for sustenance. I could hear the other two helicopters passing by the tower. As I stood to watch, Bach waved a gloved hand out of the window directly at me. Somehow, he had figured out we were up there as well, he made sure to let us see him making his escape.

I heard a buzzing noise nearby and glanced around. Laying near one of the holes torn in the wall from the gunfire was my cellphone, ringing. I hesitantly picked it up and glanced over the text 'Private Number' displayed on the screen. I thumbed the green answer button and held the phone to my ear saying nothing.

"Ah good! I was worried this phone might have been destroyed during the gunfire. How are you, Lady Von Drake?" Bach's voice leaked from the speaker.

I could feel tears of rage streaming down my face in response to just hearing him speak. I gritted my teeth, trying to compose myself.

"What the hell is that thing?!" I heard myself ask, my brain was working overtime.

"That would be Subject One. I'm sure Devon explained that to you, they always did love any opportunity to tell stories. It was nice to see them again, however brief." Bach replied.

"But what is it? Some kind of demon?" I demanded.

"Perhaps it is. Perhaps it is something else. All that matters is that I've no further need of it. Subject One is your problem now. I lament losing him, as well as you and your lover, but one must learn when to cut off loose ends." Bach laughed to himself.

I could hear radio chatter in the background of the call, but nothing clear enough to gather where they might be heading. I growled under my breath.

"My research remains intact, and with what we learned from you two, it shouldn't take much effort to find replacements. Besides, it stands to reason that if I found one, there are bound to be others. I've got leads to follow, so I won't keep you much longer." he said, mockingly.

"You'll pay for this, motherfucker." I growled, "I won't just be your plaything."

"Oh, but you aren't!" He replied, "You are a valued investor! With your initial investment, and the additional hundred million I pulled from your accounts, you have ensured that I have plenty of time to further my work."

"Bastard!"

I turned and sent a ball of fire into the sky, hoping to strike the helicopter. The conversation had distracted me from realizing how far the choppers had gotten from the building. The flames dissipated in the air before ever reaching my target. I hadn't thought about the act drawing the attention of the beast below, but that was exactly what happened.

The phone felt hot in my hand, and I dropped it as it began to spew smoke and sparks. Bach had loaded my phone with thermite, so I couldn't use it for help. He played me this whole time, using my own rage as a distraction. I was getting tired of being used.

"We've got a problem." Callie said, pointing down at the lawn.

I walked back to the edge, and as soon as I looked down, locked eyes with Subject One. He stood staring curiously at me, seemingly intrigued by my presence. He had seen the ball of blue flames I launched into the sky, and that had given him pause. Not much of one though, because he was quickly moving to scale the building.

"Should we run? Find somewhere else to hide deeper in the hotel?" Star asked.

I nodded. "You two go hide. I'm done running from this fucker though."

"What do you mean? You aren't going after it alone! Tri get serious!" Star yelled at me.

However, I had already made up my mind. I blew her a kiss, gave her a wink, and then I leapt through the hole in the wall. I heard the girls shriek, but I didn't look back. I was focused on my target, the raging beast waiting below.

Talking with Bach had awakened a pure rage inside me. It was primal and ferocious, and I could feel it calling to me. It boiled within me, churning like a great sea of power waiting for my command.

I could hear the familiar ancient voice deep in the back of my head. It wasn't loud enough for me to make out what it was saying, but I could tell it was there. I closed my eyes, focusing on the sound. The voice changed quickly from a whisper to a throbbing blast inside my mind, and I felt something else take hold of me.

Radiant blue flames engulfed my body head to toe, and suddenly I lost the feeling of falling. Instead, I felt in control, and I was gaining speed. I held my fists out before me and opened my eyes. The building was racing past me, the creature steadily approaching, and his face twisted with curiosity.

I slammed into Subject One with so much force I thought my arms would break. I could hear his leathery flesh searing from my flames as we connected. The beast screamed with pain as I sent his body spiraling towards the ground. I instinctively pulled up, and flames burst from my underside, slowing my descent some before I landed hard on the ground. The creature slammed into the earth with a thud, several feet away.

I stood there for a moment, feeling the power radiating through my body. It was like I unlocked something within myself by reaching out to that voice, and I had never felt more powerful. I felt unstoppable. I looked at my flaming hands, turning them over to take in the view. I didn't feel the heat of the fire, even though it covered my whole body. It seemed to come out of my pores, burning from deep within, but I felt nothing.

"ABOMINATION!" a foul voice echoed through my skull.

I turned and looked at the creature laying on the ground. He stared back at me, eyes fixed on mine and full of rage.

"You should not exist!" the voice said, "Only our kind should be able to call forth such power. You pig-men are supposed to be too weak!"

Subject One was speaking to me telepathically as he rose to his feet. This startled me but could not break my resolve. I stood confidently facing the beast, even as it loomed over me with its impressive height.

"That power is sacred, and yet you parade it before me. I will not stand for such insolence! What this world has become in my sleep sickens me!" he boomed.

The beast held his hands to his side and flames began to dance on his clawed fingers. I wasn't about to stand still and give him a chance to overpower me.

"Eat shit." I said and lunged forward.

"You dare... "

He started but was cut off by my fist across his fanged mouth. His head reeled to the side, and I struck him in the stomach with my other fist. Without pause, I rained blow after blow on the beast, the flames seeming to give me more strength. He staggered back with each new strike, as I advanced unleashing all the hatred and anger bottled inside me.

Each time my fist landed I roared, releasing my rage. Everything pent up inside me from this whole endeavor was leaving through my fists. His skin began to bubble with blisters from the heat, and I only continued my assault. I felt amazing, like a righteous fury burned within me guiding my hands.

The feeling consumed me, so much so that I failed to notice the beast was regaining his composure. I had stopped pushing him back, and his fists were raised together above his head, coated in his green fire. He pulled them down, striking me across the face harder than anything I had ever felt in my life, and I spiraled to the ground.

I clutched my head as the fire dissipated from me. Everything was spinning, and I couldn't find the balance to even begin to stand. As I managed to get onto my knees, a large foot connected with my injured ribs sending me across the grass in immense pain. I screamed as I tumbled along the ground, all that righteous fury had left me and now all I felt inside was pain, and likely some internal bleeding.

I spit up blood as I lay on my back, trying to get my vision to stop blurring and spinning. Subject One stood over me and his wicked face stretched into a grin.

"Weak. Pathetic, just as I thought. You are unworthy of such power! I will strip it from you, and then I will strip your flesh from your bones, swine."

His voice was like thunder in my aching head. I was exhausted, nothing left in me to fight back. I could only watch as he reached down for my throat with his clawed hand. I stared puzzled when that hand collapsed limp onto my chest as something flew past. Glancing to the side, I saw a stone-headed hand axe imbedded in the ground, just before thick, swirling, red and black blood sprayed over my face, neck, and chest.

The creature recoiled in pain, roaring as he clutched his wounded arm to his chest. I felt the creature's blood seeping into my open wounds, and it burned like hell. Wiping it from my eyes, I watched as Callie and Star came down the side of the building. Callie was levitating slowly on a chunk of concrete, and Star carried herself down on tendrils of electricity.

They advanced quickly once they reached the ground, not wanting the beast to recover too much. With a wave of her arm, Callie sent a quake through the ground racing towards the creature and causing him to lose balance. Star closed in quickly, accelerating her movements with her power, and brought a ball of lightning up into the beast's chest.

His muscles spasmed, unable to regain control against the surge of power she pushed into him. Callie brought stones from the ground and slammed them into his face, shattering his fangs and launching him onto his back. She summoned her stone axe as well, slashing at the beast repeatedly with it. Large bloody gashes opened across his body as he thrashed to get away from the onslaught.

Star scrambled over to me, clutching my hand with tears in her eyes. She frantically wiped the blood from my face, unsure how much of it was mine.

"Trianna! Are you okay?!" She blurted. I managed only a nod.

"You dumb bitch! How could you do this by yourself? Do you want to die?!" she asked, rhetorically.

I couldn't have answered if I wanted to. My whole face ached, and I didn't really have an answer anyway. I had only thought about saving Star this whole time, I had pretty much given up on thinking of my own safety. Laying there on the ground, broken and bruised, I was regretting that decision.

Callie shrieked, interrupting Star's reprimanding of me. She turned back, electricity already sparking in her eyes, and ran to aid our friend. I could only watch as they sparred with the creature, trading blow for blow, power for power, locked in combat with this strange magic beast. Callie would barrage the beast with stones, and Star would shock him to keep him from sending them back at Callie.

They were losing ground against him though. The beast began deflecting Callie's assault with bursts of wind and pulling earth up to ground Star's electricity. He fought back, harder than they hoped for. A thick backhand sent Callie backwards before Star could get enough voltage in him to stop the swing. A pillar of stone struck her in the abdomen, dropping her to her knees, where the beast planted a hard kick into her side launching her away as well. He laughed, wiping blood from his broken mouth.

"You are all too weak. I wonder, if I feast on such weak flesh, would that weakness spread to me like a disease?" His booming voice mocked from inside my head.

He coiled up a fist, and the ground rose around Callie, clenching her with a giant stone hand, slowly crushing her. With his other hand, bolts of electricity lifted Star from where she lay, the surge of energy causing her body to spasm.

"You may watch them die, my little pig friend. Do not fret, your turn will come." He mocked.

I felt my heart breaking as I watched him torture my friend and lover with his own twisted version of their powers. I felt helpless, broken, defeated. I was sure they would die before my eyes, all because of me. I might as well be killing them myself.

I could never do that. I would never do anything to hurt those I loved, I didn't have that in me. Tears streamed from my eyes as felt something stirring inside me. It brought up terrible feelings from my past, images from my childhood I had long buried away. It reminded me of the last time I had felt this helpless.

As a child, my father beat me. He would come home from work, drunk or loaded on pills, and the first thing he would do was hurl insults at me. He would mock what I was wearing, or the way I styled my hair. He called me ugly, he called me a mistake. He blamed me for ruining his life, and for any other problems he may have been having that day.

He would often tell me I was not a person, not human, but only his property. Something that he owned, and as such I must obey his every whim. I was punished for any perceived slights, even when there were none made. He treated me like I was less than nothing, a slave to do his bidding or a scapegoat for his problems.

He was incredibly violent at the drop of a hat. He would often start fights with me, just to give himself an excuse to hit me. If I wouldn't take the bait, he would hit me for ignoring him. I covered myself with makeup just to go to school, hiding the bruises.

Sometimes I would cut myself at night, thinking that if I had control over some of the pain then I could better deal with the pain he inflicted on me. He got inside my head, made me feel worthless, even more so than I do now. He treated my mother much the same.

I couldn't understand why she ever loved such a horrible person. I begged her to leave, but she always told me that it wasn't that easy. I tried to run away once, he found me and beat me for it. He called me so many terrible names and threatened to kill me.

He pulled my own knife on me once, told me he would make me squeal like a pig. He told me they would never find my body, and as a child my fear made me believe him. I could only cower and cry as he mocked me for being weak. He told me constantly how much of a disappointment I was.

I spent years in therapy because of how he treated me. It took those years to even begin to undo the damage he caused me, inside and out. I swore I would never treat anyone the way he treated me. I swore I would never let anyone treat me that way again.

That rage from those experiences in my youth returned some strength to me, as the creature laughed. I didn't have any power to save myself back then, I didn't have a way to stop the terrible things from happening to me and my mother. I couldn't stop that monster.

I could stop this one.

I was on my feet before I even realized it myself. Once again that mysterious voice returned to me, this time like a symphony. I burned with fury, and blue fire swirled around me more intensely than ever before. I raised an arm and saw that I was once more completely encased in fire. The pain was fading from my mind, as concentration and focus set in.

A ball of flames formed in my hand and raced towards the beast. It slammed into his chest, knocking him backwards to the ground. Callie and Star both dropped back to the ground now that his attack had ceased.

"You are nothing, little pig!" his voice echoed in my head as he rose. "You will squeal and die and nothing more."

He brought his arms up before him, conjuring a storm of elements to lash out at me.

"You first." I replied, my voice calm and cold.

Power surged from within me. The flames surrounding me swarmed, raging like a wildfire. Another ball of flame formed in my hand, this time drawing in from all around me. I could hear the rush in the air as the fire pulled all the oxygen from it. I drew my hand back, and then thrust it forward, sending a massive beam of fire at the beast.

The grass between us scorched away, and even the dirt began to char from the heat of my attack. I screamed with pain and anger and a wave of energy rippled through the beam of fire pushing it even harder. It struck the whirlwind in front of the creature like a freight train. He was forced to focus it into a shield to try and stop the onslaught of fire raging at him.

I focused on his terrible face, forcing every bit of my will towards him through that fire. I could feel him through it, as if it were a part of me, my anger and rage brought to life by flame. I could feel his shield failing, feel him struggling to hold me back. His power was so strong, but I was unbridled-rage manifest.

He called more power to his shield, drawing in stone and swirling winds, but I only pushed harder, burning hotter against his failing wall. I was using everything I had, but it felt like it wasn't going to be enough. Somehow, despite everything I was throwing at him, he was holding his ground.

That's when I heard the crack of thunder in the sky. With all the fire around me, I hadn't noticed the dark clouds forming overhead. Star was awakening that fury from before, when I first saw her transformed. She floated on tendrils of energy, sliding in next to me. I could barely see her through the energy coursing over her body, but I knew it could be no one else.

"You.... Are... Not Alone!" She said, body shaking with power.

Her hair stood on end, and lightning arced down her cheeks from her eyes. Her presence felt heavy on the air, even beside my own. She raised her arms and called forth her tremendous power to aid me. Lightning struck her from the sky, but only to lend its strength. She directed the bolts through her arms into my beam of fire.

I stood there, side by side with the only woman on earth that knew my true past. She knew everything about me, and her pain resonated with my own. We became one in that moment. Our hearts were joined, and we stood stronger than ever, united against such an impossible obstacle.

The lightning surged through my beam of fire and shattered the shield protecting our foe. I heard his screams of pain over the surging energy, but we did not relent. We had to end this once and for all. I channeled my rage into my fire, Star called more lightning from the sky, all of it pouring into the beast's body.

I watched as his skin began to boil away, unable to withstand the force of our relentless fury. I kept pushing, focusing on him as my fire burnt his flesh from his bones. Lightning danced through his nerves, until they too turned to ash. When we finally ceased, only his skeleton remained, charred and ruined.

A light breeze rolled through, and the skeleton collapsed, bits of it had turned to ash and the winds carried those away. A few embers glowed red at the ends of the bones on the ground. The flames surrounding me faded away, and the weight of the world came crashing back to me. I buckled under it, collapsing into Star's arms as she moved to catch me.

My vision blurred, my head spun, and I found it hard to even stay focused on her beautiful face as she leaned down to kiss me. I closed my eyes and relished the feeling of her lips against my own for a moment. I was exhausted and sore and could hold on no longer. My head fell to the side, my body went limp as sleep took me.

CHAPTER 19

I found myself standing alone in the fields outside of the facility. I was watching the walls crumble and the steel beams of the frame bending and twisting. It was serene and quiet, but the building was coming down. I was standing near a pile of burnt bones and ash. Something was coming from inside the building.

I felt its presence on the air, foreboding and massively powerful. It felt like I was standing on the beach, watching a tsunami approach. A gust of wind fluttered my hair as I watched the ruins of the building form into the shape of a skull. A raging green inferno surrounded the macabre metal sculpture as a figure stepped into view.

I blinked and suddenly the creature stood directly before me, its face only inches away from my face. Its appearance was familiar, it looked much like Subject One. This creature stood slightly taller, and its leathery skin was taught, not wrinkled. I could see the muscles moving under the skin as it reached down to the pile of ash and bones at my feet.

Instead of a dark robe, this creature wore plate armor, painted dark black with golden accents. Strange rune patterns glittered in the sunlight across the metal plating. As it kneeled, it plucked a bone from the pile that fell away as dust in the wind. I blinked again, and the creature was standing back at full height, staring down into my face.

Its eyes burned with rage, literally burning as they appeared to contain molten lava. It felt like the beast was looking through me, to something at my core. It raised a clawed hand to the tattoos running down my neck, examining them thoughtfully.

"Such insolence." The beast spoke in my mind, not moving his mouth.

I couldn't respond, I was frozen with fear. His voice was low, raspy, and sounded ancient but powerful. I felt the clawed fingers wrapping around my neck, and I struggled to breathe. Green tendrils forming some semblance of wings emerged from the creature's back, and we rose high into the air.

"I am vengeance incarnate, and you will be judged." The voice again rumbled through my head.

We floated amongst the clouds as a thunderstorm began to form. Dark clouds rolled in with ferocious speed, lightning and thunder crashing between them. The beast drew back his arm and thrust my body towards the earth once more. I watched his body shrink away from me as I fell.

I could hear him laugh in my head, rattling my skull with its tremendous rumble. I rolled in the air to watch the ground looming up towards me. I tried to call my powers to me, but no flames came. I was freefalling with nothing to slow my fall. The dirt rose to greet me, approaching fast. I screamed, but no sound emerged.

I awoke just before I hit the ground. My body jumping from the shock. I was breathing heavily, which reminded me of the pain in my broken ribs. I tried to relax and looked around the room. I was lying on a bed of hay and fur, inside of a small shack. I was back in the village.

A feeling of dread washed over me, as I thought of our friends that had died back at the compound. I didn't want to face Cherry with the news of her father's death, let alone everyone's. They had all perished trying to stop Bach's evil plan, and we let him get away. Tears welled in my eyes, and I felt like a failure.

Star reached from beside the bed, wiping the tears from my eyes as I turned to face her. She had a few bandages here and there, but otherwise looked to be in much better shape than I was. It was bittersweet to look at her, I was so happy to have her back, but my heart ached over what it took. She adjusted a loose bandage on my arm and patted my chest with her hand.

"We got him, pookie." She said, "Whatever that thing was, he's nothing but a pile of soot now."

"I know, I saw it in my dream." I replied. "Where is Callie, did she make it?" I changed the subject.

"She's in the hut next door. She took a beating, and she's banged up just like you, but she'll make it."

"Did anyone tell Cherry?" I asked, not wanting to complete the thought.

"She knows, the poor thing. She brought the others to us after everything was over. A few of them went inside and retrieved the bodies. There's going to be a funeral later, once it starts getting dark." Star replied, wiping more tears from my face.

There was a knock at the door, and Cherry pushed through the grass hanging in the doorway. Her face was solemn, carrying the weight of being an orphan with her. She was carrying a bowl of water and set it down on the table by the door. She walked over and sat down beside me on the bed.

"Cherry, I'm so sorry..." I started.

She held a finger up to her lips to shush me, and then laid down beside me, wrapping her arm around me gently. I wasn't sure how to respond, so I held her for a while. Star rested her head on my shoulder and the three of us sat in silence, commiserating over recent events.

Cherry was a strong girl, she wasn't even crying as I held her. It was almost as if she was the one consoling me, and perhaps she was.

Cherry sat up after a while and broke me out of my thoughts. She hopped of the bed gesturing to her stomach with her hand, then pointed outside.

"I think she wants to go eat." Star said, "That's an idea I can get behind."

Cherry nodded happily at Star's words and rushed out of the room.

"I swear, food is a universal language for you." I said, straining to rise from the bed.

"Hey, a girl's gotta eat!" Star replied, helping me to my feet.

We stepped outside, and I saw Callie walking into the main hall with Cherry in tow. It was good to see her up and about, if she felt anything like I did it was certainly a challenge. I leaned on Star for support as we made our way across the clearing to join the others. I was sore and exhausted, but the promise of food kept me moving.

Inside the hall, the atmosphere was more pleasant than I had expected. The few remaining villagers, about seven in total, all sat around the large table chatting away as they ate their food. Several of them even smiled at us as we joined them. I was baffled at how well everyone was processing things.

Star helped me to a seat beside Callie, and then sat on my other side next to Cherry. We all piled food on our plates, mostly eating in silence but enjoying the company of the others. I was sad to not have Devon's stories, or the lewd jokes from Lemon. I missed the chugging challenges from Twig and Holly, I missed all our friends. Still, conversing with the other villagers was enough to keep my spirits up, that or the food. I was still impressed at how well these people could prepare a feast in the middle of nowhere.

"What do we do now?" Callie asked after a while.

I thought about it for a moment, we hadn't planned beyond this, focusing on trying to get Star back and then stop Bach.

"Bach managed to escape and took his work with him. Without knowing where his other labs are, stopping him is going to be impossible." Star replied.

"We have to try. If we could get home, we would have the resources to try and track him down. I don't have any clue where we are though." I replied, trying to come up with ideas.

"Devon told us this was an island, off the coast of the US." One of the villagers added.

"I'm not sure if that helps you, but maybe it narrows it down?"

I pondered the thought for a bit, chewing on some dried meat. If we could make it back to the mainland, that would be a great place to start.

"That does. Do you have a boat or anything we could use to get back to the mainland?" I asked.

"We have a raft for fishing in the river, but it isn't sea-worthy. It wouldn't take terribly long to build something if we can salvage some materials from the compound." She answered.

I nodded, that could work. There were plenty of things left behind in the facility, despite how torn up it was. Working together it wouldn't take long to gather up materials, and I could check our room again for my purse. Bach had destroyed my phone, but at least if I found my wallet, I would have everything I needed to get into my bank account and get us home if we made it to the mainland. It was as good a plan as any.

"Okay, tomorrow we'll go search the facility for anything we can use. There's plenty of clothing and food we could grab as well, which should make this easier." I announced.

Everyone seemed to agree with the plan, and we sat down to discuss the finer details. I was impressed with the villagers' knowledge of boat construction. Reed, the one who spoke up earlier, had apparently been something of a boating enthusiast before she was taken. She had limited memory of her previous life but could remember the basics of the craft.

She laid out the plans and helped compile a list of items that could be converted for use. Fabric, barrels, wooden furniture, ropes or cords, anything that would float or hold things together would be helpful. I thought about things I had seen while exploring the facility, thinking that we should be able to find plenty of options depending on what had been destroyed. I made a few suggestions here and there for what to look for and where we might find them.

By the time we had finished laying out the plans for the boat, the sun was setting. This meant it was time for the funeral, and sadness returned to me. The others did not seem down about it, however. They moved dutifully outside to where they had prepared things earlier.

Eating had returned some strength to me, and I managed to get to my feet on my own. I walked to the door of the hall to watch the others. They had prepared a large pyre in the center of the village, and now they quietly loaded the covered bodies of our friends. They moved quickly, as if they had done this many times before, and perhaps they had. Devon had mentioned that most of those cast out as failures died, they may have held funerals for them as well.

Once all the bodies were placed on top of the pyre, the villagers gathered around it, holding hands. Cherry stood in the middle, flanked by the others. Callie joined them, but Star and I decided to hang back and observe. Reed gave a bit of a eulogy, thanking the fallen for all they had done to provide and keep them safe over the years they had lived out here.

Everyone dropped hands, and Cherry held up a torch, setting it alight with her powers. She handed it off, lighting another and repeating until they all held lit torches. Each of them stepped forward in unison, placing their torch at the base of the pyre to ignite it. It wasn't long before the pile of wood was completely engulfed. The villagers all backed away and sat down to watch the fire burn.

Star and I joined them then, and we sat quietly watching as the fire sent our friends on their final journey. Boughs of green branches and flowers had been incorporated into the pile to help mask the smell of the burning bodies. I leaned against Star, watching the smoke rise into the evening sky, sobbing quietly in mourning. I had known them for only a short time, but I felt the loss, nonetheless.

"You cry for them." Reed stated, scooting over to join us.

I nodded, "I can't help but feel as though I'm responsible for their deaths."

"You did what you could, we all knew the dangers before you left for the facility." Reed replied, placing her hand on my shoulder.

"Devon taught us of the cycles of life and death, and how to accept it for what it is. We have lost many over the years, and while it is sad to lose loved ones, at least they rest now, free of the shackles of this life." She explained.

Her eyes were calm and focused as she spoke, she seemed almost happy for them. I envied her convictions.

"If anyone is responsible, it is Sebastian and his foul experiments. That our friends gave their lives trying to stop him is cause for gratitude. We honor them tonight and bid them farewell."

"That's sweet of you. I'm sure they would be grateful." Star said.

"I will find him and end this." I said sternly, "I won't let their sacrifice be for nothing!"

"I believe you will, Trianna. You are stronger than any of us. If anyone stands a chance, it is you." Reed said cheerfully.

She shared her mead with me, and we sat quietly together for a while watching the fire. Her confidence in me was empowering, I was glad that she felt that way. I felt like I had let the others down so far, but I resolved to make up for that. No matter what it took, no matter how long, I would find Bach and make him pay for everything.

We spent the rest of the evening honoring the fallen with celebration. A couple of the villagers brought out some makeshift instruments to play music for us. We drank and laughed and told stories honoring our friends.

At one point the villagers began dancing, and while I was too sore to attempt, Star was more than happy to dance by the fire with the others.

I watched her dance and my heart swelled. She moved so fluidly, spinning this way and that, hair spinning and fluttering as she moved. Her body was stunning, and it was accentuated pleasantly by the firelight. Her movements cast a spell over me, captivating me with each step.

She was so pure, and I loved her more than anything. I could have spent days watching her dance around the funeral pyre. Her innocence was a raw force, and certainly one to be reckoned with. She was magnificent.

After a few hours, the fire began to die down signaling the end of the night. The villagers gathered up their instruments and began returning to their huts for the night. I had quite a bit to drink, so getting to my feet required some aid. Star chuckled, supporting me with her shoulder.

Callie stayed with Cherry, so she wouldn't be alone all night, and Cherry seemed pleased to have her company. They had been growing close, and that made me feel better about Cherry's situation. Callie had such a motherly aspect to her that it seemed only natural for her to cling to Cherry in her time of need. She would make a good surrogate mother for the young girl.

Star escorted me back to our hut, helping me support my weight. She was careful not to put any pressure on my injured ribs as she ushered me along. Even if my head hadn't been swimming, I might still have needed some help, my injuries still getting the better of me. Some rest would do me much good.

We climbed into the bed together, happy to be in each other's arms once again. Despite everything, our relationship held strong, perhaps it was even stronger now for sharing in these latest trials and tribulations. Star nuzzled her head up against my chest and quickly dozed off. I smiled and fell asleep to the rhythm of her breath.

CHAPTER 20

The next day we grouped up in the main hall for a light breakfast before we set out. Everyone was coming with us, since it seemed the facility was abandoned now. We shouldn't have to worry about anyone attacking us, but there was still the threat of parts of the building collapsing. The battles with Subject One had significantly compromised parts of the building, but as large as it was, most stood stable.

We ate quickly, ready to get started on the day's tasks. Reed reminded everyone of what to look for, and as we walked through the trees, we decided what groups would go in which direction. The forest seemed calm, birds chirped happily overhead, and at one point I heard a boar grunting in the distance. This was some cause for concern, as wild boars are notoriously violent, but the sound moved further away from us as we walked.

As we arrived at the edge of the forest, I stopped to survey the damage. The east wing of the building where the laboratories were, was mostly caved in on itself. The warehouse seemed intact, as did most of the west and southern wings, save for some exterior damage from the helicopter crash. All in all, the structure still seemed sound.

My eyes traced over the area in the grass where Star and I had killed Subject One. The path where my fire had burned away the grass was dark with ash, and even still some smoke rose from the edges. My memory flashed with traces from the event, and I marveled at the power I had called forth, let alone what Star had added to it. We were a force to be reckoned with, a point I would be happy to prove to Bach when I found him again.

We moved across the lawn quickly, eager to begin our search. Inside the lobby Callie gathered up some papers and drew some crude maps for each of the groups, laying out the basic path to various rooms. We all split up, some went to the warehouse and labs to look for barrels, others went in search of food. A couple began carrying out tables and other bits of wooden furniture from the dining room next to the lobby.

Star and I headed up to the suites to check for anything left that we had brought with us. Callie and Cherry came along far enough to reach the wardrobe floor to begin gathering fabrics. We were relieved to find that the other elevator was working, somehow it had not been destroyed when we dropped the first one on Subject One. We parted ways at the wardrobe floor to begin our search higher up.

Up in the suites, the walls were shredded from the helicopter attack. We didn't need any codes from Callie to get back into the room, we just stepped through the gaping holes. There wasn't much left of the room, the floor was covered in water from burst pipes. We managed to find a few of our things undamaged, hidden behind fallen furniture. Thankfully, my wallet was one of them.

We decided to leave our mostly ruined clothes, and head down to the wardrobe floor with Callie to help gather clothing for everyone else. Star, having a bit of background in the clothing industry, had kept a mental image of everyone's build. Using her memory for reference we pulled a variety of jeans, shirts in a few different sizes as well as some thick jackets to help protect from any harsh elements at sea.

Callie had changed out of my tight clothing and into something that better fit her form. I couldn't help but admire how well everything fit. Star poked me lightly in the ribs to remind me of the task at hand. We loaded everything we could on to a luggage cart to bring back downstairs, carrying some things in our arms.

The whole time we spent looking around had been uninterrupted, but I kept feeling like something was watching us. I glanced around, but never managed to spot anything. I chalked it up to paranoia and kept moving. We got the cart loaded into the elevator and started to head back downstairs.

"Oh! You know, the screens in the theater might be helpful to make a sail or something." Star chimed.

"That's not a bad idea. It's a large sheet of some kind of fabric, so I'm sure Reed can find a use for it. Let's see if we can get it down." I replied.

We punched the button for the floor the theater was on and set off to see about retrieving the screen. I had noticed Cherry staring at things the whole trip, it occurred to me she was seeing much of this for the first time. She had been born in the village, so this was her first glimpse of civilization. I wondered if she would be fearful of the real world.

In the theater she ran up and down the rows of seats, sitting on the edges of the fold up seating and letting it drop her into place while she giggled excitedly. Her innocence weighed out over any fears she may have it seemed. It was refreshing to watch her play and just enjoy being a child.

"You see this big white screen on the wall? If this place was working, we could watch a big movie on it." I said.

Cherry cocked her head to the side with confusion, it hadn't occurred to me that she had no clue what a movie was.

"It's like being told a story, only by pictures of people moving on the screen. We'll have to show you one day when we get off the island!" Star chimed in.

I walked over to where the screen hung from the wall and tried to figure out how to get it down. There was a pulley system that appeared to raise and lower the screen, but it was attached to a mechanism on the wall at the top of the room. While I pondered this, Callie waved her hands and pulled the cinderblocks from the wall, bringing the whole contraption down with it.

"That works." I shrugged.

With some effort, we got the screen free from the mechanism, folding it up as best we could for something so large. We packed it onto the cart with the clothing and headed back for the main floor. Again, as we were leaving, I got that uncomfortable feeling that we were not alone up here. The others were all downstairs, so I wasn't sure who could be up here. Perhaps there were a few drones left behind, waiting for a chance to ambush us.

We made it back to the lobby without interference, however. We rejoined Reed and a few others outside on the lawn, looking over the pile of materials that had been gathered. We had plenty of tables to make a surface, several barrels to create a pontoon of sorts to keep us afloat, and a variety of ropes, cords, and chains to hold everything together.

We had spent most of the day sifting through the compound for food and materials, and it seemed we more than achieved our goal. Now came the daunting task of getting everything down to the shore, and then of course, actually constructing the boat. Reed was confident in her ability to do so, and no one seemed to contest it.

We had found some lumber in the warehouse, and with the help of some pallets fashioned something to carry the bulk of the supplies on as a group. In the midday sun, having fewer trips to make was appreciated. It still took four or five trips to get everything moved where we needed it. We took only a short break for food, wanting to stay focused on the task at hand.

Reed began giving everyone tasks to focus on to prepare for construction. We emptied the barrels, laid out rope to fasten them to the tables, and even mixed a basic plaster from sand and mud to help seal the wood to prevent leaks. We gathered leaves and strips of fabric to cover the mud, which would hopefully keep everything water tight. We used some of the wood to create rudimentary tools with stones as well.

The rest of the day was spent getting everything prepared, and then returning to the village for dinner and rest. Everyone had been working hard all day, and the downtime was appreciated by all. We ate, drank, and chatted about nothing just to pass the time. Sleep came to us all with little effort.

We spent the next several days working in groups on the construction of the boat. We prepared food to be loaded on as well, several day's-worth, since we had no idea how far we would need to travel. It was a bonding experience for us all. Reed was a great supervisor, assigning everyone to something new once a task was completed and guiding us all through the process.

The work was hard, but with everyone contributing it came together nicely. After about five days we had something that resembled a boat, all we needed to do was test it. It took quite a bit of effort from all of us, but we managed to get the thing into the water, and it floated with little effort. Reed inspected everything several times over, patching up small holes with our mud plaster to ensure it would stay afloat.

"It isn't pretty, but I believe it's seaworthy." Reed proclaimed, tying off a line to keep the boat from escaping with the current.

"I'm impressed, I wasn't sure we'd pull it off." I replied.

"Well, I'm going to let it sit in the water overnight, see how the wood swells, make sure it stays together, but I think it'll hold up."

Most of the group had returned to the village for the night, to get things ready to leave the next day. Cherry was splashing in the waves and picking up shells. Callie sat talking with Star as they watched Cherry play. I sat down on the sand with Reed, observing the boat. We shared a drink, admiring our work.

The boat was nicer than I had expected, it had a covered area for the food storage, and enough room for us all to huddle together without much discomfort. We had managed to fashion the theater screen into a sail that Reed would work by hand to get us moving. With Callie's help pulling up some stones, we had a makeshift anchor to keep us from drifting if we needed to stop.

"How far do you think it is to the mainland?" I asked.

"It's hard to say, I can't see it from shore, but there are other islands blocking the horizon." Reed answered, staring out over the sea.

I followed her gaze, trying to make out anything in the distance, but to no avail. The view was stunning however, the sun was setting, painting both the sky and the water gorgeous colors. Given that the sun sets in the west, we at least knew what direction to set sail. We had made the trip by helicopter rather quickly, so I figured we had to be on the east coast somewhere.

"What do you want to do, when we make landfall?" Reed asked.

"Well, I managed to find my wallet up in the suites, so I can get some money and a ride for us. From there, I guess we can head to my house and start working on tracking down Bach, hopefully before he causes too much damage." I replied.

"I think I want to try to find a new life." Reed said calmly.

I looked at her curiously. I had assumed everyone would want to help us stop Bach.

"I talked it over with the others, we just aren't equipped for this revenge. We couldn't even help Cotton on hunts. I'm a builder, not a fighter." She continued.

"I can't say I blame you." I replied, "I can't stop though. I'm one for holding a grudge."

"You also have a tremendous power. Without taking the Opulentia again, we have little to contribute. None of us want to go back to it either." Reed sipped at her mead.

"You don't have to fight. You all have done so much just to survive this long. Even helping us get home is more than I could ask." I explained.

"Feels wrong, knowing our friends died for the cause, but it would be wasteful to throw our lives away if we have a chance to get away from it all. Cotton used to talk about that a lot. He wanted to run a farm, raise his family, live a simple life." Reed said, staring into the sky.

"That's a good dream. I think if you all choose to leave and pursue that kind of life, that they would approve." I said, placing my hand on her shoulder.

"I think so too. I hope you aren't angry with us for it though."

"Of course not. I'm grateful for everything you've done for us. When we get back, you guys can stay with us for a while, and I'll get you some money or whatever you need to get on your feet. It's the least I can do."

"You're a good person, Trianna. Don't let this quest for vengeance change that." Reed said, standing up and brushing the sand from her pants.

"Vengeance can consume a person, twist them into something dark. That Opulentia flowing in your veins could make it worse. Stay true to yourself."

She patted my shoulder and left, heading back to the village after checking the anchor line on the boat. I sat for a while, thinking about her words. My rage and thirst for vengeance was strong, and I had to wonder if anything inside me was amplifying the feeling. We gained these powers from the blood of that strange creature, there was no telling what that might do to us internally.

Star and Callie came over, carrying Cherry between them. She kicked her legs and laughed, enjoying the attention. I stood to join them, and we walked back to the village together.

"What were you two talking about?" I asked playfully.

"I'm leaving you for Callie, we are going to raise Cherry and a herd of goats together. I wanted to put it more gracefully, but you put me on the spot." Star chuckled, and I rolled my eyes.

"Well, I hope you'll send me some cheese and milk at least." I replied, taking her other hand in mine.

"We didn't speak of such things." Callie interjected, and I couldn't help but laugh.

"I can see you need a few lessons in sarcasm." I said, and Callie blushed.

Back at the village, we returned to our huts to have a light meal and sleep for the night. Most of the others retired quickly, exhausted from the effort we put in over the last several days. The next day was going to be even more work, so we needed as much rest as we could get. I was having trouble sleeping though.

I kept having dreams of that other creature in the dark armor. When they woke me, I would lay there lost in thought. I thought of the trip to the compound, and of several other times since, where I felt like I was being watched. I never saw anything, but the feeling was strong.

Was my dream a premonition? Was there another of those horrid creatures here with us on the island? Was it out there now, watching and waiting for the right time to strike? I had so many questions, but eventually exhaustion would get the better of me and whisk me back to sleep.

CHAPTER 21

Morning came, and we were all up with the sun. The villagers packed up some of their personal belongings, but none of us had much to bring on the trip. We convened for one last group feast of a breakfast, clearing out the last of what we couldn't store easily on the boat. It was mostly fruits and breads that were close to going bad anyway.

A few of the villagers left marked stones around the ashes of the funeral pyre, to honor our fallen friends until time eroded away the stone. It was a quaint gesture, and I even paused for a moment to pass on my respects. They sacrificed everything to get us here, I will never forget them. I owed them that much at the very least.

We gathered at the shore, where Reed inspected the boat, to ensure nothing had gone wrong overnight. She double checked every possible seal, tightened ropes and cords, ensuring every detail was in place for the journey ahead. Jumping up on the deck, she clapped her hands together, proud of our group accomplishment.

"All aboard! Everything's holding strong, we should be good to go!" Reed exclaimed.

The group cheered, and we began loading our food into the covered area reserved for storage. The boat held the weight of our group with surprising ease. There were seven of the villagers, counting Reed and Cherry, then Callie, Star, and myself. The barrel pontoons were quite strong, and for that I was grateful.

Reed drew in the anchor and pushed us away from the shore with a large stick. The boat rocked for a moment but settled back nicely into place, moving only slightly with the light rolling waves. Moving back to her place at the center of the boat, Reed whipped the ropes to open the sail and managed to find a breeze to get us moving. We cheered loudly, and then we were on our way.

"This is the first time I've ever been on a boat!" Star said clapping.

I thought about it for a moment, realizing the same was true for myself. Star watched the ocean from the side of the boat pointing out schools of fish swimming beneath us. The water was fantastically clear in the shallows around the island, you could nearly see clear to the bottom.

"Dolphins!" Star cried excitedly. "Whoa, this is so cool!"

The villagers, many of whom still had broken memories, followed her gaze to a pod of dolphins leaping amongst the waves. We watched in awe at the majestic creatures as they went about their task of catching fish and playing, or whatever else a dolphin does at sea with no current threat of predators. That thought suggested the possibility of encountering sharks, and I frowned. I hoped we didn't end up needing to recreate any scenes from Deep Blue Sea along the way.

Reed was keeping us on a westward path, carefully guiding us around small jutting rocks as we passed a few other islands. I sat next to Star, holding her hand and watching the beautiful views. It was nice to be in such a romantic setting, even though we were a bunch of mostly lost refugees escaping a deserted island. The untamed growth of nature on some of the island we passed struck me with awe, trees hanging out over the sea decorated with flocks of seafaring birds.

I wish I had studied biology more, identifying the birds might give me an idea where the hell we were. The best I could manage was telling one feathery bastard from another. The larger birds with the massive beaks were pelicans, the smaller noisy ones were gulls. Aside from that, I was coming up with nothing.

Given the length of the helicopter ride to get to the island, we couldn't be terribly far from the coast, but I had no idea how to translate flight time to nautical miles either. Thankfully Reed knew how to pilot the boat, at least. If this had been left up to me, we'd likely be on the bottom of the sea by now. If we had even made it off the island in the first place that is. Lost in thought, I hadn't noticed that we had begun to slow down.

"We're losing wind." Reed said, trying to work the rudder into a position to keep us moving.

"Well, that's not helpful." I said, standing as I tried to think of a solution. I couldn't just blast flames at it, the boat was flammable.

"Oh, I know!" I exclaimed, snapping my finger with the thought. "Cherry, how about giving us a boost?"

Cherry sat up rubbing her eyes, apparently, she had fallen asleep in the few hours we had been cruising along so far. I explained to her that we needed some wind to get us moving again. She smiled and nodded, moving to stand near Reed.

"Give us a good wind, little one." Reed said, pulling the ropes to ready the sail.

Cherry raised and arm and wiggled her fingers, calling forth a gust of wind that she ushered into the sail. The attempt was overzealous, as the wind slammed into the sails, the boat lurched violently. We had to shift our weight to keep the boat from toppling over, and Cherry dismissed the gust.

"Easy there girl, a little less vigor would be better." Reed said, bracing against the rudder.

Cherry frowned but tried again. This time the wind caught the sail much easier, and the boat sailed on peacefully. Reed nodded her approval, and Cherry smiled, turning her focus to keeping the gust steady. The group settled and returned to whatever they were passing time with now that things seemed to be back under control.

A few more hours passed, and we had gotten away from the string of islands into open water. Star had magnetized a nail for Reed to use in a makeshift compass, so we could keep our heading. I wasn't exactly sure how long we had been sailing, but I was already getting tired of the sea. A few of the villagers had developed seasickness and were puking over the side in shifts.

The sun was beaming high overhead, indicating it was somewhere around noon. It was incredibly hot, we had all stripped off much of our clothing and tried to huddle in the shade of the sail. I had tried to distract myself with food and drink, but the constant need to wipe sweat from my eyes made it difficult. Scanning the horizon, it seemed we still had quite a distance to cover before reaching land.

I looked over the scene on the boat, amusing myself with the thought of tourists reacting to a boat full of naked men and women with strange tattoos arriving on the beach. The headlines would be hilarious. 'SEA BASED SEX CULT DESCENDS ON LOCAL BEACH!' or something else equally ridiculous. It would probably also feature an interview with someone claiming that they witnessed us sacrificing a goat as we made landfall, dripping the blood on our genitals, and screaming like banshees.

"What are you smiling about?" Star asked, chugging at her waterskin.

"Just thinking of what the natives will think if we don't get dressed before we reach land." I replied, trying to think of more amusing news stories.

"Oh, my. Yeah, we should do something about that." Star said, closing her eyes again.

No one even attempted to redress though, it was too damn hot. I watched Callie passing the time by braiding her hair, delicately moving her fingers through the strands. Most everyone else was asleep or trying to be, except for Reed, stalwart in her role of keeping us moving. We had caught some more wind, relieving Cherry of her duty and she too had laid down for a nap.

Boredom was getting the better of me. I had seen nothing but water on the horizon for quite some time. I feared I might go crazy if something didn't change soon. It was better than fighting off monsters and soldiers though, so I decided not to complain.

My mind wandered often as we floated along. I thought of the creature I saw in my dreams, praying that it remained just that. I wasn't getting my hopes up though, because the last time I dreamt of one of those creatures it tried to kill me a few days later. This new one felt more intense, and I really didn't want to cross paths with him.

I also thought of our friends, Cotton, Devon, Twig, Holly, Azalea, Lemon, Birch. I had grown fond of them quickly, but our time together had been so short. I still felt pangs of guilt over their death, but after talking with the others I was feeling better. I would avenge them, and that kept me going.

I lay down beside Star, cuddling against her. The shade from the sail had grown now that the sun wasn't directly overhead, so being that close to her was now more bearable. I was grateful that Star didn't blame me for everything that had happened to us. The weight of that fear had been crushing me. I couldn't live with myself if she hated me, and thankfully I didn't have to.

She held me gently, barely stirring from her rest. It was the best I had felt in weeks. Even adrift in the ocean, just being with her again made me happy. Watching her chest rise and fall with her breath washed away my troubled thoughts. She really was something else.

"Land!" Reed cried, tearing me away from my thoughts.

"What!? Really!?" I asked, bolting up.

I looked ahead of the boat, and sure enough, there on the horizon the shapes of land faded into view. I could see other boats drifting along, likely fishing boats or tourists of some kind. Everyone on the boat began to rally, eagerly watching our approach. I suggested that we should all put our clothes back on before reaching civilization.

Even with land in sight, it took what felt like hours to reach the shore. Reed carefully steered us as close as she could, dropping the anchor once she felt dunes of sand scraping the bottom of the barrels. We cheered and exchanged hugs, simply excited that we had made it this far on our rickety little craft. It was truly an impressive feat.

Thankfully, we had not landed on a public beach, and hopefully dodged making any bizarre headlines or inspiring any stark mad interviews. The shore was littered with rocks and downed trees. We had to put in some effort to get the boat ashore and prevent it from drifting back out to sea as trash. We would have to leave it there, however, as it would be impossible to get it through the woods we were now faced with traversing.

"Well, we made it to land." Callie remarked, "What now?"

"Now, we find a phone. I need to get in touch with someone to get us a ride out of here. I need to figure out just where the hell we are though, so let's keep an eye out for signs or anything that might give us an answer." I replied, pointing into the woods.

Everyone gathered up their packs, bringing along fresh waterskins and some food in case we needed to stop for the night. I wasn't sure how far we would have to trek through these woods before we found anything. The venture through the sea was long and tiring, and we only had a few hours of daylight left. I wasn't thrilled at the idea of spending a night in strange woods, but I wasn't seeing another option so far.

We walked for hours, making our way through the trees as best we could. The denim clothes we had taken from the compound was proving to be a helpful armor from the brush. As the light began to fade, we managed to find a clearing large enough to set up a small camp for the night. I was grateful that Reed had decided to bring the sail with us. We laid it out on the ground for a sleeping surface.

We set up a small spot for a campfire, which I ignited easily. We managed to chop up some fallen logs into firewood to last the night. The villagers prepared some food, rationing out what we had been able to carry from the boat. As we ate, we came up with a watch schedule to make sure we weren't eaten by beasts in the night. We had no real plan for preventing the insects from eating us, unfortunately.

I sat with Callie, still eating and watching the fire, when I noticed Star playing a little game with Cherry. It was cute to see how well they were getting along. I hadn't put much thought into having kids of my own, until recently I was in no state to even consider it. It was all I could manage to take care of myself.

"They're cute together, aren't they?" Callie asked, realizing I was staring.

"Yeah. They truly are. I think I will ask Cherry to stay with us once we make it home. Give her a better chance at life." I said

"Oh, getting a motherly feeling, are we?" Callie jested.

"Sort of. I feel like I owe it to Cotton to make sure she's okay. We've got the means to get her some schooling and what not. It just feels right." I replied.

"If it wouldn't be too much trouble, could I stay with you too? I've grown rather fond of Cherry myself, I'd like to help watch after her." Callie asked nervously.

"We have plenty of room. I was going to let everyone stay with us, but Reed mentioned they wanted to go start their own lives again. Move on from all this." I explained.

"That would be good for them." Callie said, "Are you sure I wouldn't be imposing?"

"You can stay with us, we could use your help tracking down Bach, and even if you just want to stay and watch over Cherry that's fine too." I replied.

"Thank you, I will offer whatever aid I can. I too would like to see this all end, before he can hurt anyone else." Callie rested her head on my shoulder and smiled.

"Besides, if you don't stay with us, how am I going to help you make new memories?" I gave her a hug, rubbing her arm for assurance.

Callie looked up at me and smiled again, clearly content with my answer. I was more than happy to help her given that she had saved my life and helped save Star's as well. I could never repay her for any of that. Having her and Cherry around would certainly liven up the mood at our place.

The night wound down, and everyone cuddled up near the fire to sleep. I volunteered for the first watch, I wouldn't have been able to sleep much anyway. Sure, I was tired from travelling, but my mind was still all over the place. Trying to figure out how exactly we were going to find Bach, let alone stop him.

I could easily sell off some assets to replace the money he stole from us, that was a good starting point. We could buy some new equipment and maybe hire a Private Investigator, but I worried about the possibility of getting someone else killed in the process. I should probably get a new gun too, magic power was great, but a round to the head would put Bach down much quicker.

I frowned at my thoughts. I had never been a violent person. I'd been in my share of fights, growing up abused and different will lead to that after all, but I had never tried to kill anyone. Over the last few weeks, I had killed several people. Some deserved it, but some were just in the way. I wasn't thrilled about that, but I told myself that I had done what I had to for survival's sake. I was sure it would haunt me, though.

A few hours passed, with nothing but some distant noises to get my attention. I spent the time in my head, which was likely more dangerous, but it's not like I had any other forms of entertainment to pass the time. It wouldn't be much longer before I needed to wake up Reed for her watch. I was impressed with her tenacity, having captained the ship all day, hiking into the woods, and now taking a watch shift. She had insisted on it, though, and couldn't be talked out of it.

I watched the stars through the gaps in the trees for a while longer, and then roused Reed. I left her at the post and made my way over to the fire to stoke it up and then find Star. After placing a few logs in the pit and getting the fire roaring again, I made my way over to the girls. Star, Callie and Cherry had cuddled up near the fire, so I didn't have far to go to squeeze in with them. I wrapped my arms around her, and Star shimmied up closer to me barely stirring from her sleep.

It was a chilly night, and I was glad we thought to bring the jackets from the compound. Star had placed hers over Cherry as a blanket, and her skin was a little chilled. I held her close to share my body heat with her and keep her warm. Callie rolled over and wrapped her arm around me as well, gripping me tightly, but not waking either. It was easy to fall asleep with the comfort they provided.

The rest of the night passed without issue, and we awoke in the morning surprisingly well rested. We packed things up quickly, buried the fire pit, and set off from the campsite. We ate a light meal while moving, nearing the end of the food we were able to carry with us. Hopefully it wouldn't take long to make it out of the woods and find some civilization to rejoin.

After a few hours of walking, we stumbled across a clearing in the trees. There we found a sign, a building, and a man. The building was non-descript, the sign read

'Alligator River National Wildlife Refuge' and the man, in his forestry service uniform, held a shotgun over his shoulder, sipping coffee. He gave us a puzzled look as we approached, unsure of our presence for obvious reasons.

"Hey, there's no camping! What are you people doing out here?" He asked

"We were sailing, and our boat got swept away from the island we were on. We washed up on shore on the other side of the woods and have been trying to find a way out. We're so glad to find you!" I lied.

It wasn't all lies, really, but hopefully enough to get him to help instead of just calling the police.

"Well, you do look like you've been through some shit. You're lucky nothing ate you out there, this place doesn't see many people this far back. Could've run into wolves or bears!" He exclaimed.

"Well, that sounds terrible. I'm glad we have you to help us. Do you have a phone we could use to get a ride out of here?" I asked, batting my eyes a little.

"Not up here, ain't got no signal. I'll have to radio down to HQ and have 'em send up a tour bus to get you all out." He said.

"That would be great, you're so nice!" Star added.

"Ya'll come inside, now. I got some coffee brewed you can have while we wait." He gestured towards the door.

We headed inside and tried to make ourselves comfortable. The building wasn't very big, but there was room enough for us to sit along the wall waiting on our new friend to radio for help. He made his way to his desk and picked up the radio.

"Hey Quincy, gonna need you to send an empty bus up my way. Had a whole flock of folk just come up out the woods needing a ride. Yeah, I know, it's weird. They said they were shipwrecked and washed up here. They don't seem to want to cause any trouble, so I figure we just get 'em out of here before the lieutenant gets in and raises a fuss. Thanks, see ya in a bit." He spoke into the receiver.

His accent was thick but familiar, and I figured we had to still be in the south.

"Where are we anyway?" I asked, leaning against his desk.

"Well, this is a forestry service station in the wildlife refuge. Alligator River, just outside Buffalo City." He replied, gesturing to the brochure on his desk.

I glanced at it and realized we were near the Outer Banks in North Carolina. I thought that made for a strange place to have a hidden research facility but given all the supposedly undisturbed wildlife refuges in the area, it could likely make for good cover while keeping it hidden. He could disguise his travel with tourism traffic, and likely stay far enough away from shore to go undetected by the locals.

"Thanks again, we're so sorry to cause a fuss. We'll be out of your hair in no time." I said, a little flirtatiously.

"I appreciate that, shouldn't take long for Quincy to get the bus up here. Y'all can use the phones at the public terminal, and maybe drop a donation in the box for us keeping things quiet." He suggested with a smile.

I smiled back in agreement. Anything to keep us out of handcuffs for trespassing on government property. I made my way back over to the group to sit and wait. Southern hospitality is engrained in a lot of folks in the south, as is a strong desire to not have to deal with any excessive amounts of bullshit. Once I got to a phone and got us a ride, I'd happily leave them to their daily routine.

It only took about twenty minutes for Quincy to arrive with the bus. He and Flint, according to his nametag, had a short discussion about the matter. Flint insisted it was in everyone's best interest to get us out before their boss showed up, no questions asked. Quincy agreed, and escorted us down to the public terminal and showed me to a phone.

Digging through my wallet, I pulled out the card for my accountant. She complained about not hearing from me, and I simply told her it was a long story, and I needed some help. She ordered a rental car for us, and was having it delivered, but it would take a few hours to arrive. She tried to raise a fuss, but when I briefly explained why my account was suddenly missing millions of dollars, she got quiet fearing that I might blame her for the breach.

Reassuring her that I wasn't going to terminate her contract, I gave her some instructions to work on recouping the loss. I also gave her explicit instructions not to involve the police, as I wasn't sure I could trust them. With Bach working on such a devious plan, I wouldn't put it past him to have connections in law enforcement to help stop people from interfering. She agreed to follow my directions, and to keep everything under wraps, working for rich people she had experience in keeping things quiet.

The group had taken seats in the terminal, looking over the various books and brochures, to blend in with the tourists. I rejoined them, letting them know our way home was on the way. We'd be stuck here for a while waiting for the rental to be dropped off, but at least there was air conditioning. The vending machine had a card reader, so I was able to buy some snacks and drinks for everyone. This looked much less suspicious than the leaf-wrapped foods and waterskins.

A few of the villagers could remember candy and sodas, despite their broken memories, and were excited to enjoy them again. Callie and Star introduced Cherry to M&M's for the first time, Cherry was thrilled. I enjoyed seeing her face light up at the new experience. She munched the candy cheerfully, practically begging for more.

There were so many things we could share with her, and that was exciting to think about. I hadn't considered that aspect of raising a child. It would be fun for all of us to introduce her to the things we enjoyed, video games, movies, restaurants, zoos, the list goes on. I could get used to that kind of family life, I thought.

A few hours of waiting patiently in the terminal finally paid off as a man entered with the keys to a van with third row seating. I thanked him, waving politely as he made his exit. I directed everyone outside where they piled into the van, settling into their seats for the long ride back to our house in South Carolina.

CHAPTER 22

It took about seven hours to drive home from the wildlife refuge, despite my fast driving. We made a few short stops for supplies, most importantly a GPS. I even got us all some fast food, something of a treat for everyone. It was terrible for us, but having spent that long in the woods, it was the easiest way to get a cheeseburger inside them. It's the little things that bring joy sometimes.

We pulled up to the gate, and I punched in the code to allow us entry to the property. I waved to Gerald, the groundskeeper, who was watering some flowers as we passed, he seemed happy to see us back again. He and his wife helped us keep up the place. He handled the lawns while his wife, Beatrice, kept the house clean and fed the cat when we were out of town. I paid them well, and even had a small house built for them on the property that they lived in rent free.

I was excited to be home again. We had been away for at least a month, but it felt much longer. I could hear the villagers in the back gasping at the size of the house as we pulled up. I had found out over the course of the trip that none of them could remember being wealthy. Bach apparently had many sources for abducting people and had only targeted us for monetary gain.

Callie perked up, gazing at the grounds as we made our way up the lengthy drive to the house.

"You live here?" she asked in awe.

"You do too, now. Welcome home! We have several bedrooms, so you are all welcome to stay as long as you need to get back on your feet." I explained to the group.

Star smiled, holding my hand. I could tell she was glad to be home too. I couldn't wait to get inside, see my cat, and then take a proper shower. The car reeked of swamp ass, so I would probably need to have it cleaned before returning it. I pulled the van up by the steps leading into the house and parked it.

"We're here!" I said, unbuckling my seatbelt and jumping out of the car to stretch.

Beatrice met us at the door, with a smile wide on her face.

"Lady Von Drake! We were so worried about you, it is not like you to leave for so long and not contact us!" She scolded me as I hugged her.

"I know, I'm sorry. Our vacation took a rough turn, and we got in some trouble. We are home now though, you don't have to worry anymore." I explained.

"I see you have company?" she asked, gesturing to the flock of people emerging from the van.

"Yes! We picked up some of Star's relatives and friends on the way home." I lied, "They will be staying with us for a little while."

"Splendid news! I will prepare a meal to welcome you all home, you must be hungry from the trip." She exclaimed.

"Okay, but only if you and Gerald join us. You are always too kind to us." I said, ushering the others into the house to get settled.

The night passed quickly, Beatrice cooked up a fantastic meal for everyone, and we devoured it. The food the villagers made in the woods was impressive, but nothing beats home cooking. Gerald and Beatrice ate dinner with us, but left shortly after, not wanting to keep us up all night. They were some of the sweetest people I knew.

Once they had left, Star and I showed everyone to the guest rooms, letting them pair up as they wished. We picked out two rooms specifically for Cherry and Callie to stay in. Everyone settled in quickly, bellies full and tired from the long day. Star took my hand and escorted me to our bedroom upstairs.

"It feels so good to be home." Star said, petting Echo as she laid on the bed.

"I was worried we'd never see it again." I said, collapsing beside them.

"I knew we would, I had faith in you. I always have." Star said, caressing my cheek.

I stared at her for a moment, taking in her beauty. She leaned forward and kissed me passionately, pulling me closer to her and scaring the cat off the bed.

We were naked in seconds, bodies rolling and tangling on the bed. Passion overwhelmed us, and we lost ourselves in each other for a while. Afterwards, sweaty and panting, we laid back watching the stars over the sea from our window. Star fell asleep before me, and I gently caressed her arm until I drifted off as well.

We spent the next two weeks helping Reed and the others come up with a plan to get their lives in order. I made some calls to old friends that agreed to give them jobs, with only a little explanation of why they didn't have official paperwork. I bought a plot of land and had some modular homes delivered for everyone to live in while they figured things out for themselves. Star helped them get some clothes together, and Beatrice packed them some lunches before they left.

They piled into a van that I bought for them, luckily a few remembered how to drive. We all exchanged hugs and thanks, wishing everyone well before they left. It was bittersweet watching them go. I had grown fond of them, but I knew they needed this. They had a standing invitation to return if they needed any help at all, and that would have to be enough for now. I hoped they would be able to find peace in their new lives on their own.

Cherry held Callie's hand and waved goodbye to her friends. She was thrilled to get to stay with us in the big house by the sea. Callie was excited too and insisted on helping Beatrice with the housework. We couldn't talk her out of it, and Beatrice honestly needed the help. It didn't take long for everyone to settle into our new family unit.

We hired tutors for Cherry, to help her adapt to living in the real world, and hopefully get her able to speak. She loved to learn, and always seemed thrilled to do her schoolwork. I never had that much enthusiasm for school, but I was glad for her. Callie sat in on many of the lessons when she could, also thrilled for the chance to re-learn things she couldn't remember from her life before.

We converted a few of the bedrooms into a large office and filled it with computers and various things to help us try and track down Bach. We hired a few private investigators, asking them only to help us find him but not get too close. I didn't want them getting killed for poking their noses around Bach's plans, but they assured me they were used to danger in their line of work. I knew they weren't prepared for this sort of danger but hired them anyway.

We managed to learn that The Paradigm Corporation was merely a shell organization that Bach set up to launder money through. It had no official location and operated mostly out of hidden accounts overseas. We didn't have many other leads to go on, so things looked grim. Star assured me we would find him eventually.

One morning we as were sitting down to breakfast, the phone rang. I checked the screen and frowned at the private number on the display. I had a sinking feeling but answered anyway.

"Good morning, Lady Von Drake." Bach's voice spoke over the phone.

I slammed my hand on the table in rage but said nothing.

"I hope you are doing well. Glad to see you made it home. I know you've had people snooping around trying to find me. I'd be disappointed if you didn't to be honest. You won't be able to stop me, though." he said mockingly.

"You sure about that? I've got a lot of resources at my command here." I replied, my voice cold and serious.

"Oh, I'm quite sure. However, I suspect we shall cross paths again. I've learned that you are quite persistent. I hope you take care of Star for me, I'll be glad to take her back anytime."

"Can't find a new source for your blood drugs?" I asked.

"Oh, I already have, but she was something else. That power you both displayed was impressive to say the least. I've got to run, I just wanted to check in on my girls." He replied.

"You son of a bitch, when I get my hands on you... You'll wish you had just killed me." I threatened.

"Now that would have been such a waste. Have a nice day, Trianna. Until next we meet." He said, ending the call.

I slammed the phone on the table in rage, cracking the screen. Star and Callie looked at me concerned.

"That was Bach. He wanted to check in on us. He knows we are after him." I explained.

"Well, that means we are getting close. Maybe he's trying to get under our skin because he's scared." Star replied.

"Maybe, but I don't know. We need to catch a break soon. He mentioned he's found a new source already, and that's not good. Who knows how far along his plans are?" I said, pouring another cup of coffee.

"We'll find him Tri, we'll find him soon." Star assured me.

I nodded and sat back down at my plate of food. Echo mewed and rubbed against my leg, sensing my tension. I stroked her back to calm my nerves. She was good for that.

"Don't let it get to you, we have more important things to deal with right now. Our people are working on it, but we have a wedding to plan!" Star said mischievously.

I smiled and nodded at her. We had decided to speed up our marriage, and only had a few weeks to get everything ready. Friends and family were already booking hotels, and we still needed to find a cake. I hated all the stress of planning the wedding, but Star made it all worth it.

It helped that the others were so supportive in the process as well. Cherry had even picked out her own dress to wear as ringbearer and flower girl. Callie was helping Beatrice design a menu, as we decided to have the ceremony here. The beach in the evening would be a stunning backdrop.

Between planning the wedding, and working on finding Bach, the time flew. It was great to see old friends again at the ceremony. Jackson even agreed to be my best man. Our wedding party wasn't much of a traditional one, most of the 'groomsmen' were women.

Star had somehow managed to convince me to wear a dress, just for her, despite my strong desire not to do so. It was hard for me to tell her no, and with some coercing I gave in and let her design one for me. At least it was black, and had skulls stitched in the lace. Once I put it on, my feelings changed. It made me feel magical, as any good wedding dress should.

Star wore purple, because she knew it was my favorite color. The dress looked amazing on her, but my gaze rarely left her eyes. She was the happiest I had ever seen her, and it made my heart melt. We had a friend lead the proceedings, and I only fumbled two parts of my vows. Aside from that, everything was perfect.

We laughed, we cried, danced and drank, and the evening ended far too soon. People told stories of our friendship and spared most of the more embarrassing details of past parties. No one got too drunk to leave safely, and that was asking a lot of some of my family, my aunt had arrived drunk. Nobody even asked about why so many of us had similar tattoos. I couldn't have asked for things to go better.

Eventually everyone left, and Star and I spent some time together on the beach ruining our dresses in the rising tide. We finished off the champagne and stumbled back to our room for the next part of the ritual. Some traditions were more fun than others. Afterwards, I fell asleep still wearing what was left of my dress.

I am now married to my best friend. After everything that had happened to us, we had only grown closer. We have a larger family now, with Callie, Cherry, and of course Echo. I was taken aback at how things had turned out. We still had to find Bach, but we couldn't do

much but wait for now. Once we found him, however,
there would be hell to pay.

EPILOGUE

I stood in the back, watching the ceremony. I dressed in a black tuxedo, which allowed me to blend in nicely with the catering staff. I sampled a glass of champagne, it was exquisite. I must admit, I was impressed with the women's taste.

With this access to the proceedings, I could have easily slipped doses of Opulentia to all the guests, but I decided to keep my presence a secret. Crashing parties was quite fun, but it seemed rude to ruin someone's wedding night with a little casual revenge. I served untainted hors d'oeuvres, sticking to the back of the party to remain unseen by the girls.

They had hired private investigators to track me down, none of whom would expect me to show up at the wedding. I hadn't been invited of course, but you'd think since we had grown so close that I maybe should have been. Why had I come then? What reason did I have to be there? None, but really that's what made it fun.

I could call them once the party was over, give my congratulations, compliment the ceremony. It was quite nice, to be honest. Again, I decided against it. I could bring it up later, torment them with details of the event, reminding them that our lives are now intertwined forever. It might as well be my blood tattooed down the sides of their necks.

As things began to wind down, I made my exit. I considered leaving a gift to mark my visit but decided to let them have their fun for now. They would know the truth eventually, and that was enough for me. I hopped into my car and sped away into the night. I had business to attend to elsewhere.

I needed to make it to the airport and catch a flight to New York. I whipped my black Maserati through the litter of cars on the road. The roar of the engine no doubt turned a few heads as I passed. Expensive cars do tend to have that effect on people.

My cell buzzed in my pocket, indicating I had received a text. It was my pilot confirming the private jet was ready for takeoff as soon as I arrived. It wouldn't take me much longer to get there, late night traffic was thankfully slim, and I was able to really let the car stretch its legs. I managed to find a few strips of road clear enough to really push the upper limits of the speedometer.

A short time later I pulled into the airport, flashing my badge to the guard to get through the gate to the private hangars. My team guarding the hangar retreated inside as I pulled up beside the plane. We boarded quickly, and it wasn't long before we were in the air. First class has nothing on a private jet, I thought, stretching out on a couch and pouring a couple fingers of whiskey.

My associates assured me the cargo was loaded and ready for pickup upon arrival. I had already sent a team ahead with the packages to ensure the transaction went smoothly. I was meeting with the head of the Triads tonight to discuss a mutually beneficial transaction. If all went well, I would have a distributor for a diluted version of Opulentia, and the Triads would have the first crack at the hottest new designer drug.

I suspected they might try to act tough, scare me into giving them a better price. My team of Magi would put a stop to any shenanigans rather quickly.

The triads would also likely begin cutting the Opulentia with their cocaine or heroin, giving it a high and further diluting its effectiveness. This would no doubt give them more profit, but it would also benefit my plan in the long run. I was honestly curious to see what effects might be gained from mixing the Opulentia with another substance, but I didn't have time for such experimentation currently.

Getting this version of the drug on the streets was only part of the plan. Let people know the drug exists, let them see a hint of what was possible. I could spread this version across major cities around the world, using the local gangs as my servants. Getting the addicts hooked, and the rich intrigued. From there, the ball would be back in my court.

As the only supplier, the major organizations would have no option but to turn to me for more product. They could try to synthesize it, but my scientists have been trying that for years with no results. They would be forced back to me to buy more, which is already incredibly watered down. They make people aware of the drug, I get more money to further Phase Two.

A few hours later the plane set down in New York, and my team was already there waiting for me to arrive. I climbed into the bulletproof SUV and our little convoy sped off to the meeting. The car in front of us was full of Magi, ready to keep the peace if needed. The car in the rear had a few drones, and several cases of Opulentia.

I had a small box with two undiluted pills, as a gift for my new business partner. I had been discussing things with them for weeks, price, territory, competition, small matters. I was not at all concerned with their gang dealings, as they were simply a means to my ends. I assured them that my other buyers were in other states or countries, and that any competition they came across would be through their own network of rivals. Locking down territory was their concern, not mine.

We arrived at the shipping docks just slightly before the scheduled meeting time. The Triads were waiting in the shadows for us, guards emerging on motorcycles to escort us inside. We parked where indicated, and I got out of the car, putting on my best smile. After all, now it was show time!

A woman wearing a smart suit, with slight floral decorations near the collar, and matching pink heels, bowed her head at me as we approached. I returned the gesture with a full gentleman's bow, hoping I was showing the proper amount of respect to not draw any unnecessary guns or blades. She smiled at me, gesturing to a table and chairs she had set up prior to my arrival. One of her assistants was pouring us hot tea as I took my seat.

As I sat at the table, I extended my gift to her. I slid the small decorative box across the table, watching the curiosity grow in her eyes. I explained the contents, and that it would take twenty minutes or so for it to fully take effect in her system. She hesitated at first, likely expecting poison, and requested I take one of her choosing first. I obliged, and she swallowed the other after watching for my reaction.

We quickly went over the details of the transaction, confirming things I had already told her over the phone in the weeks prior. She, through practiced subtlety, flexed her power to intimidate me. I responded kindly and with a smile, as always, unphased by her veiled threats, but careful not to challenge them. The language of a good deal was universal.

We finished our tea and agreed on the terms of our arrangement. I was pleased that things were going smoothly. It would be a shame to ruin my new friendship so quickly. My drones brought out the cases, and her guards brought me several briefcases full of money. It was quite a successful meeting.

She started to rise from the table, and I reminded her of the pills we took at the start of the meeting. I held up a finger and summoned a small flame at the tip, letting the light dance across our faces as she watched inquisitively. I gave her the usual routine of the dark room and the torch, and she ate it up. No fire or energy came to her fingertips, and she seemed displeased.

I calmly poured a bit of water into my empty teacup and slid it over to her. I told her that each person draws power from different elements, and to instead focus on the liquid in the cup. First, I instructed her to focus on trying to push the water from the cup with a gust of air, and when that too proved fruitless, I noticed her guards' moving hands towards their concealed weapons.

I apologized, and instead instructed her to envision her finger as a vast desert amidst a drought, desperately seeking the water in the cup. She was wary of me, but I urged her on. A moment later she managed to pull a stream of water from the cup, and it swirled around her fingers. I explained that water was a tedious element, but very powerful with enough practice. She was simply ecstatic over her new-found ability.

With that crisis averted, I provided her with a small booklet Khan had written about the various elements and how to practice focusing their abilities. She took it gratefully, thanking me for my time as she retreated to her vehicle with her new drugs. I returned to my vehicle, and we were escorted out of the yard by her men on the bikes.

I couldn't have asked for a smoother transaction. Phase One was now fully underway, but there was still much to do. I had several more meetings, with various groups across the globe, scheduled over the coming weeks. Each one practically guaranteed hundreds of millions of dollars towards the cause, so long as nothing went wrong. Once I had my buyers in place, we could ramp up production from Subjects Two and Three.

I poured a glass of champagne in the car and toasted my team on a job well done. If all our meetings went this well, we would be ready for Phase Two in no time. Our convoy split up once we reached the city, my driver taking me to some expensive hotel with a name that I didn't bother to remember. I had people to keep track of such things for me after all.

I again debated calling the girls to toy with them further, but it was late, and they were likely mid coitus anyway. Another time, perhaps, for now I needed my rest. Nothing was more tiresome than the rise to grandeur.

A NOTE FROM THE AUTHOR

Thank you so much for reading! I really hope that you enjoyed it, as it was a fun adventure for me to write. It took me several years to get this story written and edited, and to be honest I almost gave up on it several times after it was written. Editing and publishing are time consuming and headache inducing and far more difficult than actually writing the story, but I digress. The story is here, and you read it (hopefully) and that's really cool!

This story was important for me in many ways, and so I just knew I had to get it out there. It started with a funny little concept of a pill that gives you magic and turned into something greater. You may not have noticed while reading but this story isn't just about Trianna and her wild adventure. This story is about me and the journey I had unpacking and dealing with a fair amount of trauma in my childhood. The story is full of metaphors for events in my life that had an impact and was a way for me to deal with being abused. I don't want to go into graphic detail but suffice it to say that this story contains a lot of emotions for me and I'm excited to get to share it with you.

I hope that this book reaches someone out there that needs to know that just because terrible things happened to you doesn't make you a bad person, and you can still contribute to the world. The world can be a terrible place sometimes, but there is beauty and safety to be found. Tell your story, create, thrive. I may not know you personally, but I believe in you and I'm so proud of you.

- Codi Morrigan Lokken